THE ENIGMA

UNLAWFUL MEN BOOK 2

JODI ELLEN MALPAS

Jodi Ellen Malpas

COPYRIGHT

First published in 2021 by Jodi Ellen Malpas

ISBN - 978-1-7360572-5-4

Editing by - Marion Archer

Proofing by - Karen Lawson

Cover design by – Hang Le

Photographer - Cory Stierly

Model - Mitch Wick

Photograph Licensed by - The Cover Lab, LLC

PRAISE FOR JODI ELLEN MALPAS

"Malpas's sexy love scenes scorch the page, and her sensitive, multilayered hero and heroine will easily capture readers' hearts. A taut plot and a first-rate lineup of supporting characters make this a keeper." *—Publishers Weekly on Gentleman Sinner*

"A magnetic mutual attraction, a superalpha, and long-buried scars that are healed by love. Theo is irresistible."—Booklist on Gentleman Sinner

"Filled with raw emotions that ranged from the deepest rage to utter elation, Jodi Ellen Malpas wove together an incredible must-read tale that fans will certainly embrace."—Harlequin Junkie on Gentleman Sinner

"The characters are realistic and relatable and the tension ratchets up to an explosive conclusion. For anyone who enjoys Sleeping with the Enemy-style stories, this is a perfect choice."—Library Journal on Leave Me Breathless

"The Controversial Princess, told from Adeline's POV, is thick on plot, rich in character development with Kindle-melting sex and the perfect blend of twists and turns, shockers and villains!" —SueBee, Goodreads Reviewer

"The Controversial Princess is an all-consuming, scorching hot, modern royal romance with twists, turns and a jaw-dropping cliff-hanger that will leave you begging for more." —Mary Dube, USA Today HEA

"The Controversial Princess provided us with the romance our hearts needed, the passion our hearts craved, with jaw dropping twists and turns that kept us guessing and eagerly flipping the pages." —TotallyBooked Blog

"A brave, cutting-edge romance...This is a worthwhile read." —Library Journal on The Forbidden

"Unpredictable and addictive."—Booklist on The Forbidden

"The Forbidden proves that Jodi Ellen Malpas is not only one of the romance genre's most talented authors, but also one of the bravest. In this raw and honest portrayal of forbidden love, Jodi delivers a sexy and passionate love story with characters to root for. The Forbidden is easily my favorite read of 2017!"—Shelly Bell, author of At His Mercy, on The Forbidden

"The Forbidden is a gut-wrenching tale full of passion, angst, and heart! Not to be missed!"
—Harlequin Junkie on The Forbidden

"Every kiss, every sexy scene, every word between this pair owned a piece of my soul. I could read this book a hundred times and still react as if it was the first time. The Protector is a top 2016 fave for me." —Audrey

Carlan, #1 bestselling author of The Calendar Girl series on The Protector

"4.5 stars. Top Pick. Readers will love this book from the very beginning! The characters are so real and flawed that fans feel as if they're alongside them. Malpas' writing is also spot-on with emotions."—RT Book Reviews on The Protector

"With This Man took this already epic love story to a whole new, unthinkable height of brilliance." – Gi's Spot Reviews

"Super steamy and emotionally intense." –The Library Journal on With This Man

"Jodi Ellen Malpas delivers a new heart-wrenching, addicting read."—RT Book Reviews on With This Man

"We really don't have enough words nor accolades for this book! It had everything and MORE with added ghosts from the past as well as a surprising suspense. But mostly, it was about a love that proves it can conquer anything and everything placed in its way. A beautiful addition to one of our favourite series!"—TotallyBooked Blog on With This Man

DEDICATION

To everyone who read ***The Brit*** *and told me to write more dark romance*

. . .

Thank you.

JEM x

THE ENIGMA

JODI ELLEN
MALPAS

PROLOGUE - PART ONE

Miami – Two Years Ago

JAMES

DARKNESS ISN'T what it used to be. Not to me. It's too much of a regular in my life now. Every day, dark. Every thought, dark. Every action, dark. It used to be scary. Unwelcomed.

Now, I *am* the dark.

And before me, a dark river. Blackness. Not even the moonlight is illuminating it, the dense clouds blocking any chance of light.

I stand on the edge, staring across the still water, waiting for the adrenalin to subside. For my shakes to leave. For my mind to clear.

Calm.

I need calm before I end a man's life. I need to be stable. Composed.

Seen.

I reach up and pull off my balaclava, breathing in the chilly nighttime air and filling my lungs with something clean. The banging coming from the car is starting to irritate the shit out of me. I look over my shoulder. "Shut the fuck up," I growl, my jaw in spasm. I should find his pleas for mercy humorous. He actually thinks I might change my mind. That his dribbling, pitiful prayers might alter his fate. Unlucky for him, it only fuels my rage. Changing his fate is about as likely as bringing me back into the light.

Zero possibility.

I take one last drag of my cigarette and flick it into the river before turning and pacing back to the car. I yank open the door. My victim stills, halting his squirming across the back seat. The bag over his head starts to inflate and deflate from the force of his heavy breathing. "Time to die," I whisper, grabbing his arm and manhandling him out onto the gravel.

"No, no, please! Whatever you want, I'll make it happen." Even his Irish accent grates on me, and I used to be a sucker for an Irish lilt. Now, people simply talking aggravates me, because no one in this world seems to have anything useful to say. No truths. Only lies.

I crouch down before him, where he's squirming on his front, rubbing into the cutting stones, his hands bound. I tug off the bag, and he stills, blinking into the ground.

He can't see me. And that won't do.

I rise and push my boot into his side, forcing him to his back. He looks up at me, fear imbedded into every pore of his pitted face, his eyes wide. "Who are you? Who sent you?" he blabbers.

I pull a blade out of my pocket and slowly turn it, catching the moonlight, making it sparkle prettily. I look up. The clouds have floated past, revealing the moon. Perfect timing. *Seen*. "No one sent me." I crouch again, my eyes refocused on the blade. "And who I am is irrelevant." I turn my stare onto him. "You're still going to die." I flick the knife out accurately, slicing across his mouth, so that when he squeals in pain, his cheeks rip. The piercing, blood-curdling sound goes straight through me. Inflames the anger more.

I pull out my gun and casually attach the silencer, taking my time while my prey writhes and wails in the dust and dirt, begging for mercy. There will be no mercy. Not for me, and not for him. I push it into his groin.

"No, please!" he screams, blood pouring from his mouth.

"You want to know who I am?" I ask, and he stills for a moment. "No one knows who I am."

Realization finds him. "No."

"Yes." I slowly squeeze the trigger and the whoosh of the bullet leaving the chamber brings a smile to my face, as does his scream.

"Enough, Kel."

I look over my shoulder, seeing the shadow of one of the only people I like. "Come to spoil my fun?"

"Finish it."

I sigh, swapping my pistol for my blade. "Fine." And I drag it slowly across his throat. Deep. Straight.

Dead.

And then I cut out his tongue before rising, using the bag from his head to wipe the knife clean. I pat his pockets down and pull out a burner phone, tossing it to Goldie. "Get into it," I say, grabbing my victim's legs and dragging him to the edge of the river. I nudge him in with my boot, the sound of his body hitting the water echoing in the nighttime air. I watch him sink. "I feel much better," I say to the water.

"As always, I'm happy for you."

Yes, I feel better, but we both know I need more than the kill. The peace. The satisfaction. I pull out my phone and send a message to Beth, organizing the rest of my evening. "I'll need some privacy," I say, stalking away, the thrill of my recent kill fading fast. I look up to the sky. The clouds are back. The moonlight blocked.

Familiar.

I've spent so much time in darkness, I have become the darkness.

I arrive back at my apartment and light the candles around my desk before taking my chair and resting back, breathing in and out, calm and controlled. My heart is steady again. Slow enough for me *not* to be able to feel the beats.

I need to feel the beats.

"Where the fuck is she?" I mutter as I rest my elbows on the edge of the glass and stare at one of the flickering flames, mesmerized by the tiny blaze. My hand extends of its own volition, and I hover above the small fire, feeling the instant, intense heat.

I stare.

I feel.

Ding!

I snatch my hand away and look up at my office door, hearing the familiar sound of heels clinking the floor. I blow out the candles and make my way to the stairs, coming to a stop at the top. I see Beth down below, helping herself to some water.

I observe her, wondering what makes her tick. I know why *I* do what I do. I do it because I'm invisible in every aspect of my life. And this? I'm seen.

"I'll be in the shower," I say, and she looks up. "Join me in ten minutes." I leave to go wash off my kill and get ready for more relief.

But first . . .

I go back to my office and collect a phone from the drawer, dialing FBI Agent Jaz Hayley as I perch on the edge of my desk. She answers quickly. Always does. "You'll find one in the river," I say coolly. "I believe they call him The Snake."

"For fuck's sake," she breathes. "You need to stop."

"Never."

"Then I'll stop you."

"Don't make me kill you, Jaz," I warn. "I'm beginning to like you." I switch on the bank of TVs on the wall and scroll through the faces of dozens of men. I imagine Jaz Hayley has a similar list, except hers will have a special place on it for me. Probably at the top. Such a shame she doesn't know my name. What I look like.

Who I am.

"Fuck you," she hisses.

I smile. "What are your plans for tonight?"

A light laugh indicates how exasperating she finds me. Frustrating. "Decorating my new place with my daughter. Picking out bridesmaids' dresses for her wedding. But you already know that, don't you?"

"She's getting married," I muse, as if I didn't actually know that. "You'll want to be around to see that."

"Don't threaten me," she warns, and my small smile widens. "James," she adds casually.

My amusement vanishes in a heartbeat at the mention of my name. Or, at least, one of them. *What the fuck?* And *how* the fuck? I know this woman is a talented FBI agent. She aced her tests and powered up the ranks. But she's not a fucking clairvoyant.

"James *Kelly*." She adds my surname for extra punch, to ensure I know she's not fucking about.

"I prefer The Enigma," I say quietly.

"Or Kellen James?"

I can't conceal my inhale. And I can't ask *how* she knows. I refuse to give her that much satisfaction when she details the journey to her discovery. But, fuck, how the fuck does she know?

"Won't your ego allow you to ask?" she says, knowing what I'm thinking. She always does. It's that sixth fucking sense. Jaz Hayley moving into Miami from New York City has been more than a pain in my arse. "Let me walk you through it," she goes on. "So I got to thinking, who could want to get to The Bear so desperately? Who could want to fuck with him, kill his men? Kill him? A fellow trafficker? No. This just feels a little more like revenge. So I started digging a bit deeper."

"I see where you're going with this."

"Impressed? I mean, I'm impressed with myself. My digging took me all the way to London, James. It took me to the estate where Spencer James's family was burned alive. All presumed dead. But what if one survived? Not the showman that was Spencer James, you sound too young, but maybe one of his offspring? Who could want revenge more than one of them?" She laughs a little, satisfied, and my teeth grate. "You're his son, and you want to kill The Bear because he wiped out your family," she adds, and I flinch. "Shame no one knows who The Bear is."

"I'll find out."

She hums. "I'll keep this information as security along with a few other things, if you know what I mean."

A few other things? Like? I refuse to ask. I know exactly what she means. She's going to make a rat out of me. "What are you saying, Agent Hayley?"

"I'm saying you're cornered."

My blood simmers with a rage that's dangerous. Cornered. I can't be at someone's mercy like that. "Stay safe, Agent Hayley," I grate in warning, hanging up, my fist clenching around the phone. "Fuck!" I throw it with enough power to shatter the glass door of my office.

PROLOGUE - PART TWO

Miami – Two Years Ago

BEAU

I PUSH my way out of the station and take in the clean air as I hold the wall, leaning down to pull off my boots. My feet are screaming, my head ringing after a twelve-hour shift. I look up and down the street, searching for Mom. Whatever possessed me to agree to her painting party tonight, I'll never know.

Once my feet are free from the constraints of my boots, I perch on the wall and pull out my phone, calling Ollie. It goes straight to voicemail, and I peek down at my watch, checking the time. He's already started his shift. "Hey," I say, looking up, seeing Mom pulling into the street. "My shift ran over. Another body pulled out of the cove near Byron Bay. I'm just reminding you that I'm going over to Mom's to help her decorate her new place and browse bridesmaids' dresses. I'll probably stay over since you're on duty all night. See you in the morning. Love you." I creak my way to standing and take the steps to the sidewalk as Mom pulls up. I jump in and slump back in the seat.

"That kind of shift?" she asks, smiling across at me.

"Brutal." I drop my boots and wriggle my toes, leaning over to kiss her cheek. "How's your day been?"

"Brutal." She smiles, but it doesn't reach her eyes. Never does these days, not since Dad fucked us over. "Plenty of men to keep me busy."

I laugh at her candid humor. "Why brutal?"

"Fucking Danny Black," she mutters, pulling away from the curb.

"Danny Black?" I mimic. "The Brit? He's dead." Has been for over a year.

"Yeah, and now every corrupt criminal fucker on the planet has seen a green light to move in on Miami."

"Oh."

"I popped into Hardy's and got supplies." She thumbs over her shoulder to the back seat, and I crane my neck to find paint. Lots of it. I sigh, and she pouts. "It's relaxing," she says, and I scoff at Mom's form of winding down. "Humor me."

"Where's the wine?"

"Shit," she mutters, smacking the wheel. "Wine. I knew I was missing something important."

I smile, but it's unsure. She's missing many things these days. Fuck my father. "We'll stop at a store," I say as my phone rings. *Speak of the devil.* I quickly reject the call, turning it face down in my lap.

Mom gives me a side-eye. "You can't ignore him forever," she says gently. "He's your father."

"I won't ignore him forever. Just until he finds his senses."

"Put your belt on," she orders, and I do as I'm bid. "What if he doesn't *want* to find his senses?"

How could he not? He and Mom have been together for over thirty years. "Then he's not the man I thought he was. We were happy in New York City."

She looks across the car at me. "You didn't have to come to Miami."

I give her a tired roll of my eyes. "Uncle Lawrence met Dexter and moved here. You and Dad moved here. There was nothing left in the city for me." She knows that. And she knows I could never be in a different state to her. My father, yes, but not Mom.

"Well, everything happens for a reason. You wouldn't have met Ollie."

Yes, my life is moving forward, but Mom's has gone back thirty years. "Are you saying I should be thanking Dad?"

She shrugs noncommittedly.

"He's a narcissistic prick who's become pumped up on power and wealth. I don't recognize him anymore." Did I say that out loud? Regardless, conversation over. At least, with Mom it is. In my head, I'm having many mental arguments with my father over his transgressions. The respected businessman. The respected businessman who's been fucking another woman. Moved her into the marital home. Paraded her around town like some status symbol. She's younger than *me*, for fuck's sake.

"I'm not sure I do either." Mom sighs. "It's his birthday tomorrow."

"I'll be sure to shit in his card."

"Come on, Beau." She shakes her head to herself, and I see with painful clarity the internal battle she's having. She hates him. My father humiliated her. Betrayed her. She's a powerful woman, taking men down daily. Every criminal in the state of Florida must have winced when they got word of Agent Jaz Hayley transferring from New York City. And yet she refuses to accept me hating him.

"What wine do you want?" I ask, seeing the store up ahead. Enough about Dad. Even talking about him makes my stomach turn. I unclip my belt before she stops the car and am scowled at as a result. "Sorry, Agent Hayley," I quip, and she smacks my arm.

"Speaking of which . . ." She looks at me out of the corner of her eye.

She has my attention, and she knows it. "Did you get inside information on the results?"

Her smile says it all. "Top of the class," she says proudly. "Fuck, Beau, you got top five percent in the country." She pulls into a parking space and turns in her seat to face me. I'm struck dumb. Top five? I'm feeling a little emotional. The FBI Phase 1 Test has consumed me. Drained me. Sent me batshit crazy. "Well done, sweetheart." She reaches for my cheek and wipes away a stray tear.

"I'm so glad I'm more like you than Dad," I say over a hiccup, going in for a hug. I feel her chuckling against me. "Thanks, Mom." There's no question, without her support, help, and maybe her genes, there's no way I would have gotten through the past few years.

"Enough now." She breaks our hug and brushes herself down. "You're in your blues. No hugging allowed."

"And when I'm in plain clothes?"

She laughs lightly. "Hold your horses, Ms. Croft. Phase One is only the first hurdle."

"Will you *not* call me that?" I mutter as she pulls something out from beneath her seat.

"A congrats present." She flashes a Lara Croft mug under my nose, and I narrow my eyes on the image of the character I've been dubbed by my colleagues. "I'm so glad I vetoed your father's idea of sending you to ballet," she quips.

"So you sent me to karate instead." I laugh, taking the mug.

"And now you're going to be as good an agent as your mom. But younger and fitter. And bendier." Her nose wrinkles. "Go get that wine."

"We should open the bottle of Krug you got when you graduated." She's kept it in its presentation box for years, dusting it weekly, admiring it, not letting anyone else near it.

"Never go near the Krug." She grabs my cheeks and squeezes, looking deadly serious. "Only if your life depends on it."

I roll my eyes and bat her away, reaching down to pull on my boots. "You've got to drink it one day."

"Maybe," she muses, looking down at her cell when it rings. Her eyebrows high, she returns to face the wheel. "You go. I've got to take this."

I don't ask who it is. Never do. She's technically off duty, but she's never really off duty. I leave her to take the call, and it's not until I'm in the store that I realize I have the mug still in my grasp. A Miami cop wandering around a store holding a Lara Croft mug.

I get a few odd looks, to be expected, as I head for the alcohol section, claiming a bottle of red *and* white. "We're celebrating," I declare to myself, going to the checkout. I pay and stuff the bottles into a bag with my mug, wandering back out of the store, trying to find some enthusiasm for the night of painting ahead.

As I approach Mom's car, I see she's still talking, and my pace slows when I detect her expression. My usually cool mother looks . . . troubled. She forces a smile when she spots me, and it drops a second later. Then I see something I haven't seen on Mom before.

Dread.

I pick up my pace, rushing toward her, as her eyes get progressively wider, her face more fearful. Her hand comes up, as if to stop me in my tracks. Of course, it naturally increases my pace.

What's going on?

"No, Beau!" she screams.

I drop my bag, her terror-filled yell slicing through me. But my feet don't stop moving. My heart sprints. Nothing could prevent me getting to her.

And then the world lights up.

My eardrums feel like they've burst.

My skin burns.

I'm thrown skyward.

And blackness falls.

1

Miami - Present Day

JAMES

I STAND UNDER THE SPRAY, motionless, my body heavy, the hot water pelting my back. It would hurt. Burn. If I hadn't survived an inferno before. I look down at my bare feet, at the last of the blood-stained water slipping down the drain.

Clean.

I step out and wrap a towel around my waist, collecting the oil off the vanity unit and tipping some into my hand. I massage it between my palms as I stare at my reflection in the mirror. The adrenalin has gone already. It's vanished, abandoned me, leaving nothing but a fresh thirst for another kill. I'm running low on targets. Then what? I can only hope and pray that the peace I need is there to greet me at the end of this road of blood and death. I can no longer exist in this world without vengeance. And without vengeance, peace. If I have neither, I'm as good as dead.

I take my hand over my shoulder and start massaging the oil into the top of my back, feeling the burning of my flesh all over again. Years later, it's still hurting. Tormenting.

There's a knock at my bathroom door, and I turn my eyes onto it. "What?"

Goldie appears. She watches me rubbing at my back before checking my facial expression. She clearly doesn't like what she sees, but she says nothing. "The man driving away from the scene. His name's Spittle. Apparently, he got bored in retirement."

"Interesting," I say, starting to work on the other side of my back. And what would a former FBI agent be doing with a contact of The Bear?

"His number." She holds out a piece of paper as she moves to the side, and I take it as I pass her, heading to my office. I settle at my desk and pull a phone from my drawer, punching in the digits and settling back.

"Agent Spittle," I say quietly when he answers. "Or ex agent, I should say."

"Who's this?"

"We need to talk about your whereabouts tonight." I smile when he inhales, and I point my remote control at the bank of screens before me, directing the curser to the *send* icon on the video displayed on the center TV. A video of him walking away from a man, Adrian Wallace, who I know has contacts in drug trafficking and was recently in touch with The Bear's men. Spittle has a briefcase in his grasp. He gets in his car outside a derelict warehouse and drives away.

Another inhale. "Oh, you've not seen the best of it yet," I taunt, just as a gunshot sounds and Adrian Wallace, also known as The Eagle, drops like a sack of shit. "That bit," I muse thoughtfully. "It's my favorite part of this movie."

"He's dead?" Spittle breathes, undoubtedly dripping beads of sweat all over his phone as he stares at Wallace's lifeless body.

"I'd say so, but his body has yet to be discovered. I've got to say, it doesn't look all too good on you, Spittle. So what were you doing meeting a man known to have associations with drug dealers? Feeding a personal habit?"

"Fucking hell," he breathes. "Who the fuck are you?"

"I'm the beginning of your end." I kill the screen and bring up Adrian Wallace's mug shot, tapping out DECEASED across his file. "Or I could be the beginning of your beginning. Up to you."

"You're British."

"I can see how you made it in the FBI." What a fucking cock. "Is my nationality a problem, or do you only bend for certain ethnicity groups?"

He laughs, and it's nervous. "Well, you British have a habit of leaving a lasting impression around here."

"So I've heard." He's talking about The Brit. The Angel-faced Assassin. Savage. Merciless.

Dead.

"What do you want?" Spittle asks.

"I'm not sure yet, but be on standby." I hang up and roll my shoulders, feeling the tightness there. Not of my muscles. But my skin.

"There's probably no good time to tell you this," Goldie says, and I shoot my stare to her at the doorway. "Beau Hayley has appealed the ruling into her mother's death."

I breathe out, old ghosts coming back to haunt me. And new ones it seems. I can feel Goldie watching me. Monitoring me. Wondering what the fuck I'm thinking.

"What the fuck are you thinking?" she asks, coming over and taking a seat on the other side of my desk. "I hate that look on you."

I cup my chin, feeling the roughness as I mold into it with my fingertips.

"James?"

I give her a moment of my eyes, my mind whirling. And then I reach for the phone again, calling Spittle back. "Find out how the appeal into Jaz Hayley's death is going."

"Jaz? What do you want with Jaz?"

"You're not here to ask questions. You're here to answer them."

"The appeal is being rejected," he says quietly.

"And the daughter?"

"What about her? She doesn't know yet."

"Yet," I murmur, reaching for my temple and rubbing away the tension. She's not going to give up until she gets justice for her mother, and of all people, I know there is no justice in this world. My back tingles, as if to reinforce it. And images of my family, my whole fucking family, parade through my mind. I quickly push those thoughts away and refocus on the problem at hand. Beau Hayley.

For fuck's sake. Does the woman want to die? I would say that was a stupid question if I didn't know her medical history since her mum's death. And I can relate. Been there. Done that. Wanted to die over and over again. Like I said, there is no justice in this world. So I learned to *make* justice *my* way. "Send me her number."

"Whose number?" Spittle asks, confused.

"Beau Hayley's."

"Why?"

"Did you just ask another question?"

"No." He sighs, sounding as defeated as a man could be. "Jesus, I'm tired."

"Me too. Exhausted. Exhausted of fucking waiting."

"Tell me who you are."

"Get me Beau Hayley's number." I hang up and toss the phone back in the drawer, breathing out my frustration.

"What are you going to do?" Goldie asks. "Call her and ask her nicely to back off?"

I turn my eyes onto her, but I say nothing. I don't need to. My face must say it all. *Fuck off, you sarcastic bitch.*

Goldie tilts her head. "It's been two years. You got Jaz's phone records. Nothing on them. I've checked all records on safety deposit boxes. Nothing. If she shared or hid information on you, your name, anything, you'd know by now."

"I have a bad feeling." I get up and head for the sauna. I need to sweat out some of this stress.

I need to burn.

Burn and know I won't die.

I strip off, leaving my clothes in a pile at the door. The heat hits me like a brick, and I look at the thermometer on the back wall. One eighty.

I sit on the top bench and collect some water from the bucket, throwing it on the unit, and steam billows up and shrouds the space.

Not seen.

Leaning back against the wood, I close my eyes. I hear the screams instantly. Screams that can only be associated with death. The screams of my mum. Of my dad. Of my sister.

All burning alive.

I open my eyes to darkness and lean forward, putting my hand over the grill of the steam unit, the hot coals only an inch from my palm. I hold still. Absorb the pain. The heat. Because I won't die. This fire won't kill me.

Clenching my hand into a fist, I squeeze away the burn and lie down, reaching up and turning the sand timer. Fifteen minutes. I'll turn it another four times before I'll allow myself to leave this inferno.

It will never be enough.

2

Miami – Present Day

BEAU

A PERSON'S ability to escape depends on their ability to imagine. I've lost my imagination. Lost everything. I'm trapped—trapped in a world that doesn't make sense to me anymore. Trapped in a body I can't even look at. Trapped with thoughts I want to physically rip from my head. Trapped with feelings that blur and blend into nothing. Happiness is a forgotten emotion. It's safer to feel nothing, to ignore that I'm a fuck-up. To disregard the fact that I'm beyond help.

Accept I am alone.

Give up on hoping—hoping I can ever be normal again.

Because without hope, there can be no disappointment.

"Have you thought of ending your life, Beau?" Dr. Fletcher asks, and I blink, looking up from my lap, woken up from my daze.

All the time. "Never," I say coolly, aware that the alternative answer will have me sent swiftly to a psychiatric hospital. Not again.

Her eyes fall to my wrists, and mine fall with them. I clear my throat and pull the sleeve of my shirt down, holding the cuff in my palm with my fingertips. "Tell me what you did today," she goes on, and I smile to myself. "Is something amusing?"

I force myself to look at her. This woman, who is so together, so calm and serene, I could easily punch her in the face and not feel an ounce of guilt. "Nothing is amusing." Not anymore. Not in *my* life.

"You smiled." She crosses one leg over the other, her slender, perfect, untarnished limbs like a horrible torture. A reminder than I am anything but untarnished. Anything but perfect. She shouldn't be a therapist. Dr. Fletcher is so flawless, it's enough to send even the sanest person over the edge. "A person smiling suggests they are amused," she adds.

"I'm amused that I'm here," I say honestly. "I'm here, and I don't want to be." She knows I'm not talking about my sessions. Sessions with various therapists that have cost a small fortune and done nothing to chase away my hatred or my demons in the past two years. I'm talking about this world. This life. And yet each time I've convinced myself that there is a way out, that small, infuriating part of my brain surfaces and warns me away from the blade. From the rope. From the pills.

The voice of my mom.

The buzzer sounds, and I breathe in, rising from the chair. "It's been a pleasure, Dr. Fletcher." I smile, and she huffs a small, disbelieving puff of laughter. I'm sure it's unprofessional, but I can't blame her. She's endured me for six months now. Six whole pointless months. And I'll keep on coming. The alternative is a hospital. I'm not game. I bust my balls every day trying to make sure everyone around me thinks I'm okay. My act doesn't wash with Dr.

Fletcher. I'm ill, no question. Poisoned by hatred and bitterness. I'm used to it now. Comfortable with it. Accepting.

"I'll see you next week, Beau." Dr. Fletcher unravels her long legs and stands, placing her journal on the glossy wooden table between the couches. "It would be lovely to hear if you'd tried something new."

"Like?" I ask as I swing my purse onto my shoulder.

"Dinner in a restaurant. Drinks in a bar. Maybe even seeing your aunt perform in one of her shows."

"I thought you'd learned to manage your expectations." I give her a wry smile, and she gives me a bright one. It's dazzling. I can't remember the last time I smiled so wide my face hurt. It makes me want to punch her more.

It was with Mom. The last time I smiled that brightly, it was with Mom.

"I won't give up on you, Beau," she says.

Isn't that what every therapist should say to their patient? "That's sweet." If wasted. "Goodbye." I leave her office and make my way down the stairs, and the moment I burst out of the door, I take in air urgently, as if I could have been holding my breath for the past forty-five minutes.

Sad truth is, I feel like I've been holding my breath every minute of every day for two years. I can't remember what it feels like to breathe easy. To not have to think about each inhale and every exhale, just to make sure I'm actually alive.

And then the inevitable sinking of my heart when I realize I am.

It's a vicious cycle. A continuous, torturous, dizzying merry-go-round I can't get off.

Misery.

~

Bang!

I jump out of my skin, despite expecting the ear-piercing boom, as I pull up at the back of Hardy's Hardware store. I have to take a few moments for my heart to settle down. Every damn time.

I push back the impending flashback and open my eyes, finding an elderly lady with a hand on her chest. "Sorry." I smile mildly as I shut off the engine of my dilapidated Mustang and get out. I don't bother locking my car, never do, and wander into the store. The smell. I take a moment to breathe it in. Paint, metal, wood—a heady mixture that never fails to ease me.

I spot Mr. Hardy behind the counter winding rope around his hand, his coveralls decorated with years' worth of service to downtown Miami. His gray, wiry hair is in his eyes, his beard looking like it needs a good groom. When he looks up, his eyes shine, and I make my way over and lean on the counter, forcing myself to *not* look at the rope and instead helping myself to one of the mints he keeps in a jar by the ancient cash register.

"Beau," he says, his southern accent heavy. "How much oil is that old jalopy of yours going to spill on the road outside my store today?"

I crunch into the mint, making him wince. "My car cries, Mr. Hardy. It cries because everyone is mean to it."

He chuckles and sets aside his wound rope before claiming a mint for himself, though he doesn't crunch into it, his false teeth preventing him. "How's business, Beau?"

"Slow," I admit, blasé. "I'm not worried. Something will come up soon."

"Then why are you here?"

"Aunt Zinnea wants me to redecorate her bedroom." I reach for one of the paint samples and start flicking through. It doesn't need decorating. I only did it a few months ago, but, apparently, she's bored of the canary-yellow and turquoise stripes. It has nothing to do with the fact that she's trying to keep me busy. "My specification in sumptuous and sexy."

Mr. Hardy laughs and leans over to scan the colors with me. "I'd expect nothing less from your aunt Zinnea. What about that one?" He points to a deep pink that's right up Zinnea's street.

I cock my head, considering what I could match it with. "Midnight blue," I say, turning the samples in search of a suitable hue. I spot it in a heartbeat, the perfect shade. "I'll have a gallon of each."

On an agreeable nod, Mr. Hardy makes his way to the paint mixing machine and starts to load it up, while I head to the first aisle to collect a new brush, the same type of brush I've always used. The brush Mom insisted on. The brush that helped make me a half decent decorator. But the space where it should be is bare. "Mr. Hardy." I poke my head around the end of the aisle. "Where are the two-inch natural bristled brushes?"

"Ah." He looks up as he slips a tin of white base into the mixing machine. "Discontinued."

"What?" Is that panic rising in me? It's my signature brush. The *only* brush I can use to cut in—to achieve a perfect straight line. Mom tried plenty of others. None compare. "They can't discontinue our brush."

"I'll let them know," he replies sardonically, shutting the door of the mixing machine and settling in front of the computer, tapping in the codes for the shades I've ordered.

My shoulders drop, and I go back to the shelf, frowning as I finger through a few other brushes. I pull down a lame alternative and make a mental note to search Google when I get home. A pang of guilt grabs me as I pick up some new paint trays and roller covers before making my way down the aisle. I shouldn't be resorting to the Internet. It feels like a betrayal. Mr. Hardy's store has been nestled in between two old factories downtown for over forty years. It's the only place I use to buy my decorating supplies

—support your locals, as Mom taught me. Plus, it's calming in here. And it's never crowded. "But he doesn't have our brush, Mom," I say quietly, browsing the shelves, as if I don't know what's on each and every one.

I stop in front of the utility knives, my head tilting.

Keep walking.

A few paces more, I come to the rope section. Rope of various thicknesses. Various colors. Various strengths. I reach forward and pull at one of the thickest options. The strongest option.

Keep walking.

I make haste to the front of the store and place my replacement brush on the counter with a little pout as the paint mixing machine starts jolting around, and the store is filled with the whirling and banging sounds. "I suppose this one will have to do," I shout over the noise.

"Broaden your horizons, Beau," Mr. Hardy replies, frowning at the machine as it jumps toward him. That machine has been on its last legs for as long as I can remember, but since I'm the only one who ever requires paint mixing, Mr. Hardy—understandably—is reluctant to replace it.

"Mr. Hardy, when are you going to retire?" He must be in his mid-seventies by now, and I know for a fact his business limps along. I'm his best customer. I could be his *only* customer. I never see anyone else in here.

"And do what?" he asks, shutting the machine off and swinging the door open.

"Relax. Take up a hobby."

He lifts another tub of white base into the machine and taps a few more buttons on the computer before shutting the door and turning it on. "My hobby is working." He lifts the lid of the first tub, and we're blinded by the brightness of the pink.

"Perfect," we say in unison.

While Mr. Hardy sees to the rest of my paint, I help myself to a bag and load my buys in, and then flick through a local newspaper that's sitting with a pile of others on the counter. My scanning eyes stop flitting when an article catches my attention, and I zoom in on the mug shot of a man I recognize. "Jesus," I whisper, laying out the paper so I can read the report.

"Oh yes," Mr. Hardy pipes in, and I look up to see he's looking at the mug shot too. "They dragged his body out of the river."

"The Snake. Mom was tracking him for years," I say quietly, swallowing hard. "He always managed to slip through her fingers."

Mr. Hardy smiles sympathetically. "Well, whoever sliced his throat before they tossed him in the river certainly didn't let him slip through *their* fingers."

"Sliced throat?" I ask, going back to the report.

"Yes. And the tongue that ordered all those deaths? Cut out. They reckon he's been at the bottom of the river for a couple of years at least."

"Nice."

"Indeed." Another sympathetic smile. I know what's coming, but before I can stop him, he asks. "What do you think Jaz would have made of it?" He flicks his head in the direction of the newspaper, and I look at the image again.

"I think she would have been pissed off that someone killed him before she could put him before a judge and jury." Actually, I don't think. I *know*. Mom always said justice wasn't served by death. It was served by being locked up *until* death. It was served by being in fear of your life on the inside, where there were endless blood-thirsty inmates just waiting to put you below them in the pecking order. Mark their territory. Wield their power. Justice was served with legal justice. Once upon a time, I would have agreed. Now? Now I don't believe in justice at all.

"What do you have in that bag?" Mr. Hardy asks as he makes his way back with my second color. I start to fold the newspaper, but something else catches my eye. Another report, one about a local businessman. My father. My lip naturally curls. There he is, all suited and booted, standing outside a brand-new building down on South Beach looking proud. A building he built. I read the article with a scowl, the journalist harping on about my dad's charity donations and service to the community making my eyes roll. He's just trying to crush his guilt. Redeem himself. Lessen the chances of him going to hell by doing all these good deeds.

"Is that your dad, Beau?"

"Yeah, that's my father," I breathe, shutting the paper on his face. "Or Saint Thomas, if you prefer." I place it back on the pile as Mr. Hardy chuckles and pulls his pocketknife from his coveralls, levering off the lid of my second color.

"Very nice."

I crane my neck to see. "She'll love it." I pull my credit card from my bag. "I have two large trays, two roller covers, and two non-Beau/Jaz brushes." I smile sweetly as he rings it through the till.

"Seventy-four bucks on the dot, but we'll call it seventy for the inconvenience." He reaches for his beard and starts his customary stroking as I pay and claim my buys. "Good to see you, Beau."

"And you, Mr. Hardy. Don't work too hard."

He laughs as I leave, the bell on the door dinging loudly. I load my things into the back seat of my car, yanking the driver's seat into place with a loud huff.

It bangs. I wince.

It clicks into place. I sigh.

Jumping in, I turn the key in the ignition and start my usual chanting mantra. "Come on, Dolly, you can do it. Come on. Come on. Come on."

Bang!

She roars to life, and I chug off down the road, calling Nath to let him know I'm on my way.

. . .

I pull up behind Nath's car at the backstreet diner, and the moment Dolly declares her arrival with another bang, he gets out of his BMW and starts shaking his head. "It makes no sense that you have that car," he says as I wander over, pulling my sleeve farther down my arm until I'm able to grip it with my fingers pressed into my palm. My move doesn't escape Nath's notice. "I know it's sentimental and all, but the damn thing scares the shit out of you every time you start the engine.

"I'm used to it," I lie. I'll never get used to the bangs, but I'll also never get rid of Dolly. "How are you?" I reach up and kiss his cheek, and his arm comes around my back, rubbing me in that friendly way he does.

"Chasing my tail with numerous cases." He pulls his phone out and checks it before sliding it back into his inside pocket. "It looks busy today," he says, tilting his head toward the diner. "You want to sit outside?"

I look through the window and see the space crowded with people around most tables. "Yeah," I reply, taking a seat in the less busy space on the sidewalk.

"Usual?" he asks, heading inside. Because he knows I won't.

I nod, pulling up the parking app on my phone and paying for thirty minutes on my car.

Nath is back with our drinks by the time I'm done. "So come on," he prompts, stirring three sugars into his coffee. "I know you weren't aching to see my face."

I purse my lips. I would ask myself if I'm that transparent, but with Nath I know I am. "Any news on the appeal?" I ask. My stomach flips in anticipation of his answer. Always does.

"No news, Beau. I could have told you that over the phone."

My shoulders drop. "I was aching to see your face," I say, and he laughs a little. “How long could it possibly take to give a straight yes or no? Yes, your appeal has been accepted. No, it hasn’t.”

“You know it’s all political in the force. The red tape is never ending. One person says yes, the next overrules them.” He leans forward, and I see that dreaded sympathy veil his features.

“Don’t look at me like that,” I warn.

“Like what?”

“Like you’re about to tell me not to hold out hope.”

He sighs. “It was cut and dry.”

My teeth clench. “It was a fucking cover-up, Nath. That’s what it was. Cars just spontaneously combust on their own, do they?”

“The tank was leaking, Beau. Forensics proved it.”

“On a one-year-old government issued Audi? Come on, Nath.”

“And she was smoking in the vehicle.”

“So it’s Mom’s fault?” I grate, my fingers aching. I look down and find my knuckles white from my grip on the cup, and I loosen it, circulating some blood. I honestly can’t recall seeing her smoking in the car that night. All I remember is the terror emblazoned across her face. She knew something was about to happen.

“I didn’t say that.” Nath sighs again. “Beau, you’ve got to let this lie or you’ll drive yourself crazy.”

“Been there,” I mumble despondently, and he reaches over, taking my hand.

“Don’t go there again.” The empathy on his face serves only to anger me. And that’s not fair on Nath. He was a great friend of Mom’s. The best partner. “Jaz would have wanted you to live. She’d want you back on the force.”

“Nath,” I lean over the table. “Something isn’t right.”

“Fucking hell, since when did you become a conspiracy theorist? Choose your battles, Beau.”

I retreat and finger my cup of coffee, admitting defeat. Just for now. “I heard you finally tracked down The Snake.”

"Yeah, at the bottom of the river. Someone obviously didn't get the memo that he was wanted alive or alive."

"Someone obviously wanted him dead more than the police wanted him alive." I raise an eyebrow, and Nath laughs under his breath. "He didn't slither away from whoever murdered him, eh?" I go on. "So who do you think killed him before Mom caught him?"

"You know I can't discuss that."

"Pretend I'm Mom." I lean in. "Was it The Bear? Did he turn on him? Or did The Enigm—"

"Your mom is dead, Beau," Nath breathes, and I wince. "Shit, I'm sorry."

"Don't worry about it." I smile, and it takes every bit of effort. "I guess it never leaves you, huh?"

"Once a cop, always a cop." He smiles and tests his coffee before downing it and pulling out his cell. "Break time's up." He groans, standing and making his way to my side. He dips and kisses my cheek before resting a light palm over my wrist. He always does that. Like he can rub away the aftermath. "Ollie says hi."

I roll my eyes. "Anything else to add that might cheer me up?"

"He's still not over you."

"That was a rhetorical question."

"I know." Nath answers his phone and strides off, jumping in his car and pulling away fast. I don't hang around to let my thoughts wander to my ex-fiancé. I leave my coffee practically untouched and head for Dolly, sliding in and starting her up. "Come on," I say quietly as she coughs and splutters. "Come on, come on, come on."

I stop forcing her to life when smoke starts to billow from beneath the hood. Smoke. So much smoke. An ear-piercing bang, and then . . . smoke. I inhale. Swallow. Push my fist into the side of my head.

I can't breathe.

Can't see.

Can't get to Mom.

Beau!

My body slams back into the seat, my breathing quick, and I physically shake myself away from the flashback, glancing around, checking my surroundings. Checking the sleeve of my shirt isn't melting or my flesh isn't burning. "Jesus," I breathe, taking a moment to gather myself. When will these flashbacks stop haunting me?

I get out, wiping away the sheen of sweat from my brow, forcing myself back to the present. As I've been told, I take deep breaths with my eyes closed, trying to *find my center*. Breathe. Just, breathe. I wait until the shaking stops and I can inhale without shuddering.

I open my eyes and frown. "Well, that doesn't look good." I know this car inside out. I know when it's going to shout, splutter, cough, jerk. But this smoke? That's new.

On a sigh, I pull out my cell and go to my contacts. Then Favorites. He's at the top. Reg the Rescue Truck.

He answers in two rings. "Where are you?"

"Downtown."

"Fred's Diner?"

"Yep." I'm not embarrassed. That stopped the fourth time Reg rescued me. Now Reg and I are firm friends.

"I'm at the Starbucks drive-thru. A few minutes away. Vanilla latte?"

I drop into the driver's seat. He doesn't even tell me I need to get rid of Dolly anymore. "Love one." I hang up and turn on the radio, sighing when David Bowie's *Heroes* joins me. Granted, he's a bit fuzzy and the crackly reception would be annoying for many, but crackly and fuzzy is my life these days. I relax back, glancing at my phone when it starts vibrating in my hand. I frown at the unfamiliar number and quieten Bowie. "Hello?"

"Hi, it's me," a man says.

I cock my head. "Who's me?"

"Me."

I pull my phone away from my ear and look down at the number again. Definitely not familiar. And as for the British accent? Never heard it. "Again, who's me?" I ask.

There's silence for a few moments, the man probably checking his cell too.

"Wrong number?" I ask.

"You're not Sandy, are you?"

"No, I'm Beau."

There's a brief silence before he speaks again. "Sorry, I was after my personal shopper."

Personal shopper? "Well, I decorate. Sorry to disappoint."

He hums, it's thoughtful, and I find my shoulders rolling back slowly. Weirdly. "Sorry to bother you."

"No bother," I say, seeing Reg pull into the road up ahead. "Must go, my knight in shining armor has arrived." I hang up, wondering where that light, jokey reply came from, and jump out of Dolly, giving Reg a wave, like he might not see the lingering ball of smoke floating above me.

He pulls up alongside me and leans out of the window, his customary cigarette hanging out the side of his mouth. "The smoke's new." He hands a latte down to me. "Jumper cables aren't gonna fix that, beauty."

I look back at Dolly, a little solemn. "But you can fix her, can't you?" I couldn't bear to say goodbye to her.

"Let's get her on the truck and back to my repair shop. If she can be fixed, I'll fix her."

"Thanks, Reg."

He sets about hooking Dolly up while I collect my bags and paint off the back seat. I load it all into Reg's truck, and as I climb into the cab, my cell rings again. I glance down at the screen as I settle in my seat, faltering pulling on my belt as I answer.

"Hi, it's me."

"Hi, me," I say, rolling my eyes.

"I have a few things I need."

I raise my eyebrows. I mean, who is this guy? "Your wish is my command."

"Sorry?"

"Anything you so desire."

There's silence, and I purse my lips.

"Pen and paper at the ready," I go on. "What would sir like? A diamond for his girlfriend? A case of champagne? A few whips for the upcoming orgy?" Reg climbs into the truck and gives me a curious look. I shrug and take a sip of my latte. "Or female company?" I add. What do rich people with personal shoppers and fuck-all problems want these days?

More silence. So much in fact, I have to check he's still on the line. He is. I bring my cell back to my ear, just catching his inhale. And I wait. "I'll take all except the diamond," he says, and it sounds rough. Dark.

My eyebrows slowly rise. No diamond. No girlfriend or wife? "How would sir like to pay?"

"With sex."

I stare at the windscreen, and he hums again. It's low. Raspy. I discreetly force myself out of my tense body, hearing him drawing breath to speak.

"But you already have a knight in shining armor," he says.

I look across to Reg, who has a freshly lit cigarette in between his lips. His beard has a few remnants of food nestled in it, his bulbus nose is an angry shade of red, and his baseball cap probably hasn't been washed since 1980. Reg obviously feels me inspecting him and turns toward me. He grins, revealing a total of five teeth. I shake my head and smile back. "I do," I reply. "I'm being rescued at this very moment."

Reg hitches an eyebrow as we rumble off down the road, and I silently contemplate that notion. Of being rescued. Of *really* being rescued.

"Then I'll stop calling you," he says flatly.

"Enjoy your sex party."

"I will."

And then he's gone.

3

JAMES

I place the phone on my desk slowly, like distance between us would be wise. It would. I look across to the pad on my desk where her number appeared next to my new contact, courtesy of Goldie. Calling her once? A stupid mistake. Twice? Silly. A third time? That would be suicide.

I reach for the pad, turning it a fraction. The two numbers noted down—Beau Hayley's and the contact—suddenly align to the correct names. I take a pen and scribble across Beau Hayley's, eradicating any chance of me fucking up again. Then I face the screens that blanket one wall and turn them all on. Each one blinks to life, showing me mug shots of all the men on my list. I don't need the screens. Each and every one of these men are etched on my sick brain. Along with the gory details of their deaths. Or impending deaths.

Kicking up my feet on my desk, I relax back with my keyboard on my lap and tap out some words across a face.

DECEASED

My eyes drift across to my next target, my lip curling. The Fox. Polish. A man with a fondness for selling young girls. Another contact of The Bear, and further proof of his reach. Of the control he has over the criminals in this city.

My email dings, and I bring up my inbox on the largest screen in the center of the wall. I open the attachment. And suddenly, lost amid the surrounding faces of criminals, is Beau Hayley.

I stare at the photograph of a young woman on the pavement of a Miami street. She's the image of her mother, the woman who relentlessly tried to hunt me down. Jaz Hayley lost her life as a consequence. And now her daughter is about to lose hers too.

"Let it go, Beau," I whisper, stroking over my Cupid's bow slowly, my stare fixed on her. In this shot, her mask is off, and her grief is embedded on every inch of her fair skin. Her eyes, eyes bordering on black, are infinite pits of sadness. She's beautiful. But eerily so.

Beau Hayley projects darkness.

And I am responsible for that darkness.

I tear my eyes away and make a call to the right person. "Hi, it's me," I say when the call connects.

"Who?"

I can't help laughing at myself. Sandy is a bloke. I didn't question the name. I didn't question the fact that my new contact appeared to be a woman.

"I asked a question." His accent is thick. Russian.

"That's irrelevant. I need some stock."

"I only do business with men I know."

"Don't take it personally. No one knows me, and since you're new to the area and business, I would have thought you'd take every buyer you can get."

"Name."

"You can call me The Enigma."

He inhales, and I smile. "Your real name."

"Don't tell me you were christened Sandy."

"Moot point," he drawls.

"Do you want my money or not?" I ask. "And as an added bonus, I'll kill The Bear. Or I could just kill you, take your guns, and leave The Bear filling The Brit's boots."

"I'm listening."

Of course he's listening.

4

BEAU

Trying to make it to the front door is like fighting my way through a rainforest. Masses of hydrangeas line the pathway, creeping into the middle, narrowing the path. With my arms full, I resort to turning and backing my way through to avoid being smacked in the face by branches and beautiful pompoms of white and pink. I make it to the front door unscathed, and with a lack of a free hand to retrieve my key, I swing a pot of paint so it hits the wood. I hear her, singing her way to let me in. Aunt Zinnea. The woman is the epitome of sunshine and smiles. Someone around here needs to be.

"My darling," she says as she flings the door open. "I was getting worried, you said you'd be back hours ago." She opens the way, relieving me of the paint, and I pass her, stopping briefly so she can kiss my cheek.

"Dolly had a hissy fit." I drop my things at the bottom of the stairs and stretch life back into my aching body. "Reg dropped me off at the end of the street." His big truck doesn't fit down our narrow road. He tried once and got wedged between two Escalades.

Zinnea sighs as she sets the paint down and flounces past me, heading for the kitchen at the back of the house, her kimono wafting behind her. "I don't know why you didn't accept your birthday gift from your father. You could still keep Dolly. How many times has she broken down now?"

Accept my father's gift? That wasn't a gift. That was a guilt crusher. I wasn't about to feed his need for absolution. Besides, Mom bought me Dolly. She's a classic. Busted, but still a classic.

I follow Zinnea into the kitchen and find Dexter at the table, engrossed in the screen of his laptop. He's still in his blues. He looks up and gives me his usual kind smile. "Good day, Beau?" he asks. Always does.

"I met Nath for a coffee," I say, and the inevitable looks are thrown between Zinnea and Dexter. I ignore them. They know why I met Nath. "And Dolly's broken again." I head straight for the fridge, pulling out a bottle of wine. "You?"

"Dead man by the ocean. Always fun." He goes back to his computer. "The Feds have moved in," he mutters, as I pull down a glass. I don't offer wine to anyone. Zinnea is almost ready for her performance this evening, and Dexter will be there admiring his love as she woos the crowd.

I pour a drink and join Dexter at the table. He smiles, not taking his attention from his screen. "No work today?" he asks.

"No."

"Is it drying up?"

"A little," I admit. More looks are thrown between them. It's long past being tiresome. "Don't say it," I warn.

"The force would have you back in a heartbeat," Dexter says, ignoring my pleas. "Years at the academy, Beau. You aced the Phase

One test. Top five in the country, for Christ's sake. You're throwing so much away."

"I'm not working for an institution I can't believe in," I mutter, taking a swig of my wine. Look where it got Mom. Dead. And they're doing fuck all about it. It's time to change the subject before they see the rage burning my insides. "I picked up the colors for your room."

"Ooh, let me see," Zinnea says, distracted, as she wrestles to fasten her bra.

I jump up and head to the hallway to collect the paint, arriving back in the kitchen to find she has abandoned her bra around her waist and now has one leg in her pantyhose. I set the paint cans on the side, pulling my keys from my pocket, using one to lever off a lid. I reveal the color, and she's across to me in a shot, holding the other leg of her pantyhose. "Oh, I love it."

"Pink?" Dexter asks from behind, and we both turn to find his glasses have been removed, his attention now firmly pointing this way. "We agreed no pink."

"Oh, won't you indulge me?" Zinnea pouts.

"No. No pink, Lawrence. We agreed."

I wince, peeking at Zinnea to gage just how pissed off she is. And not because Dexter is putting a rare foot down. "Dexter!" she barks, motioning down her half-dressed form. "What's my damn name?" Her voice has deepened to its usual manly tone, anger fueling it.

Dexter sighs. "Well, I don't know." He throws his glasses on the table. "You're standing there with your bra around your waist, one hairy leg in your pantyhose, and your balls hanging out of your satin panties. Who are you right now?"

I purse my lips, finding my wine and filling my mouth. The rules are clear, so I have no clue how Dexter fucked up so monumentally. If the wig is on, it's Zinnea. And the wig is on, albeit wonky. I can't remember when my uncle went from being an uncle to an uncle *and* an aunt all wrapped up into one. But I remember the shitstorm it created in the family. My father, the prejudice asshole, kept me and my mother away like his brother was contagious. And yet, even now, all these years later and a pile of further crimes marked against my father's name, Zinnea never badmouths him. Dexter, on the other hand, shares my contempt. Good. I need someone to remind me of what an asshole he is whenever I'm feeling weak.

"And you can keep your big mouth shut," Zinnea snaps, slapping my shoulder.

I cough over my mouthful, spraying the table. "I didn't say a word."

"You didn't need to."

Zinnea finishes getting her stocking on and her bra into place before perfecting her makeup in the mirror at the table with us. And I watch her, fascinated, as she smiles her way through her task. How easy she finds it to smile. How hard I do.

"Done," she says, smacking her painted lips. "Now I must dress." Standing from the table, she clasps the side of her kimono and breezes out of the room. "Oh, I nearly forgot," she says, pausing at the door and holding the frame as she looks back. She's still smiling, but this one has a hint of something I'm wary of. "Your father called."

I return to my wine immediately, sensing the suddenly thick atmosphere. I say nothing, looking up when I feel Dexter's eyes on me. I sip my wine, giving him a *what?* look.

"He would love to see you," Zinnea goes on, clearly cautious. "He's been trying to call you."

I close my eyes and breathe out slowly. Yes, I know. I've been purposely ignoring him. "I can't be around him and that child he calls a girlfriend," I say, braving facing Zinnea again. "Nothing's changed for me."

"*Time* has changed, my darling." She smiles mildly, desperate for me to make amends with him. "And maybe with it, your father has. He called *me*, for God's sake. Your father! He even asked how I was."

I hate the elation she's so obviously feeling. Like me, Zinnea shouldn't be giving him the time of day. I don't understand her motives. Or maybe I do. Live and let live, she says. Shake out the negativity. "He must want something," I mutter.

"Yes, your forgiveness."

My forgiveness? He'll never get that. He can continue trying to find redemption in charity work and being the consummate businessman, but he'll never get freedom from my contempt. I finish my wine and drag myself up, heading past Zinnea to the front door. I stop and kiss her cheek. "I'm going to see Mom."

She pulls me back when I break away, giving me a hug. "Send my love."

"I will."

She releases me, and I head for the door. "Beau, my darling?"

I look back, and she smiles lightly. "Let it be, I beg you. Just let it be. The upset with your father, my darling. It's the last demon you need to be rid of."

I say nothing, just return her smile and close the front door behind me. Zinnea and Dexter have worked so hard to stabilize me. I can't let on that I feel far from stable. Can't let them know of the demons that still haunt me. And my father is undisputedly one of them.

I wrestle with the dilapidated iron gate, wincing when the metal scrapes along the concrete beneath it. How it hasn't fallen off its hinges yet, I don't know. The pathway isn't much better, the slabs uneven, every single one broken, weeds bursting up from between the cracks. I tread carefully, avoiding the stinging nettles. "It's like dicing with death coming to see you, Mom," I say to myself, making it to her relatively unscathed.

I settle on the overgrown grass and put the bunch of tulips down beside me. "Hi." I inhale, my heart turning in my chest, as I stare at her headstone.

JASMINE (JAZ) HAYLEY
1965-2019
GONE BUT NEVER FORGOTTEN

"I'm fine," I assure her. "But Aunt Zinnea is definitely getting soft in her old age. She sends her love, by the way." I get to my knees and pull the stone vase free of the holder, plucking out the limp roses and emptying the old water. I take the bottle of Evian from my bag and top up the vase, arranging the tulips just so. They're Mom's favorite. Mine too. She always said they were a sign of brighter, sunnier, longer days. Nothing is bright and sunny anymore. And longer days are crueler days. "Perfect," I say, placing the vase back and tweaking the stems. Then I get myself comfortable, lying on the grass beside her grave, watching the clouds roll through the sky.

Aunt Zinnea taught me how to control my thoughts. How to channel my anger. How to shake out the negativity. How to find peace amid tragedy. It's something I never really got the hang of. A lesson I struggle to remember each day. Life is unpredictable, and death even more so. The only guarantee is that it will happen. Sometimes too soon, sometimes too late, but it will happen. "I'm thinking about buying my own place," I say, pulling at the blades of grass beside me. "Aunt Zinnea would never say, but I'm sure she must think I've long outstayed my welcome." I point to the sky. "Oh, look, the Eiffel Tower." I watch as the tall, tapering cloud drifts over us, losing its shape as it goes. "I said it was for a month." I drop my head to the side. "That was nearly two years ago." I'm thirty. I have the money. I even have the desire. But there's that tiny part of me that's scared to leave Zinnea's sanctuary. A tiny part that knows it would be stupid. And seeing my father? No. That's a sure-fire way to send me spiraling further. I can't come to terms with the fact he's still living and my mom's not. I haven't even got my head around the fact that *I* am still here.

Fear. It's one of the things Aunt Zinnea has worked so hard to push out of me. I haven't the heart to tell her it hasn't worked. I don't fear death anymore, but I fear life. I fear I'll never be rid of this bitterness. Never be rid of the pain. Never be able to keep my mind clean. Never be able to look in the mirror and like what I see. It's such an effort, an everyday struggle. And the answer to my problems is always haunting me. Everywhere I look, I see a way out.

Zinnea is my crutch.

I can't bring myself to leave my crutch. She was Mom's crutch too. And the object of my father's scorn.

I breathe out and return my eyes to the clouds, feeling around on the grass beside me when I hear my cell. I look up at the screen, rolling my eyes at the strange number that I've become familiar with today. "Isn't the sex party doing it for you?"

"You mentioned you paint," he says, seeming to completely miss my quip.

My smile is hesitant. "I did."

"I'm looking for a painter."

He doesn't sound too sure about that. In fact, he sounds agitated. "What do you want painted?"

"My bedroom."

"Is it worn out from all the sex parties?"

"How much?"

This is getting plain weird. "I'd need to take a look in order to quote."

"Tonight?"

Tonight? "I'm visiting my mother."

There's a long silence, and once again I'm checking to see if he's still on the line. He is. "Tomorrow night?" he eventually says.

I nibble my lip, wondering how to approach this. Work is sparse. I'm not concerned, it's not like I need the money. Just the distraction. The calm I find in painting. The closeness to my mom. "I'm a bit busy at the moment." I'm being instinctively wary, naturally. This is all quite odd. His calls. The conversation. I should hang up.

"Is that a no?"

"No." But instead I leave an opening, because my curiosity is raging. I damn the part of me that hasn't yet got the memo that I'm no longer a cop.

"So when can you look?"

"Let me just check my calendar," I say, pulling my cell away from my ear for a few seconds, rolling my eyes at myself. I look across to Mom. *I know. Pathetic.* "Monday evening?" I ask once I've left it long enough to check my empty schedule.

"Eight," he says, but it isn't a question. He's not suggesting. He's telling me.

And that gets my back up. "Seven. I'll need your name and address."

"Eight. I'll text it to you." He hangs up, and I stare at the screen of my phone, slightly stunned.

"Okay then," I say to myself, frowning at the sky, ignoring the part of my brain that's asking me what on earth I'm doing. The bigger part of my brain is too enthralled.

And distracted.

"Oh look," I whisper, lifting my cell and pointing it at the sky. "That one looks like the shape of Britain."

5

JAMES

Suicide it is, then. My skin tingles. I know what that means.

Danger.

Goldie wanders into my office and clocks my mobile resting on my cheek. "What the fuck are you playing at?"

She knows. Of course she knows. Since the moment I ripped a bloke off her at the back of a London boozer and battered the fucker, she's not left my side. That was six years ago. She never went back into the Marines. Their loss. My gain.

I get up, tossing my mobile on the desk and rounding it, unbuttoning my shirt as I go. "Have you eaten?" I ask, my way of telling her that this isn't up for debate. Because how the fuck am I going to explain it to her when I haven't got a fucking clue what I'm doing myself?

"No. Answer me. That woman was the next exciting thing to come out of the academy. She fucking flew through her Phase One, for fuck's sake, just like her mother. They called her—"

"Lara Croft," I murmur. "I know."

Goldie's nostrils flare. "So what are you going to do? Kill her?" She snaps her mouth shut quickly, her eyes unusually wide. "Wait. Don't tell me you're worried about her?"

I scowl as I pick up my feet, passing her. "I don't worry about people. I kill people." But the truth is, if Beau Hayley doesn't give up on her relentless need for justice, she could be opening a whole new can of worms I can't be fucked to deal with. She could also end up dead. "I'm ensuring my immunity." I need Beau Hayley to stop digging, and I haven't a fucking clue how to achieve that.

"Where are you going?"

"Out." I swipe up my car keys and march out of my office, willing myself to get my head on straight quickly before I send everything I've worked for to shit.

I get in my elevator, the doors close, and I stare at myself in the reflection. I see them clearly. The devil on one shoulder. An angel on the other.

The devil speaks louder. The angel never made it.

I blink, looking away from the man staring back at me.

The stranger.

Yet the person I know best in this world.

The doors open, and I see Otto look up from the desk in the lobby. As I pass, I glance at the bank of screens before him, footage from every angle of my building. Every empty floor, watched. Every entrance, watched. The roof, watched. "I'm expecting someone on Monday evening. Beau Hayley. Send her straight up."

Yep. Straight-up suicide.

"Beau . . ." Otto fades off, catching his tongue. But the tone in which he spoke her name was loaded with concern. "No problem."

By the time I've made it to the garage, I've still found no sense. I get in my car, start the engine, and tap in Beau Hayley's address into the sat nav.

And by the time I pull into her street, still no fucking sense.

I park up across the road and turn off the engine, resting my elbow on the door, my eyes lasers on the house. An hour passes with no signs of life. Nothing. Not even a shred of sensibility for me.

And then there's something. A taxi pulls into the street, and I sink lower in my seat. Lower still when it pulls into the space directly in front of me. She's in the back, literally meters away. She could look into my car and see me clearly. *Seen.*

I watch her, tense, once again wondering what the fuck I'm playing at, as she stares at the house for what seems like days. *What is she doing?*

Eventually, she gets out and stands motionless by the side of the cab for a few minutes. Then she gets back in, and the taxi pulls out quickly. I breathe for the first time in minutes, scrubbing my hands down my face. "Don't follow her," I warn myself, starting the engine, looking in the rearview mirror at the taillights getting farther away. A quick three-point turn has me facing the wrong direction. And only seconds after that, I'm two cars behind the cab.

I follow it to the supermarket where it drops her at the store entrance. I get out and jog across the car park. Stop. Turn around to go back to my car. Turn back. "Fuck," I breathe, following her in. I take a basket and tail her as she wanders aimlessly up and down every aisle in the quiet supermarket. But I keep a safe distance.

Safe? Being in the same country as this woman isn't safe. "Leave," I order myself, studying her browsing the aisles. But she puts nothing in her basket. She doesn't seem to be here for anything in particular.

Unlike me.

I'm here for something.

Damage control.

And yet I feel like I'm losing my grip on *all* control.

6

BEAU

On Monday evening at eight, I push my way through the glass doors into the lobby of James House, a space-age, ultra-modern twenty-story building on the east side of town. I'm immediately alarmed by the number of mirrors I'm confronted with. Every wall, every door, even the elevator.

The concierge glances up. "Can I help you?" He's a giant, with a startling number of piercings on his face and an impressive beard. Is he the concierge? Security? None of the above?

"I'm here to see James Kelly. My name's Beau."

"He said to send you straight up." He heads toward the elevator as I follow, avoiding all of the mirrors, and I peek at the desk as I pass, seeing dozens of screens. Security cameras. Everywhere. It isn't odd. But so many?

He swipes a card through a reader and the doors ping open. I'm faced with more mirrors. Stepping inside, he punches a few buttons on the panel. "It goes straight to the top floor." He holds the doors for me to enter.

"Thank you."

He nods pensively, the doors close, and I'm confronted by my reflection. I squint, stepping forward, looking closely at my eyes. Usually empty eyes that are now overflowing with curiosity. "What are you doing, Beau?" I ask quietly. "Leave." I rake a hand through my loose, dark blonde hair, combing through the long ends with my fingers, pulling the masses over one shoulder. It's wavy. Unmanageable. I sigh and pull it up into a messy ponytail, pulling the sleeves of my oversized shirt down and tying the tails into a knot.

The doors of the elevator open, along with my mouth. "Jesus," I whisper, staring at the wall of glass across the room. The skyline of Miami lies beyond, majestic as the sun sets. It's breathtaking. Mesmerizing. I step out and look around, fascinated by how the glass stretches around three walls. I'm in a giant glass box. One huge room. Literally every wall is glass . . . so what the heck is there to paint?

"Hello?" I call, hovering by the elevator. A staircase lines the far-right wall. That's glass too, with white treads on each floating step. There are candles everywhere, all lit, all flickering, intensifying the already intense space. I shudder and look down at my cell. Eight on the dot. "Hello," I call again, this time louder. Nothing. I dial him, rather than venture any farther into his glass box, and it rings and rings until it eventually goes to an automated voicemail. "Um . . . hi. It's me. I'm here, and you're not. I'm standing outside your elevator on the threshold of your glass box." I feel . . . uneasy.

I hang up and stand there, a little lost, waiting for him to appear, while I run through everything I know about James Kelly, which isn't much. He's not on any social media, and this address threw up nothing on Google, except an old real estate advertisement marketing it for sale five years ago.

Ten minutes pass, no sight, no sound. "Come on," I say to myself, checking my cell again. I look back at the elevator doors, which are now closed. At the panel on the wall that requires a keycard. And I mentally see the collection of buttons inside that require a code. I'm stuck. "Amazing," I whisper, turning and facing the glass box again. I didn't get the name of the guy downstairs. He wasn't in uniform, therefore there was no company shirt to enlighten me on who he works for. *Shit. Real smart, Beau.*

I venture farther in, cautious, slow, gazing around. "Mr. Kelly?" I call, still getting no reply. "It's Beau Hayley. I'm here to look at your bedroom." I reach the bottom of the staircase and gaze up. "Mr. Kelly?" I hear something. Music. That would explain why he can't hear me. Wherever he is. *Where is he?*

I kick off my flip-flops without thought and start taking the steps slowly, one by one, finding a whole new space at the top. A large space, with a round table in the center, and more glass walls, although these are frosted glass with frosted glass doors leading off, six in total. And still no walls to paint.

The music is louder now, coming from one of the rooms to the right. *Paradise Circle*. Massive Attack. A few chills glide up my spine as I approach the door. Knock it. "Mr. Kelly?" I call through the glass.

Nothing.

I don't know what possesses me—I should turn and leave—but, instead, my body takes on a mind of its own. I grip the handle, turn it gently, and push the door open a fraction. "Hel—"

Holy fuck!

My ability to speak is stripped from me, and I suck back my words as I squeeze the handle, my body becoming a statue. I'm wide-eyed. Open-mouthed. My tangled, shocked mind is trying to piece together the scene in the colossal room before me.

There's so much to take in, but the one thing that holds me completely rapt?

His profile.

I stare. I just stare. I stare at him as he smashes into her from behind, his fist clenched in her hair, holding her head back, stretching her throat. I allow my gaze to drift. She's chained to a frame that's anchored to the wall, extending into the room. She's blindfolded. Gagged. Bound.

They're lost.

I flex my hand on the door handle, screaming at myself to go. *Close the door. Leave.* But then something else catches my attention, tucked away in the corner of the room.

A man.

Slumped in a chair.

Naked.

Masturbating.

He's lost too, his drowsy eyes rooted to the couple before him.

Fuck.

I step back and pull the door closed, struggling to breathe. Struggling to find instruction. I stare at the frosted glass, bringing my cell to my mouth and nibbling on the edge, glancing over my shoulder to the stairs. What the hell am I supposed to do? He's obviously forgotten about our meeting.

I pull up on that thought. No. The guy in the lobby—occupation to be determined—said he was expecting me. My head starts to ache, my eyes going back and forth between the door and the stairs. He was expecting me. He didn't forget. Of course he wouldn't anticipate me snooping around his apartment, because I can't even comprehend the possibility that he wouldn't care if I saw that. So I'm left to reach the only other explanation. He's got carried away. Lost himself in ecstasy. But then our telephone conversation is suddenly trampling through my mind.

Sex party.

Jesus Christ.

I head downstairs to the elevator, slipping my flip-flops back on. "Oh my God, this is horrific." I squeeze my eyes closed, struggling to rid my mind of what I saw. Struggling to clear my ears of the sounds. The music. Which is still playing.

I go to the keypad and stare at it for a few seconds. The building. *Call the building.* I pull up Google, type in the name of the building, and search for a phone number. There's nothing. I'm going nowhere.

I close my eyes, breathing in, and accept my fate—my unthinkable, awful fate—sliding down to my ass by the elevator. He looked nowhere near done. It's all I can see in my mind. That scene. I reach up to my forehead and press my palm into it, trying in vain to suppress my thoughts.

Her moans. The sounds. The music.

His power.

I look to the ceiling, my cheeks inflating from my exhale. And I cringe, thinking back to our telephone conversation again. "Oh, Beau," I breathe, squirming harder. I can still hear the damn music. It's not helping, my brain off on a tangent, wondering what's happening up there. The man in the chair. Has he joined them?

My cell rings, and I jump out of my skin. "Fuck." I swipe to answer, grateful for the distraction. *Any* distraction. "Hello."

"Beau?"

"Hi, Reg." My eyes glue themselves to the top of the stairs. "How's Dolly?"

"Dead."

I recoil. "Break it to me gently, why don't you?"

He laughs. "You and I both know she's been on her deathbed for a while, Beau. I'm surprised you haven't come to terms with it."

I pout. "Is there nothing we can do?"

"Aside from replacing the engine, no."

"Why can't we do that?"

Reg falters. "It'll cost more than replacing the car, Beau. What with parts and labor. We're talking thousands of dollars."

"I don't mind how much it costs." I really don't. Truth be told, with all the money I've spent on Dolly over the years, I probably could have bought myself a shiny new, *reliable*, top-of-the-range Mercedes. But I don't want a shiny, new Mercedes. I want Dolly. "She's sentimental, Reg," I say, but he already knows that.

I hear him sigh. "I'll see if I can find a bargain engine somewhere."

I'd smile if I could. It's a struggle to have this simple conversation with Reg. "Thanks, Reg." He doesn't say goodbye, just hangs up, and I blink, my eyes burning from staring at the same spot at the top of the staircase for so long. What on earth shall I say when he finally finds me here?

I don't have time to ponder that. I hear a door open, and my back straightens. The music stops. I hear voices.

Oh God.

I scramble to my feet and mess with the thread of a rip in the thigh of my jeans as he rounds the corner at the top of the stairs, pulling on a T-shirt as he takes the steps. "Oh my God," I whisper, my eyes following him down the stairs.

Don't choke, Beau.

His face. He's brutally handsome, and yet almost callous. His dark hair is falling around his ears and across his eyes, wet and wavy, his rough, square jaw is tense. His body looks powerful. Hard and powerful, every muscle on his tall physique sharp.

I rip my eyes away from his bare chest, seeing the woman, now fully dressed in a business suit, following him. And behind her, the man from the chair. My mind blesses me with a quick, detailed recap of what I walked in on, although the people heading down the stairs toward me now look . . . different. Composed.

Dressed.

I wait to be spotted, feeling so fucking awkward.

"It was nice to see you, James," the woman says.

"Sure." His reply is simple and flat and with absolutely no hint that he feels the same.

"Yeah, really nice," the man adds.

James halts pulling his T-shirt down his torso, coming to an abrupt stop halfway down the stairs, forcing the man and woman to stop too. His hands remain motionless, still holding on to the material around his chest, his eyes laser beams.

On me.

I swallow.

"Beau Hayley," he murmurs, as the man and woman regard me with interest. My ability to talk has escaped me. Gone. I swallow, shift, and look away from him, needing a break from his penetrating eyes.

I eventually locate some words. They're not the words I need, but all the words I can find. "James Kelly," I whisper, willing myself to look at him. Face him. It's a task.

I exhale, my shoulders dropping with the air that leaves me.

"Thanks for waiting," he says quietly, his tone flat.

I dig deep for the woman who always remained cool and unaffected in the face of uncertainty. "No problem." I look past him to the two silent people in the background, and he glances over his shoulder.

"I'll see you out." He continues down the stairs, his naked feet padding toward me, the hem of his frayed jeans dragging the floor. He hits the call button on the wall and the doors open. I move back, out of their way, managing a small, awkward smile to the man and woman as they pass me and enter.

"Beth, Darren, good evening," James says. The doors close.

And . . . silence.

A horrible, screaming silence.

I look up at him. He's biting the corner of his lip, his chiseled jaw ticking. He's thinking. What is he thinking?

He steps back, away from me. His eyes are crystal clear pits of blue. Sharp, like his jaw, intense, like his persona, and his eyebrows are heavy, making him appear as unfriendly as he feels. His wavy hair's darkened by sweat. He's stupidly stunning. "I ran over on my meeting." His words are quiet. Rough.

I can't look at him. His eyes are too astute, his lazy gaze potent. I feel like he's tapping in on my thoughts. "I called, but you obviously couldn't hear me." *Because you were lost in some pretty intense-looking kink.* "I would have left"—I motion back to the elevator—"but I don't have a keycard or a code."

He points to the button above the slot for the card. "You don't need a card or a code to leave, just to enter."

"Oh." I inwardly shake my head to myself. I could have left? I could have spared us both this embarrassment? Yet, as I look at him, he doesn't look very embarrassed. He just looks inconvenienced. "You know, if now's not a good time, I could come back."

"Now's fine." He turns on his bare feet and heads to the open kitchen on the other side of the room. "Would you like a drink?"

"I'm good, thanks." I follow him, glancing around again. More glass. "Nice place."

"Thanks." He opens a tall glass-fronted fridge and pulls out a beer, twisting the cap off and resting back on the countertop as he takes a slug.

I don't know what it is, but I just can't look him in the eye, so I take another pointless peek around his apartment.

"Do you struggle with eye contact?" he asks, and I dart my stare back to his. He regards me as he takes another swig of his beer. "Or is it just me?"

I laugh on the inside. *Only when I've unexpectedly stumbled upon your orgy, and then have to pretend I've not seen your gloriously naked body pounding relentlessly into a woman.*

Holding his eyes, if only to make a point, I scratch through my mind for what to say. This guy is dark. How dark is yet to be determined, but my intuition tells me *very* dark. I've been submerged in enough darkness in my time to recognize a damaged soul. To sense someone's anger. To feel their pain. I'm a walking, talking example.

What's his story?

It's like he's purposely trying to make me feel uncomfortable, and I hate him for succeeding. What I was faced with before isn't helping, of course, but he doesn't know I saw.

Or does he?

He cocks his head, and I cock mine right back as he watches me. "You know, I think I will have that drink." Give me *all* the alcohol, for the love of God.

He nods mildly, pulling the fridge open, eyes still on me. "Beer?"

He's goading me, and that pisses me off. "Please." I'll feel like I've failed if I look away, so, like a stubborn fool, I maintain our eye contact, refusing to let him win. I will not give him that power.

He sets his bottle aside to unscrew the cap of mine and then hands it to me. It's all I can do not to scowl as I accept it and take a sip.

Eyes. Still. On. Me.

I'm beginning to think he knows I saw what was going on upstairs. The way he's being, this staring shit. He really is trying to make me feel uncomfortable. Why? I am Jaz Hayley's daughter. I absolutely will *not* break, and as if he's read my mind, I see the tiniest of smirks crack the straightness of his lips. And then *he* looks away, running a hand through his messy, sexed-up waves.

"Let me show you my office." He pushes himself off the countertop and heads for the stairs, and I stare at his wide shoulders as he goes.

"Your office?" I call, and he stops, his foot on the first step, looking back.

"You're here to paint, aren't you?"

"Yes, but you mentioned your bedroom." Why the hell would I point that out? I don't want to step foot in his bedroom.

"I did?" he questions. "I meant my office."

"But all I've seen is glass."

His eyebrows lazily rise, and I die on the inside, looking away. "But you've not seen upstairs."

Oh God, Beau, just leave. Go. Put yourself out of this misery. But I don't. Instead, I say nothing and follow, kicking my flip-flops off again at the bottom of the stairs before climbing them, my eyes nailed to the backs of his thighs.

We round the corner at the top and, naturally, my focus lands on the door into his dungeon. "Do you live alone?" I ask, making idle chitchat in an attempt to break the ice. I've never met a man so cold.

He passes the first door, *the* door, and looks back at me. "Yes."

"Are you always this hospitable?" It just falls out, my mind all over the place, no matter how hard I'm trying to convince him otherwise. My job as a police officer taught me how to be calm in the face of seriously fraught situations. How to maintain my cool. It's all lost on me now.

"I'm *very* hospitable," he replies, and I laugh under my breath without thought as he comes to a stop at another door, looking back at me. Good grief, his eyes are like bottomless pits of sinfulness. Magnets. He takes the handle, but he doesn't open it. "Are you sensing a bit of tension between us?" he asks huskily.

"Yes." I don't lie. I'm too old to play games.

"Why do you think that is?"

"I don't know. You tell me."

"Are you usually so awkward?"

"No. Never." I'm really not, and I just unwittingly admitted that I'm feeling uncomfortable.

"So, it really is just me?"

"Yes, it's you." I give him a sarcastic smile. "Does that make you happy?" I sense it does.

"No, it makes me curious."

"Why?"

His eyes fall down my body, and he takes his time taking me in. "It makes me curious," he whispers, returning his eyes to mine. I'm immediately hypnotized by him. Spellbound. "Because I can't figure out if you dislike me." A beat. A blatant beat for impact. "Or want to fuck me."

My lips part, a little in shock, and, God help me, a lot with desire. "And I can't figure out if you're purposely trying to make me feel uncomfortable, or whether you're a natural asshole."

He smiles. That's wicked too. "A bit of both."

I cock my head, entranced, as he opens the door and gestures me inside. I force my feet to move, passing him, feeling his shrewd stare follow me into the room. More floor-to-ceiling glass, though only on one wall. The couch could seat eight people with ease. The small kitchen in the corner is equipped with a glass fridge, a Nespresso machine, and glass-fronted cupboards with matching glass cups and saucers. His desk is more a conference table—again, glass—and his chair sits between that and the window. One of the three walls is covered in dozens of TVs. You could live in his office, and it tells me all I need to know about James Kelly. He's a workaholic. It's no wonder he's fairly anti-social. I bet he's holed up in here most of the time when he's not at work. *Or performing an extraordinary fuck for some man to watch.*

I take in the two plastered walls—large walls—and look to the ceiling. It's scattered with dozens of tiny spotlights. I grimace. That'll be a bitch to paint.

"What's the verdict?" he asks, cocking a leg and sitting on the conference table.

"It's a week's work." I wander over to one of the walls and run my palm across the paint. Smooth. Only a couple of holes to fill from where picture hooks have been. "The ceiling will be a pain with all those lights to cut in around." I look up, as does he. "A thousand."

"No, I think there's only two hundred," he replies, his eyes dancing across the spotlights.

I smile to myself, admiring his throat. "Dollars," I clarify. "Excluding paint."

His head drops. "A thousand? To paint two walls and a ceiling?"

"They're big walls and a very annoying ceiling." I'll have a seriously bad neck by the time I'm done intricately cutting in around all those lights. One hundred dollars will probably be spent on a chiropractor. Plus, my inner mind is probably trying to put him off. Trying to lose the job. I shouldn't spend any more time here than I have to, and I don't need to spend a minute. *Then why are you still here?*

Clearly because I'm too fucking curious. Or bored.

James shakes his head. "You're ripping me off. I could do it myself on a weekend."

I take a sip of my beer and hold it out to him. He takes it, if a little tentatively. "Then enjoy," I say, turning on my bare feet and leaving his office, feeling the pressure of his presence lifting from my shoulders the farther I walk away from him. I take the stairs, slipping my flip-flops on as I hit the bottom. I don't think I could spend another minute in this glass box with that glass man, let alone a whole week. He's sharp. Cutting.

Transparent?

I wander into the elevator when the doors open and turn, slowly lifting my eyes. He's made it to the bottom of the stairs.

And he just stares at me.

And despite wanting to look away, his eyes refuse to release me from their hold. His teeth latch on to his bottom lip. His hands go to the hem of his T-shirt. And he turns, pulling it up as he pads on bare feet to the kitchen.

I swallow and rest my weight on a hand against the mirror, my eyes darting across the vast expanse of his sharp back.

And the angry, deep, monstrous scar that blankets every inch of it.

7

JAMES

What the fuck am I thinking? I slump down on the couch, my eyes rooted on the elevator, my beer discarded and replaced with something hard. I neck the straight vodka and gasp. I knew what I was doing. When I arranged for some company prior to Beau Hayley arriving, I knew exactly what I was doing.

I was creating an obstacle. Making sure she hates me because she should. But with each update Goldie sends me on Beau Hayley, my intrigue grows. And those calls? Her voice? Something inside of me kicked, and I was fucked if I could ignore it.

Damaged.

Broken.

Hopeless.

Everything I once was is emblazoned over every inch of that woman. And my attraction? *That* caught me off guard. Her clear, fair complexion. Her messy blonde waves. Her dark, dark eyes. She moves with grace and purpose, and yet I've never seen someone look so obviously heavy and lost before. *Contempt for life*. I've never seen demons displayed so clearly on someone's skin.

Except when I look in the mirror.

"Fuck me," I murmur, rubbing at my forehead. I pull my mobile out and wake up the screen. Beau Hayley's face fills it.

Beautifully toxic.

She doesn't want to be here anymore.

And I can make that happen.

Do us both a favor.

8

BEAU

"I feel like I'm sleeping in a bottle of Pepto-Bismol," Dexter mutters as he drops his holster on the chaise that's adorned with regal peacocks.

I dunk my brush in the can and load it with more paint, balancing on top of my ladder to reach the corner. "She loves it."

"Of course she does. It looks like Barbie puked up all over it. Don't let her see you playing gymnastics like that."

"I'm as safe as houses." I swipe my brush with accuracy along the wall where it meets the ceiling, getting as perfect a line as I can with my new brush. "Terrible," I mutter, pulling back and inspecting.

"Looks perfect to me."

"All done," I declare, jumping down and setting my can on the drop cloth. *Perfect*. What the fuck is perfect, anyway? "They've discontinued my favorite brush." I've searched Google and come up with nothing. I curl my lip at my substitute brush as I toss it in the can of paint. "Where is she?" I ask, just as Aunt Zinnea bursts through the door looking harassed, her body encased in a floor-length red velvet gown.

"My wig," she cries. "Has anyone seen my wig?"

Both Dexter and I cast our eyes around their bedroom, across all of the drop cloths and decorating equipment. "I'll tidy up." I start transferring my tools into my box and wrap my brush and roller ready to wash.

"Beau, sweetheart?"

I glance up. Aunt Zinnea seems to have lost her panic and is now looking at me in that way she does. With concern.

"Why don't you come to my show this evening?"

I don't answer, just look at her in the way *I* do, and continue with my task of clearing their bedroom. A dark cavern of a club downtown on a Saturday night that's packed to the rafters with excited, loud fans is my worst kind of hell. She knows it. And yet each time she asks, I see new hope in her eyes.

"You look lovely," Dexter says, moving in for a swift change of subject, anything to get Aunt Zinnea off my back.

"Why, thank you." She reaches for her hair to twiddle at a lock coyly. Her smile drops. "My wig." And she's off around the bedroom like a whirlwind again, pulling sheets off furniture as she goes.

"You'll get paint on your dress." Dexter sighs. "Go wait in the kitchen. I'll find it." He claims Zinnea and leads her from the room, and I start to collect up all of the sheets and fold them away.
"She's not okay," Zinnea mutters, not for the first time this week.

"I'm sure she's fine."

"I can hear you, you know," I call tiredly, and they both stop at the door, looking back. "Uncle Lawrence is much quieter than Aunt Zinnea. If you're going to talk about me, do it when you're Lawrence."

Dexter chuckles lightly, and Zinnea shrugs off his hold with an air of indignance, throwing him a dirty look before returning her attention to me. "Let's meditate," she suggests, breezing across the room to me, holding up her dress.

I look to Dexter for help. He shrugs. "I don't need to meditate."

"You do. You haven't been yourself all week."

"Surely that's a good thing," I say over a laugh, getting my very own filthy look from Zinnea.

"I mean your *fake* self."

I get my amusement under control quickly, looking away from her probing eyes. She's right. I've been so wrapped up in controlling my wandering mind and stopping it from steering in a direction I know is totally the wrong way, I've neglected to remember to force my smiles. To make sure everyone thinks I'm okay. I even missed my therapy session. *Distracted.*

I let Zinnea take my hand and pull me out onto the bohemian-inspired balcony. A gigantic daybed is nestled under the canopy, the sheets adorned in elephants of every color of the rainbow, a few dozen cushions in clashing patterns scattered across it. Wind chimes ding, dreamcatchers sway, candles flicker. It really is a sweet sanctuary, but I'd enjoy it far more if I wasn't always here under duress. "You mustn't be late for your show," I say, knowing I'm fighting a losing battle.

She positions me on the end of a vivid striped woven rug. "Sit."

I do as I'm bid and rest my bum on my heels, and Zinnea mirrors me, though with more difficulty in her velvet gown. "Now," she says, her eyes like questioning probes on me. "What's on your mind?"

James Kelly.

"Nothing." Damn me, I look away, breaking the ultimate rule. I hear Zinnea hum, as my mind once again tortures me with a re-run of my encounter with him on Monday. So many words dance on my lips, waiting for me to speak them, to get Zinnea's thoughts. There's no question, she's liberal enough to take it. She won't gasp in horror or judge. So why don't I tell her? Why don't I share?

I finally admit to myself that my reluctance is more to do with what she'll conclude about *me* rather than a man she doesn't know. Why can't I get him off my mind? What is this curiosity? Why am I thinking about him all the damn time? He was artic cold. Unfriendly.

Spellbinding.

Darkness entices darkness.

Zinnea must see my mind reeling, because she turns her hands so her palms are facing the sky. She closes her eyes. I follow. She breathes in. So do I. She starts to talk softly, words I've heard time and again, words meant to soothe me, to settle me, to chase away the demons.

Is James Kelly a demon?

My eyes squeeze tighter, and *Paradise Circus* invades my hearing, along with grunts and moans, all mixing and blending, a montage of bodies slipping against each other, limbs entwining, hands drifting. I feel my shoulders drop. My heart slows. My breathing becomes shallow. I mustn't think about him. I mustn't see him again.

And then sirens screech, and I snap my eyes open, blinking into the darkness.

Fire.

Darkness.

Sirens.

Heat.

My hands start grappling at the floor beside me, searching for an anchor, anything to hold on to, anything to pull me up.

It's too hot.

I can't touch a thing.

It's all too hot.

Mom!

"Oh no," Zinnea breathes. "Dexter!"

I start to choke, the smoke overwhelming me. "I can't breathe," I wheeze, my mind now an abyss of unbearable memories, my throat feeling like it's clogged with smoke.

Screams.

Cries.

Panic.

Fear.

Pain of unbearable levels.

"Beau, sweetheart, take it. Breathe into it." I feel the crumpling of paper around my mouth, and I inhale deeply, drinking in the clean air. Clean. *So* clean. No smoke.

I gasp, my hand clenching the bag like the lifeline it is. My mind empties. My heart settles.

I'm alive.

But Mom is not.

I blink, finding Zinnea and Dexter before me, their faces a picture of worry. I can't bear it. I shake my head mildly, my way of telling them not to worry, that I'm fine. They won't buy it. I know that. "It's been awhile," Zinnea says, her body relaxing a smidge. "Are you still going to tell me you're fine?"

"Lawrence," Dexter warns gently, and this time Aunt Zinnea doesn't fly into a hissy fit. She simply sighs, defeated.

I give Dexter an appreciative smile. "You still keep these?" I say, handing him back the paper bag once I know I've got a handle on my attack.

"I still pick up one or two when I'm at Trader Joes." He shrugs. "Habit."

Habit. I've heard somewhere—I can't remember where—that you have to do something for an average of sixty-six days for it to become a habit. Dexter was collecting paper bags from Trader Joes for a lot longer than sixty-six days. And I used them all.

I look down at the decking, noticing I've pushed myself into a corner. *I mustn't see him again.* I blow out my cheeks and get to my feet, while Zinnea and Dexter remain on the floor, looking up at me. The cop and the drag queen. The most wonderful pair.

"I'm going to Walmart," I declare.

"How?" Zinnea asks. "Dolly's in the repair shop."

"I'll walk." Slowly.

"But it's so late," Dexter says, looking at his Apple Watch.

"All the better," I reply, moving past them, wincing for speaking my thoughts. It'll only fuel their concern. To them, my nighttime trips to Walmart are a positive step toward freedom. To me, it's one of the only places I find comfort. The blinding lights. The calm of the few people doing late-night shopping in such a colossal space. The low buzz of noise that blankets the mild sound of people's voices.

It's one of the few places on this earth that doesn't freak me out.

And I need it now more than I've felt I've needed it in years.

A voice over the speakers tells me I have fifteen minutes to finish my shopping before the store closes. I look down at the basket I'm tugging along. Empty. Coming to a stop at the fruit and veg aisle, I scan the shelves for the mangos, frowning when I see none. Who sells out of mangos? I stop a store worker, a young man with red spikey hair. "Do you have any mangos?" I ask, pointing at the empty space between the pineapples and kiwis.

"No more fresh fruit until tomorrow." He doesn't even stop, no doubt keen to finish his shift and go meet his friends.

I pout at his back, claiming my basket and tugging it along to the dairy aisle, dropping some milk into it. Because . . . everyone needs milk.

And chocolate. Everyone needs chocolate. I walk up and down every aisle to get to the candy aisle and stand for a few moments scanning the selection. My skin tingles. I look left. No one. I look right. No one.

My cell rings, but I ignore it, drained of the energy needed to reassure Zinnea, Lawrence, or Dexter that I'm okay. Instead, I text her, knowing she'll be waiting to go on stage, and she won't settle until she hears from me.

I'm okay.

I snatch a Hershey Bar, the biggest, and drop it in my basket.

Next, wine.

I trudge on, looking over my shoulder, rolling them as I do. No one.

Another announcement comes over the speakers, telling me I have ten minutes to find my wine and pay. It doesn't encourage me to rush, my feet heavy as I flip-flop along. My cell rings again. I ignore it. Again.

"I think someone wants to speak to you," somebody says, and I glance up at a man beside me, who's grabbing a bottle of expensive-looking Merlot.

"Is it good?" I ask, motioning to his hand.

He smiles. "The best."

I nod and reach for a bottle, my cell ringing off and immediately sounding again. I sigh, accepting that she won't settle until she *actually* speaks to me, my thumb going to answer. I falter placing my wine in my basket, the number on my screen making my heart boom. And I stare. For an age, I just stare at it, delving deep to find the will I need to answer, at the same time wondering what on earth he could want.

Because I can't figure out if you dislike me. Or want to fuck me.

"I can't figure that out either, James," I breathe, and let my thumb fall to the green icon that accepts the call. "Hello." I don't say my greeting as a question. He knows I know who it is.

"Beau."

"James."

Silence falls, and it's only broken when the speakers announce it's my last chance to grab the daily specials. I look at the ceiling, to all the bright, harsh light pouring down on me. It's a stark contrast to the darkness I'm feeling from down the line.

"Where are you?" he asks, his question flat and without any curiosity. Almost a demand.

"Walmart," I answer quietly and hesitantly.

"At this time?"

"It's less . . . chaotic." *Less noisy. Less busy. And it's light. So very light.* "And the risk of having the back of your legs rammed by a cart is reduced."

Rammed.

I blink my vision clear.

"You don't like busy?"

"Hate it," I answer, with no thought for what that might tell him about me. I start to wander toward the checkout, wondering, again, why he's calling me. Wondering why I'm indulging him.

"Me too," he whispers, almost to himself.

Except in your bedroom. That was far busier than it should have been. "Why are you calling me, James?" I ask, starting to unload my few things onto the conveyor belt.

"I don't know," he answers candidly, and my hand falters on its way back to the basket.

"Lonely?" I ask.

"Always."

Air catches in my throat, and it's beyond me why. *Loneliness.* It's a strange thing. You can be surrounded by many people, people who love you and shower you with attention, but still feel incredibly isolated. I'm testament to that. But James? I know nothing about him, apart from his bedroom habits, of course. And that he's possibly made of glass. "Me too," I say quietly, wanting him to hear me.

More silence stretches as I move to the other end of the

checkout and the lady behind the counter starts scanning my things. "So you called me because you're lonely?" I ask.

"No, I called you because I need you to paint my office."

I frown as I tap my card on the reader to pay. "I'm too expensive, apparently."

"And, apparently, I'm terrible at painting."

"You tried to do it yourself?" I can't imagine James painting. I can't imagine James doing anything other than brooding. And fucking. And there's part of my problem. I've imagined him fucking more than is healthy. I can't get the image of his strained, incredible body, or his intense face, out of my damn head.

I collect my bag and make my way toward the exit as a five-minute warning to the rest of the shoppers sounds.

"You have five minutes, Beau," he whispers.

"Five minutes for what?"

"To decide whether you can bring yourself to be in my company again." He hangs up, and I stare down at my cell, stunned. *Five minutes.*

I glance around me, as if the empty store can help me. No one can . . . *help me*. I walk out a little dazed and perch on a wall under a streetlight. The next five minutes feel like the longest of my life, my head overcrowded, leaving no space for me to actually decide whether I will take his offer, and only room to relive the last time I was in his apartment. And I admit to myself for the first time, I wanted to be that woman. Not so much because I want James to fuck me with that kind of ferocity, but because I want to feel as lost as she looked.

Light. Free. Immune to thinking, immune to everything, except for the pleasure.

I startle when my cell rings in my hand, and I stare at the screen for a few seconds before answering. I don't greet him. He doesn't greet me. We just breathe down the line at each other.

Lonely?

Always.

"See you Monday," he finally says.

Then he hangs up again.

The house is quiet when I get home, and I flick on every light as I make my way to the kitchen at the very back of the house. I unpack my few items. Wash my hands as I stare out into the dark yard. Go up to my room, flicking on every light switch I pass. I drop my bag on my bed and wander to Mom's special bottle of Krug on my nightstand, brushing across the top of the box delicately. "I don't know what I'm doing, Mom," I whisper, stripping out of my clothes and leaving them in a pile by my bed.

I go to my bathroom and turn on the shower before putting myself in front of the mirror, forcing my eyes to look at myself. At my arm. At my shoulder.

The scars look especially red today. Angry.

Ugly.

Alive.

I draw a line down the length of my arm to my wrist, my lips twisting, the pain raw. Dead flesh. Dead skin.

A dead soul.

Condensation starts to creep up the mirror, fogging it, until I disappear.

Invisible.

And yet when James Kelly looked at me, I felt seen.

Completely bared.

9

BEAU

The next morning, the kitchen is silent as I go through the motions of making a morning coffee, Uncle Lawrence and Dexter quiet at the table behind me, no doubt tossing each other worried looks every now and then. I slowly stir half a sugar into my caffeine as I stare out of the window at the sun trying its hardest to push through the dense clouds. The front yard has trees and bushes that place shadows across the front of the house, but the backyard is bathed in natural light from the sun. Warm. *Light*.

"How was your show last night?" I ask the pane of glass, my tone lacking the interest I hoped to find. I drop the spoon and turn, leaning against the counter and bringing my coffee to my lips. Lawrence's face is nothing short of insulted. I force a smile around the rim of my cup as Dexter nudges him under the table with his knee.

The eye roll performed by my uncle is award worthy. "Good. It was good."

"Good," I mimic, heading out of the kitchen. I feel their eyes follow me until I'm in the hallway.

"What are you doing today?" Lawrence calls.

"I was going to meet Nath for coffee," I reply, taking the stairs. "But the case he's working has had a few developments he needs to look into." Truth be told, I suspect he simply doesn't want to face me and my probing about the appeal again.

"So what are you going to do?"

Probably be consumed by thoughts of James Kelly. "Chill out," I call, closing my bedroom door and setting my coffee on the nightstand. "And drive myself insane," I whisper to myself, moving the details of a thousand apartments I'm not going to buy and collapsing on the bed. Tomorrow is Monday.

I'll see you on Monday.

Something deep and sensible is telling me that I absolutely shouldn't see him on Monday. And yet something deeper and more relentless is telling me I should.

But what if you can't, Beau?

I sink my teeth into my bottom lip and pull up the message from Reg that's telling me he can't get my car back to me as soon as he hoped. So it'll be more cabs in the day and more walking by night. Many of my tools are in my car—tools I haven't a hope of transporting without a vehicle. Sensibility grabs me for a moment and controls my movements, making me pull up my texts and send a message.

I'm afraid I need to reschedule.

No sooner have I clicked send, my cell rings, and for the first time I wonder why I haven't saved his number. Not that I need to. I know it by heart; I've stared at it so much. I answer, but say nothing, waiting for what James might say instead.

"Why?" is all I get, and although I have a perfectly good reason,

I'll be damned if I can voice it, leaving a long, lingering, expectant silence. "I asked why."

"I have travel issues," I say, trying to come across assertive but sounding hesitant instead.

"It's not an issue."

"I have equipment issues."

"It's not an issue."

I breathe out, reaching for my temple and massaging. "I have James issues."

"And finally we have the real issue," he whispers, and it doesn't escape my notice that he fails to claim this issue of mine isn't an issue. Is it an issue? I laugh on the inside. Of course it's an issue. My body and mind aren't my own around him. *Lonely? Always.* It's like he's wired into me, making me think things I shouldn't think. Say things I shouldn't say.

Do things I shouldn't do?

"What's your issue?" he asks.

"That you're not the kind of man I should be spending time with."

"You're probably right," he replies, honest as can be, no hesitation. I blink my surprise. "But I'll be at work."

"And you trust me in your apartment?"

"Shouldn't I?"

"You don't know me."

He inhales loudly, like he's losing his patience, and releases the air on a sigh I'm supposed to hear. Impatience. It's rife in him. "Stop reading between the lines, Beau. If transport is an issue, I'll have you collected. If equipment is an issue, I'll buy you some more."

"And if you're an issue?"

"Then we'll fix that issue." He hangs up, and I let my limp arm hit the bed with a thud. I have no idea what I'm doing right now.

No idea at all. All I know is that when James is on my mind, nothing else is.

10

JAMES

The heat. It's tolerated. It's a fucked-up comfort, because never will I burn alive again. Never will I feel the heat of such a savage inferno.

I stare at the glowing flame swaying hypnotically, my palm hovering over it. I raise it a little. The heat subsides. I lower it again. The heat intensifies. Lower still. Hotter. Lower again. The flame licks my skin.

I hiss and slowly retract my hand, taking my gloves from my desk and pulling them on, my eyes turning to the screens in my office. All are blank, except one with the face of the man I will kill tonight. And another with footage of Beau Hayley. She's in a supermarket, wandering up and down the aisles, aimless, no direction, no purpose.

Lonely.

I wrestle thoughts of her away with conviction, resetting my attention on the man on the screen next to her. One of The Eagle's foot soldiers. I slide my knife off my desk and inspect the blade.

"He'll be at the old scrapyard off the Biscayne Bay docks in an hour," Goldie says from the doorway.

"Who is he meeting?"

"A dealer from the streets."

I blink back the glare from the metal blade reflecting off the spotlights. The Bear's web of control is about to lose another key player on the drugs front. "They replaced The Snake yet?"

"Not yet. They only just found his body in the river. It's been two years. MPD aren't exactly the fastest at finding dead men. Vince Roake was the obvious choice. With him locked up and The Eagle dead, who the fuck knows who'll move up the ranks."

"Well, it won't be the man I'm killing tonight." I turn and face Goldie. "I need you to collect Beau Hayley tomorrow morning from her home address."

Her face. I've seen various levels of annoyance, but this is something else. My expression dares her to challenge me. But I sometimes forget, Goldie loves a challenge. "You want to fuck her."

I laugh under my breath. There's absolutely no humor in it. "Yes, I want to fuck her." I can't stop imagining that. Fucking her. Tying her up. Blinding her with something other than her mental pain. It's screwed up on every level. But then again, I long ago accepted that I'm a whole new level of screwed up.

"More than kill her?" Goldie asks.

I pull up, stalling from slipping my knife into its sleeve. That's a damn fine question. And the answer, the true answer, is fucking frightening. "No." I make tracks to my bedroom to collect my Beretta. "You can go home now," I call, stuffing my balaclava into my back pocket as I go.

11

BEAU

On Monday morning, I call Reg while I'm eating a mango and loading the washing machine to let him know I'll be there soon to collect some things from Dolly.

With my hair pulled into a low, messy bun and my body appropriately dressed in ripped, paint-splattered jeans and a signature long-sleeved, oversized shirt, I leave the house feeling a puzzling mix of trepidation and anticipation. My hand reaches for my tummy of its own volition, rubbing soothing circles as I dip and weave through the forest that is our front yard.

I make it to the sidewalk with only a few snags on my clothes and come to a screaming halt when I'm confronted by a tall, formidable-looking woman in a masculine suit, her short blonde hair slickly tucked behind her ears. "Miss Hayley," she says, her British accent strong, stoic as she motions to the Tesla behind her. I know my face must say what I'm thinking, and I'm thinking, *who the hell are you*?

"I work for Mr. Kelly."

My eyebrows jump up so fast, I'm surprised they don't detach from my face and fall to the ground at my feet. "I'm sorry?" I question.

Her impassive face remains blank. "Mr. Kelly instructed me to collect you and deliver you to his home."

Deliver? What the fuck am I, a parcel? "And how does Mr. Kelly know where I'm to be collected from?" I ask, instinctively looking left and right.

"That I can't answer."

"Can't or won't?"

A small smile breaks the corners of her bare lips. "Both." She sweeps her arm out toward the car again. "Shall we?"

I laugh, unable to stop myself. "You want me to get into that car with you when I have no idea who you are?" Did he send a woman because he thought it might make this less fucking weird?

"I work for Mr. Kelly."

"That's lovely, but I don't even know Mr. Kelly." *Or what he fucking does.* He could be a mass murderer for all I know.

She eyes me with curiosity, her lips still hovering on the verge of a smile. "No, but you *will* be getting to know him, yes?"

My shoulders straighten. What is that supposed to mean? I should ask, but, instead, like I'm working on autopilot, or idiocy, I step toward the car. *For fuck's sake, Beau. You're a cop.* This goes against everything I know and believe in. I quickly swallow. No, not a cop. I *was* a cop, and by casting my badge aside, it seems I've also cast aside my sense.

"My name is Goldie," she says, opening the back door for me. "In case knowing my name makes you feel better about accepting the ride."

"It doesn't, but thanks," I say, settling in the back seat. I'm stupid. Must be. And on that thought, as Goldie rounds the front of the car unfastening her black suit jacket, I send a quick text message to Nath, telling him to report me missing if I don't contact him by this evening.

She slips into the driver's seat. "I have instructions to take you to collect your equipment." She looks up at the rearview mirror as I pull on my seatbelt.

"The old scrapyard by the docks," I tell her. "I'll guide you."

"I know it," she replies, pulling away.

"You do?" How could a pristine, suited woman driving a sparkly Tesla know of such a place? It's dire, cars piled twenty high, old tires forming mountains, the stench of gas dripping in the air. And then there's the landfill next door, which only adds to the ripe stench, turning it putrid. Every time I get into Reg's truck, the smell hits me like a brick to the face.

Another glance in the mirror. "I do."

I nod mildly. "Okay," I say quietly, looking down at my cell when Nath replies.

Why? What are you doing?

I reply, adding a smiley face, just to ease his worry.

Going on an adventure :)

I click send and drop my cell into my lap, focusing on the woman in the seat before me. "What does Mr. James do?" I ask. She merely peeks up at the mirror on a small smile. "Okay. What do *you* do for Mr. James?" Another glance. No answer. "You're not very talkative, are you, Goldie?"

"You seem like a smart woman, Miss Hayley."

"Smart?" I question. "Then what am I doing in this car with you?"

"I was wondering that myself," she says quietly, taking a left.

My curiosity goes into record-breaking territory. But my fear? Where the fuck is that?

After collecting my painting gear from Reg, Goldie drives me to James's apartment and has my equipment put onto a shiny gold trolly that wouldn't look out of place in a five-star hotel. I don't miss the wariness of the pierced, bearded guy who frequents the lobby as he eyes my paint-ridden equipment polluting the luggage trolley. He taps in a code, Goldie bids me farewell, and I ride up to James's glass box with the guy in silence. I look up at him. Concierge? Security? There's no rule book stating what a concierge should look like, but this dude here definitely doesn't fit. So, security? Where's his uniform?

He looks out the corner of his eye at me, obviously sensing me staring. And he smiles. It's forced. A fake smile meant to assure me all is well. "What do you do for Mr. Kelly?" I ask.

Saved by the ding of the elevator arriving, he pushes the cart out, offloads my things a little heavy-handedly, as if he's inconvenienced, and then leaves promptly before I can press him for an answer.

"Morning." James appears at the top of the stairs, his fingers working the buttons of his shirt. His hair is wet. His facial hair the perfect length. He looks deadly gorgeous, even without a smile, and I find myself looking away, my chest thrumming with something I'm less than familiar with.

"Morning." I turn my attention to my things, crouching to find what I need to get started. "Have you decided what color you want your walls?" *Your two walls?*

"White."

I grab my pot of spackling, some drop cloths, and my filling knife. "And I assume the same for the ceiling?"

"Yes," he answers. I hear the sound of his shoes meeting the stairs as he makes his way down, and with every step he gets closer, my body tenses more until his shoes are in my downcast vision. "Tea?"

"No, thanks." I stand, a bit too abruptly, not appreciating just how close he is, and collide with his unfathomably rigid physique. "Shit," I murmur, staggering a few paces, dropping my knife and spackling. He catches my arm and steadies me, and I look at his fingers gripping me over my shirt. Over my scar. It tingles, and I turn my eyes up to his, finding him staring down at me, his face straight. The atmosphere is thick. "How did you know where I live?"

He doesn't answer, just stares at me, and I move back, out of his grip, rubbing at my arm. And I wait. Wait for an answer. Wait for a break in his expression. I get nothing—nothing except a laser stare that is so obviously meant to unease me.

"I should get on. Have a good day at work." Doing whatever it is you do. *What do you do?* I dip, collect my tools, and move past him, my eyes wide, my heart in my throat.

Why?

Why does he make me feel like this?

It's a contradictory mix of exciting—because I'm feeling something other than unrelenting despair—and anxiousness because I feel like I am way out of my depth.

I make it to his office, albeit on annoyingly shaky legs, and glance around the impressive space, reacquainting myself with it. All of the screens on one wall have a different channel on, all news channels, and his desk is scattered with newspapers, his laptop open on the end. His chair looks like you could sleep in it. I wouldn't be surprised if he *does* sleep in it.

I take in the walls and look up at the ceiling. It doesn't look like he's tried to paint anything. Frowning, I lay down the drop cloths in my working area and start stirring up the spackling until it's smooth and consistent as I go to the wall. I locate the holes and take my loaded filling knife to the first, pausing halfway there when he strolls in. He doesn't acknowledge me as he wanders to his desk, and my eyes follow him the whole way, my neck craning to see him. He moves a few things around and then tugs his trousers up at the knees and lowers to his chair, pulling his laptop forward.

What?

My arm starts to ache where it's held in midair, and I slowly turn toward him, staring at him in question. Either he's unaware or he doesn't care. Something tells me it's the latter. He eventually stops browsing his screen and looks across to me, tilting his head.

"What are you doing?" I ask, pointing my filling knife at him. His eyes switch from mine to the knife, an undetectable smile at risk of showing. But he won't let it loose. He'll control it.

"Working." The fingertips of each hand meet, forming a steeple at his chin, and he rests back, looking comfortable. I'm anything but.

"Excuse me?"

His eyes dance. My fucking heart gallops. No. Please tell me . . .

"I work from home."

I swallow.

"Every day," he adds.

"Every day," I murmur, scanning his office once again, for what reason I couldn't tell you. "So you're just going to . . . be here?" This close? *All. The. Time.*

"Is that a problem?"

"Yes." It's out fast, indignant and unstoppable. "I'll need to put drop cloths over everything when I start painting," I rush on.

"That wall is a good thirty feet away from me. If you manage to get paint on this table from there, I might question if I've got the right person doing the job."

I can answer that for him. I'm the wrong person. He should have someone who can keep themselves together in his presence. I expect his options will be limited. "And the ceiling?" I ask, pointing up.

His head drops back, taking in the dozens of tiny spotlights, as if they're new to him. His throat. The taut flesh of his throat. *Fuck.* This isn't going to work. The resistance I'll need not to admire him all day will kill me. "Why are you here, Beau?" he whispers.

"What?"

His laser eyes drop, but his head remains tilted back, as if he's aware of my battle to keep my eyes from that place. As if he knows I'm at risk of sinking my teeth into him. I can only imagine what he must taste like. Intoxicating. So bad but so good. "Why are you here?" he repeats.

I blindly indicate his office, and his eyes cast around the space before returning to me.

"But I make you uncomfortable," he murmurs quietly. "So I'm still wondering why you're here." He holds my wide eyes for a long, long time before going back to his screen, and the moment I'm free from his fire stare, my body starts to convulse uncontrollably. I need some air, and I'm not likely to find it in this box of tension.

I leave the room hastily, feeling his piercing eyes follow my fleeing form, and close the door behind me. And then I stand like an idiot on the other side, wondering which door I need.

"Second on the left," he says, and I jump, swinging around. The door is still shut, James on the other side.

I take backward steps, feeling his eyes on me, even with the frosted glass between us. "How did you know?"

"I can hear your heart hammering."

I close my eyes and apply pressure on my chest, feeling the uncontrollable pound.

"I can still hear it," he whispers, and I breathe out shakily.

"You didn't try to paint at all, did you?" I ask.

"No."

I don't know what that means, and I haven't the mental

capacity to figure it out. Not now. Why am I here? Easy. Because as fucked up as it is, I'm riveted. Already addicted to the distraction. But why did James entice me here? Could it be for the same reasons?

I turn and hurry to the bathroom, shutting the door, locking it, and glancing around. More glass. The tub, the sink, the tiles. And not a waterdrop on any of it, every square inch sparkling. He's one single man. How much space does he need?

I go to the sink and wash my hands, reluctantly assessing myself in the mirror. I know what I must look like—I don't need my reflection to confirm it—but the mirrored tile spanning all three walls isn't avoidable. My cheeks are pink. My eyes bright, if a little round.

I glance back at the door.

Who are you, James Kelly?

And how can you hold me captive with curiosity I know is dangerous?

I feel like every cop sense I have is dulling. And senses I never knew existed are heightening. I brace my hands on the sink and take some time to get my breathing under control. Then I retie my hair, use the toilet for the sake of it, and spend a good five minutes rubbing the sink clean with one of the luxury towels to rid it of water splashes.

I finish. Swallow. Stare at the door that'll lead me back to the unknown. I leave the bathroom feeling no more settled than when I entered, making it back to his office in no time. I take a deep breath as my hand grips the handle hard, and I enter on my exhale. He looks up, pointing a remote control at one of the giant TVs on the wall. The screen goes blank, and I look from him to the TV a few times. "Would you like me to leave?" I ask.

"No."

Then why is he looking at me like I've just intruded?

I wipe my palms down the front of my jeans and collect my

filling knife, carrying on with what I'm here to do. Painting has been an unexpected savior over the past two years. Something I get so into, I forget everything else. Right now, I need to forget James Kelly is sitting behind me. Wouldn't that be nice?

Yes.

No.

I'm debating that for the next hour as I work my way across the wall, filling in the holes and imperfections as I go. I finish up, replace the lid of the spackling, and leave the room for a welcomed break from him, heading downstairs to collect everything else I need. I gather my box of brushes, my pot of undercoat for the woodwork, some sugar soap, and my sandpaper. With my arms full, I turn to head back upstairs.

And crash right into something.

Him.

Everything falls from my arms. "Shit," I murmur, stepping back, catching sight of something in his hand as he reaches behind his back. But when his hand appears again, it's empty. I look up at him. He looks pissed off. He has a nerve. My veins are throbbing, both in fright and because of his proximity.

His eyes clear in a moment. "Let me help you," he says, crouching and gathering up my things.

Taking a deep, needed breath, I join him on the floor. "You know, I'll get this finished much faster if you give me some space," I say, taking everything from his hands. Space to work, but also more space to breathe.

I stand, my arms full, and he slowly unfolds his body from the floor. "Space," he says quietly. "I was just trying to help."

"I don't need your help." I rip my stare from his and will my feet into action, and he lazily turns his body as I pass him. Goosebumps. Jesus, my skin is alive with them, every hair standing on end.

The crazy pace of my heart isn't helping me as I take the stairs, the sheer bangs threatening to knock everything out of my hold. I make it to his office and take a few needed inhales. I'm all over the place. Rickety. Unstable. But it's a different variation of unstable. I'm more warped than I ever thought possible to endure this. To tolerate the tense atmosphere. And, worse, welcome it? It's a whole new level of fucked up.

I hold my foot out and release the roll of sandpaper from my grip, catching it on the toe of my Converse and lowering it to the floor. Then I lift my foot higher, releasing the pot of undercoat so it rests perfectly on the top of my foot. I lower that to the floor too, my balance, as always, faultless. With my hands now less crowded, I'm able to crouch and set everything else down. *Focus on work.* I collect another drop cloth and flap it out, and it wafts into the air, before drifting down and coming to rest on the floor. He's at the door. Watching. This is getting plain uncomfortable. Did he just invite me here to make me feel awkward? "What?"

He blinks. "Nothing." Heading for his desk, he slides a palm onto his nape, rubbing a little. "I'll leave you to get on."

Yes. Please do. And leave the room too.

But he doesn't, and I'm left to do my thing, feeling like I'm in a glass display cabinet, which is ironic, because I am.

And everyone knows, people in glass houses shouldn't throw stones.

The rest of the day passes by in a haze of constant and consistent unease as I prep—sanding, soaping, and wiping, ensuring all the surfaces are smooth and free from debris. I fight the urge to respond to him each time I feel him staring. And fail. Which leaves endless occasions when we catch each other's eye. I always look away first, struggling with the intensity that he seems to laugh in the face of.

By the end of the day, I'm mentally exhausted by his behavior, and also by the relentless questions circling my head. What does he do, why all the security, who the hell is he? I haven't achieved half as much work as I should have.

I turn to face him where he's sitting at his glass desk, and he looks across to me. He appears as perfect now as he did first thing this morning. He reaches for the lid of his laptop and slowly shuts it. Eyes on mine. I tilt my head, studying him. I'm a grown woman, and yet James is making me feel like a clueless little girl. I shake my head in despair and break our eye contact, pushing my things into the corner. "Do you want me to move all this out of the room overnight?"

"Leave them," he says, getting up, rising to his full, intimidating height, regarding me closely. "Have you decided whether you hate me or want to fuck me?"

"No, not yet," I lie, heading for the door.

"Oh. Do you think you'll figure it out anytime soon?"

"Why, am I driving you as insane as you're driving me?" I look back over my shoulder.

"You have no idea," he says quietly, his eyes dropping down the full length of my body. My skin beneath my clothes heats. "Goldie will drive you home."

"I would rather walk." I tilt my head. "Clear my mind. Warm up for my run tonight. Have a good evening, James."

"I will," he says quietly.

I leave his glass paradise not certain of much, except James will certainly have a good evening.

And I will spend mine wrestling with my sensibility.

12

JAMES

I watch her leave, reaching to the back of my trousers and pulling out my Beretta, laying it on my desk. What the fuck am I getting myself into? I grab the remote control and bring up all the cameras on the screens, and I study her closely making her escape from my apartment. I release air, inflating my cheeks, and rake a hand through my hair. I've done zero research today. At least, I've researched nothing I should be researching. Instead, I've trawled the Internet and various restricted case files to find out anything I could about Beau Hayley. Yes, she was in the vicinity when her mum's car exploded. No, I didn't feel particularly good about that. But in my world, there's no room for guilt or attachment. I only find out what I *need* to know. I didn't need to know much about Jaz Hayley's daughter, just enough to make Jaz believe I knew a lot. But now I do know a lot. I know she's haunted, *lonely,* bereft.

All because of her mother's death.

The letter breaking the news of Beau Hayley's failed appeal

will land on her doorstep soon. And then what? What will she do? Who will she talk to? How deep will she dig? Like her mother, I get the feeling Beau Hayley is like a dog with a bone. And like her mother, she will end up dead as a result. So why the fuck is she still breathing? She knows there is more to her mother's demise. It's that sixth sense in her. The same sixth sense her mother had. I don't need Beau Hayley getting in my fucking way. I don't need complications in my simple life.

So end it.

I growl to myself and head downstairs to get a beer, pulling up my contacts as I go. I need something to take my mind off things. Something to relax. I down a straight vodka and stare at the screen of my mobile where Beth's number glows.

Then toss it on the worktop, head back to my office, and locate the footage from today.

I stare at the moment I had my gun aimed at the back of Beau Hayley's head.

And the moment I bailed.

I can't kill her.

Don't *want* to kill her.

Fuck.

13

BEAU

Tuesday plays out the same as Monday. I'm collected by Goldie and when I arrive at James's, he hasn't found somewhere else to work. He looks up from his laptop when I enter his colossal office. Stares at me.

I stare right back, unable and unwilling to be the first to break our eye contact. What James Kelly should know is that I've faced demons far greater and scarier than him. I realized that last night while tossing and turning in bed. He's dark. But I'm darker. I bet he doesn't wrestle with black thoughts each day. I bet he doesn't have to spend every minute of his life correcting himself. Reminding himself. Pulling himself away from the easy way out. Not needing to control his urges.

I also came to terms with the reason I can't stay away. Why I'm here. Why I'm enduring these constant episodes of unbearable intensity.

Escape.

When I'm here, when I'm in his orbit, there is no darkness. Not mine, anyway, because I don't have to pretend here. *No veil. I'm fine.* It's all *his* darkness, and it is addictive. So if he wants to play this game, I'm willing. He won't find a better opponent than me.

My eyes begin to burn they're so focused on him, but I refuse to blink. To look away. And I will endure the torture and thrill of his presence all day. I'm armored up. My war paint is on. "I won't submit," I say evenly.

His expression doesn't waver, and he settles back in his chair, getting comfortable. Talking without talking. That is, until he speaks. "Why are you here, Beau?" he asks again. "I've spent all night wondering, and I've come up blank."

"You tell me," I say quietly, held prisoner on the spot, his icy eyes darkening by the second.

He hums, blinking slowly. My pulse quickens. "You're here to paint my office. Why else would you be here?" He stands and rounds his desk, passing me. "So get on with it."

My head turns, following him to the door. "Asshole," I breathe quietly.

"You have no idea," he replies without looking back, shutting the door loudly.

I bite my lip and approach the glass on light feet, coming to a stop only a foot away from the door. "I can hear you breathing," I say, my voice throaty, as I reach for the frosted pane and lay a palm on it. "And I feel your heat." My eyes dart before me, my mouth spewing words before my brain is engaging.

"Does that mean you want to fuck me?" he asks, and suddenly the door isn't frosted anymore, but crystal clear. And James is on the other side, a whisper away.

I inhale and pull my hand back, truly feeling the burn. And I retreat. Away from the door. Away from the temptation.

Away from the danger.

I don't need to answer him. I've never wanted anything more, and judging by his wicked, half-smile as the glass frosts again, it's clearly written all over me.

My body aches perfectly by the time I'm done undercoating the baseboards, and it feels so good. I rub the back of my neck as I look at the ceiling, studying the endless tiny, *awkward* spotlights. I set up my ladder and take the steps, reaching for one of the spotlight encasements and wriggling it. It pops out, giving me just enough room to swipe my brush around it. I nod, satisfied, and lift one foot from the ladder, leaning back, pulling three of the four legs off the floor. And I spin it, letting the legs lower back down slowly by counter-balancing the weight with my body. I come to rest under the next spotlight and reach up to pop the encasement off before performing the same move to get me to the next spotlight. In just ten minutes, I remove a quarter of the spotlight encasements ready to paint around tomorrow.

I descend the ladder and fold it up, propping it against the wall before crouching to tidy up, setting everything in the corner out of his way and folding up the sheets. I dust my hands off and stand, finding James perched on the edge of his desk, his palms wedged into the glass, his legs stretched out, crossed at the ankles. When did he come back? "What?" I ask. "What are you looking at, James?"

"I'm not quite sure," he murmurs, sounding truly perplexed. "What was all that?" He motions to the ladder and then the ceiling.

Oh . . .

He must have felt like he'd stepped into a circus. "I didn't realize you were in here." It's all I have.

"Very Lara Croft," he whispers, and my eyes undeniably widen. "I'll be downstairs." He pushes away from the desk and slowly wanders out of the room, pulling the door closed behind him.

I stare at the glass, my brain bending. *Lara Croft?* I go after him, fueled by irritation, and find him in the kitchen. "What was *that*?" I ask, sounding hostile and uptight.

He slowly lowers a glass of water to the countertop. "What?"

I swallow, biting my lip. Do I even want to get into this? Explain? Could it be a coincidence? "Nothing." I'm not risking it. I force my eyes from his and collect my handheld vac so I can clear up the last few bits of dust and debris.

"What are you doing?"

I hold up the vac, like, what on earth do you think I could be doing? "I haven't got the same level of sucking power as my friend here." I recoil in an instant. *Where the fucking hell did that come from?* "I mean . . ." I'm at a loss.

His lip quirks as he turns, opening the fridge, and I roll my shoulders to rid them of the lingering goosebumps, my focus rooted on his shirt-covered back.

"Would you like a drink?" he asks.

"No, thank you."

He ignores me again and slides a bottle of beer toward me. "Have one."

"Why?"

"Why not?"

I could give him a million reasons why not. My brain just won't enlighten me as to what those reasons are right now. I'm blank. Mute. Melting under the pressure of his stare once again. I've never seen such sharp eyes before. They're hard. Icy. Piercing.

Completely fucking captivating.

So, he's finished work for the day? "You must have plans."

"Like what?" he tosses back, his face willing me to go there. The more time I spend with him, the more I'm convinced he knows that I saw him in his bedroom with that man and woman. I will *not* go there.

I retreat before my mind can convince me to accept. "Good

night, James." I turn and walk away, and the elevator opens before I press the call button. Goldie steps out.

"Goldie," James says from the kitchen. "Can you drive Beau home?"

"No," I pipe up, stepping into the elevator and pressing the button. "I'll walk." I need the air.

"If you insist."

"I do." The doors close and I collapse, exhausted by another day battling enticement and curiosity. I can't believe I'm willingly putting myself through this. But the alternative is putting myself through something else. I'm beginning to wonder which is more torturous.

I dial Reg. "Please tell me Dolly's ready," I plead, needing my car back, if only so I don't have to endure more silent rides with Goldie.

"She'll be ready to collect in the morning. I've a few hours left on her."

"Thanks, Reg. I'll be there at eight." I hang up and head for Walmart. It's a long walk—two hours, at least—so when I finally make it there, it's suitably empty.

I roam up and down the aisles tugging along the basket, tossing in random things. By the time the speakers announce my five-minute warning, I have a mango, six rolls of toilet paper, a foot scrub, a nail file, and a nail polish in a new shade of gunmetal gray. I head for the checkout and unload.

"Beau?"

I freeze mid-lift of the nail file, my heart sinking, and I instinctively pull my shirtsleeve down to the palm of my hand. It takes every ounce of strength in me to turn and face him. "Ollie," I breathe, coming face to face with my ex-fiancé. I haven't seen him since he visited me in hospital when I explicitly told him not to. He looks just as I remember. Clean-cut. Shaven. On the bulkier side of muscular. He's in plain clothes. Like me, Ollie aced his Phase I Test. Unlike me, he made it into the FBI.

He takes me in for a long while, and I hate it. I hate that he's assessing me, both physically and mentally. "How are you?" I ask for the sake of it. I know because Nath takes it upon himself to tell me. I take no pleasure in single-handedly humiliating this man by leaving him at the altar, not to mention breaking his heart. *Guilt. So much fucking guilt.*

"Working," he replies. "A lot."

I knew that too. He's buried himself in his career since I left him, while I've buried myself in loneliness. I smile, it's awkward, but I have no words for him. What do you say to the man you jilted? To a man you know loved you? To a man who promised to hold you up through your turmoil? He deserved more than I could offer. It's what I told myself to ease my guilt. Truth was, I had no energy to love. Still don't. And I couldn't marry a cop. I couldn't commit myself to a man who worked for a cause I didn't believe in anymore. "It was good to see you," I say, turning and walking away.

"Beau, you don't have your shopping," Ollie calls.

I walk faster, away from him, away from the memories, away from my past.

"Beau!"

I make it to the door, to the fresh air, and drink in as much as I can, trying to keep the impending panic attack at bay.

"Beau." Ollie appears in front of me, and I look up through my watery eyes. "Jesus, Beau," he whispers, stepping into me, and before I know what's happened, I'm in his arms sobbing relentlessly, the onslaught of memories, of guilt, of sorrow, all too much.

"I'm sorry," I mumble mindlessly. "I never meant to hurt you. I'm sorry." I should have apologized before. I should have found some strength through my self-pity to give Ollie the apologies he deserved.

"I forgave you long ago, Beau," he whispers. "It's time to forgive yourself. For everything." He pulls away and holds me by the tops of my arms as I wipe at my soaked face. I don't know where that came from. I haven't cried for a long time; I'm all out of tears. "Come on." He smiles, his thumb stroking under each eye. "Let's get a coffee. Where's your car?"

"She's in the repair shop. I'm walking."

His arm goes around my shoulders, and he leads me to his car. I don't stop him. I probably should.

But I don't.

He helps me in and drives, and I don't question where. The silence isn't uncomfortable, more peaceful. It's only when Ollie pulls off a main street that I seem to wake up and realize where we're heading.

Our apartment. The apartment we shared.

My heart starts beating double time.

"I know you don't like busy spaces," he says, pulling into the parking lot. "So I thought this would be better."

I look at the door. The door I passed through millions of times. I see myself, coming and going, in uniform, dressed up, in my gym gear. Happy.

Gathering all the strength I can muster, I unclip my seatbelt and get out, forcing myself to face this. Because the alternative is to cause worry. To spike concerns. *I'm stable. I'm okay.*

I approach the apartment block slowly, hearing the jingle of Ollie's keys. I step aside to let him pass, watching as he opens the door and gestures the way. I make it to the apartment and stare at the wood as he opens the door and the way for me. I swallow, bracing myself, and the moment I'm inside, my stomach starts twisting and rolling violently.

"I'll make us coffee," Ollie says, dropping his keys in the bowl on the table before heading to the kitchen. I stare at the bowl. Just one set of keys. Not two. Not my keys and his keys. Just his. I pass the living room and glance inside. I see Ollie and me curled up on the couch on one of our rare nights off together. I see Mom in the chair by the fireplace where she always sat when visiting. *Oh God.*

I shake my head and follow Ollie, entering the kitchen. It's spotless. "Do you have a housekeeper?" I ask, lowering to a chair at the table. My eyes root to the faded red wine stain in the center from the glass that was knocked over during a passionate after-dinner *moment*. This table. We've eaten at it, laughed at it, done the deed on it.

He laughs as he prepares two cups of coffee. He doesn't ask me how I like it. He wouldn't have forgotten that. Is it terrible that I *have* forgotten how he takes his? Sugar? No sugar? Cream? No cream? Self-preservation has meant trying to eradicate everything from my past, limiting the amount of things to feel sorry about.

"No housekeeper." He sets the mug on the table. The mug Mom bought me. The mug with a picture of Lara Croft on it.

"My mug," I say, my heart clenching. *Very Lara Croft.* There's a massive chip on the rim. This mug was the only thing that survived the explosion with minor injuries. Everything else? Ruined. Dead.

"Well, I didn't want to throw it away, and you didn't take anything when you left." His words and tone aren't accusing, it's just Ollie being Ollie. Factual. "Maybe I thought you'd come back." He shrugs and joins me at the table. "So how have you been?"

"You mean Nath hasn't given you every detail of each of our coffee dates?"

"I don't see him much lately. He's working like a madman."

"Like you?"

"There's a lot of dead bodies cropping up recently." He takes a sip of his coffee, and I have a fleeting moment of missing my old job. The adrenalin. The thrill. The brilliant people I used to work with. But that was destroyed. "So . . . how are you?" he presses again, as if he needs to ask.

I blink myself back into the room. "Good," I say, sounding as convincing as I meant. "Really good, actually."

"And the new job?"

"I enjoy it." I shrug, knowing many find it hard to understand. Although my current project isn't exactly enjoyable. More compulsory.

He motions around the room. "Anytime you feel like it, help yourself."

I gaze around, seeing Mom up the ladder when we moved in, coating the kitchen walls with a vivid blue. It's no longer blue. It's an insipid shade of taupe. I see me at the counter making coffee. Mom at the table chatting to me as I did. Ollie tossing pasta in a pan. My friends drinking wine while I sat on the countertop fastening the straps of my heels. "I'll bear that in mind," I say quietly, swallowing, blinking back the memories. All happy memories.

Ollie's phone rings, and he audibly sighs. "Agent Burrows." He stands and takes his cup to the sink, tipping the rest away. "On my way." He hangs up and turns an apologetic smile my way. He doesn't have to. I know the job, and I imagine it has only intensified since he joined the FBI. "I've got to go."

I stand. "I never did congratulate you." I walk to him, reaching on my tiptoes to kiss his cheek. "I'm proud of you. I know you always dreamed of joining the Bureau."

Before I know it, I'm enveloped in his arms, being squeezed to his body. It's warm. It's Ollie. He inhales and exhales, and I deflate with him. "Yes, pulling severed limbs out of a crushing machine is *everything* I dreamed of."

I smile weakly and step back. "Enjoy."

"You want a ride?" he asks. "I'm heading to the old scrapyard by the docks so I'm passing Lawrence's. Or is he Zinnea today?" He checks his watch.

"The scrapyard by the docks? That's Reg's place."

"Who's Reg?"

"He's saved me and Dolly a few times. That's where Dolly is

now. New engine. He said to collect her in the morning, but he should be done by now. I'll come with you."

"Afraid not, Beau." He rolls his eyes. "You should know I can't take guests to a crime scene."

I pout and he shakes his head. "I only want my car."

"I'll tell *Reg* you'll be there to collect it tomorrow, *if* it doesn't interfere with the investigation." He slips an arm around me and leads us toward the door, something he's probably done hundreds of times before. His presence is calming, but it doesn't feel right for him to offer me comfort. "Anyone would think you've forgotten how to be a cop."

"I've tried," I admit, and immediately regret it. I can feel Ollie looking down at me with concern. I always noticed things other people wouldn't notice. Saw things other people didn't see. Unraveled irrelevant things and made them relevant. I achieved 98% in my Phase 1 Test. That would have made me a pretty sharp agent. I've always prided myself on reading characters well, knowing when to trust and when not to. When to avoid danger.

And yet I've just spent two days with a man who seems dangerous.

Oh how the mighty—the once wise— have fallen.

14

BEAU

For the first time in as long as I can remember, I don't jump out of my skin when I start Dolly. "She purrs," I say, smiling, and Reg laughs.

"She'll never purr, Beau. And it's only a secondhand engine, so don't expect any miracles." He walks off, his coveralls blending nicely with the oil-covered scrapyard.

"I heard you had company last night," I call.

"Swarming with cops," he yells back, throwing an arm in the air toward the end of the yard, where police tape seals off the back end. "Turned the crusher on yesterday and the damn thing spat half an arm out. An arm!"

Don't do it, Beau.

But before I can stop myself, I'm out of Dolly, leaving her running, and walking across the uneven ground toward the back of Reg's scrapyard. I duck under the tape and round the corner, coming to a grinding halt when I'm intercepted by a uniformed officer. He doesn't get a chance to warn me away. He recognizes me, and his stern police face softens. "Beau? Fuck me, it's Lara Croft."

"Hi, Jed," I say on a forced smile, looking past him.

A forensics van and endless police cars—marked and unmarked—swarm the area. "How have you been?" I ask mindlessly.

"Yeah, great. You?"

"Good." I stare up at a hydraulic arm of a machine, where blood stains the metal, my brain beginning to whirl, my old eyes searching for more.

No.

God, no.

I turn and walk away. "Great to see you, Jed," I say to the ground, refusing to relent to my curious mind. Refusing to go there. Refusing to be lured back by a damn good mystery. It used to fuel me. Inspire me. The unknown. My curiosity. But that's not where I can allow my head to go. I'm no longer a cop. No longer an upcoming FBI agent. I'm just a painter, and James Kelly is today's mystery. He's a safe bet for my attention. The FBI is not.

I get out of Dolly and admire her for a few moments. Good old Reg. He's even polished her rusty paintwork. "If I could take your keys," the pierced, bearded guy says as he joins me on the sidewalk.

"Why?"

"You'll get a ticket there, Beau. I can put it in the parking garage."

"There's a parking garage?" I ask, handing him my keys.

"Underground." He slides into Dolly and starts her engine. Her new, non-banging engine.

"What's your name?" I ask, watching as he yanks and pulls at the stick shift.

"Otto."

"Thanks, Otto." I look up the face of the building to the very top. The glass box that's perched atop is hardly visible.

Otto chugs off in Dolly, and I enter the lobby to find Goldie by the open elevator. "Waiting for me?" I ask as I approach her.

She says nothing, holding the doors open, and the moment I'm inside the elevator, she keys in a code and sends me to the glass apartment. My cell chimes, and I look down to see a text from Ollie. Sounds about right that he's just gotten home from a callout.

It was good to see you. Don't be a stranger. x

A stranger is exactly what I am. I'm not the Beau he met. In fact, I'm sure he would hate the woman I've become. I don't reply, not wanting to fuel any lingering feelings he might have. Might? I shouldn't have accepted his offer of coffee. It was cruel and selfish, but in that moment, I was a robot, and I was happy to be stripped of all control. To not think. To have the long-lost feeling of a man's arms around me. And now I'll pay for it.

More guilt.

When the doors of the elevator open, I scan the space, bracing myself for another day suffocating in James Kelly's presence. I head up the stairs, pass the bedrooms, and enter his office. He's already at his desk, every screen on the wall alive, a coffee in his hand. He gives me his eyes for a few moments before returning his gaze to the TVs. No hello. Nothing. I'm good with that.

I get my ladder out and set it up, climbing to the top and pulling off an encasement on another spotlight. I look across at him when I feel my skin being licked by the flames of his stare. He's lost interest in the TV.

I descend the steps. Move the ladder. Climb back to the top. Remove another encasement.

I glance at him again. He's still watching.

On an inhale, I descend, shift the ladder, climb back to the top, and remove another spotlight, my teeth now grating. *Don't bite.* We're adults playing a childish game of who can stand this tension for the longest. He's won. I admit it. He won days ago. "Stop it," I breathe.

"Stop what?"

"Looking." I take the steps back down and lean on the ladder, facing him. "Stop looking at me."

"Why, does it make you uncomfortable?"

My eyes narrow. "No, it just pisses me off."

He smirks. "I'm just wondering why you're going up and down that ladder like a yoyo"—he motions to the steps I'm leaning on—"when we both know you have a faster way to remove those spotlights."

I scowl at him.

His face remains impassive. Thoughtful. *Accusing*. It shouldn't be attractive. And yet here I am, attracted.

"Got any other tricks up your sleeve, Beau Hayley?"

"I was a champion gymnast until I was eighteen." It's the truth. I won't tell him that I also aced karate, judo, and kickboxing.

"Interesting," he muses.

"Why? Why is it interesting, James?" I'm done. He's exhausted me, worn me down. I feel like I need a big argument with him to clear the air.

He stands slowly and rounds his glass desk, coming toward me. I'd back away, but my body locks up. I'd breathe, but my lungs have shrunk. And then he's close, his dress shirt pushed into my chest, breathing down on me. I look up. I inhale. God, he smells so good. Spicy. Creamy. Manly. "Why is it interesting?" I ask, my words quiet but firm.

He gives me a few moments of the warmth of his chest before he breaks away, retreating. "Did you have a nice evening last night?" His question comes out of the blue, and I'm as confused as fuck by it. Why does he care?

"Yes. Did you?"

"Yes, it was enlightening." He wanders out of the room. "I'll be in the steam room."

"Is that glass too?" I call, my muscles relaxing with the growing distance.

He looks over his shoulder. He doesn't answer. He doesn't need to.

Of course it's glass.

He pulls the door closed, and I eventually find the will to breathe. Enlightening? *What the fuck, James Kelly?* I turn on the spot, taking in every inch of his office. *Enlightening.* He needs to share some of that enlightenment with me.

By six o'clock, I've finished cutting in around all the spotlights on the ceiling and my neck is stiff. I spend the next half hour dividing my time between rubbing some life into my nape and tidying up.

He's in the kitchen on his phone when I make it downstairs, a T-shirt draped around his neck and a pair of jeans gracing his long legs. He spots me and pulls the T-shirt off his shoulders. "Thanks." He hangs up and starts to cover his chest.

I blink my vision clear of the magnetic sight and make my way to the elevator. "Have a good evening, James," I say.

"A drink?"

He's asked every time. "Anyone would think you don't want me to leave."

"I don't."

I stop a few feet away from the doors, looking back. He's holding up a new beer. I eye it. And him.

"Have the drink, Beau," he says quietly. "It's got to beat roaming the supermarket until it closes."

I recoil, shocked, but he doesn't react to my stunned state. "What?" I whisper. How does he know that?

"Drink." He places it on the island, and my eyes jump from the bottle to James a few times, my mind vehemently denying my feet from taking me to the beer. To James. To the danger.

"I think I should leave," I say, regarding him closely.

"I think you should stay," he counters, resting back against the counter. It's a staring stand-off, and I swallow down my nerves, my reckless side at war with my sensible side.

Recklessness wins.

I wander over, taking the beer, and rest on the stool when he indicates one. So, now what? We're going to sit here and chat? Pretend I've not spent the past few days burning in his company? Pretend he's not throwing statements at me that are twisting my mind and spiking this insane curiosity.

"Lara Croft," I murmur. "Roaming the supermarket."

"What about it?"

"How . . ." I pause for thought, knowing I can't spike interest in him. "Why did you say those things?"

"Lara Croft?" he asks.

I nod. "And the supermarket. How did you know I was in the supermarket last night?"

"Because I saw you there," he replies, simple as that.

"And you didn't stop to say hello?"

"Why would I do that? You struggle to speak to me at the best of times."

My jaw rolls. "And the Lara Croft thing?"

"Do you have something against her?"

Jesus, my head could explode. "Never mind." I sigh, drinking some beer. "What do you do, James?" I ask again.

His eyebrows arch. "I'm assuming you mean business-wise."

"What else could I mean?" I shouldn't have said that.

"You tell me."

I look at him tiredly. Is this what's going to happen? A duel of words. Trying to decipher hidden meanings? "Yes, in business."

"It's totally boring." He takes the stool next to me, a little too close for comfort, and I inch back a fraction, just to ensure our knees don't brush. He looks at the flesh of my thighs through the rips of my jeans. "I'm in the cleansing business," he adds quietly.

"Cleansing?"

"The world."

Like the environment? Carbon footprints, that kind of thing? "Oh," I say quietly, taken aback as I swig more beer. I guess that humanizes him. He wants to save the world. Admirable. *How about saving me?*

I flinch at the wayward direction of my thoughts, and James doesn't miss it. "I also work the stock market."

I nod mildly, remembering the many screens in his office loaded with news channels.

"What do you do, Beau?" he asks.

"You know what I do. I'm doing it in your glass box."

"Oh, you mean driving me to distraction?"

I withdraw. Me? "I paint. Nothing more."

"Why?"

Why? Yes, *why*? *Why* all the fucking questions? "I enjoy it."

"And you've always aspired to do this?"

"Is this a therapy session?"

"I don't know. Do you need therapy?"

"That's debatable," I murmur, my mouth on autopilot.

James's curious eyes fall to my hand still holding the beer at my lips, and he follows it slowly until I rest the bottle on the counter. His head tilts, thoughtful, and he tentatively reaches for the sleeve of my shirt and pushes it back. I'm powerless to stop him, caught in a trance, studying him closely. Every inch of his face is unreadable. Straight. Emotionless. My scar tingles as he traces a light fingertip over the edge, and I inhale, seeing the ugliness that riddles my arm is exposed.

Exposed.

Jerking to life, I retract my arm, pulling the sleeve back down to my wrist as best I can while still holding my beer. "I won't ask about yours if you don't ask about mine."

"I don't mind if you ask about mine," he says softly.

Something tells me he's being honest; he wouldn't mind. And I can't deny I'm dead curious about the beast of a scar marring his back. Too curious. But even if I asked, he didn't say he would tell me. This is getting too deep. Too uncomfortable. I'm no longer appreciating the distraction, more resenting it. Because we're getting personal. There's too much talking. For the last two years, I've kept to my very small circle of "people." I don't strike up conversations with strangers. I keep to myself and limit interaction because I don't want anyone asking questions I can't answer. I don't want to be known. To be seen. Invisible is safer. No one wants their lives dimmed by my shade.

I can't bear the interest splattered all over his face. I knew this was a bad idea, not just the beer, but the job. I've not gained anything from taking on this project, only a ton of questions I shouldn't be asking and many I don't want to answer. I swallow, placing my beer down, and make to move. To leave. To escape.

But he stops me, seizing my arm firmly but gently. "Sit down, Beau," he whispers hoarsely, and I freeze, my skin heating. His touch. His voice. The way he's looking at me. I slowly lower to the stool, mesmerized by him. He unhurriedly shifts his hold and pushes up my sleeve again, so lazily, like he's got all the time in the world. His gaze travels back and forth, from my arm to my eyes, watching how I'm responding, clearly taking pleasure from my useless form.

Then he dips, eyes on me, and places his lips on the edge of the scar tissue. I convulse. "What are you doing?" I ask, hardly able to breathe. I reclaim my arm, and he definitely scowls. "What the fuck is going on here, James? Why the games?"

"I don't play games, Beau."

"This is a game," I assure him. "And I haven't got a fucking clue what the rules are."

"You're absorbed."

"There's a lot to be absorbed by."

"I agree." His hand lands on my knee, and my stomach cartwheels. "An awful lot. And I don't know what the rules are either."

"Then why do you seem to be playing this game better than I am?" Experience? Success?

"You're wrong." He releases my knee and gets up, walking casually to the fridge and getting a bottle of water. I stare at his back, and all I can see are the scars beneath his T-shirt. Thick, uneven, damaged skin. "You're playing the game far better than I ever could."

So there *is* a game. "How?"

"Because I'm snookered," he says quietly, and I frown at his back. "You want to be invisible," he goes on. "Forgettable. Blend into the background." He turns and tips the bottle to his lips, while I stare at him with my mouth slightly agape. "Problem is, Beau Hayley," he whispers, coming closer. Closer. Closer. "I. See. You."

My spine straightens, and despite knowing he can't possibly really *see* me, I'm wary. "You don't know me."

"Don't I?" he replies, his head tilting. "Your jokes on the phone were a poor attempt to mask your misery. Your fake carefree attitude is a poor attempt to mask your hurt."

I scoff, getting up and walking toward the elevator, which feels like fucking miles away. Is this why he wanted me to stay for a drink? So he can point out my shortcomings? Pretend to know me? "Fuck you, James Kelly," I say under my breath.

"Your anger now is a poor attempt to mask your craving."

Outraged, I swing around. I don't know when this job went from being a job to a personal annihilation. "Craving for what?"

"Many things."

"Like?" I yell, getting worked up, something that hasn't happened in a long, long time. I don't allow it. *Can't* allow it.

"Like revenge." He starts a leisurely pace toward me, and I lose my breath. "Like escape. Like darkness." He arrives before me, his fierce, almost angry face close to mine. "Like *me*."

"I don't crave you," I breathe, avoiding that he's probably hit the nail on the head with each one of his other assessments. *Revenge*. That one word hits me hardest of all.

His arm rises slowly, and he rests the tip of his thumb on my nipple, brushing the hardening nub into full erection through my shirt, making my chest concave. "Say it again. Tell me you don't crave me."

I can't talk. Can't see straight.

He works his touch up to my throat and strokes me softly. "You're as clear as the glass you're surrounded by, Beau Hayley."

"And what do you see?" I gasp, trying so hard not to lean into his touch.

He smiles. It's almost a sick smile. "I see the woman you were. The woman you're trying to forget existed. The one with power. Unbridled strength." He releases me and steps back. "But I want you to find her. Show me who she is. Show me what she can do, how strong she is."

It's not the first time I've lost my breath in the presence of this man. It won't be the last either. But it is the first time I think I understand him. He really has seen right through me. I have no room in my clustered mind to analyze how right now. No room to ask the questions I should be asking. There are too many sparks flying, and the prospect of more is too much to resist. This is a whole new world, and I'd be lying if I said I'm not getting a sick thrill from it. It's different. Overwhelming. Diverting.

"Let's get the inevitable over with, shall we?" James's face seems to darken. He's serious. "Show. Me. Who. She. Is."

I step back.

I see him brace himself. I should smile on the inside. He has no idea, but he asked for it.

Show you?

I lock, engaging muscles I haven't engaged for years.

I load, filling my lungs with air and my legs with bounce.

He stares hard, goading me, watching as I call upon the woman I used to be. The woman I need to be to take on this man. The woman with potent, limitless faith in her abilities.

I launch into the air and spin, wrapping my legs around his neck, and take him down to the floor. I land softly. He does not. Stress leaves me and something else fills me. I don't know what; I've never felt it before, but it feels electric.

I look down my body to his head that's trapped between my thighs. I don't know what I expected. A smirk was not it.

"This is going to be way more fun than I ever imagined," he says, his voice gravelly, and it's not because I'm limiting the supply of oxygen to his head. *Fun?* I have not a moment to consider it.

He twists suddenly, and I'm spun onto my front, a knee in my back, my arms restrained behind me. *How the fuck?* Disorientated, I blink, feeling warmth moving in on my ear. "Oh baby, you're going to be fun to break."

I snarl, throwing my head back and colliding with his nose. He hisses, and I spin over, jumping to my feet, breathing heavily. "I'm already fucking broken, you stupid assho—oh!" I'm caught off guard when his leg swipes out, taking me clean off my feet, and I land on my back with a thud and a cough.

James is spread all over me in a second, panting down at me. "Then we're both safe," he whispers, dipping to kiss the edge of my mouth. A volcano erupts inside of me. My want and craving break the scale. But I still fight him, trying to get my hands between us to push him away. I fail. So I sink my fingers into his T-shirt and yank hard, ripping it apart across his back. He growls, wrestling with me to win my hands, pinning them down over my head. He transfers my wrists into one hand, takes the other to my shirt, and yanks it, ripping every button off.

"Do you submit?" he whispers, dragging his palm down my torso, my body bowing violently, pleasure flooding me.

"Never."

"Good." He slams his lips over mine.

I. Am. Gone.

I don't know where, but I like it, need it, and I might not ever want to come back. I open up to him, mouth and thighs, and attack him with equal force, our tongues lashing dangerously, our kiss borderline psychotic. "Let go of my hands," I pant, sinking my teeth into his lip, straining against him.

"No." His face plummets into my neck, his groin rubbing into me, and I cry out, the stabs of pleasure cutting me in two.

"Scared of me?" I ask, bowing my back, pushing my breasts into his chest.

He bites at my throat, then sucks hard, before rolling to his back fast, sending a stool flying across the kitchen. It clatters against the cupboards as I come to rest on his waist, my hands still held in one of his. He reaches up and pulls the cups of my bra down, and my boobs spring free, aching. I lick my lips as I study him, his hair in disarray, his eyes pits of fire. His jaw ticks, enhancing every sharp inch of it. He is the most beautifully dark thing I have ever seen.

I roll my hips, rubbing into the iron rod of flesh beneath me. James hisses, swallowing hard. "I'm not scared of you, Beau." He sits up, getting his face close to mine. "I'm scared of *us*." He bites at my cheek, and my head falls back on an almighty moan as he takes my hands and places them over his shoulders. The moment my palms come to rest on his skin between the ripped material of his T-shirt, I feel the uneven flesh of his back. But I'm too drunk on lust to ask. And I can't bring myself to stall what's about to happen.

I've never been so desperate. So exposed. So raw.

"Hold on," he whispers, lifting to his feet with ease, guiding my legs around his waist. He carries me like I'm nothing up the stairs, not looking where he's going, our eyes glued, the pressure multiplying. "Want me to help you escape?" he asks as we reach the top. I nod, not questioning him. It would be foolish. He's figured me out, and part of me is glad of that. "You're about to disappear, Beau. Feel only what I make you feel. Hear only what I say."

Disappear. It sounds amazing.

He pushes a door open, and I close my eyes, bracing myself, knowing exactly which room he's taken me to. He sets me down before the wall. The wall with the wooden frame secured to it. What's remaining of my shirt is pulled off, and I close my eyes, escaping his probing eyes as he takes in my scar in all its glory. He leans into me to unhook my bra, breathing in my ear. My eyes fly open. "Give me your hands," he orders, dropping my bra to the floor before reaching for some rope that's hanging nearby. I present my wrists, and he starts to meticulously bind them, his concentration acute, as I look past him to the wall of glass, seeing tops of buildings as far as the eye can see. And in the very distance, the ocean. It's a mesmerizing view. But it has nothing on the man before me.

He tugs at the binds, testing his work, and looks at me. "Nervous?" he asks, and I shake my head. Strangely, no, I'm not in the least bit nervous. Maybe I should be, but I'm not. The promise of disappearing is too enticing. Of feeling only what he will allow me to feel. To hear only what he will allow me to hear. The tormenting voices in my head will fuck off. The persistent visions of my past will be gone. I can't pass that up.

"Are *you*?" I ask, as he guides my hands to the rail above my head, securing the ropes to it with a D-ring, forcing me onto my tippy-toes.

"A little," he says, and it surprises me. He's a man who knows what he's doing. I've witnessed it myself. "Ask me why."

"Why?"

"I don't know." He kisses me forcefully on my lips. "And that's making me more nervous." Taking his thumb, he drags it roughly across my bottom lip, his eyes becoming drowsy. "If you want me to stop, say my name." He starts kissing his way down to my stomach, and my chest pushes out as a result.

"What?" I gasp, throwing my head back. "I'll be saying your name nonsto—fuck." I moan as he trails up to my nipple, sucking hard. "James," I cry. And there's the first. It won't be the last. *I don't want him to stop.*

And he doesn't stop, yanking my jeans down my legs. "My other name," he says, so casually, and I shoot my eyes to where he's crouched at my feet, his fingers resting in the top of my panties.

"I don't know your other name." He has another name?

"Exactly." My panties are drawn down my legs, a kiss planted on the edge of my pubic bone, and he rises, pushing his front into mine.

"What's your other name?" I breathe into his face, making him smile darkly. "Tell me."

"And run the risk of you stopping this?"

"I won't stop this."

"So you're just curious, yes?" He rests his forehead on mine.

"Tell me."

"No."

I thrash and buck, frustrated, and James withdraws, tilting his head.

"Tell me your other name!" I don't know if it's my curiosity or the fact that the pressure is building to unbearable levels. I'm throbbing painfully between my legs, dripping with need.

"I think you're talking too much." A gag appears from nowhere, and I inhale, fighting against the ropes. They burn the flesh of my wrists, but nowhere near as much as I'm burning everywhere else.

"No," I beg. It's pointless, I know that. He pushes the material between my teeth, and I immediately bite down on it, my jaw tense. He secures it, and then steps back, beginning to strip, starting with what's left of his T-shirt. Every inch of his skin he reveals sends me more delirious. Until he's naked, and I can hardly breathe.

He's . . . devastating.

"And finally," he whispers, holding up a blindfold. I can only moan my desolation, shaking my head. Why would he do that? Deprive me to that extent? My hungry eyes drop down to his groin getting one last look at his prime, rock-solid erection. It's weeping. And then . . .

Darkness.

I can barely move, can't speak, can't see. But I can smell, and I get a waft of his signature creamy, manly scent. "Your skin's tingling, isn't it?"

I moan in response, and let my body go lax.

"Your hearing's hypersensitive." He blows a warm stream of air across my ear, and a wicked shiver glides down my spine. "Anything that touches you"—he pinches a nipple as he bites down on my earlobe, and a muffled cry escapes—"feels like fire." I buck, screaming in my head for him to stop. To give me more. "And when I ram my cock inside you, Beau, it'll feel like it could break you in the best possible way."

Do it!

His voice alone could bring me to climax. Add touch, add smell, add the taste of his tongue still lingering on mine, I'm a slave to his kink. I'm trapped. But the freest I've felt in too long. There's no pressure to pretend. Nothing is strained. I'm not being forced to lie about how I feel. I don't see pity. I don't see worry. I'm invisible because I can't see how he sees me. In this moment, this illicit, erotic, overwhelming moment, I can be whoever I want to be, and I want to be his slave. I want to submit. I want to hand over every ounce of power and feel no pressure to be strong. This is everything I have been waiting for. Not him, but what he's doing. How he's making me feel. It's freedom within a cage. Safety in darkness, something I haven't known for too long.

I exhale and let my arms take my weight, hanging there lifelessly, zoning out more, walking the lightest path of darkness. I feel him grab me under my thighs and lift, and the undeniable scratch of his scruff brushes the inside of my thighs. *Oh God.* The nerves in my clitoris start to spasm in anticipation. My heart vibrates. My skin burns. "So fucking juicy," he rumbles, and then his mouth encases me, and I'm sent into orbit, screaming around my gag. I'm given no time to adjust. No time to settle. No time to get hold of my violently bending body. He goes at me like a famished animal, thrusting his tongue deep, lapping greedily, biting at my flesh. The pound of my climax building is fast, far faster than I want it to be, but not at all surprising given the gift of his mouth. "Make it last, Beau," he growls, plunging his fingers deep and high. "Make it fucking last."

Another muffled scream, my orgasm not listening, steaming forward relentlessly.

James!

I'm screaming his name over and over in my head, not for him to stop, but because I wish I could see him. See his eyes, his face, his mouth coated in me. My body temperature shoots up, the burn of my skin bordering unsafe. The pressure in my head is becoming too much, my body rigid.

And his mouth is suddenly gone, my feet are on the floor, and I moan my ruin. "Too fast, Beau."

No.

"Let's try again."

God, no!

He blows air across my clitoris, and I feel the thrums slow to a manageable level, just for him to build them back up to explosion. Except he won't let me explode. How many times will he do this?

A light dash of wet, warm contact.

His tongue.

A lick.

Fuck me, save me from this addictive torture.

Heat stretches across the insides of my thighs.

His hands.

Spreading me.

Oh God, oh God, oh God.

More air drenching my sodden flesh.

His breath.

Cooling me.

I mumble his name behind my gag, wrestling with my restraints, as he drapes my legs over his shoulders again.

"Shall we try one more time?" he asks, his voice groggy with lust. "Can you take it, Beau? Can you stand it?" He doesn't give me a chance to answer, slamming his mouth down on my pussy, his tongue frantic, his kisses deep, his licks hard. I scream, by body bowing brutally, my thighs squeezing his face. The ropes cut into my skin, and unexpected emotion creeps up on me. The material covering my eyes becomes damp. I'm crying. Why the fuck am I crying when this is the best thing to happen to me in a long time?

Because it's good. A relief. And because I know it can't be sustained.

Fuck off!

I swallow hard, grit my teeth, and concentrate on keeping my relentless orgasm at bay. It's a pointless endeavor. Nothing could stop it.

Only James.

He pulls away again, and I go limp, exhausted. I can't take anymore. I mumble my pleas, praying he deciphers them.

He doesn't. Or if he does, he ignores them.

More air.

A little flick of his tongue.

A few kisses on the insides of my thighs.

I brace myself.

"And again," he whispers, licking from my thigh to my throbbing, swollen lips. Latching on to my clit, he sucks hard, rolls his tongue, sucks, bites, licks, bites, sucks. I choke, flinging my head back as the blood gathers again and rushes forward, my orgasm regaining momentum. I try to stop it. With everything I have, I try to stop it. But all I feel right now is uncontrollable need. It brews, brims, very nearly bursts.

And he pulls away again.

No!

I breathe in deeply through my nose, try to gather myself, as my release subsides, abandoning me. This is the best kind of pain imaginable. I'm suffering but not suffering. Hurting but loving it. Feeling and craving more of it.

This really could be the best thing that's ever happened to me.

And the worst.

I go limp, unable to hold myself up, my full weight resting on his shoulders. It doesn't hinder him. James rises to standing, holding me with one hand on my lower back. I hear the clang of metal, and suddenly my arms are falling from the suspension rail, though my hands are still bound. No more? Another hand meets my back, and he walks a few paces, his face still snuggled in between my thighs. Softness meets my back, and then hardness meets my chest. "Your orgasm is going to be so fucking powerful, I need my cock to absorb it, not my mouth." He fiddles with my gag, and a moment later it's gone. I swallow, trying to find some moisture. "Here," he rasps, sweeping his wet tongue through my mouth, sharing his saliva. And once my mouth is wet again, he kisses me deeply, moaning, pulling back, pushing forward time and again.

"I want to see you," I beg, not with any confidence that he'll grant my wish. "Please."

"Let me see *you*," he counters, pulling my blindfold up. I blink and squint, finding his blue eyes quickly. "Let me see you, Beau."

I stare at him. He's seen me. But . . . "Let me see you," I counter softly, absorbing every inch of his complicated, beautiful face. His kink. His mood. His coldness. His other name. Who am I looking at? Who am I seeing?

"You will." Another kiss, this time delicate. "I've no doubt about it." He scans my face. "Do I need protection?"

"No. Do I?"

His hips swivel, and he thrusts into me on a gruff bawl, me on a broken cry, my neck cracking with the speed that I throw my head back. He pumps hard and fast, hitting me unfathomably deep. The pain is unfamiliar but comforting. A pain I can handle. A pain I like.

"More," I cry, closing my eyes, absorbing his blows, smiling on the inside when his pounds become harsher. "More," I say again, and I hear him growl, striking me harder still. It's agony. It's amazing. "More," I whisper, disappearing into a never-ending abyss of pleasure. Sound becomes a muffled white noise, my body weightless, my heart light. I'm being jolted constantly, I'm drenched through. "More," I mumble, willing everything he has to give, rising to meet his drives, turning my head slowly to the other side, hiding my face in the crease of my raised arm. Every horrid woe leaves my mind one by one until there is only this moment. Him. Me. Our sweating bodies, his power, and my acceptance.

"Beau!" he barks, and I'm snapped back into the room, my eyes springing open. He's looking down at me, his hair soaked and falling into his face, his skin glistening, his eyes crazy. *Not* in control. Wild. With me. "Stay with me, baby," he says more calmly, and I force my eyes to remain open and my head in the game. He pulls free, grabs my thighs, and thrust them up until my knees are by my ears, his arms braced against them. He slams back into me on another grunt, and I choke, the change of position sending him even deeper. "More?" he asks, studying me as he withdraws slowly, the slickness of his cock gliding like ice.

"More," I taunt, staring him down, egging him on, asking for it.

He smiles and slams home again on a yell.

"More," I scream.

I'm pinned to his bed, folded in half, taking his mercifulness, and I want more. So much fucking more.

Bang!

"More!"

Bang!

"More!"

Bang!

"More!" I scream.

"Fuck!" He releases my knees and spins me over onto all fours, running a palm over my core, groaning at the saturated flesh he finds. "Jesus, Beau Hayley, you are a fucking surprise." He pushes a palm down in between my shoulder blades, forcing my face to the sheets, and with the most delicate of touches, he runs a fingertip down the length of my spine to the crease of my backside. As I stare across the mattress, something appears in my field of vision. His hand. Holding a leather paddle. "Kiss it," he orders, putting it in front of my mouth. I do as I'm bid, pushing my lips to the leather, as his thumb pushes against the tight ring of muscles in my ass. I tense without thought. "Relax," he commands, and with that one soft word, my entire being loosens. I'm praised, his thumb slipping past the barrier, and I moan, the leather paddle being dragged down my back, his thumb circling a forbidden place. "I'm going to put something inside you."

I don't question what. I don't question where. I've handed all power over and it's therapeutic. No worries. No concern. No pressure.

His thumb is suddenly gone, and his hand appears again. "Suck it." He pushes a butt plug past my lips, and I close my eyes, sucking the cold metal. It pops free, and he drags that down my spine too, until he reaches my ass. I inhale, feeling it pushing against me, and swallow as it slips into me, my muscles gripping it hard. Then his fingers slip inside me, sweeping far and wide.

"James," I breathe, feeling sensation overload.

"What, baby? What's wrong?"

Wrong? Is this wrong? "Nothing's wrong." I murmur, closing my eyes, floating away again. His fingers slip free and his cock slips in. "Oh, God," I say over a sigh, my body shaking, my skin tingling, my core gushing.

He takes my hair and thrusts gently, and I feel the leather paddle smoothing over my bottom again. It leaves my skin. I brace myself.

Slap!

I jolt, the sting biting, but he thrusts on.

Slap!

I hiss, pushing my face into the mattress as blood floods to my head and my clit.

Thwack!

He drives deep at the same time. "More," I beg.

And he gives me more.

His pace increases, and with the increase of pace comes more thrashes. My ass is full, my pussy full, my skin blazing. I'm being attacked full force in various ways, and I want more. I zone out, hypnotized by his ferocity, walking the path to nothingness. I go nowhere. I hear no words. I see no evil.

I taste only freedom.

My internal walls quiver as the friction builds. The slickness. The heat. The power. And then the tell-tale sign of a release is within reach, and it brings me back into the room. I gasp, drinking in air, starving for it, my clit pulsing. My thighs tremble, and with each drive, each spank, each constriction of my ass muscles, it edges forward, almost prowls, creeps, giving me time to prepare for it.

"Go on, Beau," James yells over the ear-piercing sound of our colliding bodies. "Let it bend you. Let it break you."

It hits me with so much power, it makes my eyes water. My body jacks off the bed. James fingers dig into my hips, holding me tightly, and he bangs on, slamming my orgasm out of me. I scream. My head's spinning. I choke on nothing, gritting my teeth, as bolts of pleasure tear through me like a monster, leaving limp, listless muscles in their wake. The sensitivity becomes too much, my jaw aching from the force of my clenched teeth.

I really am utterly broken. Unable to move. Unable to speak. Unable to even think. James pulls out, and he helps me to my back. I can't see him. Even my vision has failed me. Once again, he pushes my knees to either side of my ears, and I feel him watch me as his head falls south. His tongue meets the ring of muscles holding the butt plug in place, and he circles it slowly, working his way up through my pussy as he pulls the plug free with his fingers. He releases my legs. Kisses my navel. Each breast. And then my lips.

I force my heavy eyes to remain open, trying to clear my vision. Trying to see him. He spreads himself all over me, my bound hands fall limply over my head, and he enters me again, this time slowly. The fog leaves my sight.

And there he is, looking out of this world, soaked, like he could have just stepped out of the shower. His pace now is meticulous and lazy. He glides in and out with ease, in no rush, and when his piercing blues seem to turn up a notch in the brightness stakes, his face strains, and he quickly pulls out again, walking on his knees until they're positioned either side of my chest. He wraps a fist around his girth and pumps over my face, the lust in his eyes crazy as he looks down at me, his lips parted. I don't think I've ever seen anything so magnificent. So powerful.

He reaches down and pulls at my bottom lip, and I open my mouth. He comes hard on a hiss, the tip of his cock bursts like a volcano, cum spraying my boobs, my face, hitting my tongue. I would close my eyes and savor the salty taste of him, if I could bear taking my eyes away from what's towering over me, exuding supremacy, screaming sex.

His back arches, his hips push forward, the thrusts of his hand starting to slow, and then he falls forward onto a fist, struggling to hold himself up. "My God," he whispers, dipping to kiss the corner of my mouth, not bothered by his seed spread all over my lips. "I'm broken." He collapses and blankets me with his body, completely crowding me.

I have to agree.

I'm broken too.

But this kind of new broken hurts so good.

15

JAMES

There's a fine line between want and need. Sometimes you can want something so much, you convince yourself you actually need it. Or, worse than that, think you're entitled to it. It makes the withdrawal symptoms more prevalent. I no longer allow myself to want something. I refuse to fall into the realms of need.

I'm used to the misery.

The darkness.

The never-ending cycle of hate. Hate for the world. Hate for my family's deaths. Hate for every person on this planet living.

Hate for myself for surviving.

Hate is easier to feel than love. It's a consistent, reliable form of self-torture I'm in full control of. Other emotions are not. With that tainted, unnamed emotion, someone else is in control. Someone else delivers the torture.

I'm only capable of hate.

But as I stare at the woman beside me, her skin still damp, her screams of ecstasy still ringing in my ears, I feel no hate. I feel only purpose. I see a lost soul who's fighting to navigate this world. I see desperation to escape. I see an equal, diabolical, deep-seated need for vengeance. And her scar? I reach forward and stroke down the length of her arm, from her shoulder to her wrist.

I see red. A mist of fury descends. It's unstoppable.

I get up off the bed and stalk out, needing to walk it off before I wake her up and give her truths that unveil my darkness. *No. Not happening.*

I land at my desk and pull up the screens, loading the stock market and scanning the numbers. All numbers I like. There's nothing to take my mind off things here. So I pull up my inbox and reply to every email. And once I've done that, I call Otto to check on the burner phone he's been tracking for two years. Nothing.

Then it's just me, my thoughts, and the darkness again. I close my eyes, and the first thing I see is our house. My family home in England. My father at the head of the table smiling as the maid serves dinner to his wife, son, and daughter. As the butler pours wine and water. As his best man, Otto, gives him a nod that all is well. In that moment, it *was* all well. The men were guarding the gate, ensuring we were safe. My father, the prolific Spencer James, lording it up on his country estate after finalizing a deal with the Serbians to supply London's richest with the finest cocaine.

I was twenty-two years old. A master shooter. A fine gymnast. An unrivaled fencer. A genius mathematician. A university graduate. And my sister? An aspiring historian. Beautiful like our mother. Smart like our father. Nothing made Spencer James prouder than his multi-talented offspring. Nothing made my mother smile harder than her boy and her girl. That evening, my father declared world domination. He told us our future was bright and crime free. And the same evening, our home was blown up by the men my father took from.

My family lay in thousands of pieces amongst bricks and

rubble. I dodged death. But watching Otto pull the teeth from my parents, my little sister, and our staff's cindered remains, and then forcing me to neck half a bottle of vodka before he took one of mine, made me want to die.

And eventually, it made me want to kill.

16

BEAU

I open my eyes and stare at the ceiling, feeling James lying next to me. My breathing is still heavy. My wrists still bound. I turn my head on the pillow, finding him sprawled on his front, his eyes lightly closed, snoozing.

His back.

I use my stomach muscles to sit up, my body aching like it's never ached before. Not even when I was recuperating after being bedridden for weeks. Not even when I've run miles and miles.

I get the full force of his injury. Every last millimeter of his flesh is scarred, uneven, and angry. It's a sobering sight. It puts my own scar to shame. The front of this man is perfect. His chest, his thighs, his unfathomably stunning face. Even his messy hair is perfect. But the back of him?

I wince.

It's gruesome.

Ashamed of my thoughts, I divert my stare to my wrists, wriggling to loosen the rope, the sores beneath raw. I hiss, the burn painful, and give up. I don't want to wake him—he looks so peaceful. But I need to go home.

I glance around the room, wondering how many people he's had in here. What has he done to them? And why does he do it? I look over my shoulder to his sleeping form. He looks too angelic, too perfect to be so . . . ruined. My eyes fall to his back again. Imperfection stares back at me.

He's broken.

Like me.

Did he see right through me because he's the same as me? Feels the same as me? Hates like me?

I'm distracted from my endless questions when I hear something in the distance. My cell phone. I shuffle to the edge of the bed and gingerly place my feet on the hard floor. I expect it to be cold. It's not. Naked, with my hands tied, I go to the door and negotiate the handle, pulling it open. The sound of my cell gets louder before ringing off, and I take the stairs at a safe pace, finding my purse in the kitchen. I flip my cell onto the counter and see missed calls from Lawrence. It's after nine o'clock. I've vanished for three whole hours.

I call him straight back, pressing the speaker icon and propping my elbows on the edge of the counter to get closer to my cell.

"Hey," he says when he answers, with a ton of questions in his tone that he's trying so hard to disguise.

"Hey." My throat is dry, my voice hoarse. *More*. "Everything okay?"

"Yes, of course. It's just you're not home and you usually are. Are you in Walmart again?"

I smile. It would be easy to say yes. I look down at my bound wrists. "No."

"Oh." He's dying to ask where I am, but he won't. "I'm not worried."

"I'm glad." He's lying through his teeth. "Do you have a show tonight?"

"I'm on in five minutes. Dexter just arrived. He said you still weren't home when he left. I just needed to check you're alive before I go on stage, else I'll fluff my words."

I look across the kitchen, seeing the stool we sent flying still on the floor. "We'll talk tomorrow."

"Why tomorrow?" he asks.

"Because I'll be in bed by the time you're home."

"Oh, yes. Of course."

"Uncle Lawrence?" I say, despite knowing he's actually Zinnea at the moment.

"Yes?"

"Ever wanted to disappear?"

He's silent for a moment. Contemplative. "Every day, sweetheart. But I have my coping mechanisms. I hope one day you'll find yours."

I stare at the glass countertop, worried I already have found it. "See you in the morning."

"Be safe, be careful." He hangs up as I assess the blisters on my wrists. They're sore, yes. But they have nothing on my old injuries. I wander into the middle of the room, circling on the spot. Darkness has fallen, the city illuminated by millions of lights, whether from buildings, streetlights, or monuments. I feel like I'm in a goldfish bowl. And at the same time, standing on top of the world looking down. Not closed in. Not suffocated. Naked—physically and metaphorically.

"It's freeing, isn't it?"

I whirl around and find James standing at the top of the stairs. He's still naked too. Unbothered. And as he slowly takes the glass steps, I get time to admire the perfect side of him. The undamaged side. His legs are so long, so defined. His shoulders the perfect width. His torso forms the perfect V. God was kind to him. Yet somehow, I know that's not true.

"Are you okay?" he asks as he approaches me, a small frown marring his perfect forehead. I immediately worry that he thinks I may have been snooping.

"I heard my cell ringing." I nod toward the kitchen area across the room, where my cell remains on the counter. "It was a bit of a challenge finding and answering it." I lift my wrists, showing him why.

"Here." He steps into me and starts to unravel the rope, and I watch him with interest, his concentration sharp, his care great. When the ropes are gone, I flex my fingers and roll my wrists. "Does it hurt much?" he asks, taking one hand and checking the sores.

"Not really."

"And your legs?"

"Achy."

"Would you like a bath?"

I step back, pulling my wrist out of his clasp as I do. "I can take a bath at home."

"I'd prefer it if you had one here."

"Why?"

He takes my hand and leads me toward the stairs. "It's all part of the service," he says quietly, and I can't help but laugh on the inside. He didn't bathe that woman I saw him fucking. He escorted her right out, along with the man. "Then we'll eat. *Then* you can go home."

Fuck me, bathe me, and feed me. "I don't need you to be all attentive, James. I asked for what I got."

"Did you?" he replies, not looking back.

I pull my hand from his when we reach the top of the stairs, but he doesn't stop, just carries on to the bathroom I used earlier. Not *his* bathroom. Not the bathroom in the room we just fucked in. Did I get what I asked for? "Yes, I did."

He stops. Looks back. "Did you though, Beau?" He disappears through the door, leaving me standing naked at the top of the stairs, stumped.

My other name.

I pad slowly to the entrance, finding him sitting on the edge of the impressive egg-shaped glass tub as water pours from a waterfall faucet. "I remember saying *more* many times," I remind him. I goaded him. Begged for it.

"You did."

"You asked me to give you what I had, and I did," I go on.

"You did." He tips a small bottle of oil into the water, and the waft of lavender is instant. Isn't lavender supposed to be calming? Does he think I need calming?

"James?" I ask quietly, and he looks at me. His eyes aren't so cold now. They're sorrowful, and it throws me. "Are you okay?"

"I don't know yet, Beau." He rises to his full six foot four and eats up the distance between us with three strides of his long legs. His palms rest on my shoulders, and a few flexes nearly has me folding to the floor in pleasure, his firm fingers working deep into my screaming muscles.

"What do you mean?" I ask.

"I mean what I said. I'm yet to determine if I'm going to be okay."

"Your scar," I breathe, compelled to touch it. Feel it. Show him that it doesn't bother me.

"You think it's ugly."

I lift my arm. "This is ugly."

He stares at my damaged skin, stroking my arm, his eyes

flicking to mine. "You're yet to encounter ugly, Beau," he whispers, dipping and kissing my scar. I breathe in deeply, caught between enchantment, wonder, confusion, and lust.

It's so much better than being caught in limbo, between life and death.

My head falls back as James returns to working my muscles. Part of me wants him to leave them tight and painful; the ache will last a long time. The longer the better. But his touch on my skin is like nothing else.

He starts walking backward toward the tub, and I follow robotically, powered by his working fingers. "There," he says, flipping the faucet off and feeling the water. He takes me under my arms, lifts me from my feet, and places me in the water. "Take as much time as you need."

And then he turns and walks out, leaving me alone in the bathroom. I look at my naked body. At my scars. At the welts on my wrists.

Need. Take as much time as you *need*. I don't *need* anything.

Especially not time. Especially not to think. And I definitely don't want to lose the intense ache I'm feeling on every part of my body. It's masking things I've struggled so hard to mask for too long.

I wash quickly, leaving my hair, and get out to dry myself with one of the crisp white Egyptian cotton towels. I go to the bedroom to find my clothes, snatching them up from the floor and tugging them on. I approach the mirror hanging on the wall. The whole of my front is exposed, my tattered shirt gaping open. I can't go out in public like this. I glance around the room, not holding out much hope of finding anything to wear. This isn't even his bedroom. It's his kink room. The room he brings many people to and fucks them wildly with an audience.

Of their own volition, my teeth clench, and I hate myself for letting foolish resentment cloud the serenity. I spot a closet across the room, and, desperate, I go to it, pulling the doors open. I'm presented with another room. A walk-in closet. Floor-to-ceiling rails and various width drawer units span the circumference, and an enormous snuggle chair sits on an angle in the center. His closet. This *is* his bedroom?

I look back over my shoulder to the various contraptions attached to the walls, the cabinet full of toys, the leather chaise in the window.

Clothes.

I work my way through the rails trying to find something suitable, an old T-shirt or something. All I can see are suits, dress shirts, and jeans. I can't go waltzing down in any of those. "Shit," I mutter, starting on the drawers. I yank the first open. Boxers. The second. Socks. The third. "Watches?" I murmur, casting my eye across dozens of timepieces resting in cushions. I slam it shut. Where does he keep his plain old T-shirts?

I turn, seeing another unit of drawers. Wider drawers. I hurry over and pull the first open, being presented with a perfect pile of perfectly folded, crisp black T-shirts. There must be a dozen, all the same style. I grab one, discard my shirt, and pull it over my head as I make my way downstairs.

As my feet hit the staircase, I hear voices and see a couple sitting at the island with James. He's leaning on the glass counter, supported by his forearms, and he's now dressed in jeans and a black T-shirt to match the one I've just taken from his stash. They're talking quietly, and my steps falter, my hand taking the metal rail. A couple. A man and a woman.

I pull myself together just in time for them all to turn and find me hovering on the stairs. Uncomfortable doesn't cover it. James pushes himself up slowly, his laser stare holding me in place where I stand.

I look away. “Sorry to interrupt.” Convincing my legs to move is a task, and I take the steps slowly, feeling terribly unstable, as I’m watched by all three of them. I glance at my work tools by the door, torn. I can’t carry it all, so I gather what I can manage—I’ll come back for the rest—and hit the elevator call button.

“Beau,” James says softly, and my shoulders rise, like tensing can protect me. The doors open, and I lift a foot to step inside. I don’t make it over the threshold. He takes my arm, keeping me where I am, and I look at his long, capable fingers wrapped around my scarred flesh.

“Let go of me,” I whisper, not wanting to make a scene in front of these people.

“Leave your things here.”

I swing a stunned look up at him. He thinks I can come back? “I don’t think that’s a good idea.”

He takes everything from my hands and places them back where they were. “Why?”

I look to the people in James’s kitchen instinctively, while James keeps a firm hold of my arm. They’re not watching now. They’re looking at something together. A laptop.

“That’s Pierce and Michelle,” James says, pulling my attention back to him. He’s showing no expression. No emotion. Giving me nothing to tell me what he’s thinking or how he’s feeling. Why does that irritate me? “They track my private stocks.”

“Oh.” I immediately feel like a fool. He knew what I was thinking and that my thoughts were bothering me. “You’re obviously busy.” I gently try to tug my arm free, and his grip slides down to my wrist, catching one of the welts. I flinch. He’s doesn’t miss it.

“You didn’t spend very long in the bath.” He steps back, giving me space, and tucks his hands into his back pockets. “You should have soaked a while; it would have eased the discomfort.”

I reach for the call button again, the doors, at some point

during the past few moments, having closed. "It's fine. I'll soak in the tub at home."

"I'd rather you did here."

The doors slide open again as I show him my absolute confusion. "Why?"

"So I know you've taken the necessary measures to ensure the fastest recovery time."

"You fucked me, you didn't beat me," I say, louder than I planned, my frustration getting the better of me. He regards me quietly, still with nothing to read on his face. He looks over his shoulder to his people, and I follow his direction, nearly dying on the spot when I see they've stopped what they're doing and are looking this way. "I'm sorry," I say quietly, humiliation engulfing me. "I'll be going now." The doors have closed again, and I bite down on my teeth, smacking the button.

"I want you to get back in the bath," James says, moving in closer.

"I do not need to get in the damn bath."

"Beau, let's not fall out over this," he whispers. "My request is simple and for your own benef—"

"I don't want a bath, James," I hiss, anger replacing the frustration. I take backward steps into the elevator when the doors open, and James follows me, backing me into the corner with his imposing frame.

"Why?" he asks, his chest pushing into mine. "Why don't you want a bath, Beau?"

My eyes climb his torso to his stoic face. His beautiful, stoic face. "Because I like the pain," I say through my clenched jaw. It's a pain I can deal with. A comforting pain. A pain that reminds me that I *can* escape. A pain that didn't suggest I was fragile, that I needed to be treated with care. *Flogging. Paddling. Hammering.* Intense, welcome pain. Everywhere.

His eyes remain clear, his face straight, and he rests a hand on the wall behind my head, moving in until our noses are touching. My shakes are violent. "Take a bath," he whispers. "Soak off the ache." He kisses the corner of my mouth, and I close my eyes, breathing in deeply. "Because we're doing it all again tomorrow." He takes my hand and places something in it. A small box. He's breathing in my ear, and it racks my body. "Goodnight, Beau." He pushes away from the wall, backing out, eyes on my useless form. "Sleep well."

The doors close.

And I slide down the wall until I hit the floor, in a complete state of shock, when I should really be angry. Angry by his persistence. He was so fucking insistent that I take a bath there, while he discussed business with his employees downstairs. So, where is that anger? Why am I not fuming?

I open the box and find a tube of cream and a small bottle of lavender oil. I laugh under my breath. Does he have these little care packages at the ready?

"Fuck." I drop it to the floor and rest my head back. "What are you doing, Beau?" I ask myself, just as the doors slide open. Goldie looks down at me where I'm on my ass. "I don't need a ride home," I say before she offers. Her eyes fall to the box on the floor before slowly returning to me. "I used to be smart."

"A handsome, fucked-up man can make any smart woman stupid." She offers her hand, and I take it, letting her pull me to my feet. I don't miss her taking in the welts on my wrists. "And a beautiful, fucked-up woman can make any smart man stupid." She says it so quietly. But I hear her. Is James being stupid?

"Who are you to him, Goldie?" I ask, with no confidence she'll answer me.

She steps inside and hits the buttons. "Take it easy, Beau." The doors close, and I stare at myself in the mirror for too long. My cheeks are still flushed. My wrists red raw. My hair a crazy mess.

I swallow, turn, and walk through the lobby in a haze, a

complete muddle, collecting my keys from Otto as I pass. "I brought your car up from the garage. It's on the street."

"Thanks."

I make it outside and look up to the dark sky, gulping down air, trying to get my breathing under control.

God help me.

17

JAMES

The figures on the screen all blend and blur, my concentration shot, as the people in charge of my fortunes tell me where it's stashed, invested, and how trading's going. "Email me the reports," I say, eager to get them out so I can resume the mindfuck that is Beau Hayley.

"Sure." Michelle gathers up her things as Pierce shuts the laptop, and I see them to the elevator.

"Thanks for accommodating the late hour." The doors open, revealing Goldie. Her laser stare tells me I'm about to cop it.

I turn and head to the drinks cabinet, seeking some backup from alcohol, as she sees off my guests. I take my vodka to the foot of the glass pane that spans the side of my apartment and stare out across the city, my mind in chaos.

"Otto is with her," Goldie says from behind, and I nod, taking a swig of my drink.

"And the guy she saw last night?" I ask.

"Agent Oliver Burrows. FBI and ex-fiancé. They shared a hug outside the store. Obviously, I don't know what they shared once they were at his place."

I scowl at the window. "Thanks." So the ex-fiancé is sniffing around again?

"Does she know yet that her appeal has been denied?" Goldie asks.

"No," I answer with certainty, since Spittle confirmed the official letter has only just been sent.

"Do you know what you're doing?" she goes on.

"Not a fucking clue."

"Want some advice?"

I laugh under my breath. My answer won't mean a thing. "No."

"She doesn't deserve to die."

"I know." I turn to face Goldie. "But I'm not the only one who needs her dead, am I?"

"So you fucked her?"

That wasn't a fuck. That was an experience. "It seems like a better alternative to killing her." I raise a sardonic eyebrow, and Goldie rolls her eyes. "It's nothing," I go on. "Get over it. I need to keep her close until I know I'm in the clear." It wasn't nothing. It was everything. Like our darkness and torture blended, melded, and the weight of it wasn't so fucking heavy anymore. It was as if we shared each other's agony, and in those moments, it wasn't as painful. The hurt, shared. Pain, welcomed. *Scars, meeting.*

A connection.

A fucked-up connection.

And I'm fucked if I know what the fuck I'm supposed to do with it. I need to keep her close. She has a purpose, but regardless, Beau Hayley is a dead woman walking.

Because if I can't bring myself to kill her, someone else will.

18

BEAU

As I climb out of Dolly, I thank every god in existence that Lawrence and Dexter aren't home. My arms are bare, showcasing my new collection of welts, my scar is, unusually, on full display, my hair wild, and I'm wearing a man's T-shirt. I'm a walking box of guilty signs.

I slip my key into the lock, pushing the front door open and flicking on the lights in the hallway.

I come face to face with Lawrence.

My arms instinctively go behind my back. "What are you doing here?" I ask, sounding as alarmed as I know I must look. "You're supposed to be on stage." Although he's Lawrence right now, he has the remnants of Zinnea's lipstick smeared across his lips.

He looks me up and down, taking in the black T-shirt that isn't mine. "Are you okay?" he asks, as Dexter appears in the kitchen doorway behind him, his glasses resting on the end of his nose. His eyebrows get gradually higher as he takes me in too.

"I'm fine." I edge past my uncle and take the stairs. "I just need to get out of these clothes."

"Why of course you do, Beau," he calls. "Because half of them aren't yours."

"Lawrence," Dexter warns quietly.

I stop at the top of the stairs and breathe in.

"Where have you been?" Lawrence implores, ignoring his husband's warning.

"Did you come home especially so you could grill me?" I ask tiredly. "I'm a thirty-year-old woman, Lawrence."

"And when we spoke earlier, you asked me if I ever wanted to escape. You can't say things like that and not expect me to worry."

"You don't need to worry." I lock myself inside my bedroom, perching on the edge of the bed, my hands joined, my mind racing.

We'll do it all again tomorrow.

I bite down on my lip. Once was an experience. Twice? I'd be closer to it becoming a habit, and everyone knows habits are hard to quit. "Oh, God, Beau," I breathe, getting up and going to my bathroom. I run a hot bath, adding a few drops of the oil James gave me, and I strip. Climb in. Sink down beneath the hot, soothing water. Close my eyes.

There are no flashbacks of my past assaulting me. There're only memories of today. There's no lingering, familiar pain. There's only the intense, unfamiliar ache of my body and sting of my wrists. There's him. Every word he said, every move he made, every look he gave me. I need another habit. One to replace my terrible habit of suffering, but I know that habit shouldn't be James.

I sink deeper into the water, falling into a slumber. It's been a long time since dread hasn't monopolized my dreams. Too long. I feel my mind shutting down. My body becoming heavy, a deep sleep upon me.

Peace.

Calm.

James.

I got what I asked for.

Have you, though, Beau?

I shoot up, startled, water splashing everywhere, my breathing shot. I'm freezing and feel incredibly stiff. Reaching across to the vanity unit, I grab my cell. Midnight. I glance around my bathroom as I drop it, bewildered, my eyes heavy with tiredness.

I need to get out.

Lying back, I plunge my head under the water, enduring the cold for a little longer to wash my hair. "Jesus," I gasp, my teeth chattering, my skin riddled with goosebumps. I lift out of the water as soon as the suds are rinsed from my hair and grab a towel, wrapping it tightly around my chilly form.

As I'm wiping my eye makeup off with a cleansing cloth in the mirror, my cell rings and my hand lowers slowly from my face as I see the screen. It's past midnight. I breath in deeply, taking his call. I don't speak. But he does.

"Hi," he says, low and gravelly. "It's me."

I look at myself in the mirror. I'm smiling. "It's late."

"And you're awake. Why?"

I can't tell him that I fell asleep in the tub and fantasized about him. It sounds as sappy as it is, and though I don't know much about James, sappy he's not. "I don't sleep well," I admit.

"Me neither."

"Why?"

"Too much on my mind."

"Like?"

"Many things," he replies as I lower to the edge of the tub. "One of those things today is you."

Today. Perhaps not tomorrow or the next day. Just today. "Why?" I ask.

"Because I never imagined I would meet someone as fucked up as me," he says honestly. "And yet here I am, living the dream."

It's probably inappropriate, but I laugh to myself. He's being straightforward, and I appreciate it. I'm glad he's confirmed he's fucked up, because I was silently beating myself up about reaching that conclusion. His kink shouldn't make him fucked up. His scar shouldn't either. But his broodiness and apparent lack of emotion certainly pointed to it. "Why are you fucked up, James?"

"Maybe you'll find out in time. And perhaps in time you'll feel comfortable enough to share your demons with me."

My eyes dart across my bare knees. *In time*. How much time is that? "Maybe," I murmur, quite certain that all the time in the world wouldn't be enough for me to be comfortable.

"But in the meantime," he continues, his voice rough, "let's just carry on dodging our reality."

"Isn't it unhealthy to bury your head?"

"What's the alternative?"

"I don't know," I admit. I've done therapy, seen shrink after shrink, taken medication, become a zombie because of it. Nothing worked. Nothing saved me from myself.

"Or maybe we just accept it," he says.

"I accepted it long ago."

"Me too."

"Then why are we having this conversation?" I ask, a bit bemused.

"Because I wanted to hear your voice."

I recoil, so much so, I nearly fall back into the bath. That just doesn't sound like something James would say, and I'm thrown by it. His voice has been like ice—brittle, angry, cold. *Arousing*. He has elicited so many different responses from me. But I can't deny, hearing his voice is settling. *Because I wanted to hear your voice.* Like I *needed* to hear his.

"How are you feeling?" he asks, probably sensing that I don't know what to say to that.

"I feel fine."

"Did you use the oil and cream I gave you?"

"Do you give a recovery package to every woman you fuck?" I get up and go to the mirror, placing my cell on loudspeaker and setting it behind the faucet. I take the cream and squeeze a little onto each wrist.

"No."

"Then why me?" I ask, starting to rub it into the angry welts.

"It's more for my benefit than yours."

"Why?"

"To ease my guilt for hurting you."

"Why would you feel guilty?" I ask, my broken skin seeming to get redder with each word he speaks. "I'm a grown woman, James. I knew what I was getting myself into." That's a complete and utter lie. I had no idea of the places James could take me to. No idea at all. But I do now. And, God, I want to go there again.

"Beau," he breathes. "You have no clue what you're getting yourself into."

My massaging fingers falter, my mind struggling for how to respond. He keeps alluding to this. It's like he needs to share something but can't. "Then tell me."

There's a brief silence before he speaks again. "Sleep well." He hangs up, and I stare at myself in the mirror for an eternity, coming to terms with the fact that I'm as much in the dark about him as he is about me. Treading murky waters.

But will I drown in them?

Or just drown in James?

19

JAMES

She's home. That eases me, but I know I'd feel a fuck load better if she was in my bed. I place my mobile down and try to focus on the spreadsheet Michelle's sent over. I can't focus. Not on anything, and that's fucking dangerous. I click out of my current screen and pull up Google. Type in a name.

The results show me a good-looking guy, early thirties, well built. Oliver Burrows.

I sit back and study him, for the first time in my life considering killing a man for reasons less than worthy.

He wants Beau back.

And if he doesn't stop pursuing her, I can't promise I won't end him.

I snap my laptop closed as Otto strolls in, Goldie on his tail. "You're gonna get a call," he says, slumping down in a chair and helping himself to the remote control on my desk. He aims it at the screens and pulls up ABC News. A reporter is standing outside the scrapyard on the docks, a swarm of police cars and forensic vans behind her.

"It made the news," I muse.

"The owner clearly has dollar signs in his eyes," Goldie says, joining Otto. A phone rings, and all our eyes fall to the top drawer of my desk. My skin prickles as I slowly reach for the handle and calmly pull it open, swiping up the ringing phone, clicking to answer and putting it on loudspeaker. I rest it on my desk. "Your men are dropping like flies," I say quietly.

"Who the fuck are you?" he breathes, and I smile.

"You sound agitated." Well and truly pissed, actually. His nifty voice distorter can't disguise *that*.

"You're hindering my business activities."

"Maybe you should move out of Miami," I say, kicking my feet up on the desk. "I hear Hell is nice at this time of year." Translated: you're a dead man.

"Fuck you. This ends now."

I smile. "Is the big bad bear afraid?" Most definitely not. But certainly pissed off. Apparently, he saw the demise of The Brit as an opportunity. Thought he could swoop on in and mop up in Miami. It was rich pickings. The Russians out. The Romanians out. The Brit out.

Shame The Enigma is *in*.

"I will find out who you are." His words are a threat, and I roll my eyes.

"Good luck with that. In the meantime, I look forward to picking off your men one by one." I hang up and flick the phone away.

"Ever thought about what you'll do once they're all dead?" Otto asks, and Goldie settles back for the show, obviously wanting an answer to this question too.

"Why's it always about me?" I ask tiredly. "What would you two do?"

"I'm going to walk in the park eating an ice cream," Goldie declares, and Otto laughs.

I smile across at her. Goldie doesn't talk much about her childhood. I have minimal details. She was unwanted. Was in foster care. Jumped from one children's home to another. Her childhood was stolen. She's never strolled in a park for pleasure, relished the sunshine, listened to the birds tweet. And to eat an ice cream while doing it? For her, that's bliss. She joined the Royal Marines at eighteen and seemed to find her place in the world. Until some fucker gave her a stark, brutal reality check. She's a woman. And women are targets for rapists. "Don't be greedy," I say, thoroughly enjoying the look of pure exhilaration on her face, just at the thought.

Her nose wrinkles, and she looks to Otto. "What about you?"

"I'll buy a ten-bedroom villa on an island and fill it with women."

"Pig," Goldie mutters, and Otto chuckles. They both deserve those simple things and more. I'll make sure they have them. Otto served my father loyally for years before he served me. He knows only this life. He claims it's enough, yet I know his loyalty to my father won't allow him to walk away from me. I'm not the young man he knew. My father wanted my sister and me to build a life away from the crime that gave him his name and money. I'm more of a criminal than my dad ever was, and while I know Otto struggles with that at times, I also know he seeks vengeance for my family as much as I do. But he dreams of more.

"And you?" they ask in unison, returning their attention to me.

I think.

Revenge. Peace. Death.

"There'll always be people to kill." I get up and leave them to fantasize about ice creams and endless women, calling Spittle as I go. "I need the report on Jaz Hayley's death. I want to know who was on the scene, who filed it, who approved it."

"I can't access that information."

Can't or won't? I know the file has been compromised. I know what's in there is a pack of lies, which means The Bear has someone on the inside. What seems to be im-fucking-possible is getting the file to determine *who* has tampered with it. "Try," I order, hanging up. There's a bright side here. If Spittle can't access it, then Beau Hayley hasn't a cat in hell's chance. But there's always someone else who can. This should be dead and buried. *God damn you, Beau.*

20

BEAU

When I walk into the kitchen the following morning, the silence is excruciating. Dexter is nervously spooning Cheerios into his mouth, his face tired after his night shift, and Lawrence is wiping down the countertop with fast, furious swipes. Dexter shrugs when I throw him a questioning glance. I imagine he's had earache since he got in from work. "Morning," I say, flicking on the coffee machine.

"Morning," Lawrence grunts, attacking the countertops with more cleaning spray.

"I think it's clean."

He huffs and slams the bottle down. "I thought you could tell me anything," he snaps, and Dexter sighs loudly, dropping his spoon and reaching for his eyes under his glasses, rubbing into his sockets.

I collect the pot of coffee. "I can," I reply. *Most of the time.*

"Then why the silence now? I know something's going on."

"Nothing is going on." My words are robotic, my patience wearing thin. I abandon my coffee and throw my bag over my shoulder. "I'm going to work."

"Where? You've not even talked about this new job. You always tell me what you're painting, where you're painting, what colors you're painting. You've not murmured a word about this one."

I hurry toward the door, Lawrence on my tail. "It's an office," I call back, the front door in sight, my escape close.

"Beau, please. I'm so worried about you."

Guilt grabs me and squeezes hard. God damn guilt. I slow to a stop and face my uncle. The true concern splattered across his smooth face only enhances my shame. I go to him and wrap my arms around his shoulders. I hate making him feel like this. I really do. He and Dexter had a fabulous, easygoing life before Mom died. That was hard for them too, but then I crashed into their orbit with my pain and sorrow. They've taken me in, shown me nothing but unconditional love, and I am so extremely thankful for that. For *them*. I need their love, but I also need them to respect some boundaries too. I'm not a child, just a woman whose world imploded very suddenly. This thing with James? It's respite. Like therapy. "You've nothing to be worried about." I kiss his cheek. "Promise." I break away and jolt when Lawrence grabs my wrist, pulling me to a stop again. My hiss of pain isn't avoidable, and Lawrence drops his hold fast, alarmed. I cringe, feeling at my wrist over the sleeve of my shirt. *Fuck.*

Tension floods the hallway, and I swallow, yelling at myself to leave. Get out of here. Go before—

He lunges forward and yanks the sleeve of my shirt up, revealing the red, blistered skin on my wrist. His gasp is loud and shocked enough to bring Dexter crashing into the hallway. "Beau?" Lawrence asks quietly, looking up at me through glazed eyes. I can't bear the questions in his voice. Can't bear the worry.

Can't explain, either.

I turn and rush out of the house, feeling shame I don't want to feel and remorse that matches the routine feelings of secret self-pity. This is not how I want to feel. It's no good going through blissful escapism if your reality is going to be ten times worse when you have to face it again.

I jump in Dolly and start her up. She doesn't bang to life, but she does splutter a few times, and I don't will her to get moving as she starts to chug down the road. I have no words, not even to encourage my dilapidated old car. I reach the junction. I should be turning left to go to James's. To finish his office. Turn left to do it all over again.

I turn right.

After stopping at my regular florist, I go to see Mom. It's a gray day, the clouds heavy with rain waiting to pour, the sun a dull haze a million miles away. I let myself through the rickety gate and tread my way through the long grass, weaving around the headstones to the far side by the derelict stone wall that separates the graveyard from the world. The tulips I left over a week ago look sad and droopy, so I set about changing the water and flowers, busying myself for over an hour, weeding and fiddling around Mom's grave. I ignore the texts that come in from Lawrence and Dexter. I'll talk with them later. *Maybe.* I also ignore three calls from James. He's undoubtedly wondering where I am.

On his fourth attempt to get hold of me, I've finished fixing the tulips. I take a deep breath and take his call. "Where are you?" he asks, sounding a little indignant.

"I'm not coming."

"Why?"

"Because this can't last, James." Not just whatever is happening between us, but the feelings he provoked in me. It's not sustainable. That's been proven this morning by my confrontation with

Lawrence and the onslaught of shittiness that followed. It would be a wholly unhealthy cycle of relief and shame. I'd be jumping out of the frying pan into the fire. Setting myself up for a bigger fall. No. I need to call my therapist. James will have to find someone else to finish painting his office.

"And you need it to last," he says simply, with no judgement.

"I don't know what I need."

"What if I do?"

"You could never even comprehend what I need, James." I cut the call and sink to my back on the grass, chasing the clouds with my eyes, willing them into various recognizable objects. I spot a car. A dog. An enormous heart. The clouds are being kind to me today.

My cell rings again. "Stop," I order him quietly, lifting my arm to see the screen. But it's not James. It's someone else—another person I'd rather not speak to. But a mindless phone call every so often keeps him at a distance. I don't have to see him. Face him. Restrain myself from unleashing my anger on him.

I answer. "Dad."

"My darling girl."

My teeth grate, my smile tight. "How are you?" I ask. I only have to look in a newspaper to find that out.

"You missed my birthday."

"I did?"

"You can make up for it. Come to dinner with us."

Us. Him and his girlfriend. I cringe. "You know I can't do that."

"I'll book the entire restaurant out. It'll be just us three."

You can't knock the man for trying and usually I wouldn't have a problem declining, whether politely or not. But today? "Can I think about it?" *What the hell?*

"Yes, yes, of course."

I can't bear the hope in his voice. The happiness. "I'll call you." I hang up and sigh in despair. I can't forgive. *Won't.* But surely that's a healthier option than this madness I'm going through with James. It has to be.

I don't know. I honestly don't know, and that's why I hate this life. *I. Don't. Know.* I was never indecisive in the past. I was on top of life.

Was.

Was.

Was.

What am I now? Desperate? Bitter? Twisted? All of the above?

Again . . .

I. Don't. Know.

I chase more clouds, these ones darker, and the sky finally relents, the rain falling. It comes hard and fast. I don't run to the church for cover. Instead, I lie there, being thrashed by the angry bullets of water, letting it numb my skin.

The thunder clashing matches my loud, crowded head.

Lonely?

Always.

It's getting dark by the time I find the will to move. There have been many days when I've sat with Mom for hours, but today is a record. I'm drenched through, my clothes stuck to me, my hair heavy. I trudge through the sodden graveyard and slide into Dolly, looking up into the rearview mirror and wiping under my eyes to get rid of the black smudges.

Then I drive to Walmart.

I grab a cart and start my usual route through the aisles, finally ending up at the alcohol section. I grab a bottle.

"I'm not following you, I promise."

I glance to my left. "You sure?" I ask, as I place my wine in the cart. "Because you look as guilty as sin."

Ollie shrugs, stuffing his hands in his pant pockets. "I didn't think you still did this anymore."

"Shopping?" I question, and he rolls his eyes as I start walking. This habit of mine started only a week after I was discharged from the hospital. Everywhere just felt so crowded, even our spacious apartment with only two of us living there. But when Ollie would get home from work, the suffocating feeling would overwhelm me. So I'd come here. He found me on numerous occasions when I'd go missing, roaming the aisles.

I arrive at the checkout and place my wine on the belt, and Ollie grabs a bag and flaps it open, slipping the bottle inside once the lady's scanned it. "Let me get this," he says, pulling out his wallet.

I smile, but it's sad. I should never have had that coffee with him. Should never have fallen apart on him. Definitely shouldn't have let him take me back to the apartment we shared. "You don't have to."

"I want to. It's been a long time since I could buy you a drink."

I don't have the energy to fight him, offering a small smile instead. He's just an additional element to my ever-increasing mindfuck.

He pays and we walk toward the exit together. "So are you going to tell me why you look like a drowned rat?" he asks, looking me up and down.

I reach for my shirt and pull the cold, wet material away from my stomach. "I went to see Mom. I got caught in the downpour."

"It's not rained since three o'clock." He looks down at his watch, as if checking it's as late as he thinks it is.

I don't bother explaining. "Anymore dead bodies at scrapyards?"

"Stop it," he warns, giving me a playful nudge. "Just think, if you go back to work, we could talk all day long about the mutilated remains of various wanted men."

"So he was wanted?" I ask, ignoring everything else.

Ollie rolls his eyes. "One of The Bear's men."

I blow out my cheeks. "There's gonna be no more bad guys for you to lock up soon."

"Hmmm," he hums, thoughtful.

"Are we talking serial killer?"

He sighs, and I see him cave under my questioning. And perhaps just his need to keep my attention. "Do you remember hearing about The Enigma?" he asks, and I nod, knowing the name well.

"Assassin. Mom's nemesis," I confirm. "She swore she'd catch him before she retired. Or at least find out who he was."

"Yeah. He went quiet for a while. After your Mom . . ." Ollie looks down at me, pensive. Nervous. "Well, the last three bodies suggest he's back. Or has been resurrected. Or that we're now finding the bodies given one was a few years old."

"Wow," I breathe, my mind racing. The Enigma. He was top of Mom's list. What would she think if he was caught? If it was *me* who caught him?

Shit.

"You sound like you have a lot on your plate," I say, getting my thoughts back under control. Nothing could make me return to the MPD. Nothing.

"Coffee?"

I slow to a stop, as does Ollie, and I hate the hope I see in his brown eyes. "You don't want me back," I say evenly but softly, because I just know where this is leading. "Really, you don't."

"Don't tell me what I want, Beau. You did that when you left me at the church too. That was twenty months ago, and I still want you."

"I'm a different person."

"You mean bitter? Twisted?"

I look away.

"I still love you despite that."

"You shouldn't." I return my eyes to him. He was a popular guy at the force, with his male colleagues, and definitely with the female ones. I can't imagine that's changed since he's moved on to the FBI. He could have had the pick of the bunch. And he chose me. *Mistake.* I tried so hard to see our wedding through. I sat by Mom's graveside in my dress, a mess of a woman, willing her to give me the sense and courage I needed to marry Ollie four months after she was taken from me. She didn't speak to me. I couldn't go through with it.

I sigh and loop my arm through his, getting us moving again. "How many women have you dated since we split up?"

He scoffs. "None. You know I'm shit at dating."

I smile. He obviously hasn't improved since our first date. He was so nervous, and the nerves made him clumsy. It was endearing and hilarious all at once. And aside from his fine build and handsomeness, it was one of the things that attracted me to Ollie. How together he was as a cop, and how utterly disastrous he was as a date. The two sides of him were contrasting and lovable. "How many women have you slept with?" I ask, wincing at the mere thought, wondering why the fucking hell I'm asking such stupid questions.

He stops us and turns into me, his expression irritated. "Don't try and do that thing women do. When they try to be your friend as a consolation prize."

"I'm not a consolation for you, Ollie. I'm a lucky escape."

His hand drags through his hair roughly. "You're so fucking self-destructive, Beau. Resentment is eating you up inside."

"I'm getting better," I say, unable to get angry with him. Anger is exhausting, like hate. I'm too tired right now to feel either. "I really am."

He sighs, and I see something in him settle. Defeat. "I just need you to have peace again," he says. "There are no questions to be answered, Beau. It was a freak fucking accident, and you need to move on."

Move on. I hate those words. Only people who have never lost someone they love use those two insensitive words. "Something doesn't feel right," I mumble, swallowing, and he exhales, pulling me in for a hug. I sink into his hard chest, my eyes closing. "I need you to stop believing you can give me peace," I say, letting my arms hold him. This hug feels so final. Does he sense that? "Let me go, Ollie," I order gently, opening my eyes. He doesn't ease up, and I don't reinforce my request. Because something has captured my attention across the parking lot in the distance.

James.

He's standing by a silver Range Rover, watching me. Watching *us*.

What the hell? I pull away from Ollie and step back. Not because James is watching, but because Ollie is hoping. "It's time for you to move on too," I whisper, reaching for his arm and giving it a squeeze.

He nods slowly, beaten, handing me my wine and dipping to kiss my cheek. "Take care, Beau." He turns and walks to his car, and the moment he's pulled away, I seek James out again. He hasn't moved.

I wander over, feeling resolute and calm, but when I make it to him, just a few feet away, I can't seem to find the right words.

"Who was that?" he asks. They're not the right words from him, either, and definitely not a question I'm interested in answering.

"Why are you here?" I must change my hiding places. Two men have found me in twenty minutes.

"Who was it?"

"You think you can show up here and demand answers to questions you have no right to ask?" I sound calm. I feel anything but.

He has the decency to look mildly ashamed. "I didn't like it."

"What?"

"You with that man," he more or less snarls. "I didn't like it."

Unbelievable. "You're jealous?" Is he serious? One night of madness, and he's jealous?

"I didn't like it," he grates.

"I don't like the code language you use."

He opens the door of his car. "Get in."

I gawk at him. "Excuse me?"

"Get in the car," he hisses.

"I have my own car."

"That's not a car, Beau. It's a fucking death trap."

God help me before I slap his obstinate face. "Tell me what you meant," I snap, squaring up to him. "Your other name, what I'm getting myself into. Tell me."

"No."

"Then why the hell say it?"

His jaw twitches dangerously. I'm with him. "Because I can't seem to control my fucking mouth when you're around."

"Tell me!"

"No."

"Then I'm leaving." I back away. "And you're going to let me."

He inhales, gathering patience. "I don't have much choice, do I?" He shuts the door of his car, regarding me for a short time. "You don't want it again?"

I take another step away from him, trying to escape the range of his magnet. "No," I answer, not nearly quickly enough.

His nostrils flare. "You'll come back," he says surely, drilling into me with his penetrative eyes before he gets in and pulls away speedily, drawing the attention of a few shoppers leaving the store.

I breathe out, deflating, my head spinning. I don't even know what the fucking hell just happened. He came, we yelled, and he left before I had a chance to. But he left apparently certain that we're not done.

I don't want him to be right. But I fear he is.

I slowly walk to my car, looking at the bottle of wine. Drink it all. Every last drop.

I'm interrupted from my recklessness by my cell. I don't have the heart to ignore Lawrence's call. So I answer, getting in Dolly and turning the heaters up. "I was with a man," I say when I answer. I'm a grown woman. I shouldn't feel like I have to hide this. Lawrence doesn't need the details, and he doesn't need to get excited about any future prospects, but he does need to know I was doing something relatively normal. Like having sex. The sordid details beyond that aren't necessary. He's seen them on my wrist, anyway. "That's where I was last night. With a man." Lawrence remains silent, and I frown at the windscreen. "It's the man I am . . . *was* working for. It just happened, and I didn't try to stop it. It felt good." He should love that. He should relish the thought of me feeling good, even if it was brief. "There's nothing to read into it past that. It was a one-off." His lack of a reaction is starting to annoy me. "Don't you have anything to say?"

"A letter's arrived."

My cell becomes heavy in my hand. My heart heavy in my chest. "Open it."

"Come home, Beau."

"Open it," I repeat, turning off the heaters, suddenly roasting hot. Nervous. Hopeful. "Please."

"Not until you come home. We'll open it together." He hangs up, taking away my options.

"Damn you, Lawrence." I smack the steering wheel and pull out of the parking lot as fast as Dolly's capable, and I drive home in a haze of panic and fear, my body racked with shakes.

Jumping out of my car and racing up the path, I ignore the scratches from the overgrowth, not bothering to knock them out of my way.

Bursting through the door, I hear Lawrence and Dexter in the kitchen, and I make my way to them, my heart pounding dangerously. They're at the table, and they fall silent when I walk into the room.

The letter sits between them, a harmless piece of paper waiting to ruin me or cure me. Lawrence jumps up and comes to me, taking my arms just above my wrists. "Promise me this is the end of it," he begs, stroking up to my shoulders and gripping hard. "Whatever is in that letter, it's the end. We put it to bed."

I rip my eyes away from the letter on the table and look at him. I hate the doubt lingering on his face. The fear. I move past him and slide it from the table with a shaky hand. I work the seal open. Take a deep breath and pull out the paper, unfolding it.

I read the first line.

It's all I need to see.

I loosen my grip and the paper floats down to my feet.

"Beau?" Lawrence rushes to collect it, scanning it as I stare out of the kitchen window into the darkness.

"They're not re-opening the investigation." I turn and walk out in a haze of devastation, feeling crushed, desolate, but most of all angry. So fucking angry.

"Beau!" Lawrence yells, coming after me. "Beau, wait." He seizes me, swinging me around to face him more violently than is in him. "Where are you going?" he asks, frantic. "Stay here. Stay with us. We'll meditate. We'll talk. I'll help you."

I don't need meditation. I don't need to talk. I don't need pills or therapy or sectioning. "I'm going out." I pull myself free and open the door.

"To him?" he asks, his panic rising. "To the man who did that to you?"

I look at my hand on the door handle.

"Who is he?" he goes on. "Who did that to you?"

"He did nothing I didn't ask for." I walk away, hearing my uncle crying my name repeatedly, and I look back as I reach the bottom of the pathway, finding Dexter has intervened, pulling Lawrence back, trying to calm him.

"Let her go," he soothes.

I've never seen disappointment on my uncle's face.

Until now.

21

JAMES

"She's heading toward your apartment," Otto says as I dry off after my shower.

I hang up and stare at myself in the mirror. I don't know what I hoped to achieve in the car park of Walmart. Seeing her in the arms of her ex clouded my purpose in that moment. I aimed to stall her. To delay her finding out that her appeal had been denied. To delay the repercussions and to stall her grief, even if only for one more day. All I did instead was discover I have a jealous streak, and I'm shaken by that. But seeing another man soothe her?

Rage. Rage spiked by jealousy, and that's fucking new.

I reach for my jaw and rub a hand across my scratchy face, tilting my head back, but I keep my eyes on the stranger in the mirror. The face of a man I no longer recognize. He's distorted by grief. By a relentless need for vengeance. And by a heavy, misplaced sense of responsibility. He could cure Beau Hayley. He could also end her.

This isn't a case of *fix me*. I'm beyond that. Yet, scarily, I've discovered Beau certainly eases the torment. Masks the pain. She also injects my black soul with fragments of goodness, purpose beyond my only purpose. And perhaps the growing guilt I'm feeling, because I'm the reason she's lost. I'm the reason she's grieving her mother. I'm the reason Beau Hayley is so utterly damaged, both spiritually and physically. I can't ignore the opportunity to redeem myself. Maybe give myself some light relief in more ways than one.

I pull on some boxers and go wait for her.

22

BEAU

When I walk into the lobby of James's building, Goldie is sitting at the reception with her legs up on the desk, a can of soda in her hand. She glances up from the computer screen, says nothing, and gets up, walking to the elevator and punching in the code needed to take me to the very top. To James.

I enter, avoiding her eyes, and the doors close, the whirling of the mechanisms kicking in. I ride up, questioning for the first time if James knew I'd come. Goldie's reaction to my arrival suggests so. And I hate that. I hate that he was right.

The doors open, and my eyes find him immediately, sitting at the bottom of the stairs in his boxers. My question is answered. He knew.

But he doesn't know *why* I'm here.

I step out as he rises to his feet, unfolding every glorious inch of his body. There he is. My path to oblivion. His hair looks darker. His eyes lighter. His physique sharper. The air sizzles in the space between us, and I reach for the buttons of my shirt and start to unfasten them. His face remains impassive as he turns and starts taking the stairs, his steps measured and slow, his scarred back a beacon of ruin. I drop my shirt to the floor and follow him, reaching back to undo my bra, dropping it to the steps.

When I reach the top, I kick my shoes off and start on the fly of my jeans, watching as he bypasses his bedroom and goes into his office. I don't question it, my feet naturally following him. I arrive at the open door, finding him in his chair, reclined back. Waiting for me. And then suddenly we're joined by music, and the track is no accident. I stare at him, struggling for air, as Labyrinth's *Still Don't Know my Name* plays.

I don't want to know his name. I don't care. I just want this. *Him*. These sensations.

He says nothing, scanning my face. Trying to read my emotions? Trying to figure out why I came when I refused him not so long ago? His eyes journey the length of my legs, and I take his silent instruction, pushing my jeans down my thighs, catching valuable air as I do, loading up, preparing. It's a pointless endeavor. Nothing will prepare me.

His sharp stare lands at the juncture of my thighs and stays there as I remove my panties. He pushes back in his chair a little, and once they're on the floor at my feet, I step out and wander around his impressive desk to him. He looks up at me, watching me closely as his hands find my hips and guide me until I'm standing in between his legs. He leans forward and pushes his mouth onto my stomach, and my body folds in pleasure, my hands finding his shoulders, my fingers feeling the start of the scarred flesh of his back. Soft kisses are placed across my stomach, every inch of it, and I breathe in deeply, closing my eyes. He turns his face into my arm, licking the inside of my elbow, sending shivers surging through me. I look down at the back of his head, my hand finding his hair and stroking through the wet waves. I'm here. I was always going to be here, and he knew it. Was ready. Waiting.

He looks up at me, his hands sliding onto my ass. His stare is hard yet soft. Revealing yet disguising. Reaching for my arms, he inspects my wrists, smoothing over the welts softly with the pad of his thumb. His moves are so tender, and yet his expression remains hard. Contrasting. Confusing? No. I feel like I'm beginning to read him. Understand him. He needs this too. What I don't understand is why.

He slowly encourages me to turn away from him and pulls me down to his lap. I rest against his chest, the back of my head settling on his shoulder, feeling his soft bristle against my cheek, his hardening cock behind his boxers pushing into my ass. He takes one of my legs and guides it up until my foot is wedged against the edge of his desk. He repeats with the other, and then places his palms on the insides of my thighs, pulling them apart so I'm spread wide open to the room. My arms curl back around our heads, and he turns his face into mine and kisses me softly. How he knows I need this moment of gentleness doesn't escape me. I certainly didn't expect it, not from this dark, complex man. The chemistry is electric, but I feel so incredibly calm. And yet the nerves between my legs are screaming, my flesh dripping.

James reaches for something on his desk, and the next moment, the screens before us come alive.

And on all of them . . .

Us.

A still image of us.

Me, blindfolded, gagged, shackled, hanging from the suspension bar, and James standing before me naked. The same scene on every screen, but dozens of different angles. I inhale, scanning them all, taking in each one. My eyes home in on the center, largest screen. It's a close up of his face. His wild, beautiful face. He looks drunk, dozy eyed, completely lost. *In me. He* was lost in *me.*

Completely. He didn't like seeing me with Ollie, because he's watched this. He's watched us. And it's a sight to behold. Mesmerizing. Spellbinding.

Magical.

This, us, what we do, how I feel. It's magic.

The sheer sight floods me with even more need, and I turn my face into him. His eyes are fixed on the screen, and he starts to walk his fingers down my stomach.

"Shall I play it?" he whispers, turning his eyes my way as his fingers scissor and slip through my pulsing flesh. I inhale fast, tensing, the sensitivity too much already. He holds the remote control up, his thumb hovering over the play button. I nod, and then jolt when he rolls a fingertip around my clit painfully slowly.

"Relax, Beau," he orders gently, pressing play and sliding the remote control onto his desk. "Enjoy the show." He takes my jaw between his fingers, kissing me hard, and then turns my face toward the screens.

It's like nothing I've ever seen before. Sex personified.

And I am rapt by it.

He massages me gently between my legs with one hand, his other tracing light circles around my nipple, and my head drops back, my eyes heavy, but I keep them rooted to the screens, unable and unwilling to look away. I watch as the James on the screen plays with me, tortures me, denies me of an orgasm, and my body bucks and bows in response, all the while my body *now* getting hotter and hotter, his touch getting firmer and firmer. I push my feet into the edge of his desk, my back into his front, my pants becoming loud, the fire inside raging. He spreads my need far and wide, fucking me with his fingers brutally, pinching my nipple, thrusting his groin upward constantly. I don't know what I'm going to do if he pulls away. If he halts the climax building. My mouth drops open, more air needed, and I grapple for the arms of the chair, clawing my nails into the soft leather. "James," I breathe, starting to shake, my body locking up, pinning down the rush of pleasure steaming forward. His fingers roll harder, plunge deeper. "More." My head is limp, my drowsy eyes struggling to keep focused on the screens. Tingles start to attack me, my skin hypersensitive, the sounds from the TV mixed with my sounds now a sensory overload. "More!" He persists, circling his long fingers wider, pulling them free and spreading the wetness. My heart is hammering. My body blazing. My mind spinning. My feet push farther into the desk, sending us back a few feet in his chair.

And suddenly we're not facing the screens anymore. James spins us to face the wall of glass, and my feet instinctively find the window, looking for an anchor. I press my soles into the cold pane, my arms flying up to cradle our heads, my hips thrusting up into his drives. The lights of the city meld and blur, creating a rainbow splash of color under the moon. Everyone miles away. The world miles away. Misery, miles away.

Freedom is here. Serenity. Detachment from the world.

I turn my face into him and nuzzle his rough cheek, prompting him to look at me. His working fingers never falter. My heart doesn't slow. He stares at me as he continues to blitz my mind and body with his incomprehensible capabilities, the real world gone. Because James can't be real. This can't be real. I want it to be, because this, here, us, how I feel? I don't know how I will survive life without it now.

He moves forward, sealing our lips, plunging his tongue deep into my mouth, and my hands find his hair, my tongue finds his pace, my lost soul finds . . .

Relief.

I come on a moan into his mouth, a tug of his hair, my hand resting on his over my breast and squeezing. I'm breathless. Exhausted. Stiff from tensing so much. The waves of pleasure rack my body to no end, my legs ramrod straight, braced against the window, as I let it consume me whole. Every last bit of it.

His fingers slip free and softly circle my twitching clit, his lips slowing until they're unmoving on my mouth. He breaks away and wraps his arms around my belly, turning the chair so we're facing the screen again.

Together, we watch the end of the show, the track still playing, James's heavy breaths behind me, not a word murmured. I observe as the onscreen James rolls off me and my eyes become heavy, both on the screen and in reality. I can't hold them open anymore. I sigh and give in to my tired muscles everywhere, and he holds me tighter in response to my body softening, tenderly kissing my cheek. "I'm glad you came back to me," he whispers.

And I'm gone.

23

JAMES

It was all about her. I didn't come. Didn't want to. But I desperately needed her to need this.

Peace. Peace found in intimacy. It's new. Unexpected. A bit like the jealousy that found me when I saw her with Oliver Burrows.

I remain in my chair, Beau on my lap sleeping, and rewind the footage to the beginning. And I watch it again, my concentration split between her face and mine. Both are fascinating. Hers because of the sheer pleasure, mine because of the sheer pain.

I didn't know what I was doing last night when I tied her up, but I knew I couldn't stop it.

I'm hooked on her. On us. But she doesn't know me, and that will inevitably change everything. I fuck women to be seen. I take them with an audience because it's the only time in my life that I can really show myself. I'm known as James Kelly, a private stockbroker, but no one knows *who* I am. Where I come from. *Why I'm here.*

But Beau *sees* me. Even if she doesn't know what she's looking at. And I sure as shit see her. She's blinding. Soft. And though she feels weak, she's strong. I have to show her that.

My phone bleeps from the desk, and I gently ease forward to claim it, checking that Beau doesn't stir. I open the message from Otto. A picture of a well-dressed man appears on my screen, and I narrow my eyes on his chubby, cheerful face. He reeks bent. Swiping away from the screen, I dial Otto.

"Who is he?" I ask quietly.

"Judge Ferguson. He's taking back-handers from someone in exchange for the manipulation of evidence on a man. A man under The Bear's umbrella."

"Vince Roake," I hum to myself. Otherwise known as The Alligator. Jaz Hayley got him in cuffs before I got my knife to his throat. "Could the judge know who The Bear is?"

"No."

Makes two of us. And it's as frustrating as fuck. "His movements?"

"I'm on it."

"Thanks." I hang up and get the image of the judge back up on my screen, airdropping it to my laptop. I look down at Beau. Dead to the world. Turning on my screens, I drop the judge's face into the mix, scowling at his photo. Otto was right. The Bear will always add to his army. Until I find the fucker and end him.

My eyes scan across the bank of TVs, landing on the last two. Blank screens. One reserved for The Bear, and the other for who he's got on the inside. Because that's a given.

I look down at Beau's peaceful, sleeping face. "Stop chasing the truth, Beau Hayley." *Because that ends in death.*

I gather her up and take her to my bed, settling her down gently, fighting the odd compulsion to crawl in behind her. *No*. I have shit to deal with. Beau Hayley is a complication. A *big* fucking complication. She was before I fucked her. Now? "Fuck," I mutter, scrubbing a hand down my face and backing out of the room. I head downstairs, coming to a gradual stop when Otto steps off the elevator. He holds up a file. The man works fast.

"The judge's schedule. He's a busy man." He drops it on the table and backs up into the elevator. "Can I ask you something?"

"No," I answer, knowing that won't stop him.

"Are you going to tell her who you are? What you do? What you *did*?"

"Do you think she'll handle it?"

He recoils and reaches for his beard, stroking it thoughtfully. There's no denying the worry emblazoned across his pierced face. It's the same as the worry I'm feeling. I'm inviting disaster. "You might not have to even tell her," he says quietly, glancing up the stairs where she's sleeping. In *my* bed. Cozy. Warm. Safe. "Are you forgetting something here, Kel?"

I don't know, am I? Probably. My head's completely bent.

"She's an ex copper, boy. And a talented one at that. Just because she's quit, doesn't mean her instinct has. Once a cop, always a cop."

"You think she'll hand my arse to me on a plate?"

"You'll have to kill her before that."

I swallow and retreat before Otto can bend my head further, going up to my dressing room and dragging out a case ready for Goldie. I check the contents, pull out a few parts, and polish them until they sparkle before slowly piecing the rifle together. I admire my work, slowly turning the gun in my grasp. Beau Hayley is searching for an answer.

And she's sleeping with it.

I'm breaking the fucked-up scale.

24

BEAU

The stretch of my muscles is something dreams are made of; the delicious pull lengthening every one of my limbs blissful. The warm, soft sheets radiate James's heady scent, creeping into my nose, waking up my senses. I open my eyes to a soft, hazy, apricot glow in his room. It's quiet. The room *and* my mind. Both quiet.

I sit up and tug the loose hair tie from my waves and pull the sheets around my naked body. He's not here. Shuffling to the side of the bed, I get up and go in search of him. I start in his office. No James. At least, not in the flesh. But the screens are frozen on our sleeping forms in his bed. I reach up to my lips. They don't feel sore or bruised. My body doesn't feel tender and damaged. This time was a very different experience, but the result was the same.

Blitz my mind clear.

I pull the door closed and make up way down the stairs. I hear him before I see him on the couch, tapping away at the keys of his laptop. He's pulled on some lounge pants but left his chest bare. It's quite a welcome. How can something so dark be so beautiful?

He looks up when I reach the bottom step, and his laptop is forgotten. He blindly reaches for the screen and pulls it down, placing it on the footstool by his feet. Then he sets an elbow on the arm of the couch and props his chin on his hand, his finger brushing thoughtfully over his Cupid's bow as he watches me pull the sheet in tighter around my body.

My move seems to amuse him, and the hint of a smile moves the corner of his mouth. As a result, I risk a smile too. "I was going to eat," he says, rising from the couch. "Are you hungry?"

I don't know if I'm hungry, to be honest. I can't feel anything past the peace. "And then will you bathe me?" I ask, making his eyebrows rise a fraction. He doesn't answer but, instead, collects me from the bottom of the stairs, walking me to the island and lifting me onto a stool. He bends and leans into me, and I find myself reclining back, if only so I can keep his entire striking face in my sights. His lips purse. He leans in more. So I recline farther, and his head tilts, his expression curious. And he comes closer, prompting me to lean back even more, to the point my stomach muscles are screaming and I'm parallel to the floor.

He's looming over me now. "Do you want to be on your back for me again, Beau?" he asks, reaching for the front of the sheet and pulling it open, exposing my front. "Just say the words." His palm splays my chest and drags down to the apex of my thighs. My breath undeniably hitches, meaning refusing him would be laughable.

"Who are you?" I ask out of the blue, the question surprising us both. He recoils a fraction, but quickly gathers himself.

Taking my hands, he pulls me back up to sitting. "Those aren't the words I was expecting."

"I'm sleeping with a man who's an enigma."

His eyes dart to mine, cautious for a fleeting moment, before he corrects it, rearranging the sheet around me, his focus set on his task. "You didn't google me?" he asks, his eyes fixed on mine, reading my reaction. He knows I have, and it makes me wonder if he tried the same with me. He won't have found much—the FBI will have made sure of that. "Does it matter who I am?" he asks, stepping back. "Does it matter who *you* are?"

That soon wins him back my attention. His questions are loaded. Could the answers be an explosion? But at the same time, I'm wondering if it really does matter. Do I need to know who he really is? Do I want *him* to know the dirty details of why I am who I am, because I'm sure as shit he knows *what* I am. Because he's told me.

Broken.

"Why did you come back to me tonight, Beau?" he asks, sounding harsh. Judgmental.

"Because I love where you take me." I'm honest. That much he can know. "How did you know I'd come back?"

"Because I know you love where I take you." He steps into me and lifts my chin, making sure he has my full attention. He has. From the moment I set eyes on him, he has. But what he doesn't know is what he's taking me away from. That shall remain undisclosed. "We seem to have a mutual connection in that area," he whispers.

"Then we're both safe," I murmur, repeating his words.

"Safety is an illusion, Beau." He kisses my forehead, lingering for a long time. "I'm happy to provide that illusion."

I swallow and let the warmth of his mouth sink into my skin. "See?" I whisper. "An enigma." He speaks words I don't understand. Looks at me in a way that baffles me. Like I'm his redeemer. And at the same time, his ruin. "You make no sense to me."

"I don't need to make sense to you." Feeling my nape, he

massages gently, and despite my whirling mind, I loosen under his touch. "Accept this for what it is."

"What is it?"

He lifts me from the stool and places me on the countertop, pulling the sheet apart and muscling his way in between my thighs. My body responds in a nanosecond, tingling back to life, ready to take him on again. My ass is seized, and I'm pulled in close. His condition behind his pants presses into my naked pussy. "This is beauty amid endless pain, Beau." A palm pushes into my chest, forcing me gently down to the counter. He pulls his arousal free and starts torturously rubbing the swollen head around my flesh.

"Oh God." I arch my back, willing him on, the wildfire inside back with a vengeance.

He pushes into me on a grunt, sinking his fingers into my thighs. "And isn't it fucking beautiful?" he asks, yanking me down onto him. The flames are fanned, the burn intensifying. I cry out, clawing at his forearms, trying to find my anchor. And that's the thing with James. There is no anchor. Nothing to keep me grounded when he's got his hands all over me, and that feeling of absent control is cathartic. It's deliverance from evil. It's the therapy I need.

I look at the ugly scars on my arm as James finds his pace, alternating between smooth grinds and hard hits, beating constant cries of ecstasy out of me.

"They're not there," he grunts, and I shoot my eyes to his. They're glazed. His jaw is tight. He looks almost angry. "They're not there." He drives forward at an eyewatering speed, punching me deep. "They're not there," he whispers, retreating, the smooth flesh of his iron erection gliding with ease, stroking my walls. I look at my arm again. The scars have gone. I don't see them. Don't feel the pain that's so fresh in my mind. He makes all the terrible disappear and replaces it with magic. "Look at me," he demands, moving a hand to my throat, laying it there. I do as I'm bid, and the sight will never leave me.

He's about to come. I want his release. *For him. For me.* The sight of him staring at me, holding his breath, his body rigid, every last muscle in his arms and chest protruding.

I lift my arms above my head, finding the edge of the counter behind me, and grip it tightly. I'm going to need it. "Come," I order calmly, and he roars at the ceiling, his pace reaching maniac territory as he thrashes me repeatedly and mercilessly.

I've never seen anything so spellbinding. Never heard anything so poetic. He's out of control, and I am in my element. I don't need to orgasm. I just need to watch him.

"Fuck," he chokes, sucking back air, his body vibrating violently, his skin slick with sweat. He collapses onto one hand, his head hanging, and he starts to grind firmly, hissing his way through his climax. I go limp, staring up at the ceiling, as the sensation of him filling me, of his cock pulsating against my walls as he releases, overwhelms my body.

"It doesn't matter," I say quietly, heaving, fighting for breath. "Who you are, who I am, it doesn't matter." I don't want details. Don't want to give them either. This. I just want this. Whenever I can have it, just this.

"What if I ever want to tell you?" he asks, bringing his front down to mine. His head lays on my chest, and I look at his dark waves.

"If it'll change this, I want you to resist."

"Is that a condition?"

"Of what?"

"Of you continuing to see me. You want nothing. Just this."

"Just this," I confirm.

"You sound like most men's dream woman."

"I'm no one's dream," I whisper. I'm their nightmare. So yes, this agreement works for me, because if I don't know about him, he can't know about me.

And as if he understands, he takes my deformed arm and kisses my scars. Such a gentle move, and I'm unsure whether I like it. "But I'm not most men," James says, turning his stare up to me, holding his mouth to my arm. I look away, avoiding him seeing whatever it is he's looking for in my eyes. "What about opera?"

I frown and look at him with curiosity. His chin's now resting between my boobs. "Opera?"

"Yes. Is opera allowed?"

"Along with fucking?"

"With fucking," he confirms, deadly serious. "Or escaping. Or disappearing. Call it what you will."

I'm bemused. Opera? When I first met this man, he was frosty, unreadable. Now? "Are you asking me on a date?" James doesn't seem like the kind of man to date. Opera, yes, I can see it. But dating?

"Do you want to call it a date?"

"No."

"Then no."

"But you want me to go to the opera with you?"

"Yes."

"Why?" Don't tell me he's short of women ready to let him lavish them with his expert fucking and a touch of opera on the side.

His head drops tiredly, and he sighs. "Why not?"

"Because it falls outside the scope of our relationship." *And I can't be in crowded spaces.*

James swallows, and it looks like a patience-gathering move. "Fine. No opera." He pushes himself up, and we both hiss as he slips free of me. "Here." He unravels the sheets and starts to wipe the inside of my thighs meticulously, and I study him as he does, my fascination growing. But fascination should be avoided. It could lead to questions I don't want answers to.

He finishes up, adjusts his pants, and takes the sheet into a room off the kitchen. I retrieve my shirt from the floor by the elevator, and just as I'm fastening the buttons, the doors slide open. I freeze, a deer caught in the headlights, when Goldie appears. Her gaze travels from the tips of my toes, up my half-naked body to my wide eyes. She doesn't bat an eyelid. I smile awkwardly, backing away, making sure the shirt covers as much of me as possible.

"Evening," she says, looking past me. I turn to find James by the island, motionless, watching me wilting on the spot.

"Evening," he says, his face straight, almost angry. "Give me a second." He disappears up the stairs, leaving Goldie and me alone with a lingering, unbearable silence. Good grief, I can't stand it. I reach for the tails of my shirt again and tug them down. She catches it, smiling out the corner of her mouth.

"Still being smart?" she asks, her smile turning wry.

I laugh under my breath as I back away. "What does your gut tell you?" I ask, motioning down my naked legs.

"I don't listen to my gut. Only my head."

"Okay. What does your head tell you?"

"It tells me to brace myself."

I withdraw, surprised, my backward steps slowing to a stop. "Brace yourself?" What does she mean? "What for?"

"Here," James says from behind me, interrupting. I swing around, finding he's holding out a fancy briefcase to Goldie. The black leather is highly polished, the gold latches sparkling.

She takes it on a nod and goes back to the elevator. "Enjoy the rest of your evening," she says dryly, giving James eyebrows so high they're blending with her sharp hairline. I cast a look over to him. He's not scowling at Goldie, but he's not far from it.

"I will." He heads to the kitchen, and Goldie dazzles me with a smile that's as sarcastic as could be. Everything about the past few minutes is making me highly regret my silent vow to not ask questions.

"It's time to feed you," James says, opening the fridge and pulling out a dish. I look from him to the elevator doors a few times, my mind reeling. What exactly does Goldie do for James? She's always just . . . here. And Otto? He's no concierge, and he doesn't work for a security firm. But security is definitely involved. My brain starts to burn.

"You know, I should probably go." He wants to feed me, and what will we talk about, because I can think of nothing other than the millions of questions gathering at the front of my mind. Questions I should file away forever. But that's the problem. My mom raised me to question everything. It's innate. She taught me by osmosis how to put puzzles together, and it's why I was a good cop. Something about this glass world that James hides within deserves a lot of questions, but I will resist. I'll do anything to keep this . . . calm.

James slides the dish onto the counter, his move slow. Everything this man does, he does deliberately. Thoughtfully. His mind is reeling too. Which means I should definitely go. I head for the stairs, mentally locating my jeans, but I get no farther than the first step, my body jolting when it meets some resistance. I'm backed up against the wall a moment later, James's bare chest compressed to mine, my eyes on his throat.

I'm shocked. Stunned. But I'm still breathless. "What are you doing?"

"Convincing you not to leave." He bends a leg, running his knee up the inside of one thigh and forcing my legs apart.

"You could have just asked," I breathe, my mind lost.

"I'm asking." His hand creeps under my shirt and brushes across my flesh. I moan. "Are you staying?" His fingers drive high, and I whimper, pushing myself farther into the wall. "Because I believe I owe you an orgasm."

"Yes."

"Thought so." He kisses my cheek and moves away, and I stumble forward with the sudden absence of his support. My hands meet his chest, his arm curling around my waist to catch me. I look up at him, my lips parted, my breathing shot. He blinks slowly, his lashes fanning his high cheekbones. "Shall we eat before I fuck you senseless again?"

Senseless. It's apt. "I think you've chased away my sense for good."

"Same," he whispers, turning me in his arms and placing his hands on my shoulders. He guides me to the kitchen and puts me back on the stool, and I watch quietly as he makes his way around, collecting various things and placing them on the island. "Wine?" he asks.

"Why not," I murmur. It's not like alcohol could make me any more stupid. My rational side is warning me that I'm getting myself into something I shouldn't be. But what? And yet my impulsive, desperate side is goading me, willing me to take the medicine James offers. I just hope that medicine doesn't turn out to be poison.

Safety is just an illusion.

"Do you mind if I make a call?" I ask, accepting the glass he hands me.

"Do you need some privacy?"

I smile over the rim of my glass. Is that chivalry? "Yes."

"I'll take this to the couch. Join me when you're done." He starts collecting the plates and dishes from the island, and I follow his back across the vast space to the rug in front of the window.

I find my purse by the door and retrieve my cell, dialing Dexter. "Is he okay?" I ask when he answers.

"He is *she* right now, and she's wailing like a banshee. Where are you, Beau?"

I look over my shoulder. James is on the rug, his back against the couch. "With a man."

"Who is he?"

I don't know. "Just . . . a man."

"Do you know what you're doing?

No. "I think so."

Dexter sighs. "You think so?"

"Will you let him know I'm okay?"

"Are you? Okay?"

I don't know. "Yes. Don't wait up for me." I don't know if staying meant *staying.*

"Fine," he breathes. "Be safe, Beau."

I smile and hang up, making my way over to James. He looks up at me. "Everything okay?"

I nod and lower to the rug next to him, scanning the mini feast. "This is all very romantic."

"Have you decided yet whether you hate me or want to fuck me?" he asks, and it's tactical. James isn't romantic. He's simply feeding me. Then he'll probably fuck me again.

I take a sip of my wine, ignoring his question. It's been answered a few times now. But what will we talk about, since we don't want to actually get to know each other? "How long have you lived here?" I ask, gazing around the glass box.

"Five years."

"You were born in England."

"Yes."

"How long have you been in the States?"

"Five years," he answers swiftly, sounding wholly uninterested. "Who was that man?"

My wine glass pauses on its way back down to rest on my thigh, and I shake my head, silently telling him we're not going there.

He regards me coolly. "A friend? A relative?"

"James—"

"An ex?"

"Okay, I'm going." I stand and step over his legs, going to find my jeans. We've got nothing to talk about. Nothing that falls into the safe box, anyway. This was a mistake.

"Going? Or running away?"

I screech to a stop, staring at the steps before me. He sounds so critical. I signed up for freedom, not condemnation. Picking up my feet, I keep moving, unwilling to get into a fight with a man I hardly know over something he has no clue about. I find my jeans and shoes and slip them on.

James is standing at the foot of the glass panel opposite the elevator when I get back downstairs, looking out across the city. I stop and take in his naked, mutilated back.

"You choose to run, Beau," he says to the glass, before turning to face me. His hard stare could turn me to ashes. Does to an extent. This is the James I want. The one who fucks like an animal. The one who strips me of hate and replaces it with craving. The ice-cold man. "Maybe I'll get tired of chasing you."

"I've never asked you to chase me."

"And there's the problem with us," he whispers, while my jaw ticks dangerously.

There are many problems. Many things we should ignore, except I'm finding that easier to do than him. Probably because I need this more than James. And that's dangerous. It means I'm at his mercy. "And what is that, James? What's the problem with us?"

"You think you have bigger secrets than I do."

My mouth snaps shut, my legs taking me back a step.

My other name.

Do you, though, Beau?

I know there's more to James than meets the eye, but I'm not ashamed to admit that I've been ignorant to it. Pushed my insane curiosity back, because, God help me, there is a lot more than meets the eye with me. Add the fact that knowing too much about him might find my lost sensibility, I've been, and will carry on being, blissfully ignorant. Until he ruined it. "You keep your secrets, James," I say, turning and leaving. "And I'll keep mine."

"So you're running again?"

I pause. "This isn't running. This is choosing to walk in an alternate direction." I don't look back.

My admiration just turned into hate.

More hate to stir into the pit of my demons.

25

JAMES.

I need to be rid of this incessant need to make her talk. To tell me things I already know. It's driving her away when I need to be luring her closer, and not only because of this fucked-up desire for her.

I text Otto.

Watch her.

The elevator opens, revealing Goldie.

"I'm not up for being nagged," I warn, glancing at my phone when it dings. I ignore the message from Beth. Not tonight.

"Tough."

"I'm taking Beau to the opera." I push my phone away and head toward my gym. Since my method of relaxation has just left the building, I need to relax in another way.

"Are you crazy?"

"Insane," I murmur to myself.

"Why? Why would you do that?"

"Because it'll look fucking odd if I'm there solo," I retort, turning when I reach the top of the stairs. Goldie has made her way to the bottom. "And we'd look a bit weird together."

"Yes, I'm sure people will think you're punching way above your weight, you arrogant fuck."

"Such a lady," I mutter, getting on my way. "Make sure Otto got my message."

"He just left."

"I want updates."

"In case she sees her ex again?"

"My interest in that is only because he's a copper."

"Of course," she practically sighs. "And while you're balancing in the gym, can you try to balance your fucking head as well?"

I laugh to myself. I'll try. God knows why Goldie's still so fucking loyal to me. I'd never let anyone hurt her, she knows that, although she's learned a lot from me since I stepped in, a total stranger, and ripped that lowlife rapist off her in that alley in London. She can defend herself, but this, me, my life, is now all she knows. She has a purpose now, beyond her time in the military. She has people, albeit limited people, who respect her and value her. She feels like she owes me. It's been a long time since she's seen me do something so contrary to the plan. Her anger is understandable. She won't allow herself freedom until I find it for myself, and Beau Hayley is seriously screwing with that plan.

I push my way into the gym, heading straight for the horse. I take the handles, flexing my fingers, getting the best grip, and slowly pull myself up, bringing my knees into my chest, before unbending my arms and lengthening my legs until I'm vertical, my body straight. Blood rushes to my head, my balance faultless, and I remain in a handstand, arms at full length, my eyes closed.

Just focusing on remaining steady.

And, inevitably, with the absence of Beau here to distract me, my thoughts turn to a past I've tried and failed to forget.

To the shell who mourned his lost life for years after his family was wiped out. To the hollow man who drowned in alcohol and drugs. To the pitiful, broken mess who attempted therapy battling —and not defeating—his black thoughts.

And to the monster who was eventually born.

The monster I am now.

The monster I will always be.

26

BEAU

Sleep feels like a slow, unending torture. I close my eyes, I see him. I wipe him clear, I see Mom. I wipe Mom away, I see fire. Smell the stench of burning flesh. Hear her screams.

Hear *my* screams.

I fight it all from my dreams and see the letter denying me the answers Mom deserves. The answers I *need*.

I don't need *anything*.

Except that.

A movement at my door pulls my attention to the wood, and I see the handle move ever so slightly. But Lawrence doesn't come in. I sit up and grab my cell, checking the time. It's seven. I've been lying here for hours at war with my head, battling with sense and reason.

I pull up Nath's number and dial, falling back to the pillow. The sounds of a bustling coffee house seeps down the line when he answers, the gurgling of the machine, the scrapes of chairs on the floor. "They denied my appeal," I say mechanically.

Nath's silent for a brief moment, and for the first time I consider that he already knew. "Beau—"

"Did you know?"

A brief silence. A sigh. "I knew."

I reach up to my forehead and try to rub away the headache that's threatening. Of course he knew. And Ollie probably did too. "Why didn't you tell me?" I ask for the sake of it. I know why, and it isn't only because it would have been top-secret information. Nath knows as well as I do that my life's been hanging in the balance for two years, unable to move forward until I've found my peace. I'm trapped. Caged.

"Beau, you have to move on."

"To what?" I ask. "What do I have to move on to, Nath?"

"Anything you want."

Anything I want? I want my mom back. I want my life as I knew it back. I want faith and hope and daily justice. I can have none of it anymore.

"The MPD would have you back in a heartbeat. You've got too much potential for them to lose permanently."

"You mean enough potential to stir more shit?" I ask. There's only one reason the force would have me back now, after my relentless attempts to prove Mom's death wasn't a *tragic accident*. To keep me close. To keep an eye on me. To keep me quiet. No. "I won't let this rest. Someone knows something, Nath."

"You're out of options."

I close my eyes and swallow hard, refusing to accept he's right. But there's a power far greater than me at play here. I can't beat them. But it'll finish me off if I give up hope.

"You free tomorrow?" he asks softly. "Let's push the boat out and do lunch as well as coffee."

"Sure," I mumble, getting up and pulling on my robe. It's not Nath's fault he works for an institution of liars. And he's a good friend. One of the only ones I have now. Mom trusted him with her life. I trust him too. "Let me know what time and where." I hang up and stare at the door. I can feel the tension in the house even locked away in my room. I can't bear it. I look at the piles of apartment brochures on the sideboard. Perhaps it's finally time to get my own place. A big glass box on top of a building, all spacious, peaceful, and light.

Maybe. Is that what I need? Or is it simply the glass man inside?

No.

I take a deep breath and leave my room, forcing my feet to take me to Lawrence before my head has a chance to foil my plan. I push the door to his bedroom open, finding him lying on the bed in his silk robe that's embellished with flamingos. He's twiddling his thumbs, chewing his lip. "You'll get scabs on your lip and your lipstick will clog," I say, pacing over and dropping to the mattress beside him. I turn my head on the pillow to face him. "You need a shave."

He reaches up to his jaw and feels, grimacing. "I was too busy whittling about you last night. I forgot." Reaching for my hand, he pulls it to his mouth and kisses my knuckles. The arm of my robe slips down, revealing my welts. They're still red. Still fresh. I don't rush to cover them. "Tell me about him," he says, shuffling down the bed and mirroring me.

I indulge him, if only for his sanity. Even if it might send *me* over the edge. "His name's James." *And he has more secrets than me, which pretty much makes him the most enticing man I could find.* And his ways in the bedroom make him all the more tempting. "We spent the first few days of our professional relationship avoiding each other's eyes." That's a lie. I avoided. James goaded. "And then one evening when I was leaving, he said something that triggered something in me."

"Triggered what?"

"Lara."

Lawrence gasps, and I nod. He knows what I'm capable of. He knows I'm lethal when I put my mind to it. "Did you disengage him?"

"Yes." I can't help secretly smiling as I picture James's head trapped between my thighs. "And he threw it back at me. Played me at my own game." I frown. It wasn't *my* game. It was totally his game. "I was on my back before I realized I was moving. And then he kissed me."

"And tied you up." Lawrence reaches for my wrists, wincing when he turns them over.

"I asked for it."

Did you though, Beau?

I fall to my back and stare at the ceiling. James wasn't talking about what he did to me in the bedroom. He was talking about something else, and I'm so fucking furious that it's playing on my mind.

You think you have bigger secrets than I do.

"It was nice. To be that lost, it felt freeing. While James played games with my body, my mind was wiped clean for the first time in a long time," I admit.

"It can't be healthy," Lawrence whispers, and I turn my head on the pillow to find him.

"And this is?" I ask, motioning down my body. "This invisible cage I'm trapped in? The relentless need for retribution? The never-ending cycle of hate, pity, and anger? That's healthy, is it?" My time with James made all of that vanish, if only temporarily. Not that it matters. It's done. James and I are done. I lean over and peck my uncle's cheek. "I'm not seeing him again, so you don't need to worry."

"Why? If he's all that to you, why aren't you seeing him again?"

I get up and go to the door. *Because he started asking too many questions. Because he could become a habit. Because I'm a little bit afraid of who he is.* "Because my wrists can't take it," I say on a smile, pulling the door closed on high, cheeky eyebrows. And as soon as the wood is between us, my face muscles give in to the effort it's taking me to smile.

"Beau?" Dexter calls from downstairs.

I lean over the banister and find him at the front door in his blues, a box across his arms.

"Delivery for you."

I frown and make my way down, pulling the lid off while it's still in Dexter's arms. I'm greeted by a pile of black lace. My frown deepens as I reach in and pull it out.

Dexter breathes in as the material unfolds, tumbling to the floor. A dress. "Good grief," he says, taking it in. "Do *not* let Zinnea see that; it'll be gone forever."

I'm still staring at the gown, my mind blank, when I hear thundering footsteps coming down the stairs.

"Too late," Dexter sighs.

"My God, would you look at that." Lawrence swoops in and seizes the dress from my hands, holding it up. "Italian. I just know it." He looks for the label and sings his joy when he discovers what he's looking for. "I've never seen anything so beautifully made."

I can't see his face, the dress is concealing it, but I can hear his utter glee. I peek in the box, spot a card, and seize it while Lawrence and Dexter are distracted. Of course, I know who it's from, but I don't know why. Or what the heck I'm supposed to do with it. I wander to the kitchen while my uncles drool over the lace gown, pulling the card from the envelope.

Secrets are only secrets if *no one* knows about them. No one knows my secret.

I frown down at his handwriting. *No one knows my secret.* Therefore, it is, in fact, a secret. Is he suggesting he knows my secrets? "What?" I murmur to myself, so fucking confused. But more than that, intrigued. And isn't that his point? Intrigue me. Lure me back into his sex chamber. But why? "Fuck this," I mutter, marching out of the kitchen. The dress lowers, revealing Lawrence's and Dexter's stunned expressions, their wide eyes following my path. I stomp up the stairs, find my cell, and dial him. I pace. Around and around, I pace. He doesn't answer, and I growl, dialing him again. No answer. "God damn you, James." I throw my cell on my bed, frustrated, and so very angry. He knew what he was doing.

And I've given him exactly what he wanted.

"Everything okay?" Lawrence and Dexter appear at the door, both looking a bit sheepish.

"Fine."

"Oh. Okay, then." Lawrence takes a few, cautious steps into my room. "I'll just hang this up. Be a shame to get it all creased."

"No," I snap, sounding harsher than I intended. I can't help it. I'm mad. "You keep it."

"What?" Lawrence clutches the dress to his chest, like he's scared I might change my mind and snatch it back.

"I want you to have the dress." I go to him, encouraging him to turn, and then gently and firmly guide him out of my room. I shut the door before I'm questioned as my cell beeps from my bed. I don't rush over, despite my curiosity going through the roof. I take calm, measured steps, hoping my temper settles as I do. I see a text from him and open it.

Tomorrow night at eight. My secret won't be a secret anymore.

"You bastard," I breathe. The manipulative, immoral, *clever* asshole. I dial him again, intending on telling him exactly what I think of him. He doesn't answer, and I picture him staring at my name flashing up on his screen, his face impassive. Satisfied. My thumbs lose all control and start hammering away at the screen.

I don't want your secret.

I just want *him*. No. I just want his gift.

Outside the Ziff Ballet Opera House at eight.

I drop to the bed. His evasion of my statement is warranted, because we both know my claim is utter crap. And as if my conscience is joining the persuasion party, it reminds me that I haven't thought of anything else but James in the past ten minutes. It doesn't matter if those thoughts are infuriating. I look at the marks marring my skin. His mark. The angel on one shoulder is screaming at me not to do it. Don't bend. Don't play his game. The devil on my other shoulder is daring me to extend the distraction.

I startle when my cell bleeps the arrival of another message, but this time there are no words. Only a video. I open it and stare at a piece of footage from our first encounter. I'm on my back, my knees pushed up to my ears, and James is fucking me violently. I can only see his profile. But it is heart-stopping all the same. He knows that's what I want. He knows that's what I need. His dark, fierce fucking. *Merciless.* Glorious. "Bastard," I murmur. The beautiful, depraved, dangerous bastard. He's stunning, and I simply do not want to resist watching, listening to his grunts, studying his moves. I'm already wet.

I wander to my bathroom, shrugging off my robe and letting it fall to the floor. After flipping on the shower, I step into the stall, resting my back against the tile. I don't feel the shock of cold.

I slide down the wall, skim my hand down my stomach, and let my fingers slip over my throbbing clit. I inhale, my head falling back. But my eyes never leave the screen of my phone.

I come on a murmur of his name.

And on the screen, he comes with me.

27

BEAU

I stand outside the diner the next day at noon, staring in through the window. It's busy. Too busy for me. Only half the tables are taken, but still too busy. I glance left and right, to the free tables outside on the sidewalk of the quiet backstreet.

"You can do this, Beau." I whisper to myself, taking a deep breath and pushing my way through the door, batting down my climbing heartbeats. I hurry to a table at the back and sit, pulling out the brochures of apartments for sale and setting them in front of me. Distraction. Focus on the brochures. I start flicking through the one on top, a two-bed, top-floor apartment overlooking the ocean.

"Good afternoon, can I get you a drink?" the waitress asks, setting a menu on the table. I look up at her on a smile I'm forcing to within an inch of my life. "Just a sparkling water, please," I say, rolling my shoulders, so uncomfortable. "And a Coke with ice."

"No problem." She leaves to fetch my order, and I return my

attention to the details of the apartment. It's too perfect. I need something that requires a full redecoration. I discard it to the bottom of the pile and begin on the next, a converted factory on the west side of town. My cell rings. It's Nath.

"Hi," I say, looking past all the people to the sidewalk outside. As I expected, he's standing there looking up and down the street for me.

"You going to be long?" he asks.

"I'm here."

"Where?"

"Inside," I reply, and he turns and looks through the window, confusion rife on his face. I wave, and he cocks his head, going to the door. "Don't make a big deal of it," I warn as he approaches the table, doing exactly what I did. Counting the amount of people in here. There's thirty. Too many. One person for every beat of my heart per second.

"I won't," he says, taking his jacket off and hanging it on the back of the chair. "But . . . well done."

I give him a tired look, vehemently ignoring the fact that this isn't about sitting in a semi-busy diner. It's a step in the right direction, yes, but a backstreet diner isn't quite the same caliber as an opera house.

The waitress sets our drinks on the table and tells us she'll be back to take our order. Nath clocks the piles of brochures before me. The poor man must be wondering what the hell is going on. I'm wondering myself. "Just looking at my options," I tell him, pushing them aside. "Lawrence and Dexter's place was supposed to be a temporary solution."

He smiles. "I bumped into Lawrence yesterday."

"Did you get an earache too?"

"A bit. He just worries about you. As do I." He takes a sip of his Coke. "And Ollie."

"Ollie needs to move on."

"And you?"

I show the ceiling my palms, taking a quick look at our surroundings. It shuts Nath up. Good. The waitress returns, and I pick up the menu and scan the options. "Cajun salad, please."

"And a BLT on white for me," Nath says, collecting my menu and handing it to the waitress. "So who's this guy you've been seeing?"

I sag in my chair. "Lawrence needs to stop gossiping." I fiddle with the straw in my water, wondering if the gossiping stopped there or if he went into explicit details. My gaze inadvertently goes to my wrists, and I reach to pull the sleeve of my shirt down a little more, checking to see where Nath's attention is. He's staring at my wrist too. I clear my throat to say something, anything to break the uncomfortable quiet, but no words come to me.

"So, who is he?"

"No one you know," I quip, looking at Nath in a way that suggests I'm not game for this conversation."

"Name?"

"You going to run checks on him?"

"I don't know. Do I need to?"

Nath's question oddly spikes a few goosebumps, and I rub over the sleeve of my arm. I don't know. Does he? Regardless, I'm not giving him his name, because he absolutely will run checks on James. Why does that bother me?

Because he might find something.

I fall into thought, staring at the silver fork on the napkin. The police database could shed light that Google can't.

My other name.

My heart beats a little faster.

"Beau?"

I blink and look up, and Nath smiles, though it's hesitant. "What?" I ask.

"Will you?" he asks, his smile turning into a grimace.

"Will I what?"

"Take me to the dealership."

I'm lost. "Why do I need to take you to the dealership?"

"My car's in for a service. I need you to drop me back at the dealership to collect it."

The dealership.

It hits me like a brick. A memory. I stare at Nath across the table, my face blank, as I dig deep for every scrap of the moment in history I can find. My heart's pounding now, it is way beyond my control, and my eyes dart across the table. "Her car was at the repair shop," I murmur, the conversation coming back to me, all of it, every word spoken between Mom and me. Where has this memory been? Why is it only coming back to me now?

"What?"

I look up at Nath, and he moves back in his chair, obviously not liking the expression on my face. "They said Mom missed the routine service on her vehicle. She didn't. I called her about an appointment we had the next day for my dress fitting. She sounded out of breath because she was walking to collect her car from the dealership."

"She said that?"

"Yes." It was a fleeting part of the conversation, forgettable, as proven, just a little joke made on the side of the subject at hand. My wedding. She said she needed to up her cardio game, but I remember it now like we had the conversation five minutes ago. "It was a couple of weeks before she died," I whisper, my head about to explode. Nath is silent, pensive, looking at me like he's unsure if I'm insane or a genius. They say there's a fine line between the two. "It must be on the records." I reach forward and seize Nath's hand. "Her car was fine."

"Beau, you must have your dates wrong."

"I don't." I shake my head, adamant. "Nath, please. Just check the records. Maybe then I can convince them to reopen the case." I can see he's torn, and I hate putting him in the middle, but he's my only hope. "Please."

"Jesus," he mumbles, closing his eyes briefly. "Okay. I'll check."

He thinks I'm mistaken. I'm not.

Mom's car was fine. Which means I'm not going insane at all.

I don't know whether to be relieved or afraid.

28

JAMES

Watching Beau go into the diner threw me. And those brochures she was looking at? I'm not so sure I like where that's going. Neither did I like that she met Agent Nathan Butler. After learning of the news that they're not entertaining Beau's appeal, that could mean only one thing. Beau Hayley is about to dig.

Fuck, I wish she'd stop.

This is getting a bit too close for comfort. I laugh, mentally awarding myself with a medal for supreme idiocy. This got too close for comfort the moment I invited Beau Hayley into my world. Because the truth needs to remain buried if Beau is going to live and I'm going to remain hidden.

I sit idle by the curb and watch her leave the diner with Nathan Butler. They get in her old, battered Mustang. I shake my head to myself. She lives a simple life. Appears to have no desire for material things. She has the money—I know she has the money, not to mention a father who's famously loaded. So why the fuck does she drive that old banger and risk her life?

The answer isn't one I'm comfortable with.

I pull out and follow her at a distance, to a dealership a mile or so away. Nathan Butler gets out and smacks the roof of the car, and she drives away, the car chugging and spitting all over the place. I answer my cell when Otto calls, keeping three cars back. "All okay for tonight?" I ask.

"Yeah. Where are you?"

"Surveillance."

"You mean following the girl."

"She's business."

"And you're a tool."

"She's digging, Otto."

"And there's nothing that can be found. We've been over it a hundred times."

"Someone knows something, and Beau's suspicious. If she gets too close—"

"She's already too close."

She'd die.

I see the signal light of Beau's car start blinking, and a quick scan of the area tells me she's pulling into a Walmart. It's early afternoon. The store will be packed. *What the fuck is she thinking?* "I've got to go." I hang up and follow her into the car park, parking on the other side, out of sight. But I see her. She sits in the driver's seat for an age, looking at the store. Then she makes a call. To whom?

I rest back, watching her closely, hoping she'll change her mind and drive away. This is too much in one day. The diner, the store, the opera tonight.

But she gets out, pulls her bag onto her shoulder, and walks with purpose toward the entrance. I don't know if my increasing heartbeat is because she's exposed, or because I am.

What the fucking hell is she doing?

29

BEAU

After I drop Nath off at the dealership, I head for Walmart, trying desperately not to pin all my hopes on my newfound recollection. Nath has a point. I could have my dates wrong. I could be clutching at straws, making small things into big things, or even nothings into somethings. I'm driving myself wild going over the conversation that happened over two years ago, reciting it word for word, trying to iron out the sketchy parts. I keep coming back to the same thing. Mom's breathlessness.

The parking lot is packed when I pull into it, the afternoon shoppers out in force. This has got to be on par with an opera house, hasn't it? Or maybe worse. People at opera houses are considerate and dignified. There is nothing dignified about fighting your way around Walmart on a Saturday afternoon. It's each person for themselves. Survival of the fittest.

I park and call Lawrence. "Do you need anything from the store?" I ask, my mind blank, even the essentials disappearing.

"Huh?"

"I'm at Walmart."

"Why?"

Because I'm preparing myself for a trip to the opera. "I got my period. I need Tampax," I mutter, and cringe immediately with it.

"Really, Beau? I know your cycle. It's like clockwork, and you're not due for a few days. Besides, you have a stash in your bathroom vanity."

"You've been through my bathroom vanity?"

"I needed some tweezers."

I sigh. "It's all I could think of. Put Dexter on."

"Fine," he grunts, and the line muffles as Lawrence tells Dexter who it is and why I'm calling.

"Milk," Dexter says softly, soothingly, when he comes onto the line. "We always need milk. And bread. And wine."

"Keep going," I order, putting him on loudspeaker and pulling up my notes, starting to compile my list.

"Coffee. Make sure it's not decaffeinated."

"Because what's the point in that?" we chant in unison, and I laugh a little.

"Tea bags, eggs, and some lubricant."

"Because that's essential in our house," we say together, both laughing again.

"Thanks, Dexter."

"Block it all out, Beau. You can do it." He's not making a big deal of it. God, I do love that man. He's the calm to Lawrence's chaos. The logical to Lawrence's irrational. They balance each other perfectly, and their love? The richest kind. Lawrence's favorite story always begins: *Let me tell you about the time a cop walked into a drag bar . . .*

I jump out of my car, mentally repeating Dexter's mantra as I collect a cart. A basket would do, but I need some kind of armor. Some protection. On that thought, I pull out my earbuds and pop them in, finding my music app and putting on some . . . opera.

Perfect.

Pie Jesu starts to serenade me as I push my cart through the doors of the store. I immediately have to dodge a woman who's stopped in the middle of the busy entrance. And then someone else who abandons their cart and dives across the aisle to grab something off an end display. And then a kid who spots the toy aisle. It's bedlam, total chaos, and my lack of hearing the madness doesn't lessen my building stress. "Jesus," I breathe, taking it all in, alarmed, my muscles becoming tenser by the second. I walk in a zigzag, navigating the store carefully, stepping left and right to avoid crazy shoppers, constantly stopping and starting to avoid being knocked to my ass. Lord, what was I thinking?

I can't do this.

I can't do this.

I can't handle the chaos.

It's too much.

I turn up the volume and round a corner, finding a man racing toward me with arms full of groceries, looking harassed. I stop in the middle of the aisle, frozen, the shopper's face morphing into fear rather than stress. And he's suddenly not alone. He's joined by a stampede of frantic people running scared.

I blink, shaking my head violently, clearing my vision and my flashback. I see the harassed shopper again. He's alone. No stampede.

I really can't do this.

I release the handle of my cart, trying to convince my legs to move. I need to get out. Leave. Go. I turn on the spot, my lungs tight, my heart tighter.

Get out. Get out.

I jump out of my skin when my phone screeches in my ear, and

I reach up quickly to yank my earbuds out. I shouldn't have. The bustling noise of the supermarket hits me hard, and I scan my surroundings frantically, searching for the one thing that might get me through the impending panic attack. A paper bag.

No paper bags.

"Fuck." I look at the screen of my phone, starting to hyperventilate. "James," I murmur, answering it quickly as I shove my buds back in. "Hello," I yell, making an old lady startle as she passes.

"Hi, it's me." James's deep voice sinks into my ears. "Why are you shouting?" I close my eyes for a moment and listen to his breathing. "Beau?" he says calmly, and for some extremely strange reason, his voice eliminates everything else. Everything. My heart slows. My breathing settles. I look at my hand that was trembling moments ago. Steady. "Where are you?" he asks.

I look around me at the unrelenting bedlam. "Shopping." I locate my cart and seize the handle with both hands, anchoring myself. But it's not the cart quietening my demons. It's James, and that's a frightening thing to admit to myself.

"Why, Beau?"

He's right. Why would *anyone* tackle Walmart on a Saturday? Least of all me, with my phobia of chaos. "Because I wanted to make tonight easier," I murmur, not holding back. I haven't got the mental capacity to lie. "Anything has to be easier than this." I chance a risky peek around me. God, it's getting busier. *Focus on James.*

"You're there because of me?" he asks, surprised.

"I'm not doing it for you." I'm doing it for myself, although I'm wishing I hadn't. Superstores at night are far nicer places to be.

"So you'll come to the opera with me?"

I close my eyes. "What do you think?" I'm not braving Walmart in the middle of the day on a Saturday for my health.

"You stormed out Thursday night."

"I've answered your call, haven't I?" Even if it was a little selfish. Besides, his message insisted. Is he surprised I'm complying?

"Are you saying we should never hold grudges?"

I smile, and it's unstoppable. If he only knew of the grudges I hold. But with him? He's offering me too much respite. "I have a list," I say, changing the subject.

"What's on your list, Beau?"

My mind blank, I locate my notes and reel off my list.

"And what have you got so far?" he asks.

"Nothing."

"Shall we start with milk? Nice and easy."

"What?"

"I'm coming shopping with you."

"What?"

"Turn around."

I slowly pivot and lose my breath for all the right reasons when I see him at the end of the aisle. My lip wobbles. *Why is my lip wobbling?* My heart gallops. I don't need to ask why that is. I disconnect the call and pull my buds from my ears, my focus on James and James alone. The store and all its crazy disappears. He looks perfectly rugged and unshaven, his messy hair poking out of a baseball cap, his body casually covered in some sweatpants and a zip-up hoodie. He's perfectly calm. Perfectly impassive. It's James on a weekend, and I like it.

I force a smile, as if to assure him I'm okay, and he shakes his head, looking almost angry. It's me who should be angry. I know he must have followed me, but it doesn't weird me out. I'm too relieved he's here.

He strides toward me, and once he makes it to me, he takes the handle of the cart with one hand and tucks me into his side with the other. He walks us to the milk aisle without a word, while I gaze at him in wonder. He's like a shot of valium. A balm for my tortured soul. Does he know that? Part of me hopes so. Another part of me hopes not, because I shouldn't offer him more ammo to use against me.

I collect a gallon of 2% milk. "A mango. Eggs. Coffee. Bread," I say quietly.

He hears me, and that's where we head, collecting each thing one by one. He's quiet and patient. His presence is powerful, attention falling on him from all directions, and yet he's unassuming. Oblivious. It's as if he's walking in a world where nothing else exists to him. Surroundings. People. Sounds. I'm envious. So envious of his ability to blank out everything.

He looks down at me nestled into his side and pulls me in tighter.

I exist.

And I'm in so much trouble. Yet denying myself this feeling is impossible. It would be cruel. Almost barbaric. I'm done punishing myself.

At the checkout, I unload while James packs, and I discreetly watch him, unable to stop my small smile. "Is me packing groceries amusing?" he asks without looking up, his focus set on his task.

I pay, joining him at the other end. "You following me is amusing."

"You weren't supposed to know I was following you."

"Then you need to work on your stealth skills."

He smiles lightly as he slips the milk into a bag, and it's a vision to behold. "Clearly." He collects my shopping and we head for the exit, and when we make it outside, I stop and look back at the store doors, where the chaos continues inside. Chaos that I was apparently immune to with James by my side. I mustn't read too much into that, and I can't be proud of myself, because those kind of shopping trips—ones only with James—aren't viable.

"Beau?"

I pull my eyes from the crowds and notice he's stopped a few feet away. His casual form renders me unable to move for a moment, my eyes happy to admire him, my heart hammering for the right reasons.

So. Much. Trouble.

I swallow and join him, beating back the swirling questions, because I promised myself I wouldn't ask. And beating back my awe because darkness shouldn't be admired.

We make it to my car and James slips the bags onto the passenger seat. "You don't lock your car?"

"I don't think anyone would steal it," I say on an ironic smile.

He looks up and down the battered length of Dolly a few times. "You should lock it." His eyebrows slowly rise, a clear sign of him wanting my agreement. I think if James asked me to walk on hot coals mixed with broken glass in this moment, I would do it.

"I'll lock her," I confirm, falling into the driver's seat. James is crouching by me in a second, assessing the inside of Dolly. The threadbare seats, the worn carpet, the ripped cloth of the roof lining. "She's sentimental," I tell him. "My mother bought her for me."

His eyes soften, and I quickly look away, quite stunned by my openness. "Her?" he asks.

"Dolly," I say on a shrug. "We named her after my uncle. His stage name. Zinnea Dolly Daydream." I expect an unsure smile from him, but instead his heavy brows become heavier. Something comes to me, something that's been playing on my mind in between all the other shit I'm dealing with. "James, the video you sent me. Of us." How many are there? How are they stored? How do I express my concern? Ask these quest—

"Just for you and me," he says, not needing me to ask. "You have my word, Beau."

It's all I can expect or ask for, I suppose, so I nod, oddly trusting him on that, and start Dolly's engine.

Bang!

I jump, alarmed, but my fright is forgotten when James all but dives on me. His arms are wrapped around me like ivy, so tightly, my face buried in his chest. A few seconds pass, me wondering what the hell just happened and James breathing heavily. "Shit," he whispers, gingerly releasing me and breaking away, refusing to look at me. Is he embarrassed?

"She shouldn't do that anymore," I say quietly, studying his profile, his cut jaw buzzing from the force of his bite. "Reg replaced her engine." But Dolly's returned shouting habits are not my main concern right now. "Are you okay?"

"She's loud." He seems to shake his head to himself, once again assessing the exterior.

"You get used to it." That's a lie. For years, every time I've started Dolly, I've had a mild heart attack. But driving her offers me a comfort that I've failed to find anywhere else. Until now.

James nods, thoughtful, and gets himself together, rising, then leaning in and kissing me straight on my lips. It's chaste. But I still solidify in my seat. "Drive carefully," he says seriously.

"Are you going to tell me your secret?" My words are so quiet, hardly decipherable. But he hears loud and clear. He nods, but why does it feel like a reluctant nod? Has he changed his mind?

"Tonight." He shuts the door of Dolly and steps back, giving me room to pull out of the parking space. Except, my feet won't work, and my brain won't enlighten me on which pedal does what. I stare at the dash. *Tonight.*

My forehead becomes heavy, and I grab the lever on the door and wind down the window. "Just fucking," I reiterate, whether that be for me or him.

"Just fucking, Beau." He strides off, and with those few words exchanged, James knows I'm not only going to the opera with him because I'm curious. I'm going because . . .

"Oh God," I murmur, slamming Dolly into reverse and pulling out of the space. "No, Beau."

I cannot develop feelings for a man.

Especially a man like James.

Which is what? What is James like? Apart from brooding and sexy and a huge fucking comfort?

An enigma. He's an enigma.

And I want him to stay that way.

30

JAMES

I give Otto the nod when I pass his car, and he pulls out immediately, tailing Beau out of the car park. I get into my Range Rover and stare at the wheel, shellshocked. Not only because Beau might have just unwittingly shared something, but because I am getting wholly obsessed with her. *Just fucking.* I close my eyes and breathe out. I see me. All those years ago, it's me. Lost. No purpose. No outlet. I'm giving her an outlet. Not answers, but an outlet.

"Fuck." My phone rings, and I answer to Goldie.

"The exchange is arranged for tomorrow evening at South Beach," she says. "A case will be left between two beach chairs. Look for yellow towels."

"Sounds clean and simple, huh?"

"I thought the same."

And nothing is ever that clean and simple in my world. I start my car and pull out of the car park fast. "I have a new name for you to search."

"What?"

"Dolly Daydream."

She laughs, and I don't blame her. "Are you kidding? It sounds like a porn star."

"Not quite."

"Then what?"

Why all the questions? Fuck me, since I met Beau, it's all I'm getting. Question after fucking question. "You're pissing me off a lot lately, did you know that?"

"Fuck off." She hangs up, and I clench the steering wheel tightly, anger brewing. Because for the first time in forever, I wish I didn't have to kill a man tonight. And such a perverse headspace is more dangerous than my need to continue my never-ending killing spree.

31

BEAU

As I unload the groceries in the kitchen, I try to pluck up the courage to find Lawrence and claim back the beautiful black lace gown. He's going to be devastated, and not only because he loves the gown. I put the milk in the fridge and face the door to the hallway, taking a few steps toward it. I can do this. Play it down. It's no big deal.

I'm a joke.

I pace to the bottom of the stairs in assertive strides and take the first step.

That's as far as I get.

I hear a door open, followed by a breathless sigh, and then Lawrence appears at the top of the stairs.

As Zinnea.

In *the* dress.

Shit.

"Isn't it a showstopper?" she sings, picking up the bottom and flouncing down the stairs. "My God, I'll be the talk of the circuit. I look lethal!"

I move aside to let her pass, my heart sinking. "Gorgeous," I murmur, just as Dexter comes through the front door in his uniform.

His face is a picture. "Wow," he blurts, and Zinnea squeals.

"I know!" She breezes to the other end of the hallway where the floor-length mirror hangs by the kitchen door, swishing the skirt of the dress dramatically like she could have just walked onto the stage. "I'll wear it tonight." She turns around and inspects the back. "It's like it was made for me."

My shoulders drop, my whole being sagging. What the hell am I going to do? I can't break her heart, and I have absolutely no opera-worthy dresses. "It's uncanny." I smile tightly, playing it cool, while mentally carving out a plan. It involves an emergency dash to the Midtown shops. On a Saturday afternoon. I start to sweat. And the shakes take hold. And my breathing goes to shit. I can feel the panic attack looming, ready to trap me in its claws and bring me down a peg or two.

I walk to the kitchen, my legs like lead, and start yanking open drawers, searching for where Dexter might hide those paper bags these days.

"Here." One appears in front of me, and I grab it, scrunching it around my mouth and taking long, deep breaths as I find a chair and flop into it.

"Well," Zinnea says, sitting opposite me and taking my hand. I look at her over the ballooning bag. "When I said I look lethal, I wasn't wrong, eh?"

I shake my head, feeling so incredibly beaten. I did the diner, which was nothing compared to Walmart. But I only survived the store because of James. I'll do the opera—again only because of James. And then what? When there is no James? I pull the bag away. "I need that dress back," I tell her calmly. I don't know what happens beyond this minute, so trying to figure out tomorrow or next week is a waste of time and energy. Today is now. I have to do what I can and hope I can keep up the momentum when James inevitably isn't around anymore.

Zinnea's shoulders push back, her palm resting on the intricately detailed lace covering her chest. She looks horrified. "Oh." She clears her throat, and I peek at Dexter, who's holding back an epic grin of both amusement and delight as he pulls the belt out of his blue pants. "And may I ask why?"

"You know why," I counter quietly, hoping she's not going to force me into details.

"That man."

I place the bag down and draw in some courage with air. *That man* was the only reason I made it around the store at a peak time today. That man is the only reason I *haven't* thought nonstop about the letter I received denying me a chance of justice. That man is a walking, talking mystery, and he could be the only reason I make it through the latest shitty news about Mom's death. I won't be sharing my earlier memory of the conversation I had with Mom. Not until I know if it's something worth sharing, anyway. "His name's James," I say, giving Zinnea my eyes.

"I thought you said it's not sustainable."

"It's not."

"But if he's helping her now, what's the harm?" Dexter pipes up, joining us at the table. He reaches for my hand and squeezes, and I cast him a surprised look.

What's the harm? It's a loaded question with endless answers. I don't know what the harm is, but I do if I don't see him again. Which makes this all very easy, really. "I'm going to an opera with him."

"What?"

"It's just opera."

"To everyone else it's opera," Zinnea says over a laugh. "To you, it's hell on earth."

"Not with James."

She recoils, flicking worried eyes at Dexter. And then those worried eyes fall into the realms of sadness. "I've offered to take you to many places."

Dexter lets out a bark of laughter, and both Zinnea and I jump. "But not to heaven, right, Beau?" He gets up, his eyebrows rising with him, and for the first time since I can remember, I blush a little, evading their eyes.

"Heaven?" Zinnea questions as she reaches for the sleeve of my shirt and pushes it up. "Really?"

I quickly pull away, yanking it back down. "I don't expect you to understand." How can I when I hardly understand this craziness myself? "All I know is James is a much better alternative to everything else." I smile lamely, silently praying for her blessing. She looks sulky. It doesn't suit the vivacious Zinnea Dolly Daydream. "So can I have the dress back?"

"Don't have much choice, do I?"

I shake my head.

No, she doesn't.

And neither, it seems, do I.

32

BEAU

At seven thirty, I stand in the hallway gazing at myself in the mirror. I don't recognize the woman before me. She's elegance personified. Perfection. I've let Zinnea at me with her bottomless supply of makeup and hairspray, and I'm beginning to regret it. Not because she hasn't done an amazing job—she totally has—but because it's been a long, long time since I've seen this woman in the mirror. A long time since I carried a dress like this. I'm not sure if I know how to anymore.

I peek down at the strappy Jimmy Choo heels that haven't seen the light of day in two years. And at the YSL purse that's been stuffed at the back of a drawer for as long. Years ago, I walked out most weekends in heels like these for drinks with friends or work colleagues. Now, I don't know if I could make it to the kitchen a few feet away.

"It's like riding a bike," Zinnea says, pulling my attention to the bottom of the stairs. She's halfway ready for her evening on stage, her hair and makeup on point, her body wrapped in a tropical kimono. I offer a small smile, silently thanking her for not mentioning where I'm going and with whom again, but rather concentrating on getting me ready for where I'm going and with whom. I'm so thankful for them.

Zinnea must see my gratitude, because she matches my smile and comes up behind me, smoothing my French pleat again before attacking it with more spray. "You look gorgeous, Beau," she says on a massive sigh, and I see her inside conflict. This is the old me. At least, the old me when I wasn't in uniform. She's pleased to see me again, and yet the circumstances of my transformation are less than comforting for her.

"The taxi should be here by now," I say, glancing down at the sleeves. Long, lace sleeves. James has me covered. Literally.

"And will you be home tonight after your date?"

I flick a knowing smile up at Zinnea as I brush my front down. I hope not. I want to walk the path to nothingness with James.

A car horn sounds outside, and I take in air, silently chanting words of encouragement. "Have a good show," I say, dropping a kiss on Zinnea's cheek.

"Be careful, Beau," she whispers. "Just promise me you'll be careful."

"I promise." I pull the front door open, glaring immediately at the bushes closing in the pathway. "We really need to get these bushes trimmed."

"If you're going to trim bushes, darling, you should do it *before* your date."

I gasp and fly around, finding my aunt leaning against the doorjamb with a wicked grin on her face, and now Dexter is with her, laughing like a hyena. I can only shake my head in dismay. "Goodnight," I say as they back up, closing the door. I walk carefully and slowly down the path, trying not to catch my dress on any of the bushes.

"Evening."

I glance up, surprised, finding James leaning against the side of his car. In a beautiful black suit. Crisp white shirt. Black tie. My knees go weak under my dress and my tummy flutters as he takes me in, top to bottom, all very slowly. And I do the exact same, every inch of him I explore sending my insides further into bedlam. "Evening," I murmur. "I was expecting a taxi."

He pushes off the side of the car and wanders casually over to me, his hands deep in his pockets. He comes to a stop before me, and my eyes rise to keep contact with his. "You look out of this world," he whispers, removing one hand from a pocket and reaching for the edge of a sleeve, brushing delicately over the material.

I swallow, unable to return the compliment while he's touching me.

"Do you like the dress?" he asks.

"I do, thank you," I all but whisper. He doesn't smile. Doesn't speak. He looks pensive. "Is everything okay?"

"No," he answers, letting his touch slip to my fingers. My heart sinks, dropping into my belly, seeming to dislodge the anxiety and questions. Damn me. I don't want to be curious about him. I want to be ignorant. I just want to feel and not think.

I step back, and James frowns, moving in closer. His fingers weave through mine, his eyes watching them closely. "Just feel," he murmurs, as if reading my mind, placing a fingertip on my collarbone and circling it slowly. My skin is instantly ablaze. My breath catches, my body folding. He watches it all, remaining expressionless. "We'll be late," he whispers, dragging his fingertip down to my breast.

"We will," I reply, swallowing hard, my insides twisting and turning. I'm dreading the opera for a very different reason now.

Resistance.

"Are you ready?" That fingertip turns into a flat palm, and it falls slowly to my stomach.

"Ready."

He takes my hand and places it over his groin. "Me too." Now, *he* swallows hard, and I go dizzy with the feel of him pressed into my palm. We're standing on the sidewalk, his hand now resting over my pubic bone, mine over his arousal. I'm flooding between my thighs. My nipples are bullets. My lips are parted, my sight hazy, my skin tingling. I don't want to go to the opera. I want to go to paradise.

I look up at him, pleading with my eyes, and I see the same level of want in him. "You masturbated thinking of me, didn't you?" He takes my hand from his groin and brings it to his mouth, kissing the tips of my fingers.

"I watched us," I admit.

"Me too. On repeat. And I wondered why the fuck I was watching when I could be doing." He reaches for my nape and hauls me into him, slamming his mouth over mine and kissing me greedily, his grip of my neck harsh, his tongue violently lashing through my mouth. It doesn't help our cause. But I'll be damned if I can stop it. My body melts into his, my breasts aching against his chest, my body alive with anticipation. It's a long kiss. But not long enough.

He groans and pries himself away, his eyes closed, his forehead pushing into mine as I pant in his face. He looks troubled, angry all of a sudden, and I'm wary of it. I shouldn't ask. I *won't* ask.

The sound of the front door opening has James's eyes snapping open, and he stares at me. He heard it too.

I can feel her eyes nailed to me, and I swallow, pulling away and peeking cautiously out the corner of my eye. Zinnea is a statue in the doorway, staring at James. I squirm, the silence awful.

"Hello," James says after clearing his throat, obviously deciding someone needs to break the ice, and it's not going to be me or my aunt. "James Kelly."

Zinnea's face is a picture of indignation, and it kills me. God, this is horrible. I will her to find it in herself to be polite, to push away her grievances. But my aunt remains a statue at the door. And me? I continue to die, not knowing what to do. Her acceptance was short-lived. Just an act.

"We should go," I say, taking James's arm and gently tugging him back.

"Is there a problem?" he asks quietly.

"No, no problem." I smile awkwardly when he looks at me, trying to force him away, but he remains unmoving. Then his stare drops to my wrists and understanding floats onto his face. His jaw ticks as he looks up at me, and I mildly shake my head, begging him to leave it. He shakes his in return, and I know in that moment that he won't. He faces my aunt again. "It was consensual. Nothing happened that Beau—"

"Didn't ask for?" Zinnea finishes, her nose high. I fold, giving up on trying to get James moving. He's unmovable.

"Indeed," James replies, reaching back and taking my hand as Dexter joins Zinnea at the door.

"I said leave her," he whisper hisses, taking Zinnea's arm. "She's a grown wom—" He catches sight of us on the sidewalk and freezes, taking us in. I smile lamely. *Yes, this is him.*

"It was nice to meet you, Zinnea." James turns us both and leads me to his car, and I look back, seeing Dexter now trying to get her back inside. I throw a pleading look that my aunt misses. Or ignores. I fear it's the latter. I've never seen her so hostile. Yes, she can be a diva, or even a bitch when she wants to be. But never hostile. And I'm not sixteen, for fuck's sake. *Come on, Zinnea. This is too much.*

Our eyes meet as Dexter pushes the door closed, and I hate the anger I see swirling in her usually happy gaze. She shakes her head, disappointed, and then she's gone.

And I feel like utter shit. Like I'm committing a terrible sin. Like this is wrong. James and I are wrong.

"Stop," James says when we get to the car, his tone warning. He opens the passenger door but prevents me from getting in, holding the top of my arm firmly. I look at his fingers wrapped around me. "You showed her?" He sounds angry.

"No, not voluntarily." Does he think I offered the information? Gave her a blow-by-blow account of that night?

His jaw ticks harder as he stares at my welted wrist for an age, silent and brooding. Don't tell me he feels guilty now, because *I* certainly don't. But when he reaches for my arm, brushing a thumb over the start of my scar, I realize he's not looking at the damage he caused, but the damage caused by someone else. *You think you have more secrets than I do.* I can hear his mind spinning. He wants to ask me so many questions.

I desperately don't want to know anything.

And he wants to know everything.

"We'll be late," I say, withdrawing from him, pulling the material back into place.

He glances up. "We will." His arm gestures to the open door, and I slide in, my head in turmoil. It started so well. And now?

Now I'm full of shame and hurt. Anger. Judgment. Disappointment.

Wasn't the purpose of tonight to avoid that?

33

JAMES

I'm trying to figure out why the fuck I'm so bothered, and why she is now mute. The car feels like it could explode, the tension is so powerful. I need to clear my head. Get in the right frame of mind. Going in for a kill with anything less than composure isn't wise.

I look across the car to her. She's here but not here. And I think about the look on her aunt's face. And her partner's? His was equally disgusted. Shocked. Disapproving. They don't like me. It was as plain as Beau's withdrawal now. If they knew me, I'd understand. But they don't know me, and they *won't* know me.

"Why do you live with your uncles?" I ask, digging for information I already know.

"Because my mother is dead, my father is an asshole, and I left my ex at the altar on our wedding day."

And she doesn't want to be alone.

"You were going to get married," I muse quietly, as if it's news to me.

"It's historic."

"To the man outside the store?"

She turns her eyes onto me. They're cold and empty. She doesn't need to tell me to back off. Every fiber of her being is yelling at me to.

And I should.

34

BEAU

When we arrive at Ziff Ballet Opera House, the unbearable atmosphere between us hasn't shifted. He asked some questions, I answered. That's all he's getting, and I know he must sense that because he's been silent since. Silent and thoughtful. Angry.

He pulls the door to the lobby open for me, and I stand stock-still on the threshold, taking in the bustling space. My feet feel like they're blocks of concrete, my pulse booming. James's black mood isn't helping. I'll never get through this without him helping, and he looks in no mood to help.

Which means I can't do this.

I pick up the bottom of my dress and turn, walking away, calm finding me the farther away I get from the building.

Or is it because I'm getting away from James?

I hate my final thought. Hate it.

"Beau," he calls, but I keep on walking, unable to shake the awkward vibes or the displeasure on Zinnea's face. I could endure it, maybe even disregard it, if I had any kind of reward. But her revulsion, James's mood, and now this shitty atmosphere, has me wanting to do what I've become a master at.

Hiding.

My pace increases as a result, and I see the road approaching, the bus stop within reach.

"Beau!"

I step into the road.

"Beau!"

Look right.

"Beau, stop!"

But I don't look left.

"Beau!"

I whirl around, seeing a car coasting toward me, and I freeze, paralyzed by shock. I'm grabbed and hauled back onto the sidewalk as the car zooms past, and I look up at James, startled. His face. It's grave. "God damn it, Beau, what the fuck are you playing at?"

I blink, swallowing.

"Why are you running away from me?"

My eyes drop like stones to his chest. "Why are you angry?" I ask quietly.

"I'm not angry. I'm . . ." He breathes out heavily, as if trying to expel that anger. "I'm tangled."

"Tangled?"

"Inside," he goes on. "I'm in fucking knots, Beau."

I look up at him. "Why?"

He closes his eyes briefly, as if gathering patience, like he doesn't understand why I don't get it. His hand slips onto my neck, his thumb circling my cheek, his spare hand on my hip, encouraging me closer to him. He dips and places his lips over mine, and the storm inside settles. Soft James. "I want to get to know you, Beau Hayley. And that's come as a massive fucking surprise."

I jolt in his hold, shocked. "What?" It's all I can say. Being curious about me is one thing. But getting to know me?

Pulling back, he makes sure he has my eyes, and he stares so deeply into them, I fear all my secrets can be seen. It makes me look away, makes me feel vulnerable. This wasn't part of the plan. I've fought my curiosity, so he needs to too. I feel like I've been derailed. He wants to get to know me. Does that mean he expects me to spill my dirt? Offload my demons and . . . and then what? We live happily ever after? And all of this is before putting mind to the fact that the first time I saw James, he was stark naked fucking a woman while a man watched.

"Why are you pulling away?" he asks.

I step back, and his hands fall to his sides. "This won't work," I murmur to my feet, feeling like I'm dying on the inside. "You, me, it can't work." A veil of bricks falls around me, protecting me. "You've fucked me. You know everything I want you to know."

He lets out a puff of laughter. It's a laughter of disbelief. And it's as condescending as could be. The hollows of his cheeks start pulsing, his stare hard and unforgiving. I wonder what comes next, but before I can start hedging my bets, he seizes my hand and starts pulling me toward the opera house.

"What are you doing?" I ask, unable to pry my hand from his vise grip. "James!" He continues to ignore me, pulling me, my feet moving fast to keep up with him. "James, let go of me."

He yanks the door open and pulls me through. The foyer is quieter now, only a few people milling around, everyone having taken their seats. I'm more than happy about that, but not so much about being manhandled into the building.

"Sir," an usher says, approaching, his eyes flicking to me. "Can I help?" I can hear the sounds of a tenor in the distance.

James goes to his inside pocket and pulls out some papers, virtually slapping them in the man's hand. "Which way?"

The usher looks down at the tickets. "A box?"

"Yes, a box. Which way?"

He points to the elevators on the other side of the foyer. "Top level. Farthest on the left." His eyes fall onto me again, and then to my hand being squeezed by James's. "Are you okay, ma'am?" he asks, flicking a nervous look to my rattled companion.

"I'm fi—"

"She's fine," James grunts, snatching the tickets back and pulling me on. When we reach the elevator, we're escorted to the top level, and then to the very end. "Thank you," James says, sending the usher on his way as he opens the door to the box. "Inside, Beau," he orders, releasing my hand. I flex my wrist, pushing back the emotion clogging my throat.

And I step inside.

35

JAMES

My phone vibrates, and the timing is fucking shit. I take a quick look. I don't need to open the message. What I can see of the preview tells me everything.

I found a record from 2 yrs ago at the Mid Bank for a safety deposit box under the name Dolly Daydream.

I stuff my phone in my pocket; this news is a bombshell to be dealt with another time. There's a safety deposit box. Does Beau know about it? And what the fuck is in it?

Fucking hell.

I don't give her a chance to appreciate the unrivaled view of the stage. No chance to absorb the exquisite sound of the orchestra. I push her into a chair and fall to my knees in front of her. I need her back with me. In every sense. Especially after that fucking shock of a message.

My palms land on her knees, and I stare at her as I slide her dress up until its gathered around her thighs.

"What are you doing?" she whispers hoarsely, despite there being no chance of being heard over the overture—a dramatic instrumental of the theme from Phantom of the Opera. Her fingers claw into the plush velvet arms of the chair, her body pushing back. No escape. She doesn't really want to escape. She stepped into this box of her own freewill.

She glares at me, and if I didn't know better, I would say she hated me. She should. And I hate myself for *not* wanting her to. "James."

"Shut up, Beau." I take her knickers and start dragging them down her thighs. "We've done enough talking tonight." Way too much talking, and it's my fucking fault.

She reaches for my hands to push me off, and I instinctively flick her away with ease. She grits her teeth, anger rampant on her face. And she tries again to push me off. She's just being stubborn. Trying to gain some control. I rise to my knees, pushing my front forward, bringing my face close to hers. The smell of her, the sweet, fruity gorgeous, uncontaminated smell of her hits me like a ton of bricks. "Stop it."

"You stop it," she breathes.

"Why?"

Her nostrils flare. She can't claim our location is making her uneasy. It's simply my earlier statement making her question everything now. But she was a total fool assuming she could maintain immunity. And I was a fool for ever thinking *I* could. I feel like I want her to know everything there is to know about me. Every dirty, disgusting, illegal, immoral detail.

I lift each of her feet in turn and slip her knickers off, holding them in the air before her. Then I flick my wrist, and her underwear disappears over the side of the balcony. Beau's mouth falls open. I remain impassive.

Don't underestimate me, Beau. Never do that.

I pull a pair of cuffs out of my pocket and get to my feet, wandering casually and slowly around the back of her chair.

I take her arms.

Pull them behind the chair.

Snap the cuffs over her wrists.

And she lets me.

The music suddenly seems to intensify, and it is one hundred percent apt. The sexual chemistry in this small balcony is charged. I round her again, satisfied to see her panting, struggling, unable to yank her eyes away from me. I slowly lower to my knees and place my hands on her thighs.

Spread them.

My first kiss on the inside of her knee sends her eyes rolling to the back of her head, her moan long and deep. "More," she breathes, the word coming naturally. The second kiss on her other knee brings on the shakes. The third, slightly higher, instigates a gentle, consistent, visible throb in her clit. The fourth, a fraction higher than that, makes her arms jerk, the metal clanging. The fifth on her inside thigh makes her head limp. The sixth just shy of her entrance makes her stiffen. And when I cover her completely with my mouth and suck, her body jacks, and she lets out a suppressed cry. I forget where I am. What I'm doing. Why I'm doing it. Her pussy throbbing against my tongue is absorbing. Mind-numbing.

"More," she pants, rigid in the chair, her thighs tensing around my head. I suck harder, my fingers digging into her flesh. "Oh God." She starts to pant, and fire races through my veins, my skin prickling. "James." I kiss, suck, bite, swirl. "James!"

I hum, gorging on her sweet pussy, relishing her squirming, loving her constant cries of my name. I could stay here all fucking night. But I can't.

I increase my pace, change my rhythm, and introduce my

fingers, pushing them deep and high, feeling her walls grip and hold.

She comes as the music hits the crescendo, and she screams her way through it, staring at my face buried between her legs, feasting on her flesh, her body trembling around me. I sweep my fingers through her slickness and feel her internal walls roll as I slow my attack and lick her softly through the aftermath.

Calm. It's mine again.

After a delicate kiss on the very tip of her clit, which makes her spasm, I reach for her dress and work it down her thighs. She looks at me, dazed, drowsy, as I anchor my hands into the arms of the chair and push my way to my feet. I lean into her. Close. Kiss her delicately, sharing her release. If I could, I'd unzip myself and shove my hard, throbbing cock into her willing, gorgeous mouth. But if I do that, I won't leave this box all night. "That is why we won't stop," I whisper, and she closes her eyes, swallowing. She gets it. "I'll be back." I lay a palm over her cheek, and she nuzzles into it. She *really* gets it.

Then I turn and walk out, leaving her cuffed to the chair.

36

BEAU

He's gone, and I'm left alone, still restrained, in more bedlam than I was before. The sound of the music is almost haunting. So sad. And despite James taking me to paradise, my mood matches the solemn echoes of the soloist who's currently singing to the heavens.

I zone out, disappear completely from this box, from the opera house, from life itself. And I walk through every minute of my time since I first heard his voice. Then saw him. Has the universe finally delivered my savior? One wrong phone number, and here we are? It feels too convenient.

The song is finished, another has begun, and the stage setting has changed. I look over my shoulder to the door. Where is he? As if forgetting I'm restrained, I shift my hands, wincing when the metal rubs into my sore flesh. I'm going nowhere, unless I want to open the existing wounds on my wrists. Was that his plan?

I return my attention to the stage, my options limited, and I watch, allowing myself to become captivated by the story playing out before me. I'm serenaded by another performance, and with each minute that passes, I become increasingly worried about where the hell James could be.

I'm just considering the merits of calling for an usher when the door opens and James strides in. He doesn't look like he's cooled off. In fact, he looks angrier.

"We're leaving." He dips behind me, and a few moments later, my hands are free.

"It's not finished," I say, looking at the stage, rubbing at my sore flesh.

"Neither am I."

My hand is taken, and I'm pulled up. He spends a few moments checking my wrists. "You fought the bonds," he whispers, stroking over my skin, looking into my eyes. "Never fight the bond, Beau."

He doesn't give me a chance to reply, turning me and resting his hand on my hip, leading me out.

Bond.

Never fight the bond.

At a loss for words, I let him guide me to the elevator in silence. We travel down in silence. Walk through the lobby in silence. But our bodies are screaming. I look up at him, seeing his focus set firmly forward, his face cut with so many emotions.

Stress. Anger. Craving.

We cross the deserted lobby, and I look over my shoulder, feeling eyes on me. The usher who met us when we arrived is observing us quietly, and what he's undoubtedly assuming bothers me. So I consciously smile, leaning into James, resting my head on his arm, a silent message to the worried man that I'm fine.

I'm not fine.

I don't know what happened in that box. I don't know what James's point was. That I'm a fool for attempting to walk away? For fighting the bond? He could be right, because now, as he marches us out of the opera house to finish what he started in private, the thought of walking away is inconceivable. I'm alive.

I return my focus forward but quickly shoot my eyes back when something catches my attention, exiting the ladies'.

What?

She looks left and right, pulling in her suit jacket with one hand. Because the other is holding a case. The same case she collected from James's glass apartment. I frown, just as she spots us by the door, my body slowing automatically. Her face noticeably drops, and then she walks swiftly through a nearby door, and I watch her disappear, coming to a stop, making James halt too.

"Beau?"

The door closes. She's gone. "Goldie," I murmur, turning my gaze onto James. "I saw Goldie."

He looks across the lobby. "Goldie?"

"Yes." My arm lifts, pointing to the door. "She left through that door." It's only now I notice the sign above it saying "Restricted Access."

"You must be mistaken." He claims my hand, and I glance up at him, cautious and really fucking suspicious. I'm not mistaken. She looked me right in the eye and made a very speedy exit, but something tells me that information would be wasted on him. He left me alone in that box, handcuffed to a chair, for over twenty minutes. Men don't take that long in the restroom. *What's going on?*

As James leads me away from the opera house, I realize he never said he was using the restroom, I just assumed. So if he wasn't, then what *was* he doing? My mind's spinning.

Why the fuck was he with Goldie when he asked me to the opera, played me into submission, and then left me? And what the hell was in that briefcase? I'm too fucking curious for my own good.

Who are you, James Kelly?

37

JAMES

I've fucked up. Leaving before the opera ended was a monumental fuck-up, and Goldie is about to go psycho on my arse. Beau seems to make me consistently fuck up. *Shit.*

I played her claims down. Told her she was mistaken about seeing Goldie. She wasn't buying it. Wouldn't have even if she wasn't hailed the most exciting thing to enter the training academy in years. And that's my problem. I keep neglecting to remember that Beau Hayley was on course to become one of the FBI's best agents. She's Jaz Hayley's daughter after all.

I killed a man tonight. Put a bullet clean through his corrupt skull. I'm not concerned that I might get caught. I'm concerned Beau will figure it out, and that begs the fucking question why I even bought her here.

The answer is hard to admit.

I can't let her out of my sight, but more than that, I don't want to. Close. I need her close. I want her close. I want every pain she shoulders, every hate-filled thought she has. And I want to free her from it all. It's fucked up, considering I'm the reason she's here in the first place. Totally fucking fucked-up.

I put Beau in the passenger seat and reply to Goldie's earlier message as I round the back of the car.

Get me all the details. I'll call you ASAP.

I get in my car and glance across to Beau. She vehemently looks away, staring out of the window. I need to get her talking. Get her comfortable. Make her *want* to share. So then when I spill my fucked-up truths, maybe she won't be as shocked.

And maybe I'm a fucking dickhead.

38

BEAU

When we arrive back at James's apartment, my mind hasn't quieted down, and James and I still haven't murmured a word to each other. He's still brooding, I'm still fucking curious, and Goldie is at the desk in the foyer, her head down as we pass. I drill holes into her, willing her to look up, to face me. She doesn't. And James doesn't even bother asking if she was at the opera house this evening. Because he knows she was.

Curiosity. Suspiciousness. I don't want to feel either, but it's the lost cop in me. Or is it simply James?

I'm put in the elevator, and as it carries us to James's glass box, he starts unraveling the knot of his tie, staring forward. I can't deny the bang between my legs. Or my shortness of breath. Even moody, he's stunning. Even when he's not touching me, anticipation is churning my stomach. Even feeling enormously uncertain, I still want him.

The doors open, but neither of us exit, and he slowly drags his tie from around his neck, still staring forward. "Take off your dress," he says quietly, starting to roll the material of his tie into a tight coil, his focus never wavering from the space before him.

Crazy as it is, mad as I feel, there's only one way for us to speak in this moment.

I step out of the elevator and drop my purse to the floor as I walk, reaching back for the zip of my dress and dragging it down. I come to a stop at the foot of the stairs and pull my arms out of the sleeves, letting the lace plummet to the floor and pool on my strappy shoes. I step out of it, everything inside of me thrumming, but everything completely stable as I climb the steps one by one, feeling him close behind me. Following. "Take off your suit," I murmur, removing my bra and dropping it on the steps.

Naked.

I cast my hungry gaze over my shoulder. He's halfway up. Bare-chested. His face a masterpiece of craving. His torso a blanket of dense muscle.

He comes to a stop, kicking off his shoes, letting them tumble down the steps to the bottom. Then he starts working his fly, his stare concentrated, burning through me, his lips straight, his cheeks hollow. I return my eyes forward and pick up my feet, taking myself to his bedroom. I push the door open and gaze around. To the wall. To the cabinet. To the bed.

Cold Water Music by Aim is suddenly pouring from the speakers, drenching the space. My shoulders roll, and I swallow.

Talking.

Without talking.

I pad across the carpet and crawl up the sheets, turning onto my back and settling, my legs bent, my heels pressed into the mattress. He appears at the door, pushing his trousers down his thighs, and his eyes fall to between my legs. I slide my hand down my stomach, scissor my fingers, and glide them across my flesh, bowing my back subtly. His trousers and boxers hit the floor. My desire hits the roof. His cock, weeping and hard, juts from his groin proudly. Circling the base with a palm, he draws a slow stroke down his shaft on a loud inhale, and I moan at the sight of him, as well as the slippery friction I'm creating myself, my nerves sizzling. I don't know what I'm doing. Why I'm doing it. It's all just happening, and I have no inclination to stop it, or to even take a moment and consider the consequences. Because by doing that, I'll be kicking off a war between my body and my mind, and I'm truly scared which one will come out the other side in one piece. I'm here. James is here. The insane chemistry is here.

We're both at its mercy.

My body starts to tense, my fingers hardening, my strokes building in rhythm. And in response, James starts to thrust his fist faster. His expression is firm in its indifference, but his body is communicating, screaming, telling me he's as desperate as me. As hungry as me.

As broken as me.

I can feel my walls beginning to swell, the pressure building, the blood pumping relentlessly, as I work myself up higher, my view unrivaled, the sight of him doing more than my own touch ever could. His stomach is steel. His face is straining. His biceps bulging.

He's going to come.

My lips part, and I take my spare hand to my boob, grabbing it roughly, crying out. I begin to writhe on the sheets, my heels sinking deeper into the mattress, my hips starting to thrust up. James hisses through his teeth, taking the doorframe for support, struggling to remain upright, his pumping becoming violent. My eyes climb his body until they reach his face.

And his eyes.

The entrance to the land of freedom.

To another me.

My orgasm hits, and my world explodes around me, my body

out of control, shaking, jacking, my cries long and deafening. I remove my touch on a sharp inhale, the sensitivity too much, as I'm riddled with endless stabs of pleasure, the force of them crippling.

James convulses, his shoulders jerking, his bark labored. "Fuck, Beau," he wheezes, his fingers clawing around the doorjamb, his body folding, as he watches me watching him come undone. He looks like he could collapse at any moment, but I can't remove my eyes from his to check the stability of his legs. I expect they're wobbling. I know I am. I'm shaking to my core. Blitzed. Falling apart but together.

He turns into the door, resting his forehead on his arm, breathing erratically. James Kelly post orgasm is a hypnotic sight. James in his magnificent, naked, trembling glory. And I did that. I made him fall apart.

The power I feel in this moment—not helplessness, not dependance, not pain—is as dangerous as the sense of escape he provides.

Full control.

And I haven't had full control in years. Not of my body, my emotions, or my pain.

I turn my head on the pillow and gaze out of the endless glass, to the world beyond. A world I never thought could be good for me again. A world I thought I couldn't fit into. But in this glass box, I fit, and it feels good, irrespective of the secrets shrouding us.

"You said you wanted to get to know me," I say to the dusky skyline, my body still rolling in the aftermath of my release.

"I do."

"What about other people?" I turn my head, finding him still propped up by the door, his head still buried in the crook of his arm. "Do you want to get to know other people?"

"No."

"What about fucking them? Do you want to fuck other people?"

Silence.

I don't know how we arrived at this moment, but it's time to share some truths. "I saw you," I say, my voice strong. Unashamed.

More silence, leaving my statement hanging heavy in the air. I don't need to extend. He knows what I'm talking about.

I watch him using too much effort to stand on his own, pushing his body off the doorjamb. "I know," he finally says, facing me.

"How?"

He turns, giving me his disfigured back, and walks away, not telling me to follow. But as I'm learning with James, he doesn't need to speak for me to understand him. I edge to the side of the bed and reach down to unfasten my shoes, kicking them off and following him. He enters his office, and by the time I make it to the threshold, his naked body is propped against one of the windowpanes. He points at the wall of screens. I'm filling them. Every single one of them is the same footage of me. And I'm standing in the doorway to his bedroom watching him fuck that woman. I don't know if I'm immune to shock now, but I feel nothing. No surprise. No annoyance. He's known this whole time.

"Why do you do it?" I ask, looking away from the TVs.

"Release. Wildness. The thrill." He picks up the remote control and points it at the wall, and the images of me standing in the doorway to his bedroom are replaced by images of me sprawled on his bed at the peak of an orgasm. Five minutes ago. "But my past encounters," he says quietly, "pale compared to what's on these screens now." I feel him approaching, and he takes my naked hips, holding me.

"You have cameras everywhere?" I turn my eyes up to the ceiling, scanning, but I see nothing.

"They're hidden."

"Why?" Surely if this was a security issue, he'd have them on full display to deter people.

"They're an eyesore."

"That's not the reason," I reply without thought.

"No, it's not." He circles me, putting his imposing, hard body before me, and I tilt my head back to look at him. Now, I *am* surprised. I don't know how I knew he wasn't being honest, but I knew. And that's adding to the scary that's building. "But you don't want to know my secrets," he reminds me quietly. "You just want this." His fingertip meets my nipple, and they're immediately hard for him. I inhale, my knees instantly weak. "Don't you, Beau?"

Confusing emotion creeps up on me. I feel like he's holding me hostage. Playing with me. "I don't know *what* I should want."

He removes his touch, and it's painful. So painful. "I'm not stopping you from leaving."

Is he for real? "Yes, you are," I breathe, my voice wobbly. "You know exactly what you're fucking doing, and I don't know why you're doing it." I need to get out of here. Collect my thoughts. Find space to find reason. I back up toward the door, mentally locating all my things as I go.

"Beau?" he says.

"If I go now, will you leave me alone?"

"No." He reaches for me, and I swipe my arm out fast, knocking his intended touch away.

"Why, James? Why won't you leave me alone?"

"Because you need me."

Infuriation flames. I can't control it, but I keep backing up. "And what about you? What do you need?"

"I need you to stop fucking running."

I halt at the door, incensed. "Then start being honest with me!" I don't know what I'm saying, anger fueling me, driving me.

"You want that?" he asks. "Do you, Beau? Because I already tried being honest with you, and I've spent the rest of the evening trying to stop you from walking away from me."

"Then stop trying," I say calmly, turning and hurrying away, not knowing what the fuck I'm doing. Do I want to go? Do I want to stay? My head is a fucked-up mess of I-don't-knows.

I reach the stairs and grasp the handrail, my feet taking the steps fast. I only make it halfway down before my wrist is seized and I'm swung around. Pain radiates up my arm, his hot skin heating my wounds, and I hiss. I expect him to drop his hold. He doesn't. I expect him to apologize. He doesn't. I look up at him, damn tears clouding my vision.

"Maybe you're right, Beau." He takes a few steps down, maintaining his hold, until he's looking up at me. "Let's just fuck. Every morning. Every evening. All fucking day, let's just fuck."

"Fuck you," I whisper, my treacherous body singing for him. Begging. "So you can build a library of videos of us?"

"I didn't hear you complaining when I got you off while we watched it together. I bet you weren't complaining when you fucked yourself with your fingers when you watched it alone."

I blink, looking away.

"Don't turn away from me." He grabs my cheeks and forces my face to his. His eyes are raging. His body poised, ready to pounce. "It's time to show your hand, Beau. What do you want from me?"

"Escape."

"Why?"

My teeth grind under his fierce grip. "I want escape, and I don't want to be forced into explaining why. What do you want from me, James?"

"Peace."

I recoil, stunned, and my eyes fall to his shoulder where his scarred skin ends and the perfect, flawless flesh of his chest begins. "What happened to you?" I whisper.

"I got caught up in an explosion."

My body jolts, staggering back, and I grab the handrail to keep me upright. James's hand falls from my face, and I gaze at him, shocked to my core. An explosion. My arm is suddenly burning, my head invaded by screams. And in James's eyes, I see a replay of the scene, of frantic people running, escaping the fireballs bursting up to the nighttime sky. Escaping the vicinity of the car I'd got out of only ten minutes before. The car where my mom burned to nothing. I look at my scar that pales in comparison to the beast coating James's back. And shame grabs me. Shame I can't bear. "How?" I whisper.

He removes himself, stepping down a few more stairs, putting too much space between us. "Right place, wrong time," he replies stoically, and I can see with perfect clarity that he's struggling to talk. Which begs the question why he's been so adamant about sharing secrets. "Do you want to know more?" he asks, offering to kill my curiosity with information that I honestly don't know if I want. Or, selfishly, can handle. And, again, will I be expected to reciprocate?

I know nothing right now, nothing at all. Except one thing. I extend my hand, my lip quivering, and wait for him to accept it, and he does, slowly, watching as our bodies come together again, albeit only our hands. It doesn't matter. It's still earthmoving. I move in, taking the steps down to meet him, and curl my arm around his neck, burying my face there. It's not an answer to his question. James knows that. I'm simply instigating what we both need. To give each other control.

He slips his forearm under my ass, lifts me to him, and carries me back to his room, placing me gently on his bed. He crawls up, spreading his body over mine, and my hands circle his back and stroke over his scars as he draws faint lines up and down my damaged arm.

I doze off to the sound of James's light breathing close to my ear, his lips on my throat.

His soul blending with mine.

39

BEAU

I wake with my cheek on James's chest, the sun rising over the buildings, the weight of my thoughts still heavy on my mind. I gently ease myself up, being careful not to wake him, and I stand at the edge of his bed watching him. He looks so peaceful. So serene. Every muscle on his face is relaxed, smooth, nothing cutting his features or tarnishing his handsomeness. Last night, something altered between us. Understanding. Yet, ironically, I don't think either of us know what we're trying to understand.

Pulling my eyes away from him, I find a T-shirt and pull it on as I go down to the kitchen, collecting my strewn clothes and purse as I pass, checking my cell, certain I'll have plenty of missed calls from Lawrence. I'm wrong. There's nothing. My mind wanders to the standoff outside the house last night, to my uncle's face. The disappointment. The judgment.

I sigh, flicking on the coffee machine, looking out of the window, following the path of a bird as it flies across the tops of some nearby buildings, gliding gracefully, swooping and climbing. Swooping and climbing. So free.

The machine churns in the background, and I rest my forearms on the counter, my eyes circling, following the bird. Its moves seem to become more elaborate, its swoops lower, its loops bigger, like it's aware I'm watching. My own private performance.

I'm mesmerized.

And then the coffee machine beeps, and I'm yanked from my trance, seeing steam rising and dissipating. I look back to the view. The bird is gone. Flown away.

Fly away.

I glance around the kitchen, to the endless frosted glass cupboards, and start opening them in search of cups. The first reveals stacks of glass plates and bowls. The second endless glasses. The third glass coffee cups. Glass. So much glass, so much transparency. Is it indicative of the man asleep upstairs?

I got caught up in an explosion.

I feel awful for wishing he hadn't told me. It makes it all too real. Makes me more curious. It also deepens the connection that I'm feeling, and that's not good. His burn is of a similar severity as mine, but bigger. So much bigger. A deep partial thickness burn. One layer of skin away from destroying nerve-endings. I often thought that would have been a blessing. No nerves, no pain. Instead, we both endured excruciating agony, and now unsightly scars. *We're the same.*

I bite my lip, pondering that, as I make two coffees, finding my way around his kitchen with relative ease. When I make it back to the bedroom, James is still sound asleep. I place his cup on the nightstand and take mine to the window. I feel like an ant, surrounded by giant buildings. Not seen. But so very exposed.

I hear movement behind me and turn with my cup to my lips, finding James propped up against the headboard. I smile mildly over my coffee. He swallows, casting his eyes to the side, finding his own. "Did you sleep well?" he asks, raking a hand through his bedhead before reaching for his cup.

"Too good." I pad over and settle on the side of the bed, unable to resist a leisurely jaunt with my eyes up his bare chest. "You?"

He takes a sip of his drink, resting back. "Too good," he replies, taking me in, quietly observant. "What are you doing today?"

"I don't know. What are you doing?"

He releases a hand from his cup and takes one of mine, caressing the back of it slowly. "I have a few errands to run. You could hang out here if you like."

"I should probably go make peace with my uncle."

His lips twist a fraction, but he nods, if mildly. "And later?"

I study him, unable to hold back a small smile. I feel like he's taking the long route to where he wants to be. Where I want to be too. "Would you like to do something?" I ask, looking at his thumb circling the top of my hand.

"Like?"

"Opera we won't watch," I say, peeking up for his reaction.

"Or dinner we won't eat?" Naturally, there's no reference to Goldie. "Or asking questions we won't answer." He hitches a brow, and I discreetly roll my eyes, pulling my hand free and standing, setting my cup down.

"I saw that," he says lowly.

"You were supposed to," I counter, heading into his bathroom. "What errands do you have to run?" I ask, the question falling out of my mouth. I stop at the threshold of his bathroom and frown to myself. I can feel his eyes on my back. "Never mind."

"I have a safety deposit account I need to close," he says, almost tentatively.

"Why?"

"Because I don't need it anymore."

"Do people even have safety deposit boxes these days?"

"I do."

I turn to face him. "And what do you keep in it?"

He raises his brows at my annoying curiosity. "Personal effects. You don't have one?"

"A safety deposit box? No." I have nothing sacred worth hiding in a safety deposit box. I pick up my feet and go to the sink, splashing my face and ruffing up my hair as I take in my reflection. I look . . . rested, which defies reason when my mind is racing with endless questions.

As I pat my face dry, James appears past me in the mirror, his coffee in his hand. He holds my eyes as he sips. I don't like the assessment I'm under. The judgments being made. I feel like he's taunting me. Goading me, tempting me. The air around us feels awkward, and that's not what I'm here for. "I'll leave you to your day," I say, placing the towel on the unit and approaching him. He doesn't move from the doorway, his big body filling it, blocking me. I stop before him, virtually toe to toe, and I tilt my head back to get him in my sights. "Excuse me." I sound assertive. I feel anything but.

His gaze lingers on me for a while, until he slowly moves aside, letting me pass. I collect my shoes and hurry down the stairs, locating my dress and shimmying it on. I press the call button as I fasten the zip, and the doors open.

I step in.

Turn around.

He's in the elevator with me, his naked, imposing frame crowding me.

I step back until my back meets the wall. I can feel the pounds of my heart in my stomach. Can feel my skin sizzling under his closeness. Dipping slowly, eyes glued to mine, he pushes our mouths together and moans. I give him immediate access, opening up to him, speaking in a language he understands. His warm tongue is soft, his lips firm. I taste coffee. I taste all man. This kiss has purpose. It has meaning. My body reacts, and just as I'm about to climb him and take it to the next level, beg him to take me back to his bed, he pulls away, panting, and wipes his mouth with the back of his hand, leaving me stumbling back into the wall, dazed. *This is what I crave.* This freedom from pain, from thinking, from grieving.

This release.

"Call me later," he orders softly, backing out of the elevator, tilting his head, waiting for my compliance.

He doesn't need it.

The doors close, and I urgently pull air into my lungs. "I will," I say to myself.

Of course I will.

I've never stood outside Lawrence's house for so long, just staring at the door. Dreading what's waiting for me inside. This house has always been a haven. Now? Now it feels like a cage of discrimination. On a needed injection of bravery, I slip my key into the lock and turn it tentatively, pushing my way inside. I hear them in the kitchen, knives and forks scraping their plates as they eat their breakfast. I glance up the stairs. I could go straight up. Hide. Delay facing their looks of disapproval.

No.

I drop my keys in the glass bowl on the table, making a loud clang, and the sounds of metal scraping on plates stops. I wander down the hallway into the kitchen and go straight to the fridge, and their eyes follow me the whole way. "Morning," I say.

"Morning," Dexter replies, sounding tentative. "Nice evening?"

I grab a bottle of water and twist the cap off as I turn to face them. "Lovely," I reply simply. *And mysterious. And curiosity inducing. And enlightening.* Uncle Lawrence regards me for a few, uncomfortable moments, taking in my lace dress. Then he goes back to his breakfast without a word. The silent treatment. I give Dexter tired eyes, and he smiles tightly.

"You could have been civil," I say, taking a seat at the table, my focus on Lawrence. If he wants to be a child, fine, but I won't be a child with him. Dexter shifts on the chair, setting down his cutlery before standing. Lawrence pretends like I'm not even here. "Lawrence, come on."

"Don't ask me for my blessing." He pushes his plate away. "I tried, but I cannot bless . . ." He fades off and turns his eyes onto my wrists.

"One of the things I love most about you is your open-mindedness." I get up from the table, knowing I'm fighting a losing battle. He needs to pull his head out of his ass. "But right now, you're behaving like my father." I turn and walk out, just catching sight of his horrified expression and Dexter's blank face.

"I am nothing like your father."

"Then stop being so narrow-minded," I call, taking the stairs. "I'm a big girl. I know how to say no."

"Then say no!" he yells, sounding unusually frazzled. "There must be better ways to let loose."

"Better?" I laugh. "I know where you keep your bondage gear, Lawrence." I turn at the top of the stairs, hearing him scuttling down the hallway.

"I do not have bondage gear."

"No?" I ask.

"No."

I shake my head and make tracks to their bedroom, letting myself in and zooming in on the French cabinet I shifted not too long ago so I could decorate. I yank a drawer open and swipe up the leather crotchless panties. "No?" I ask again, waving them over my head. Then I grab the bra that sports more spikes than a porcupine. "No?"

He lands in the doorway and assesses my finds. "They're

Zinnea's," he barks, marching toward me and swiping them from my grasp, stuffing them back into the drawer and slamming it shut.

"I guess this is too?" I ask, seizing a whip. "Don't tell me this doesn't cause injuries."

He gasps, his mouth falling open. "That's Dexter's."

"Hey, leave me out of it," he calls from downstairs.

"Don't judge me," I warn, sidestepping him and leaving the room. "Next time you see James, be nice," I order, turning at the door, following up my words with a stern look. I've never seen my uncle shrink before. It's a novelty.

"So you'll be seeing him again?"

"Maybe."

His nose wrinkles. "I don't know why you can't date a normal man."

Like Ollie. Kind. Sweet. *Normal.* "Are any of us normal, Lawrence?" I ask. "Do you consider men who never dress as women and don't have a stage name normal, Lawrence? Are you not a prime example of someone who can accept and enjoy things that others cannot?" He sighs, looking down, probably trying to find the perfect counter. "Everyone is a certain level of fucked up. Leave me to be blissfully fucked up, will you? Because you don't understand what *fucking* someone who isn't into missionary gives me. It might only be temporary, but I'm taking it because it gives me moments where I'm not lost or grieving or angry. And surely I deserve that. Surely."

His entire being shrinks. "I'm hearing you, Beau. I just want you to be okay. I love you."

"I love you too. And Dexter. I'd be lost without you both. You know that. But judging me or the men I see is not supporting me. It's just making me feel like shit."

He looks ashamed. "I'm sorry."

I nod and carry on to my room, shutting the door, and start

wrestling my way out of my dress, turning in circles to find the zip. My eyes land on the piles of apartment details.

I forget the zip and drop onto my bed, scooping up the stack and starting to flick through. And, weirdly, most of the properties I'd previously dismissed suddenly aren't so bad anymore. One in particular is giving me good vibes, a lovely two-bed top-floor apartment in Biscayne Bay. I pout when my stomach performs a little flip. Excitement?

I grab my cell and call the agent. "Hi, my name's Beau Hayley. I'm interested in viewing a property you're marketing."

"Sure," the guy replies. "Can I ask what your position is? Anything to sell?"

"Nothing."

"And are you financing through a bank? Mortgage?"

"I'm a cash buyer."

"Available this afternoon?"

I smile and stand, reaching back for my zip again. "I'd prefer late evening." And not only because it'll keep me busy while I try to avoid gravitating back toward James's apartment. It's time to take some positive steps.

On my own.

40

JAMES

"What is she doing there?" I ask Goldie as I scan the beach, watching the busy space as I sit, relaxed, sipping a coffee, my laptop before me.

"Right now, she's admiring the water."

She's not at home. She's not at the supermarket. She's not at the diner or at my place. She's out there, exposed, and that makes me feel immensely uncomfortable. "I don't think Beau knows about a safety deposit box."

"She must know," Goldie says. "Her mother surely left everything to her."

"Well, I pressed as best I could without rousing suspicion and got nothing." What if Beau doesn't know Jaz left a key for it? What if she's completely unaware? "Watch her until I get there," I order, my eyes falling to the two beach chairs not too far away, each with a beach towel laid across them and a suitcase nestled in between. "Closely."

"Got it. How's it going?"

"I'm watching." I look up when a man approaches my table, his feet shuffling, his face overgrown, his clothes tattered. "I've got to go." I set my mobile on the table, scanning the area.

"Got a spare smoke?" he asks, motioning to my full packet of Marlboros on the table.

"No," I answer flatly, going to my laptop. I feel tense, and it isn't because of this exchange with my new contact.

"You have, right there, look."

I glance up at him. "You want a cigarette?" I ask, picking up the packet, passing it from hand to hand.

"Yeah."

I hold them out. "Here."

He falters, unsure, and slowly takes them as I cast my eyes across the sand. I reach into my pocket and drag out some notes, slapping them on the table and setting my lighter on top. "You want this too?"

He slips the smokes in the pocket of his tatty coat. "What are you, my guardian angel?"

I smile. "One good deed deserves another. There's two beach chairs down there with yellow towels. Bring me the suitcase that's in between them. Simple."

His greedy eyes rest on the pile of money. "That's it?"

"That's it."

He shrugs and leaves, ambling down to the beach, and I rest back, collecting my coffee and sipping, watching him. He plods through the sand, moves in on the case, and starts to drag it away from the chairs.

And as I predicted, two guys nearby abandon their volleyball game and move in, flanking the down-and-out on either side, escorting him from the beach.

My lip naturally curls, I snap my laptop shut, swipe up my cash and lighter, and leave the café casually, dialing Goldie. "Trap," I say, not looking back.

"Surprised?"

"Not at all." A criminal that's *not* in The Bear's pocket seems to be a rarity.

So I'm rare, but, frankly, the Russian, Sandy, is the least of my worries right now. Knowing Beau's out there is making me uneasy. Her predictability has been a comfort. And while a sense of pride fills me, because she's getting braver, more like her old self, I never considered how that might make me feel.

Nervous.

I have a purpose to rid Miami of the sewer rats. I don't feel like control has ever slipped from my fingers, and yet, as Beau stirs back to life, I feel like I'm dancing on a double-edged sword.

Either way I fall, it'll be the end of me.

41

BEAU

I stand on the edge of the bay at seven fifteen, leaning against one of the railings, taking in the magnificent sight. The walkway lining the water at the foot of the apartment block is wide and spacious, the people still milling having plenty of room to hurry to wherever they're going. Little cafés and a few restaurants spill out onto the pedestrianized area, and benches are dotted sporadically along the route. The water is peaceful, boats chugging up and down, and the chaos of the city seems so far away. It's more perfect than I thought.

Finishing my latte, I toss my cup in a trash can, fishing my cell out of my purse when it rings, as I wander to the apartment block entrance. I inhale and answer. "James."

"Where are you?" he snaps.

I recoil, slowing to a stop, taken aback. "I didn't realize I needed to run every move I make past you," I retort, hanging up on him, outraged. "Asshole," I grumble, forcing my feet into moving, trying to locate my earlier excitement. I only make it a few paces before he's calling me again. I lift my palm to my forehead, rubbing, squeezing my eyes closed. *God damn him. And God damn* me. I answer with silence.

"I'm sorry," he breathes. "I didn't mean to sound so curt."

"Bad day?" What did he do? What were those errands?

"Had better," he says, only making those questions circle faster. "So where are you?"

"Why?"

"Because I want to see you."

"What about what I want?" I retort. It's stupid, but I won't let him believe I'm at his beck and call, however much I'd love to be his cure for everything. *But nothing could cure those scars.*

"Stop it, Beau," he says tiredly. "Where are you?"

"Biscayne Bay."

"Why?"

"I'm viewing an apartment." My declaration receives silence in reply. "I thought it was about time I moved on from Lawrence and Dexter's." I don't want to even imagine the reaction I'll get from my uncle. He won't see this as a good thing. Not now that he's met James.

"Interesting."

"Why's that interesting?" I ask, scowling at the ground.

"What time's your viewing?"

"In ten minutes."

"I'll be there. Send me the address."

"What?" I blurt. "But it'll take you over half an hour to get here from your place."

"Who said I'm at my place?"

My shoulders straighten, and I start circling on the spot, my eyes scoping the space around me. It wouldn't be the first time James has followed me. "Where are you?" I ask, suddenly feeling like I'm being watched, the hairs on my neck standing on end.

"Just dealing with some business."

I laugh under my breath. "That didn't answer my question." And it sounds very dubious.

"Send me the address, Beau," he orders before hanging up.

I slowly, reluctantly, tap out a message to him, all the while wondering . . . what the hell is going on here? Not the weird stuff, the curiosity, the mysterious happenings. But between James and me? I'm looking at an apartment to buy, and he wants to come. Why?

I ponder that while I wait outside the foyer of the block, my mind turning in circles. Does he want to give his approval? Check everything is in order? I spin my cell in my grasp, checking left and right, keeping an eye out for him.

"Miss Hayley?"

I swing around toward the doors, finding a young hip guy in a suit so tight it's *got* to be uncomfortable. "You must be Dean."

His eyes light up. "Pleasure to meet you." He takes my extended hand and holds it for too long for my liking, the dollar signs virtually pinging into his eyes. I know what he's thinking. He's thinking young cash buyer, and I'm here alone. I'm not being presumptuous. "Likewise," I say without thinking, flexing my fingers for him to release me.

"Oh." He drops my hold, and I smile awkwardly. "Shall we?" He swoops his arm out toward the door, and I look over my shoulder, searching for James.

"Actually, I'm just waiting for my . . ." I snap my mouth closed. My what? "Friend," I finish, finding no sign of James.

"We can let her up when she arrives," Dean suggests, encouraging me into the lobby. His smile is going to break his face if he doesn't ease it a bit. "So there's a twenty-four-hour concierge," he says, indicating the desk, where a middle-aged guy sits, looking utterly bored. Now *that* is a concierge. Otto is definitely no concierge. Dean pushes the button for an elevator and stands back, giving me a cheesy grin. "I'm assuming security is important."

"Why?" I ask, stepping in when it arrives, Dean joining me.

He falters, looking incredibly awkward. "Well." He coughs. "Isn't it for everyone?" Another cheesy grin. He dug himself out of that one quite speedily.

"Oh," I say, looking up at the panel that's ticking up through the floors. "I assumed you meant because I'm a single female."

"God, no." He laughs. "I'm a modern man, Miss Hayley."

I smile to myself, wondering what the hell a modern man is. I won't ask. I can't bear to see him squirming.

The doors open, and I step out, looking up and down the corridor. It's clean. Tidy. A bit soulless, but it's just a corridor.

"Last door on the right." Dean lets me lead on, and I expect it's all part of his modern-man philosophy.

We reach a solid wooden door, and the number 7 on a plaque on the wall to the side sparkles.

"Lucky for some," he says as he slips the key into the lock and pushes it open, entering first. He's taking this modern man thing too far now. "The owner is away on business, so we have the place all to ourselves." Another cheesy grin.

"Great." I step inside and gaze around, my eyes naturally falling to the floor-to-ceiling windows on one side. It's not quite the level of James's floating glass box, but it's probably about as much as I can expect for my budget. "Amazing view," I say, approaching the glass and taking in the skyline.

Dean joins me, holding out an envelope. "The details."

I accept, despite already having them. "What's the owner's position?" I ask, backing up and heading to the kitchen space across the room.

"He's not in a rush to sell."

I smile, opening a few cupboards. Translated: don't try to knock him down on the price. "But I'm a cash buyer and ready to move quickly," I point out, running the tap. "That carries some appeal, right, Dean?"

He chuckles lightly, resting his leather folder on the island. "Like I said, he's in no rush, but I'm sure I can work my magic for you, Beau."

So it's *Beau* now? "Assuming it's what I want," I say, wandering to the back of the apartment, taking in the spacious but cozy lounge as I go. It needs redecorating; the walls are scuffed and a bit grubby. "The bedrooms are this way?"

"Yes, with two very generous bathrooms."

I enter the master and am pleasantly surprised by the size. "Good space," I muse, walking around the cream rug.

"The bathroom is just through there."

I follow his pointed hand, entering. He wasn't kidding. Very generous. The walk-in shower is minimal, just a sheet of glass fixed to the tile and anchored to the wall by a silver bar.

"So what do you think?" Dean asks, standing in the doorway.

I hold back my thoughts, tampering down my enthusiasm. "It's got potential," I say quietly, running my palm across the wood-veneer vanity unit.

"Can I ask what you do, Beau?" he asks, sweeping a hand through his slick hair. What do I do? Good question. Currently, I'm floating between heaven and hell. Usually, I'd be distracting myself with some painting, although not much of that has happened of late. I must finish James's office.

My cell rings, saving me from Dean's question, and I take James's call as I peek in the mirror-fronted cupboard hanging over the sink. "Hey, I'm in the apartment. Head into the lobby." I close the door of the cupboard and turn toward Dean, who nods and gets straight onto his cell, calling the concierge.

"Yes, show her up." He cuts the call and slips his cell into his pocket. "I'll let her in."

"Thanks." I follow him out of the bedroom on a smile,

wickedly looking forward to the moment when Dean learns that *she* is in fact a *he*. A big *he*. An impressive *he*. A fierce *he*. We wander through the open living area, and I hear the sound of an impatient knock as we pass the kitchen.

I hover to the side of Dean as he swings the door open, smiling brightly. "Hi, I'm . . ." His head tilts back, and he reverses his steps, his smile falling.

"This is my friend," I say, biting my lip furiously to restrain my smile. "James, this is Dean, the real estate agent."

James gives me a narrowed eye when he catches the amusement I'm doing a terrible job of hiding. Nor the thrill of how ruggedly handsome he looks in trousers and a shirt, open at the collar. He's dressed rather smart for errands on a Saturday.

James grunts, looking nothing short of pissed off, giving Dean a glare paired with a curled lip. Poor Dean doesn't know where to look, his persona changing in an instant.

"What do you think?" I ask James, trying to distract him from whatever's gotten under his skin today. It could be me. I don't know. It probably is.

"I think I need a tour," he says quietly, wandering over to the kitchen. I follow, a little wary. "Has he made a move on you?" he asks, not nearly quietly enough, nothing but displeasure on his face.

I tilt my head. "Would that be a problem?"

"Yes." He doesn't beat around the bush, scowling over his shoulder, and I glance back, seeing Dean's smile is now more nervous than cheesy. "That would be a huge problem."

"Why?" I ask, not certain that I want the answer.

James looks at me in question, definitely wondering the same as me. Do I want to know? Is this another bout of jealously? Something tells me I'm about to find out. "Beau and I are going to take another look around," he says to Dean, eyes still on me. That gaze is threatening. And electrifying. I start to shift on my feet, and James doesn't miss it.

"Sure." Dean lowers to a stool. "Take your time."

"I will." James cocks his head at me, and I inhale, my chest expanding. My waning stability becomes ricketier as he seizes my hand and pulls me, and I feel Dean's stare follow us.

"The TV room," I say as he tugs me through, my skin tingling, preparing, bracing for his touch.

"Lovely."

"The view." I look over my shoulder, smiling awkwardly when I discover Dean looking at us, alarmed.

"Great," James mutters.

"The dining area." I blindly point at the table and chairs I know to be somewhere in this vicinity.

"Amazing." He drags me on, unperturbed.

"James," I hiss as Dean disappears from view and I'm yanked into the master bedroom. "Bedroom," I breathe, and James releases my hand and places a palm on my shoulder, walking me forward. To the bathroom. I hear the buckle of his belt clang, and then the unmistakable sound of it being pulled free of the belt loops of his trousers. *Oh Jesus.* My mind is yelling at me to stop this, but my body is absolutely begging for him. "Bathroom," I whisper on a shaky breath when we enter, hearing the door close. My purse slips from my hold, hitting the floor, and when I glance at the mirror, he's looming behind me, looking ready to strike. Jealousy. Possessiveness. It's written all over him, and I'm wary of it.

His eyes turn to something, and I read him, following his gaze to the solid metal bar that's suspended from the ceiling, attaching the shower screen to the wall. I'm damned if I can say no. And he looks far from prepared to accept a refusal, anyway.

I wander across to the shower and stand below the bar, raising my arms, and his chest is pushed to my front in a second, his hands working expertly and blindly above me, his intentions burning holes in me as he stares, daring me to back out. I won't. Can't. There's no room to consider where we are. Not past the inexorable lust. I'm out of my mind on James, and that's the best kind of crazy I've ever felt. And, strangely, I realize what's about to happen isn't intended to release *me* from anger, from pain, from fear. But him? This will be a possessive fuck. *He* needs *me.* But just fucking someone shouldn't involve possessiveness or jealousy.

The warm leather of his belt rubs against my wrists, and I look up to see my hands bundled together, bound above my head. I breathe out. It's wobbly, my heart thrashing double time. I feel James's palm frame my cheek, and I let my gaze lower. I've never seen so much conviction in a stare. The agent could breeze on in here at any moment, although after encountering James, he might think twice. But that could be part of the game for James. The risk. He said it himself. I know firsthand that being watched isn't a problem for him.

Jesus, what am I doing?

"Did you miss me?" he asks, dragging his fingers down to the buttons of my shirt. He starts unfastening them one by one as I battle to find some air and some words. "Beau?" His hands stop, his head tilts, his eyes blaze. *Demand*. He's not rushing. He really couldn't give two fucks if Dean walks in on us. "Did you miss me?"

"I missed *this,*" I say quietly. Today was as long as a day could be. I was restless, my thoughts chaotic, jumping between James, Lawrence, Zinnea, and whether Nath has found out anything about Mom yet.

"*This* is me," he says roughly. "*This* is us."

"What are you saying?"

He pulls my shirt open and yanks the cups of my bra down, and I jerk, harder still when he takes my breasts and molds firmly. "I'm saying there is no *this* if there is no *us*." He undoes the fly of his trousers, unfastens a few more buttons of his shirt and pulls it over his head, and then works my fly, tugging my jeans down my legs to my ankles, leaving them there, effectively restraining my feet too. I look at the ceiling, every brain cell consumed by a need inside simmering dangerously, ready to bubble over and have me screaming his name. But I still manage to read between the lines of his words. What he's saying, James-style, is that only *he* can do this to me. No other man. No one. Only him.

"What are you going to do?" I pant, knowing there's no chance of penetration when my legs are unable to spread. "Tell me what you're going to do." I need to prepare. It's a crazy claim. I could never be prepared for James. But always ready. Always willing.

When he doesn't answer, I find him again. His thick cock rests in his hand, being stroked slowly, every muscle in his chest rolling smoothly. "Oh God," I breathe, knowing the level of torture I'm about to face, restrained, unable to touch him *or* myself. This won't be escape. This will be hell. "James." I look at him with pleading eyes, shaking my head. I will have to depend on him, and something tells me he's not in an accommodating mood. I'm blaming Dean. Or James for being unreasonably possessive.

His smirk is salacious. Dirty. It's knowing. "I want you all to myself," he whispers, guiding himself to the juncture of my thighs and slipping the throbbing head of his erection across my pulsing flesh. I cry out, bowing violently, straining against my bonds. "Is *that* a problem, Beau?"

"Stop," I beg, as he circles my clit with his cock, his free hand grabbing my jaw.

"You want me to stop?" he asks, slipping his thumb past my lips and circling my tongue. "Then say my name."

"Which one?" I gasp, and then yelp when he changes the direction of his flesh slipping on mine, pushing closer toward my opening.

"The name you know."

My internal walls scream, trying to grab his cock and pull it in, trying to get the friction it needs. My jaw tightens, my eyes narrowing. "Stop it," I order. He knows I'm not telling him to stop *this*. I'm ordering him to stop purposely fueling my intrigue.

"You stop it," he counters, tackling my mouth hard, fisting my hair at my nape, holding me steady as he starts increasing the friction between my legs, driving me wild. The feel of his arousal, firm but soft, plays havoc with my nerve-endings, tickling them, teasing them. Our tongues tussle, our teeth clash, our moans collide. "You're burning up down there, Beau," he pants, biting at my lip and returning to my mouth, continuing the clumsy, frenzied kiss.

Heat sweeps through me, working its way to my head. My muscles start to stiffen. My mouth becomes urgent on his, my arms yanking and pulling at the restraints, my legs solid. I'm going to come so hard, and there isn't a doubt that Dean will hear it. "James," I say in warning, though all the signs tell him.

The friction is suddenly gone, his mouth missing from mine, and I growl my frustration as my orgasm retreats. He reaches down and yanks my jeans off, taking my flip-flops with them, and then seizes behind my thighs and yanks me onto him. He slips into me with no guiding. No holding. No encouragement.

"Yes," I whisper, my forehead falling onto his shoulder. "Yes, yes, yes."

He groans, holding still, and the feel of him beating inside of me brings my vanishing orgasm back with a vengeance. "How are your arms?" he asks, his voice still hard.

"Numb," I admit. Every ounce of blood in me seems to have gone to my head and my core. "Finish it," I order, and he rolls teasingly, turning his face into my neck and kissing me way too softly.

"This will never be finished," he murmurs.

I open my eyes, gazing across the bathroom to the door. "Good." I lift my head, turning into his face, finding his eyes. I see too much freedom in his gaze. Too many promises. And too many secrets. I hold his stare, lowering my mouth to his and nibbling at his lip. He quickly turns it into a kiss, and then gets moving again, thrusting into me steadily and firmly, no rushing, no urgency. But my release soon comes, and when James's fingers dig into my thighs, his hips becoming rigid, I know he's with me. It seems to hit us simultaneously, and we both jerk and whimper, prisoners to the pleasure. Our bodies roll. Our groans meld. James chokes a little, releasing one hand and grabbing the rail above us, clinging on, holding us both up, as our rolls transform into shakes and our groans become broken rather than smooth, the nerves of my clitoris pounding, my walls squeezing him unforgivingly.

He stills, and I become limp, the strain on my wrists becoming painful. The sound of our labored breathing is golden. "It's a no from me," he pants into my shoulder, and I sigh drowsily.

"You don't like it?"

"No."

"What's not to like?"

He peels his skin from mine and lowers me to my feet, reaching up to the leather holding me in place. "You living alone, that's what's not to like." My hands are quickly free, and they fall like lead to my sides. I wince, and it doesn't escape James's notice. Taking an arm in turn, he starts massaging some life back into them, checking the welts, which are red and raw again. "I don't see why you don't just stay with your uncle. What's the rush?"

"There's no rush, hence I've been at Lawrence's for nearly two years."

"Then what's the problem?" He looks up at me, and I detect something in his cool eyes I haven't seen before. Worry. I'm sure it's worry. I'm surprised James is encouraging me to stay with Lawrence after my uncle was so rude to him. So, is there more to this?

"There wasn't a problem, but now you've made me feel like there *is* a problem." I gently pull my arm from his hold and find my jeans, pulling them on while I watch him closely. "You're making me suspicious," I admit, but what I could be suspicious of is beyond me. He's a stockbroker, for God's sake. Wealthy, lives in a glass castle, has cameras *everywhere,* fucks random women with no apology. Everything I learn about James results in more intrigue, and it's getting to the point I'm losing the battle against my head, which is telling me to keep my mouth and ears shut. *Just take what you need, Beau. Take that and nothing else.* "Is there a problem?"

James fastens his trousers and gets his shirt back on, tucking it in. "Why are you asking if there's a problem? Because if there is, you're going to tell me you don't want to know what the problem is." His lips straighten, and my eyes narrow.

"I fucking hate your riddles." I fasten the buttons of my shirt with a heavy hand, and James stares at me as he coils the belt in his hands.

"They're not riddles, Beau." He steps into me and kisses me gently, nibbling his way across my lips. "But if they were, the answers are right here waiting for you."

I get lost in his attention. It's a given. "Do you hate how much I don't want to know?" I ask around his mouth, looping an arm around his neck.

"No, I hate how much I want to tell you." My ass is seized, and I'm pulled up his body, my legs wrapping around his waist. I pull back and get his face in my sights. His gorgeous, manly, handsome face. I drop a kiss on the corner of his otherworldly lips and sweep my hands through his waves. And as I'm breathing him into me, relaxed, my mind seems to open and piece together the endless things James has said.

His other name. How much he wants to tell me. How he thinks I'm getting more than I bargained for. His errands today.

Oh my God.

It's so fucking obvious, I don't know how I didn't consider it before.

I stare at the wall past his shoulder, my twisted thoughts all straightening out.

He's a dad. He has a kid.

I pull away and look at him in question, my mind spinning at one hundred miles an hour. How did I miss this? He hates how much he wants to tell me, because sharing that part of his life is a serious business—something a man would only do if he was thinking of introducing someone to their child. Right? Is he thinking of introducing me? And what does that mean? Me? A kid? Fucking hell, I couldn't inflict my gloom on a child.

I try to detach myself from him, but he stands firm, keeping me hanging from his torso, dipping to get my purse from the floor. Then he turns and walks out, and I catch sight of the fogged mirror. My face is distorted. Blurry. Unclear.

I don't bother telling him to put me down. I don't think I can walk anyway, not after that orgasm, and not while my mind is so focused on my latest revelation.

"It's a no," James says to Dean as he carries me through the apartment.

Dean's face is a picture as he stands from the stool, walking slowly into the middle of the room as he watches us leave. I raise a hand and offer a small, guilty smile before the wood of the door comes between us.

Only once we're in the elevator does James put me down. "What's up?" he asks, assessing me closely, blindly hitting the button for the first floor. I don't like it. Not at all. I can't look at him. Being involved with a man who's a dad is no joke. It carries responsibilities. I'm not equipped. God damn it, and I feel awful for thinking it, but I'm pissed off. Pissed off that he's ruined the illusion. Tarnished my escape.

"Nothing." I thank all the gods when my cell rings. Nath's name on my screen fills me with dread and relief all at once. "Excuse me," I say to James, stepping off the elevator when the doors open. "I need to take this." I wander to the seats in the lobby, but I don't sit down. "Nath?"

"Hey, you free?" he blurts, no greeting, no enquiry into how I am.

I'm not imagining it, he sounds tense, and Nath doesn't do tense. He's as cool as a man can come. "Now?"

"Yes, now."

"Is everything okay?"

"I don't know," he says, and I feel every muscle in my body harden.

"Is this about Mom?"

"Can you meet me at mine?"

"Why your place?" I have never, not ever, met Nath at his place. In fact, I don't think I've ever stepped foot in his house. I've picked him up. I've waited outside while he went in to fetch something. But I've never been inside. He's always claimed it's too messy, that he's ashamed of how undomesticated he is.

"An hour," he says, not answering me. I glance at my screen, seriously disliking the pinching feeling all over my skin. He sounded out of breath. Stressed.

"Okay?" James asks, approaching with caution.

"Yeah." I back away, and even though I don't like the call with Nath, it's a perfect excuse for me to gain some space from James to get my thoughts in line. "A friend needs me. I have to go."

He can't disguise his displeasure. Or his suspicion. But I have to make him believe it's nothing much, because the alternative will open a whole can of worms that I absolutely do not want to share with James. "Man trouble." I shrug lamely. "Call you later?"

He looks shell-shocked. "Sure," he replies, gathering himself. "Can I drop you anywhere?"

"I have my car." I point aimlessly to a wall. "Up the road, but thanks." This is getting more awkward by the second, and in an effort to try and kill it, I step forward and kiss his cheek, a better attempt to convince him that I'm fine. I'm not fine. Not at all.

I only intended to make it chaste, but James grabs me and

holds me close, deepening our connection. I'm literally a prisoner in his arms. I try so hard to match his soft swirling tongue, but my mind is elsewhere, and I never would have thought it possible while James kissed me. It's disheartening on so many levels, because isn't it the whole fucking point of seeing him?

"I have to go," I whisper, wedging my palms into his chest and pushing him back.

I turn. Walk away.

And I don't look back.

42

JAMES

I'm left in the lobby of the building with a scowl bigger than Miami. What the fuck just happened? I don't waste too much time wondering. I follow her, keeping a safe distance. She rounds a corner, her pace hurried, and I watch in fascination as she constantly zigzags from one side of the road to the other. She crosses the street three times by the time she's made it to the end of the road. She's avoiding the crowded pavement. Removing herself from the busy sides of the street as and when needed. And she wants to live here?

She zips around the corner, and when I make it there, she's halfway up the next street. I spot her clapped-out muscle car in the distance. "Shit," I mutter, mentally locating my own car. Half a mile away. I pull out my mobile and call Goldie, spewing my exact location.

"I'm two minutes away," she says.

"Make it one." I glance up and down the street, assessing my situation. Beau will be gone in less than a minute, even in that old jalopy she calls a car. "Fuck." I spot a grocery store across the road, the outside lined with carts of fresh fruit and veg.

Stall her.

I rush over, grab the side of a cart, and upend it, sending the endless piles of fruit spilling into the road. I hear the sound of brakes immediately, a cab screeching to a halt in the middle of the road, its horn blaring. The traffic is soon backed up, Beau's car trapped in its parking space. I go back to my phone, dialing Goldie as I pace up the street. "Come in on the north end." By the time I've made it to the end of the street, keeping close to the buildings, Goldie is stuck ten cars back in the jam.

I hop in the passenger seat.

"What's going on?" she asks, crawling forward with the traffic, craning her neck to see down the street.

"Not a fucking clue. She was fine, she took a call, and then she bolted." I motion to her car up front, the nose butting out of the space.

"And what was she doing here?"

"Looking at an apartment she won't be buying." I pull on my belt as Goldie starts to creep forward. I can feel her worried attention splitting between me and the road. "Don't say a thing."

"Fuck you," she says on a laugh. "What are you thinking?"

Thinking? Am I thinking at all? My mind is as tangled as fuck. "Just follow her," I mutter as the traffic breaks and we start to pick up speed. Someone up front give's Beau the right of way, and she pulls out, startling everyone within half a mile radius when her car backfires.

"Fuck me," Goldie breathes, and I nod in agreement, my eyes laser beams on the death trap up ahead carrying Beau to . . . where?

I don't know, but I'm fucking raging.

43

BEAU

I rumble down the cobbled street toward Nath's place—a converted attic space above a row of garages—and turn off Dolly's engine, getting out and putting all my weight behind me to shut the door. I look up at the Juliet balcony. No lights are on. It's not dark, but there's definitely not enough natural light to warrant that.

I approach the door and knock, unable to shake off the lingering sense of caution since I took his call, every inch of me dreading what he has to tell me. I hear no movement beyond. No doors opening or feet coming down the stairs. I knock again and frame my eyes, squinting as I try to see past the opaque glass of his door. Nothing.

I pull back, thoughtful, my mind racing. "Where are you?" I say to myself, knocking again, this time harder, more relentlessly. Shit, I need to rein myself in. What would the old Beau do? Once a cop . . .

I can't think straight. "Nath?" I call, stepping back and peeking up at the window. "Nath!"

No Nath.

Pulling out my cell, I dial him, checking the street for his car. No car. But it could be in his garage. His phone goes to voicemail, but I don't leave a message. Instead, I try knocking again. And again and again and again. "God damn it," I mutter, trying someone else instead, my worry multiplying with each minute that passes and no appearance or word from Nath.

Ollie answers immediately. "Hey, it's Beau." I start pacing outside Nath's front door, up and down, constantly looking at the window. "Have you spoken to Nath today?"

"Yeah, only a while ago actually."

"Where?"

"At the office."

"And he was okay?"

"Yeah, I think so."

"You sure?"

"Beau, what's with the twenty questions?" Ollie asks, exasperated.

I shake my head, exhaling heavily, trying to find reason and expel my worry. "I was supposed to meet him at his place. He's not here."

"Hey, I'm sure it's nothing to worry about," he says gently. But Ollie doesn't know what I know. I pause for thought. What exactly do I know?

"I've called him repeatedly."

"He's probably been called to a scene."

I realize everything Ollie is saying is reasonable and, I pray, true. There have been plenty of times Nath and I have had arrangements that have changed at the last minute because something came up at work. A dead body. An armed robbery. But he always called. Or texted. "Can you check?" I ask, aware I'm clutching at straws. There was a time Ollie would have told me anything I wanted to know, because I was one of them. Not anymore.

"You know I can't, Beau."

I laugh under my breath. "You can, and you would have if I was still a cop."

There's silence for a few beats, silence except for me hammering on Nath's front door again. "Let me see what I can find out," he says, defeated.

My hand stops just shy of the wood again. "Thank you."

"No problem. Now go home before one of Nath's neighbors puts a call in to the police."

"He has no neighbors," I point out, scanning the row of garages that Nath's apartment is spread over. If he had neighbors, I would have hammered on their door as well to see if they'd seen or heard from him.

"Go home, Beau," Ollie says gently. "I'll call you."

I relent, backing up to my car, my eyes taking one last glance up at the window. "I'm going." Hanging up, I get in Dolly and start her up, worried out of my mind.

What would have Nath so damn rattled?

44

JAMES

I slowly move out of the recess, watching her chug up the road. Goldie pulls up beside me, her window down. "Stay with her," I order, and she speeds off immediately, no questions asked. She senses something's not right, and it's not just my foul mood.

I cast my eyes across to the mews apartment spanning the row of garages. Assess the roof. The windows. The front door. After a quick scope of the area for cameras and people, I walk casually over the road, pulling out my wallet and a credit card. I tug my shirt out of my trousers and push my hand into one of the tails, taking hold of the handle, slipping the card into the small gap by the lock and sliding it up a fraction. The door releases, and I hold it open only an inch, waiting for any chimes to indicate an alarm. Nothing. I peek through, searching for sensors. Nothing.

Pushing my way in, I elbow the door closed again, listening carefully. Silence.

I climb the stairs up to the apartment slowly, quietly, on high alert. It leads to an open plan space at the top, and the first thing that hits me is how immaculate the room is. I would have put my life on the fact a woman lives here. Until I see the art on walls. All women. All naked. All abstract.

But no photographs. I wander through the kitchen space, the counters sparse, and into a bedroom. Definitely a bloke's bedroom. A laptop sits on a chair in the corner, and I wander over, crouching before it. I hit a button with my knuckle, and the screen comes to life, just as my phone starts vibrating in my pocket. I dig it out. "Otto," I say, staring at the empty box requesting a password.

"The burner phone that received the message from The Snake's cell ordering Jaz Hayley's death."

"What about it?"

"It was switched on briefly last night."

I stand slowly, my eyes darting. "Trace it."

"Done," Otto mutters, always one step ahead. "I'm texting you the address." My phone dings, and I pull it away from my ear, opening the message. "I'm running a search to find out who lives there," he goes on.

"The fuck?" I breathe, looking up and glancing around.

"You recognize it?"

"Motherfucker."

"I'll take that as a yes."

"I'm at that address now."

"What?"

"I'm there. Standing in the bedroom."

"Are you fucking joking?"

"No, who the fuck lives here, Otto?" I ask, going to the window and checking the street below.

"Give me a sec, it's just coming thro . . ." He fades off, and my heart pumps faster as a result. "Fuck."

"What?"

"You're in FBI Agent Nathan Butler's apartment."

Ice glides through my veins. “Butler is their inside man.” I hang up and call Goldie, going to the nightstand and pulling open the drawer, rifling through. Nothing.

I slam it as Goldie answers. “She’s heading east,” she tells me. “Home?”

“Nathan Butler’s their inside man,” I spit urgently, stalking out of the bedroom. “Do *not* let Beau out of your sight.” Fuck me, all this time, her friend?

I hang up and leave, my mind in chaos, constantly circling around the fact that Butler called Beau and she came straight here.

To kill her?

45

BEAU

On my drive home, I battled with the pull of the steering wheel, fighting the urge to head to James's and find my escape. A swift recap of my earlier conclusions soon pulled me into line. It also brought the unreasonable feeling of resentment crashing back. He's a dad. A father. He's responsible for a person and, God save my soul, I'm injured that that person isn't me. That all his attention and dedication can't be just for me—to free me, to take me away, to distract me from life. Anger rises. It's unreasonable, but I can't stop it.

I park Dolly, pull my purse onto my shoulder, checking my cell for the thousandth time, and trudge up the path as I try Nath once again. No answer.

I still at the front door when a message flashes up from James.

Hope your friend is okay. Come over when you're done.

I reply before I can talk myself out of it.

I'm home now. Tired. Speak soon.

I hit send and cringe all over my cell. Speak soon? There are a thousand meanings in those two words, and none of them mean I want to speak soon. *No child needs my brokenness in their life.*

The moment I open the front door, I see Lawrence coming out of the lounge, and he stops, taking me in, his persona no less hostile than this morning. The atmosphere is spikey, the air tense. "Hi," I say, closing the door, trying to break the ice.

He nods and continues to the kitchen, looking back over his shoulder. He smiles. It's small. Nervous. I cock my head in question, and he inhales. "What's up?" I ask. Perhaps it's a silly question, given the words we've had recently, but that smile? It was apologetic. I pick up my pace and the moment I'm on the threshold of the kitchen, the lingering, crappy atmosphere explodes.

"Dad," I mumble, seeing my father at the table with Dexter.

"Hello, Beau," he says, not getting up to greet me. To hug me. To kiss me. He hasn't seen me in over a year, and all I get is a *hello*. Not that I want anything more. Not that I expect it. But still, every single time we're in this place of awkwardness, I wonder why he finds it so fucking hard to embrace me.

"I'll make tea," Lawrence sings, starting to clang and clatter around the kitchen, his nerves shot. It only serves to piss me off more. He shouldn't have invited this man into his home. Not only because of what my father's done, but because of how he treats Lawrence. It's nighttime. He should be Zinnea right now, vivacious, bright, and loud. But he's not. He's Lawrence, and not even the true version.

All because this man is here.

My teeth grate, and every transgression my father is guilty of steamrolls through my mind. His affair, his abandonment of me and Mom. His absence when she was taken from me. His absence when I hit rock bottom.

"No tea," I say to Lawrence, my burning eyes on my dad. No. He's not my dad. He's a man I'm sorry I used to love. A man I'm sorry I wasted any time on at all, wondering what was wrong with me. Wondering why I wasn't good enough. Why he struggles so terribly to give me any affection or praise. The more his success and power built over the years, the less loving he became. His gain. My loss. "What do you want?"

He laughs, and it's nervous. My dad isn't the nervous kind. He's bold and unapologetic. He's thoughtless and insensitive. Then I realize something is missing, and I scan the kitchen, looking for *her*. For what point, I don't know. You'd spot Dad's girlfriend in a crowd of a million, with her masses of fake blonde hair and rubber lips. "Where's Amber?"

"She's shopping with friends."

"I'll make tea," Lawrence says again, making more noise. I peek at Dexter. He looks about as comfortable as a cow outside a steak house.

"You didn't call about dinner," Dad says, standing from his chair and fastening the jacket of his expensive suit. "I thought you might be free now."

"I'm not," I say automatically, cringing the moment the words fall out of my mouth.

"But you just got home."

"I'm going back out." I smile awkwardly, thumbing over my shoulder. "I have plans with a friend."

"Oh." He looks truly disappointed, and for the first time when dealing with my father, I feel guilty. And I hate myself for that because he feels no guilt at all. "You can't rearrange?"

Not for you.

His eyes drop to my wrists, and I instinctively pull the sleeves of my shirt down, glancing across to Lawrence, who's eyes are nailed on my wrists too. He looks up at me, and I know immediately he's been telling tales on me. My jaw rolls, the anger I was feeling doubling. How could he? My father does not need more ammunition to persecute me. He doesn't need reasons to label me unstable and have me committed. Not for my own good, but for his. His image. His ego. To get me out of the way.

"I'm afraid not," I say quietly.

"Who's your friend?" he asks, his tone accusing.

I can't believe Lawrence has thrown me under the bus. My father has no right to information on my private life. He surrendered that when he walked out on Mom and abandoned me in my darkest hour. "No one you know." Good God, someone get me away before my head explodes.

"I heard you missed your session with Dr. Ferguson."

"How did you hear that?" I ask, knowing Lawrence couldn't have betrayed me to that extent because I didn't tell him. "You called her, didn't you? She's breaching patient confidentiality telling you that."

"She didn't tell me."

The devious fucker. "I need to go, I'll be late."

"I'm here in peace, Beau," Dad calls. "Why can't you accept that? I just want my little girl back."

"I'm not a little girl, Dad."

"You'll always be my little girl."

"So where were you when Mom died? And when I was in the psychiatric hospital?" He was busy making millions and rubbing shoulders with the best of them. His unstable daughter would have tarnished his sparkly reputation. "You had me sent there and just left me. No support. No love. And worse still, you told anyone who asked that I was on vacation." I had never felt so desperately alone, terrified . . . *abandoned.*

He has the decency to look ashamed. "I can make up for my

wrongs. I should have been there for you." He takes another step forward, and before I know it, I'm wrapped in his arms, his lips on the back of my head. And I soften. For the first time in years, I soften against my father. "I will make it up to you."

Tears. Wretched tears pool in my eyes, and I lift my arms, clinging to him. "Okay," I agree easily. And at the same time, I wonder . . . is this all I needed to help fix me? My dad's apologies? His comfort?

He breaks away and takes my cheeks in his palms, smiling down at me. His dark eyes, an unmistakable match to mine, shine at me. "Come to dinner with me."

"Where?"

"A little Italian downtown. Lovely place. I'm meeting a friend, and I'd love you to meet him."

"Who is he?"

He smiles, but it's unsure. "Frazer Cartwright."

I recoil, backing out of his arms. "The journalist?"

Dad shifts a little, uncomfortable. "He's a friend."

Is he for fucking real? Journalists aren't friends. They're a means to an end for men like my father. My God, what was I thinking? This man is incapable of changing. "Mom might have agreed to put on a show for you so your reputation wasn't tainted when you left her, but you won't get the same cooperation from me." I turn, begging my feet to keep moving. The alternative would be to go back and trash the kitchen, and it's not the kitchen's fault.

I slam the door behind me and take in valuable oxygen, gasping, blinking the fog of fury away. The door quickly swings open behind me. "Beau," Lawrence says, stepping out and pulling it closed.

"Do not try to reason with me, Lawrence," I warn. "He was only here for his own gain. Let's tell him to take you to the lovely Italian to meet Frazer Cartwright."

He looks down, and I immediately feel awful. My father's

approval isn't something Lawrence should want but somehow needs.

"I'm sorry," I sigh, pushing my fingertips into my forehead. Once again, darkness and grief eclipse my soul, every shitty emotion returning full-force and putting me back endless steps. But did I ever truly make progress?

I need one thing, and one thing only.

Escape.

The doors of James's building are locked when I arrive, and I'm taken aback by it. The calming feeling that was settling as I drove over starts to subside, stress beginning to build. Locked. He's not here?

I swallow, tugging on the handles again, pushing back my panic. What will I do? *Breathe, Beau.* I turn, leaning against the door, feeling at my throat. It's clogged. Panic. It's coming. *Just breathe.*

I jump a mile when the glass bangs behind me, and I turn, finding Goldie on the other side. Relief. Jesus, it's overwhelming. She unlocks the door and pushes it open for me, and I walk slowly and quietly past her, not fazed by her steel expression.

"Not at the opera tonight?" I ask as I come to a stop at the elevator, unable to hold back. I get nothing from her as she taps in the code, no look, no words.

The doors open, and I step inside, not for the first time wondering what the hell I'm doing. And not for the first time, I laugh at my own stupid question. That threatening panic attack was very real.

I ride up, pulling myself back together, settling, and when the doors open onto James's glass box, I scan the space, searching for him. No James. I glance up the stairs, and the faint sounds of music reach my ears.

London Grammar. *What a Way to Lose Your Head.*

I swallow, the irony making my head spin, and drop my purse, taking the stairs, feeling every stress and woe lift from my shoulders the closer I get to him. I follow the music to his bedroom. The door is open, the sound of the shower spray dulled by the beats of the track. I approach slowly, the tiniest part of my brain ordering me to turn and run away from this madness. But the biggest part is willing me on, yelling at me, telling me the only madness in this world is outside of this glass box.

I stop at the door.

James is a blur beyond the foggy shower screen. But crystal clear. And the music is louder. I glance up and see speakers dotted across the ceiling, nestled in between the spotlights, which are dim. Moody.

Calming.

His hands sweep through his hair, his back rolling, the scars undetectable through the misty glass. He is a perfect way to lose my head. Lose everything. It's unhealthy. To bury my head in the sand, it has to be unhealthy, because outside of this glass box, the world still exists. It's still filled with a father who abandoned me, grief for a mom who I lost far too soon, and a crazed agony that sent me to a psychiatric facility at the lowest point of my life. But, while I'm here, while I'm in James's orbit, I'm not that bereaved woman.

I'm free. It's addictive . . . dangerous.

I'm at its mercy.

James stills, and then he turns slowly, his head lifting as he does, reaching for the screen and sweeping a hand across it, clearing part of the glass of condensation. His face. Just the sight of him. He radiates power. His persona screams hazard. But beyond every masculine, strong, capable piece of him is a gentleness that's grown since we met. He knows who I am, what I need, without even knowing.

Fireworks explode inside of me, my bottom lip trembling. I'm at *his* mercy.

He jerks his head, a silent instruction for me to go to him, so I step forward, my hands lifting to the buttons of my shirt, and when I make it to the edge of the enclosure, he reaches out and pulls me in fully clothed. One swift move has me turned, my back up against the tile. He breathes down on me, his eyes roaming every inch of my face. "Is your friend okay?" he asks quietly, nuzzling into my face. My head drops back, giving him access to my neck, and I nod as best I can, instantly out of my mind. He knows damn well there is no friend with man troubles. "Speak soon?" he asks, and I swallow, clenching my eyes closed. "Do you want to speak now?"

"No," I reply, my voice thick with need.

He slips a hand onto my nape and directs my head back down. His eyes harbor a million strands of knowing. "Me neither."

His mouth is on mine fast.

My shirt is ripped open.

My jeans are wrestled down my legs.

My panties ripped away.

And he slams into me with a force so hard, I'm unsure how the tiles don't crack behind me.

I scream.

And it drowns out every other thought plaguing me.

Just as I planned.

46

JAMES

The relief I feel that she's here is spilling out of me in the form of anger. I can't stop it. And by the feel of her nails in my shoulders, she doesn't want me to, which leaves me wondering what went down at her uncle's place. Goldie reported Beau's father was there. She said Beau stormed out. And now she's here, seeming as stressed as I am.

And I need to do everything I can to make sure she doesn't walk away again. I need to ensure she knows that being here, being with me, is her only option. Not only because she's in danger out there.

We're going at each other like animals, our mouths dueling chaotically, our hands grabbing and scratching at each other, my growls primal, hers equally so.

I spin her and push her front forward into the tile with my body, kicking her feet apart. She cries out, and I bite her wet shoulder. "James," she yells.

"No fucking talking, Beau," I warn, taking my cock and tracing down her arse. "You said no talking."

I don't want this to be rough and hard. I need to give her more of a reason to stay, more than the crazy fucking. *Let's just fuck.*

No.

I slow the pace and ease into her gently, and she moans to the ceiling. "Hard," she orders, and I still, submerged, my body shaking with the effort it's taking not to thrust.

"What?" I pant, and she rolls her forehead on the tile, her fist balling and pushing into the wall, as if she's angry with herself.

"Not soft. I don't need you being all soft and gentle with me. Not now."

Not now? Or not ever? "Why?" I'm trying to locate a harder tone. I'm trying to hold back the fear in me. Yet I can't avoid the need.

She doesn't answer. Because she doesn't know.

All I can think about in this moment was our first encounter. The encounter that set the wheels in motion for us. She wants that. And it pisses me off.

I withdraw, and Beau hits the wall with her fist. "Come with me," I order, taking her wrist and pulling her out of the shower. The cold air shocks my skin, and with both of us dripping wet, I pull her into my bedroom.

"What are you doing?" she asks, trying to remove herself from my grip. "James!"

I stop by the wall and position her by the wooden frame. "Do you want me to stop?" I ask, dipping and taking her nipple in my mouth, rolling my tongue around the solid pebble, her skin chilly.

"Yes," she grates, and I pull away, stepping back.

"You want hard emotionless fucking, do you, Beau?" I ask, wrapping my hand around my dick, working myself back up, my fury intensifying.

Her eyes drop to my groin. "Yes." The anger in her clear eyes is satisfying. It mirrors mine.

"So we have some issues to vent?"

"Fuck. You."

My jaw tightens, and I move in, taking slow, even strides until I'm pushed up against her front. "Do you want me?" I ask quietly, reaching forward and taking a nipple between my thumb and forefinger, squeezing hard. She inhales quickly, her jaw rolling. "Do. You. Want. Me?" I ask again, every word punctuated.

"Yes."

"What for, Beau?"

"This," she says as I lower my face, my eyes on hers, and suck her nipple into my mouth. I bite down, and her torso concaves, her arms shooting up to my shoulders.

"I'm going to drive you insane," I whisper, pulling a belt off one of the rails. "Lift your hands to the bar." I sound brusque, impatient. Just how she wants me to be. "I get your point. I understand. So lift your fucking arms."

She glares at me. "What's my point, James?"

"Need. Except you're forgetting something, Beau." I grab her hand and direct it to my dick, making her hold me. And she squeezes. Massages me. I swallow, at her mercy. And isn't that *my* fucking point? Her thumb circles the slippery wet, pulsing crown, and my body starts to fold. "You're not the only one here in need."

"I've never denied that," she says quietly.

"But I'm not the one always walking the fuck away from this, am I? I'm here. Always here."

"And yet still an enigma," she whispers, scanning my eyes. Then she drops my weeping cock and lifts her arms to the suspension rail. "I'm here now. So make the fucking most of it."

I wrap her wrists in the belt blindly as I watch her silently goading me. "Don't fight the bond," I whisper, and her nostrils flare as I look over her naked, suspended body, casually deciding where to start. She'll get no respite this evening. There will be no breaks between her orgasms. My eyes fall to the apex of her thighs, and I rest a palm on her skin and start stroking my way up until I'm cupping her. She pulls in a long breath and holds it.

"No sleep tonight," I say on a whisper, thrusting a finger into her. She bucks, her face pained, and I glance up to see her strain against the belt as I fuck her gently with two fingers, sweeping wide, stretching her. She's biting down on her lip, her gaze pure fire. "Everything that happens will happen because I allow it." I withdraw and wipe my fingers across her lips, spreading her condition across her face before leaning in, getting as close as possible. "It'll hurt."

She absorbs my hard stare and hard words, and slowly lowers her eyes to my lips. Then she leans forward, trying to capture them. I pull away, shaking my head, and she whimpers. She's regretting it.

Good.

I dip and sink my teeth into her breast and my fingers into her pussy, and she screams, bucking and wriggling. She's felt nothing yet. And unlucky for Beau, she's only made me angrier with her fucked-up intention of making this work for her. I have no choice but to make it work for me too.

I take her behind her thighs and lift, and like a man possessed, I pound into her on a guttural bark, impaling her to the hilt, no easing in, no soft approach. I roar, and Beau screams in shock at my ruthless move, her legs dangling lifelessly around my hips. I don't allow her time to adjust. To accept me. I lift her and yank her back down, over and over, showing her no mercy. Unforgiving. Hard and brutal.

"James," she yelps, wrenching and pulling her wrists as I pound on savagely, taking her aggressively. She knows exactly what I'm doing. And she asked me to do it.

I reach down and take her other boob in my mouth, biting. Marking.

She comes undone, screaming her way through an orgasm that takes us both by surprise. And the moment she goes limp, I start all over again. "It's going to be a long night, Beau." I strain the words, and her drowsy eyes drag open.

"Stop talking," she murmurs.

And I smile. Because even without words, we speak.

And what we're saying to each other in this moment is significant.

Hours. I go for hours, over and over, orgasm after orgasm, my anger fueling my adrenalin. I only stop when she submits. When she asks me to.

She's nestled into my shoulder, her teeth sunken into my flesh, virtually asleep. I unravel the bonds with one hand, and then carry her to my bed, laying her exhausted body down gently. I'm beat.

But I have shit to do.

Dropping a kiss on her forehead, I cover her naked body and leave the room, stopping in my dressing room to slip on some boxers and grab a black bin bag of clothes, before passing my office to get a phone. When I get downstairs, I dump the sack by the elevator and drop onto the couch, dialing Spittle.

His hello is tired. Wary. "Tough day?" I ask.

"They're still dragging Russians and Serbs out of the cove three years later. I've been pulled in to try and identify some of the bodies."

"The Marina massacre," I say thoughtfully.

"Yeah, Danny Black likes to leave his mark."

Likes. I hum as if in agreement, but my head is quickly whirling for other reasons. Reasons I don't have time for. "Do you have anything for me?"

"Nothing. All the files on Jaz Hayley's death have been archived and I can't access them."

"Under lock and key," I muse. "Convenient."

"No, just archived. I'd have to get someone to sign them out, and forgive me, but your interest is making me reluctant."

"So you've not even tried?"

"I need more information if I'm going to knowingly expose myself."

"Are you forgetting about our dead friend?"

He laughs, and it gets right under my skin. "How could I? I just heard Wallace is being dragged out of the sea."

I smile, knowing I'll be receiving a call from The Bear very soon. "What is he paying you for?"

"I . . ." Spittle fades off, and I silently will him to be wise. Be wise or die. "Information."

I roll my eyes and shift in my chair, feeling every muscle tug painfully. "On who?"

He stalls, and I wait patiently for an answer, my mind replaying his earlier fuck-up. *Likes*. Not *liked*. Present tense, not past. "Vince Roake."

"The Alligator," I muse.

"You know him?"

You could say that. I just killed the bent judge taking his case. "I know everyone."

"But no one knows you."

It's time to put him out of his misery. "They know me. But they don't know me."

He inhales and releases the air on two words. Two very fucking powerful words. "The Enigma."

"Well done, Agent." I smile to myself. "Sorry, *ex* agent."

"Jesus."

I can see him in my mind's eye. Sweating. Pacing. Wondering

what the fuck he's got himself into. "Get me that fucking file, Spittle."

"Okay," he breathes. "I'll try. Is that it? Just the file?"

"No. I'm going to give you a name and you're going to find him."

"The name?"

"Brendon Brunelli."

"Who is he?"

"Inmate for two years in London." I refuse to die until I find that motherfucker. Refuse.

"London?"

"You have contacts, I assume."

"Fuck me, my life, retirement, was supposed to be easier with The Brit gone."

"Sorry to disappoint. I'll call you." I hang up and dial Sandy immediately.

"You played me," he says in answer. "Well done."

"Thanks." I slide the remote control from my desk and turn on the screens. Sandy's face greets me. "Looking forward to dying?"

He laughs. "I was going to ask you the same question."

I blink slowly, ending the call, falling into thought. It's beginning to feel like the underbelly of Miami is resurrecting, and it's going to be a fuck-load worse than when Danny Black ruled it.

47

BEAU

I come round to the sounds of clatters and clangs, my sleepy brain struggling to gather my bearings. I tense my stomach to sit up, and every muscle I possess screams in protest. I wince and hiss, so sore between my thighs. It's no surprise. I was given no respite throughout the night. No time to take a breather. Not a moment to recover from one orgasm before he instigated another.

I get myself to the edge of the bed with some effort, my legs hanging over the side, and glance at my naked breasts. Bite marks and a collection of small round bruises decorate each one. I turn my wrists over, scanning the welts. Uninhibited. Carnal.

Necessary.

Another clatter sounds, and I inch my ass off the edge of the bed, taking a moment to stretch, trying to loosen myself up. My body is tight, my brain foggy.

I find my shirt on the floor, still sopping wet. No buttons. My panties lie in a pile of ripped material next to it. I snatch a T-shirt off the back of a chair, pulling it on as I stand before the wooden frame by the wall, wondering how many women have been tied to it. Strangers. I step forward and run my hand over the glossy, highly polished wood, my touch meeting a few divots as I go. On closer inspection, I see dents, pieces of the wood damaged, the wood stain worn off. From friction. From fighting.

Don't fight the bond.

I look over my shoulder to the door when I hear more sounds. "Don't fight it," I whisper to myself, following the sounds until I'm standing at the top of the stairs. James is moving around in the kitchen space, cupboard doors and drawers opening and closing, utensils hitting the countertops. I would ask what he's doing down there, if my mind wasn't elsewhere in this moment. I back up and peek into his office. Every screen is alive with various news channels from across the globe, his enormous desk is busy with paperwork, and tucked away in the corner are all my painting tools and paints. God, it feels like months ago that he asked me to paint his office. I still need to finish it too.

I back out, pacing past the glass bathroom, and quietly open the next door onto another bedroom. It's stark, basic, white furniture and bedsheets on white walls. And glass. Endless glass. Not at all child friendly. I bite my lip and close the door, trying the next door. Another bedroom. Another stark space. The final room I enter is a gym, all the equipment set at the foot of the glass spanning two sides. A workout with a view. A steam room. A sauna.

Glass.

And still nothing to suggest a child has ever stepped foot in the place.

I close the door and rest my back against it, my mind whirling. I should just ask him. But do I want confirmation, because then it's real? Yet I know I can't ignore it. It's about time I took my head out of my ass and face what's in front of me.

But what *is* in front of me? Who is James?

I head downstairs, seeing him still moving around the kitchen. He's bare-chested. His hair is beautifully mussed, his face stunningly rough with stubble. He doesn't notice me, and I stop at the bottom, feasting on the mere sight of him, watching him cutting some fruit before sliding it off the chopping board into a blender. The lid is placed on, his hand over the top, and then the whole space is filled with the whirling sound of spinning blades.

He's making breakfast. Something so simple and yet so satisfying to see. I lower my backside to the step and get comfortable, every ache and sore on my body forgotten. And I just watch him. Transfixed. Mesmerized.

Falling.

But am I falling in love with him, or am I falling in love with this feeling?

I swallow and shake my head clear, just as the noise cuts. "Okay over there?" he asks, pulling the lid off and tossing it in the sink.

"Sore," I admit, reaching for the handrail to pull myself up. I wince when my thighs howl their objection. Jesus Christ, I feel like I need a sports massage. I straighten, feeling like every bone cracks to get me upright, and James's expression is nothing short of utter satisfaction. How is he not feeling it?

"Here," he says, nodding to one of the stools opposite him. "Have some of this."

I make my way over gingerly and ease myself onto the hard wooden seat of the stool. "What is it?"

He pours the contents of the blender into two glasses, pushing one toward me. "The first step to your recovery," he says quietly.

"Really?"

"Or was the first step to your recovery our first kiss?"

I shoot my eyes up to find his, startled. "What?"

His smile is faint as he reaches over and places a fingertip on the bottom of my glass, helping it to my mouth. "Drink, Beau."

"What's in it?" I ask quietly, accepting and taking a sip of the concoction. I get blueberries. Banana. "Is that broccoli?" I ask, swallowing and holding the glass in front of me, assessing the green slop.

"It's loaded with protein to repair your muscles." He downs half in one fell swoop. "I added some mango too."

I still, watching him finish the other half. "Why would you add mango?"

"Because you like it," he says, straight faced. "Drink. You need it."

Need. How can a man I hardly know be so sure of what I need? But he does. And it isn't only this drink. I slowly work my way through the glass as James watches me, and when I'm done, he takes it, sets it down, and leans over the counter. "I thought I wasn't going to see you again after you left Biscayne Bay."

"You weren't," I admit. No playing games, no lies.

He nods mildly. "So what happened to bring you to my door again?"

"Do you have a kid?" I blurt out of nowhere, and he recoils, blinking. "Actually, don't tell me."

"Why?" he asks, pushing his palms into the counter and straightening.

Oh God. He has. He has a kid. "Forget I said anything."

"No," he says. "Would it be a problem if I did?"

I nibble brutally on my lip, damning myself to hell and back. Yes, it would be a problem, and I hate myself for that. I look away. "I don't think I'm the kind of woman a man should consider introducing to their child."

"Why?"

Why? Isn't it obvious? On the outside to most people, I'm relatively together. Relatively content. But on the inside, past the mask, I'm a mess. Bitter. Twisted. And James knows it. No parent should inflict such darkness on their child. More than that, and, again, God save my soul, I don't want to share him. I don't want to have anything infiltrate this glass box and remind me that I'm living in the clouds. That real life is happening, and it needs to be dealt with.

"Why, Beau?" James pushes, and I peek at him, feeling stupid, guilty, deplorable.

"You wouldn't understand."

"Try me." He isn't going to let this go.

I sigh and relent. "My dad abandoned me."

"Oh, so you have daddy issues," he says, and I laugh, truly amused by his perfectly timed candor. I have way more than daddy issues, but . . . if it makes him happy.

"He's not a very admirable man. Well, to me. Everyone else thinks he's God's gift."

"Why?"

I roll my eyes. "Why do you have to push everything?" I ask, exasperated. "You ask, I tell, and the next thing I know I'm having twenty questions thrown at me."

"Oh, of course, I forgot. We just fuck, right?" He curves an eyebrow, taking the blender to the sink and rinsing it. I narrow my eyes on his back. His beautifully damaged back. I'm not sure at what point it went from ugly to beautiful, but it has. What does that mean? "I don't have a kid, Beau," he says to the faucet.

I blink, moving back on my stool. "You don't?"

"No. What made you think that?"

"Your other name. The fact you've said repeatedly I'm getting more than I bargained for."

He sets the rinsed jug on the side and comes back to the island, resuming his position, leaning in toward me. He reaches for my arm and runs a light thumb over my wrist. "Way more than you bargained for."

I look at the broken skin. "And your other name?"

"So you want to know?"

I look up at him, my eyes annoyed slits. His are dancing,

thrilled by my turnabout. "No, I don't," I grate. *Damn it, I do.* "Will it change things?" I ask. "If I know your other name, will it change things?"

His smile falters, but he quickly corrects it. But not quick enough. What was that? "It won't change a thing. Not for me."

"But it could for me?" I ask.

"I don't know."

Frustration flares, powerful and unstoppable. I growl to myself and pull my arm free, getting up and walking away before I show him how desperate I am to know. To know everything. I do want to know because he's dangling the carrot unapologetically. Fuck *him*. And I don't want to know because it might change things for me. Fuck *me*. I'm in an impossible situation. I can't do this anymore. The release . . . God, the release is good. But the ever-present tension? *That* I don't love.

I scoop up my purse and yank my cell out, checking the screen. Nothing. Not from anyone and, more worryingly, nothing from Nath. "Fuck," I breathe. What happened to him last night? Why hasn't he messaged me to tell me what's going on?

James shakes his head, as if disappointed in me, unbending his body to his full height. "Sit the fuck down, Beau."

"Excuse me?"

Something seems to pop in him, and he throws his arm out aggressively. "I said, sit the fuck down on the motherfucking chair," he bellows, and I recoil, taken aback by his explosive rage. Taken aback, yes, but more than that, he's just revealed something vital. He's worried about sharing this too. He's stressed out, though he's done a stellar job of concealing it. Until now. And it all begs the fucking question: why is he so adamant about me knowing? "Sit down now!"

"What's your other fucking name?" I yell, slamming my purse and cell to the floor, truly hating myself for needing to know. "Tell me."

His jaw spasms, his arm trusting toward the stool. "Sit."

"No." I need to be on my feet in case I'm leaving.

Nostrils flaring, James paces toward me with conviction, seizing me and carrying me back to the island. I'm dumped on the stool with little care. "Don't fucking move." His finger waves in my face, and I smack it away. Who the fuck does he think he's talking to? I snort and immediately remove myself. And I'm instantly seized again.

"Get the hell off me," I yell, shoving my elbow back. I hear the crack before I hear his grunt of pain.

"Fuck," he hisses, releasing me, and I quickly turn and find blood pouring like a waterfall from his nose. He takes his hand to his face, and it seeps between his fingers, still spilling relentlessly. His eyes are pooling, watering terribly, as he blinks repeatedly, startled. *Oh God.*

He steps back, looking down at his hand. "Are you going to calm the fuck down?" he asks tightly.

Me? "I'm calm," I grate, hating the guilt that finds me. "You?"

He closes his eyes, collecting himself. "I'm calm." Going to the sink, he runs the faucet and starts splashing at his face, and I approach behind, seeing the water stained red, the bleeding constant.

I collect a dish towel and flip off the water, taking his arm and leading him to a stool. He sits without instruction, and I move into him, taking the cloth and holding it to his nose. He watches me as I dab and pat. "I think I broke it," I murmur, my guilt multiplying. "I'm sorry."

He replaces my hand with his on the towel, keeping it in place, and pulls me onto his lap. "I'm sorry for losing my temper," he whispers, letting his forehead fall onto my shoulder. Soft James.

I lift my arm so I can get it around his shoulders, threading the fingers of my other hand with his on my hip. "What's your other name, James?" I ask. This ends now. No more games. No more ignorance on my part. I need to deal with this and then deal with Nath. Deal with everything.

"Let's get a shower first," he replies, lifting his head, leaving behind smears of blood. "Then we'll talk."

My stomach cartwheels as he negotiates us up from the stool and takes my hand. Talk. We're going to talk, with words rather than our bodies. I swallow hard as he walks us to the stairs, but just as he takes the first step, the elevator dings. We stop and turn, and Goldie steps out. The usually cool ice maiden looks less than her usual cool self as she exits the elevator with haste, but when she spies us by the stairs, she jars to a halt, and the cool, impassive mask falls into place.

"A word," she says, her eyes flicking to me. I frown, trying to assess her. She's unreadable.

I'm forced to rip my inquisitive eyes away when James puts himself before me, blocking my view of Goldie. I look up at him and wince at the sight of his blood-smeared face. "Go," he says, dropping a light kiss onto my forehead. "I'll join you when I'm done."

I start backing up the steps, and Goldie comes into view again beyond James. She's still and quiet by the elevator, her hands joined before her. Both of them watch me as I ascend, neither of them moving, neither of them speaking. They want to make sure I'm out of earshot.

I turn at the top and round the corner, coming to a stop, listening carefully. I hear nothing, and given the openness of James's apartment, that means they're whispering.

Plagued by curiosity, I force myself into James's bedroom and go to the bathroom, turning on the shower and pulling off the T-shirt. I step under the spray. Whispering. Whispering means someone doesn't want to be heard. As a cop, I never believed whispers. Whispers mean distrust, so therefore I shouldn't trust James and Goldie. And yet, I am the interloper. I have no idea how long they've worked together, or what they actually do. Do I even have the right to know?

I growl to myself and take some shower gel, furiously swiping my hands across my wet skin, washing away the blood and heavy scent of sex embedded into every pore. I shampoo my hair, rinse, and by the time I'm squeaky clean, James still isn't here.

I shut off the shower, wrap myself in a towel, and pluck a toothbrush from the holder. I scrub my teeth, comb through my wet tresses with my fingers, and rub the towel all over to dry myself.

Still no James.

I enter the bedroom, set to go find him, but stutter to a stop when I see him standing in the middle of the room, his hair wet, all blood gone from his face. He's dressed too. And he's showered.

But not with me.

He looks up as he threads his belt through the loops of his jeans, the same belt he tied me up with yesterday. I give him questioning eyes. He looks away. "I have to be somewhere," he says, going back into his dressing room and appearing moments later pulling on a jacket. "We'll talk when I'm back."

"Is everything okay?" I ask. He seems tense. I don't like it.

His smile of reassurance is feigned terribly, and I'm not sure if my ability to read his persona so well is a good thing. He comes to me, snakes an arm around my waist, tugs me close. "Everything is fine." A small kiss on my lips. "Will you be here when I get back?"

"How long will you be?" I ask. I need to find Nath. But I also need to talk to James.

"I'll be an hour, tops. Okay?" He looks at me with imploring eyes.

"Okay," I breathe. I'll call Ollie just as soon as James leaves. See if he's found out anything about Nath. I can easily say I won't leave because . . . where will I go?

He presses his lips to my forehead and holds them there, breathing through his kiss. He must feel my frown because he pulls away, rubbing his thumb across my brow, smoothing out the lines. “Back soon,” he says, turning and walking out.

And I’m alone.

Alone with only my mind, which is about ready to detonate with the questions filling it. I look down at my towel-wrapped body. Then around the bedroom. What am I going to do, other than kick my heels, waiting for James to talk? What will he tell me?

I shake my head and formulate a plan to keep myself busy until he gets back. I’ll call Ollie. Then I’ll go to James’s office and distract myself with some painting, given I’ve still not finished what I was here to do in the first place.

Hurrying down the stairs, I find my cell on the floor and call Ollie. It rings twice before he answers. “Did you find anything?” I ask, pacing at the foot of the windows.

“Nothing out of the ordinary.”

“Nothing at all?” I ask, stilling by the window.

“Beau, are you going to tell me what this is all about?”

My lips press together. “I’m just worried.”

“I think sometimes you forget I lived with you and know you inside out.”

He used to know me. Ollie doesn’t *know me* anymore. I hardly know myself. I pull my phone down and check the time. It’s only eight o’clock. It already feels like I’ve been up all day, and I barely got any sleep last night. I start pacing again, and my muscles pull, as if to remind me *why* I didn’t get any sleep last night. “I’ll keep trying him.”

“Listen, Beau, he’s probably just crashed into bed and slept through. You know what it’s like after a tough call out.”

I close my eyes and try to allow Ollie’s reasonable explanation for Nath’s absence settle. He could be right, of course, and I would have accepted that, had I not got Nath’s odd call. “Yeah, I know.”

“Fancy a coffee later?”

My eyes flip open. “A coffee?” I parrot like an idiot.

"Yeah, you know, that brown stuff people drink over chitchat."

"Chitchat?" I murmur, and Ollie sighs loudly.

"I want to see you, Beau."

Oh God. I can't tell him how much that isn't true. He won't listen.

"I heard your dad's been in touch," he goes on.

"Oh." Ollie knows of the contempt I feel toward the man who played a part in bringing me into this world. "I'm fine."

"Sure," he mutters. "Sure, you're fine."

I should never have cried on him. I should never have contacted him about Nath. I should have called someone else. I feel like I've given him false hope, and I take no pleasure in dashing that. Although, I kind of did already outside the store. I thought he got the message. "I'm seeing someone." I startle at the sound of my words, immediately wishing I could grab them from the air and stuff them back in my big fat mouth. I kick myself around James's apartment, cringing.

"I know," he eventually says.

"What?"

"Lawrence called me."

My mouth falls open, my brain unable to compute this. Why on earth would Lawrence do that? What was he hoping to achieve? And, more worryingly, what else did he tell my ex? "He had no right to do that."

"He's worried about you."

That statement tells me all I need to know. Lawrence has shared more than he should, which should have been nothing at all. "It's none of his business, and it's definitely none of yours." I quickly hang up before I say anything else, something I might regret. "Damn you, Lawrence," I mutter, hammering out a text message to my uncle, telling him how pissed off I am with him. I hit send and toss my cell on the couch, before marching to the kitchen and finding a glass. I fill it with water and drink it all, slamming it down and breathing through my rage. I literally feel like the world is against me.

Paint.

I rush up to James's dressing room and rummage through his drawers to find something I can throw on, something that he won't mind getting soiled. I spot a clothes hamper in the corner and riffle through, dragging out a T-shirt and some shorts. I pull the T-shirt on and bend to get the shorts on.

Something catches my eye.

I still and slowly lower to my knees, peeking under the snuggle chair in the center of the room. It's shiny, partly concealed by a shadow. "What the hell?" I murmur. I can't be seeing right.

I instinctively look behind me to check I'm alone, before covering my hand with the shorts and carefully pulling it out from beneath the chair. A 9mm. A shell casing.

My mind explodes, and I drop it like it's a grenade, panic grabbing me. I quickly shove it back where I found it, getting up and facing the room, glancing around. I breathe deeply, in and out, trying to untangle my head, looking at the ceiling, the walls, searching for cameras. *They're hidden.* How does a shell casing get into a room this small? Who fired the gun and at whom? Why—

Paint.

I clumsily pull on the shorts and run to James's office as I hoist in the waist, setting up the ladder and mixing the white paint. I scan my work area. Climb to the top and start frantically swooping around the spotlights. Paint. Just paint.

A shell casing.

My other name.

You're getting more than you asked for.

"Fuck!" The silence is too loud, my thoughts louder. I hurry down the ladder, rush downstairs, find my cell and my earbuds, and shove them in, returning to James's office as I search my playlists. I find the perfect track, play it, and turn the volume up to max as I slip my buds into my ears.

Everyone You Know *When The Sun Comes Up* blares, and it fills my head perfectly. I climb back up the ladder, take my brush, and let the painting and music take me away. My shoulders sway. I sing along.

I forget.

Just for a moment. Just for now.

I lose myself, cutting in around the remaining spots, working my way closer to the door, not bothering to get down from the ladder to move it, but simply shifting my weight to cock it onto one leg and effectively walking it across the room, holding the ladder with one hand and the paint and brush in the other. The tracks shuffle, each one like it could have been perfectly selected to consume my senses.

By the time I've made it to the other side of the room to the door, I'm forced to get off the ladder to get to the final spotlight. I push the door closed, negotiating the ladder to sit square in front of it, and climb back up.

My brush doesn't even make it to the ceiling again. The door flies open, smacking the side of my ladder. "Fuck!" I yell, not able to hear myself, wobbling precariously, trying to regain my balance. The can of paint topples, and I toss the brush aside to free a hand, wedging it into the ceiling above me in an attempt to hold myself in place. But the ladder's already tilted too far, and before I can even think to plan my fall, I'm crashing down, the ground growing closer rapidly. I hit the floor with force.

The music is loud.

But I still hear the sound of my wrist cracking.

And the sharp flash of pain confirms it.

I hiss, and, like an idiot, push my weight into my hands on the floor to sit up, disorientated and dazed, creating more pain. "Fucking hell," I cry, grabbing my wrist and applying pressure. I blink, forcing back the black mist that's creeping into the sides of my vision. Shit, I think I'm going to faint.

James appears before me, crouching, panic emblazoned across his face. His mouth moves fast, and I squint, unable to figure out why I can't hear him. The music. I reach up to my ears with my good hand in turn, pulling out the buds. He watches, confused.

And then he's not confused. He's angry. "For fuck's sake, Beau," he yells, stressed. I flinch. "I cannot believe you went up a ladder behind a fucking door."

"Okay," I yell. "Stop shouting at me." I look at my wrist and cringe. Busted. "I think it's broken."

"No fucking shit." He kneels and gathers me up, carrying me to his desk and setting me on the glass. "Let me see." He takes my arm gently, and after he's inspected it, I see the guilt that's been masked by rage shift to the front of his emotions. "Fuck," he whispers, his expression pained. "God damn it, Beau."

"It's my fault," I say, trying to ease him. I won't tell him *why* I was up the ladder. Or why the music was blasting so I couldn't hear my thoughts. Now, as I look at James, all I can see is that shell casing.

"Does it hurt?" he asks.

"No."

"Adrenalin," he concludes. "We need to get you to a hospital."

I press my lips together, forcing my confession back. "It's fine."

He laughs, though it is not with humor. "Shut up," he snaps, pulling his cell out of his pocket. He makes a call on loudspeaker. "I need you to take us to A&E. Beau's broken her wrist."

"You two are quite in the wars today, huh?" Goldie says, and her words make me take in James's nose. It's definitely swollen.

"We'll meet you downstairs." He helps me down from the desk. "Can you walk?" He takes in my clothes. "Are those my shorts?" He lifts my T-shirt, revealing the bunched material where I've rolled them so they'd cling to my waist.

I shrug. *Why's there a shell casing in your dressing room?* "I needed to paint." I shouldn't have said that. "To finish." I look away, avoiding his immediate worried expression. "I needed to finish the job."

"I'm so pissed off with you," he mumbles, pulling his T-shirt up over his head and ripping it clean down the middle. A few folds and knots later, he's putting it over my head, gently resting my arm in his makeshift sling.

"Where did you learn to do that?" I ask, and he falters, his eyes remaining on his task.

"Boy Scouts," he says, bracing a hand on the edge of his desk on either side of my thighs. "What were you thinking?" He leans in, his head tilted, his expression annoyed.

I wasn't thinking. That's the whole fucking point, and yet I can't share that with James. "It was an accident."

"This body," he whispers, his tone strained, his palm resting on my throat and dragging down my front, "is delicate. It's delicate, it's precious, and it's fucking mine, Beau Hayley." He gives me a look that dares me to question him, as I swallow down my surprise. "All I ask is that you be careful with it."

"You're annoyed with me," I murmur, my eyes falling down his bare chest to his stomach.

He pushes away, standing tall, his jaw pulsing. "Annoyed is an understatement."

My jaw starts to match his, twitching. "Are you done scorning me like a child?" I ask, slipping down and passing his imposing frame, keen to escape his annoyance *and* the vision of him bare-chested. *Don't lose your head, Beau.*

I make it only a few paces before I get a severe head rush. "Shit." I grapple for the wall, searching for something to cling on to, as the mist I managed to push back steams forward with a vengeance. "I'm going to pass out," I say out loud, warning him, needing him to catch me, as I start plummeting forward, my body becoming light and cold, my arms coming up instinctively to save myself.

"Beau!"

That's the last I hear. And James's fierce, panic-stricken face is the last thing I see.

Along with a shell casing.

48

JAMES

"Goldie!" I bellow, catching Beau just before she hits the deck. "Fucking hell." I get her onto her side, working around her arm, putting her into the recovery position. Goldie crashes into my office, finding us on the floor. "She's passed out," I say, assessing every inch of her, fraught with concern.

"Jesus, you two are a liability together," she grumbles, joining me on the floor. "What happened to her arm?"

"She was up a ladder behind the fucking door." I still can't believe she did that. Fury and worry start to fight for poll position, and Beau starts mumbling nonsensical words.

"She's coming around."

I stroke at her cheeks. "Beau, baby, come on. Open your eyes." I tap at her face, and she flinches, her eyes blinking open. "There you are," I whisper, dipping and nuzzling her cheek.

"Bullet," she rasps, and I freeze, letting that one word sink past the fog of my brain. I pull away slowly, and she looks me square in the eye. Then her head rolls, along with her eyes, and she passes out again.

"Did I hear that right?" Goldie asks, going to her phone, undoubtedly checking the CCTV. Then she stalks into my dressing room, reappearing seconds later holding up a shell casing. "Fancy leaving this around for her to find."

I say nothing, gathering Beau into my arms and carrying her out of my office. "Get me a T-shirt and call her uncle." It's the right thing to do, though I don't relish the thought of facing the condemnation. Because that's what it'll be. A trial. A judgment.

A persecution.

By the time we've made it to a hospital, Beau's slipped in and out of consciousness endless times. I'm no doctor, but I know when a body is in protective mode, whether protecting itself from physical pain or mental trauma. I fear I'm dealing with a bit of both.

I carry her into the reception, and the lady behind the pane of glass immediately jumps up from her desk. "A broken wrist and six episodes of fainting. Low blood pressure." I reel it off as she guides me down the hall into a room.

I settle Beau on the bed and make space for the doctor to move in and assess her. "Her name?"

"Beau. Beau Hayley."

"Age?"

"Thirty."

"And you are?"

I snap my mouth closed, looking across to Beau's unconscious form. "Boyfriend," I say quietly. My worry now, my pain seeing her like this? There's only one explanation. It's fucked up on every level for me to have allowed this to happen.

And yet here I am, falling for the fucking enemy.

"Mister . . ."

"Kelly."

"Any allergies?"

"None that I know of."

"And is she or could she be pregnant?"

I recoil, surprised, shocked, and a whole heap of other things. "Pregnant?" I mimic like an idiot. "No." I look across to Beau. "I don't know." Could she be? Is that why she's passing out left and right? *Fuck, I don't know.*

"This way, please, sir," the nurse presses, and I look blankly at her, dazed. "I just need some details from you."

"Yeah, sure," I murmur, following her gesturing arm like a zombie.

Once we're outside, I answer all the nurse's questions, and it's an achievement given my mind is a total haze. "That's all," she says, as Goldie comes barreling into the hospital after parking her car.

"Okay?" she asks, and I nod, bewildered. "Sure?"

I clear my throat. "I shouldn't have left her."

"You had no choice."

I did have a choice. There would have been another opportunity to take out The Shark's second-in-command. But like with any of the men I kill, I get another opportunity to discover who The Bear is. Will they be with him? Make a call to him? Lead me to him? It's not happened yet, but I won't give up. "Did you call her uncle?"

"On his way."

"Good."

"There's something else."

I look at her, hoping and praying she doesn't hit me with another known location for one of The Bear's men, because I'm going nowhere right now. "What?"

"Otto called. The tracker's moving."

"Keep me updated."

"And Brad Black's had an attempt on his life," she says, and I recoil.

Brad Black? "But he's lying low. Out of the game." The guy's been running a nightclub for over a year now. Totally legit.

"I guess they want all of Danny Black's roots gone. Doesn't sound like The Bear's willing to risk any recourse."

I don't like where this is heading. Brad Black is of no consequence to The Bear and his web of power. Not unless . . . My mind goes back to Spittle's clumsy words. *Likes*. "What happened?"

"Dodged a bullet."

"Fuck," I breathe, falling into thought. *The roots of Danny Black.*

"And Spittle's been in touch."

Jesus, anything else? "I haven't got time for him right now."

"You sure?" she asks, cocking her head, telling me there's only one right answer.

Naturally, I'm immediately wary. "What is it?"

"He wants to meet you."

"The fuck?" I hiss, looking at Goldie like she could have just sprung another head. And then . . . "Why would that be?" I ask quietly. Brad Black's had an attempt on his life. Spittle wants to meet me. "The answer is no." I turn and walk away. Spittle must have a fucking death wish.

49

BEAU

I open my eyes and instantly slam them shut again, shying away from the harsh glare of lighting. My head is banging. My wrist though? I can't feel a thing. I gingerly lift it from the bed and peel one eye open. Bruising. Heavy. A bone that's protruding. I wince.

"Beau?"

I let my head drop on the pillow, finding James sitting on the edge of the bed. He reaches for my arm and slowly lowers it back to my side.

"How do you feel?" he asks, and I sigh.

Sleepy. I feel so sleepy. "Fine."

"I've called your uncle."

"Great," I murmur.

"It's a clean break," a man across the room says. The doctor. "A few weeks in a cast will fix it, and the cut on the back of your head is superficial. Mild concussion. A nurse will be along shortly to clean up the cut and we'll get you fixed up with a temporary cast until the swelling settles."

"Thank you."

"Beau," the doctor says. "Could you be pr—?"

"Is there any water?" My mouth feels parched, my throat rough.

"Here." James reaches for a bottle on the unit beside the bed and unscrews the cap, and I start shuffling up the mattress. As soon as I'm sitting, he holds the bottle at my lips. He is *not* feeding me water.

I try to take the bottle and get nowhere. "I'm not an invalid, James."

"You're going to argue with me? Now? Just drink the damn water, Beau."

I look at him incredulously as the doctor backs out of the room. "I'll give you a moment."

The door closes. "Glad your mood's improved since I last saw you," I snap, and his jaw twitches wildly. He's fucking rich. I've found a shell casing in his apartment, and he's the one mad with me? Then I realize. He doesn't know that I found that in his apartment. So I tell him. "I found a shel—"

"Beau!" Lawrence barrels into the room, overwrought, and shoots around the side of the bed, taking me in, feeling me everywhere. "Oh my goodness. What happened?"

"I fell," I mutter, reaching for the water again, and this time James lets me take it. "I'm fine."

"Fine? You're in a hospital!"

James remains silent by the bedside, while my uncle fusses around me. "I'm fine, Lawrence," I say. "Just a cut on my head and a broken wrist."

"Just?" He looks up and glares at James, and I quickly realize why. It's obvious James does too, judging by his mild head shake. Lawrence thinks James did this to me? For the love of God, has he lost his mind? But my uncle doesn't say anything. And James doesn't appear in the least bit surprised by his conclusion. *Or* offended.

The tension in the room is thick, to the point I can't bear it, so when the nurse wanders in, I'm grateful. "Okay, then, missy. Let's get you all sorted out so you can go home." She pulls a bed tray over and goes to the sink to scrub her hands.

Lawrence moves in, crowding me, basically cutting off James's access. I hate the genuine worry on his face. Hate it. Because he's worrying over something he should not be worried about. "I'll cancel my show," he says, stroking my hair from my face. "We'll order your favorite ice cream. Veg. We haven't done that in ages, have we, sweetheart?"

Oh God, I wish everyone would stop panicking. "You shouldn't cancel your show," I murmur, glancing across to the nurse, mentally hurrying her along. I just want to get out of here, separate Lawrence and James, and be rid of this God-awful tension.

"But I must," he insists. "So I can look after you."

I flick my eyes to James. He's standing a few feet away, keeping his distance, holding himself back. *Not happy.*

"Okay, can I get some room, please?" the nurse says, shooing Lawrence away from my bed.

"Why don't you wait for me outside?" I suggest.

Lawrence recoils, looking injured. "And him?"

I turn my attention James's way. He's still glaring. Still tense. "He can wait outside too." With Lawrence panicking and James brooding, I can't breathe. Can't think. Add in the matter of a shell casing, my pounding head is spinning.

James says nothing, backing out of the room, his expression fierce, and Lawrence reluctantly follows, leaving me alone with the nurse. I flop back on the bed and hiss when my head brushes the pillow. I reach up and feel at the back, finding matted, damp hair.

"I think we'll clean your head first."

"Thank you," I murmur, closing my eyes and turning onto my side as ordered, giving the nurse access. I feel like I could sleep for a year. The door opens again, and the doctor slips back into the room. I know it's only because he deems it safe now James has left.

"I just have a few more questions," he says, settling in a chair by the bed, facing me. "Your boyfriend said he didn't know of any allergies."

"My boyfriend?" I blurt without thought, and the doctor looks back over his shoulder, indicating the door.

"The man who just left with your . . . uncle?"

"Oh yes. Him." I smile tightly. "No allergies." *Except James Kelly at this moment.*

"And are you or could you be pregnant?"

"No," I answer instinctively, but his question makes me pull up. Makes me think. Tomorrow. My period's due tomorrow. "Why do you ask?"

He stands. "Just routine questions. We need to ensure the medication we prescribe is suitable."

"Medication?" Something flares inside, my defenses flying up naturally. Do they think I need to be committed again? Has he read my records and assumed I'm a danger to myself?

"Painkillers." He smiles, and there's sympathy hidden within it. He's definitely read *all* my records. "I'll leave the nurse to finish."

I swallow and close my eyes.

Half an hour later, the wound on my head is clean, a cast on, and a sling holds it in place. As I perch on the side of the bed looking at the wrist that's covered from my fingernails to my elbow, I can't help but feel slightly pissed off that I didn't break my other wrist. My scarred one.

"Do you have any shoes?" the nurse asks as she finishes up.

I peek down to my dangling feet. Then up my body to James's

shorts and T-shirt. "No." I slip off the bed, my arm feeling like a kettlebell held against my chest.

"Then you'll have to get that big, strong man to carry you." She gives me an impish grin that I struggle to return. "I'll let him know you're ready." She leaves, closing the door behind her, and I take a moment to build up the courage I need to face my uncle and James. I bet the tension outside this room is horrific. I also need to think about what the heck I'm going to do, because I know James will be expecting me to go home with him and Lawrence will be expecting otherwise.

I pad on my bare feet to the door, pensive, and pull it open. James is the first person I see. He's sitting on a plastic chair, leaning forward, his forearms resting on his thighs. His face is a roadmap of angry lines. Then I clock Lawrence. Standing. His face is a roadmap of contempt. My eyes pass between the two, my mind giving me no heads-up of what to say.

"You're coming home with me," James says, breaking the uncomfortable silence, rising from the chair.

Lawrence snorts his thoughts on that. "She's going nowhere with you."

I inhale some patience. "I—"

The doors down the corridor burst open and Ollie appears, pacing determinedly. And with him, Dexter. I fold on the inside, sighing. Anyone else?

And like a fucked-up, sick omen, my father breezes in too. *Who the hell called him?*

Ollie's expression is pure concern. Dexter looks plain wary. And my father, someone pinch me, looks genuinely troubled.

Another few elements just got added to the already prickly mix. I don't need this. Not now, not ever.

Ollie spots me and rushes over, scanning me from top to toe. "Jesus, Beau, are you okay?" I'm hugged awkwardly around my cast, and there is nothing I can do to stop him. "Lawrence called me."

I clench my teeth, closing my eyes to avoid whatever look might be getting tossed this way from James. I can't imagine it's pleasant. Lawrence needs to back the hell off. "I'm fine," I whisper, leaving my good arm dangling by my side, unable and unwilling to return his embrace. I wriggle a little, breaking away. "You shouldn't have come." I risk a peek at James, and turn to ash where I stand. I can see he's physically holding himself back, his eyes raging pits of fury.

"What on earth happened?" my father asks, his fine-suited form muscling Ollie out of the way, his big palms taking my shoulders and holding me in place. I look at him, blank. Devoid of feelings.

"I fell," I say quietly. "I'm okay." I move back, uncomfortable with my father fussing over me, which is plain backward after years of wondering why he finds it so hard to give me affection. And I can't deny my fear that with one call from him, I could be sent back to a psychiatric hospital.

"Beau?" Dexter asks quietly, ever the pacifying, gentle soul. I look at him, and his expression alone, never mind his soft tone, makes my lip wobble.

"I'm fine," I say for the thousandth time.

"I'll take you home." Ollie moves back in. "Why are you wearing a guy's T-shirt and shorts?"

The sound of a throat being cleared fills the corridor, courtesy of James, and I watch, nervous as shit, as Ollie turns to find the source. "They're mine," James says clearly.

Fuck.

I don't need this. Two men snarling, me between them. "Who the fuck are you?" my ex asks.

"Good question," Dad pipes in, as if he has the right to that information. James doesn't entertain their demands, remaining silent, so Ollie turns to Lawrence.

"Is this him?" he asks, motioning to James.

"Who?" Dad asks, his eyes swaying back and forth between James and Ollie. "Not the man she's been seeing?" He turns a hostile look James way. "You? You did this to her?"

I stare at my father, flummoxed. Don't tell me he's choosing now to play the protective father?

"I'll have you locked up," he spits, as Ollie starts pacing toward James, his arm locking and loading. Oh no.

"Ollie!" I yell, going after him. "Ollie, stop."

"You *ever* touch her again . . ." he snarls, throwing a punch.

"Ollie!"

He misses when James leans back, the force of his swing sending Ollie spinning, but he gathers himself quickly, heaving, and has another go. James's hand flies up and catches Ollie's fist in his palm, and he claws his fingers around my ex's clenched hand, squeezing, holding it in place before his face. He says nothing, just stares at Ollie, who is a little wide-eyed, his eyes bouncing between James's lethal expression and his seized fist.

I swallow and move in, separating them. "Are you done?" I ask Ollie.

"You're not going home with him." My ex discreetly flexes his wrist, his ego seriously bruised.

"Ollie, you know me," I say, fighting for calm.

"Yeah, I *know* you," he retorts, goading, making James bristle harder.

"Would I ever allow a man to physically hurt me?"

He looks at me, and I hate the pain I see past the anger. "But you're not that woman anymore, are you, Beau?"

I step back, injured, despite him being right. No, I'm not the woman he knew. Carefree, happy, ambitious, stable. "Thank you for coming, but it wasn't necessary." I don't know whether it's insistence when James has no right to insist, or whether it's my incessant need for some answers, but I turn to James. "I'm ready," I say, before I sidestep his towering frame and pad on bare feet to the doors.

"Beau," Lawrence calls, and it kills me, but I ignore him, my mind made, my focus set.

"Beau, sweetheart, come back," Dad yells. "What the hell is going on here? Ollie, Dexter, stop him!"

I make it outside into the fresh air and look at my feet. "I'll carry you," James says from behind.

"No." I look back over my shoulder, seeing Ollie glaring at us in utter disbelief and my father looking nothing short of furious. "No need to rile anyone further." I've made a good enough job of that myself. I'm surprised by James's restraint. I could see it was taking everything out of him not to flatten Ollie and my father. I know he's capable. And while I'm thinking of capable, what else is he capable of? I look up at him. I shouldn't be so attracted to a man who's such an enigma. "I found a shell casing under the chair in your dressing room," I say, straight up and with no emotion. "And I'm still coming home with you."

He doesn't flinch. He's shows no surprise. Not a thing.

"That's why I was up the ladder painting," I go on. "That's why I had the music blasting. I was trying to drown out the nagging, screaming questions."

His gaze drops to my cast, and guilt grips me. I didn't splurge all those words to point blame or to make him feel shitty. I simply needed him to know that I know. But I don't know what the fuck I know, and it's sending me to crazy town. Enough is enough.

"I want to know who you are. I want to know your other name. Why you think I'm in too deep."

"I'm in too deep too." He looks at me, and I back up, alarmed by the apologies in his eyes.

"Will I want to leave when you tell me?"

"Probably. But I won't let you."

"Why?"

He steps into me, taking my cheek, smoothing his palm down my face. "You're not going anywhere because despite my better judgment, I'm mad for you." He drops a kiss on my parted lips, and then each of my closed eyelids. Warmth seeps into me. A warmth I'm baffled by. "Let's go home." He lifts me from my feet, and my good arm goes around his neck, holding on.

Clinging.

James paces to his car, and I study his profile the whole way, wondering what he's going to share and how I might feel once he has.

Despite my better judgment, I'm mad for you.

I'm mad for him too. So maybe now, it simply won't matter what I learn.

50

JAMES

I carry her from the car to my apartment, and once inside, up to the bathroom. I place her on the loo and start drawing a bath, loading it with lavender. "Aren't we going to talk?" she asks.

Talk. She suddenly wants all the words, and I'm now unsure if I can speak them. I crouch before her, taking her hand and placing it on my rough cheek, holding it there and closing my eyes, leaning into it. Feeling her. Just feeling her touch and hearing her breathe. She chose to come home with me. But still, I can't talk until I've reinforced something. And it won't be rough. It won't be hard. "We need to do something else first." I open my eyes and take in every bit of her.

"What?" she whispers. But she knows.

My hand goes to her thigh, and she instinctively clenches them together. She's trying to halt the onslaught of desire from steaming forward. And I understand. It's been too easy to bury herself in my touch. My attention. To ignore the constant red flags. Be ignorant to them all. She's clever, observant, but it feels like she's shut down that side of herself since she met me.

Because she's scared. She has every reason to be.

"We need to fuck, Beau," I breathe. "Every inch of me needs to touch every inch of you, my cock plunging, your moans drenching my apartment."

"Talk," she whispers, vehemently shaking her head. "We need to talk."

My hands land on her knees and spread her legs, and she whimpers, somewhere between distress and desperation. "There's something else I need to say first." My fingertip draws a perfect line down the inside of her thigh to her knee. "And this is the only way."

She convulses, her breathing becoming ragged. She wants to stop this. And yet she can't.

"Kiss me, Beau," I order, and she dives forward, her flaky restraint gone, and smashes her lips on mine, taking out her frustration at me with this kiss, whipping her tongue through my mouth.

"That's it," I growl, standing, dragging her up with me, returning her crazy pace. "Give me all you've got, baby."

She whimpers, and I snake my arm around her waist, lifting her and walking to the vanity unit, placing her on the edge. I yank at the waist of the shorts, loosening them, before tugging them down her legs, her kiss never faltering, my actions blind but efficient.

"Spread," I order against her mouth, and she immediately makes room for me as I undo my fly and pull out my cock. I break our kiss and pull back, panting, looking her in the eyes as I guide myself to her. "Don't look away," I warn, and she inhales, feeling the warm, wet head of my erection brush across her opening. "Never look away." I slip in slowly, my face strained, my bite on my lip harsh. And the sensations, every inch of me buzzing, take me to where I need us to be.

Her dark eyes are magnets, hypnotizing, luring me further in. "Could you ever look away?" she asks quietly, her spine lengthening little by little with every inch I sink inside her.

As if to make my point, I let my forehead fall onto hers, our lashes now nearly touching. I advance a bit farther, and her inner walls clench, squeezing me. "Never," I breathe, pushing forward the final few inches, hitting her deep. Her injured arm rests between us, her good hand behind her, supporting her weight, and I start to pump steady and slow, in and out, each drive smooth, each retreat measured, each grind slow. I'm burning up, the bathroom air becoming wet with condensation, the T-shirt she's wearing starting to stick to her skin. And yet, despite us both being partially dressed, me more than her, it's the most intimately I've ever taken her.

It's her eyes.

Eyes full of the unknown.

Eyes she refuses to take off me.

This isn't fucking. This is making love. It's a form of manipulation. I know that.

There's something else I need to say first.

I'm mad for you.

"You love me," she whispers, and I still abruptly, swallowing. Shocked. But my eyes? They don't break with Beau's. "Is that what you're trying to say now?" she asks.

"I don't want to love you, Beau," I admit, drawing a delicate line across her eyebrow. Beau is fierce, strong, despite what she thinks of herself. Her losses are great, but her determination, her fire, her bravery to find justice is formidable. Admirable. But love is dangerous, as I saw with my parents. My dad loved my mom to his death. He protected her. Worshipped her. I saw his devotion, how his eyes followed her because she was his light. Like my eyes have followed

Beau since the first moment I saw her. *Knew her.* But like there was with my dad, there will be an enormous cost for loving Beau. And not only that . . . "There's no place in my life for love."

"Then what am I doing here?" she asks, not appearing at all hurt. She simply needs to know.

"You're here because I can't seem to leave you the fuck alone."

"Try."

I shake my head and take her hips, picking up my pace again, but this time I'm not as gentle, and Beau ups the ante too. She's frustrated. With me. With herself.

I can relate.

I don't want to love either.

And yet here I am, in love with her.

51

BEAU

For the first time since he demanded I shouldn't, I look away from him. I can't fall if I can't see him. I have to stop myself. Stop this.

There's no place in my life for love.

My jaw is grabbed, and my face forced to his. "I said, do *not* look away from me."

"Fuck you." I slam my eyes closed and yell when he punishes me with a hard buck of his hips, his cock filling me to the brim. "Fuck you, James."

Bang!

No more making love. Because this isn't love. It's fucking.

Bang!

I yelp, gritting my teeth, enduring his brutal pounds.

"Beau," he grates, and I turn my face, fighting his hold, further maddening him. And the pleasure just keeps on coming, strike after strike. My clammy skin burns, my insides burn, my brain burns. I will take this pleasure, this mind-numbing bliss. I will take everything he has to give. It's the only thing I'll allow between us.

"More," I hiss, letting my head tilt back. "Give me more, you asshole."

Bang!

"More!" I tense my arm, immune to the pain it spikes while he's taking me so brutally.

"Fuck!" His body jacks, his groin rolls, and I'm taken out, screaming to the ceiling as my release tears through me like a destructive hurricane, ripping apart everything in its path. My mind. My heart. But our souls? They remain intact. Still joined. Still together. Still one.

The feeling of his hot essence filling me burns, and I open my eyes, finding his brow dripping with sweat, his eyes glazed, his lips parted. I gasp in his face, tingles riddling my body, electric and addictive.

"Are you done?" I ask.

"With you? Never."

I flex my hips, and he groans, his torso folding forward. "So I just stay here, do I? Stay here and let you fuck me as you please. Tie me up. Restrain me. Shove things in my ass and record it all?"

"What else are you going to do?" he pants, his cock still pulsing within me.

"Live."

"You don't know how to live, Beau." He drops a kiss on my forehead and pulls out on a hiss. "That's the whole fucking reason you're in my apartment." He moves away, fastening his fly and turning the faucet off before leaving.

I close my legs. I can't argue with him. Never has anything truer been said.

Slipping down off the vanity unit, I grab some tissue, wiping him away from between my legs. *Could you be pregnant?* My head feels ready to pop. With . . . everything.

I follow him into his bedroom, stopping at the door and eyeing the wooden frame. "Has anyone else been tied to that thing since you met me?" I ask, my question unstoppable.

"Are you asking me if I'm fucking other women?" he asks, going into his closet.

"Yes, I am."

"Don't insult me, Beau."

"That's not an answer."

"It's a fucking answer," he yells, appearing again, wrestling on a sweater and stomping to the door.

"Why is there a shell casing in your dressing room?"

"You're not ready to know," he says over his shoulder, not even having the decency to look at me.

"What?" I almost laugh. "You said we'd talk."

He glances back at me when he gets to the door. "I've said what I wanted to say." His eyes drop down my body, detached and cold. "Did I make myself clear?"

"Crystal."

"And if you're not here when I get back, I'll hunt you down and bring you back." He closes the door, and I stare at the glass, incredulous.

No.

He is not doing that. I march after him, swinging the door open, but before I can step out onto the landing, I hear the elevator doors, and then Goldie.

"Are you out of your fucking mind?" she asks.

"Definitely," James grunts quietly.

"You can stop this."

Silence follows, and I wait with bated breath. Stop what? And why? "I really can't," he replies, as the doors slide closed.

I creep to the top of the stairs and look down, seeing the space empty of life. And as I lower to the top step, trying to process everything, trying to decide what the fucking hell to do, something comes to me. I look up and around, searching for any signs. Nothing. No cameras. But he'll be watching. Without a doubt, he'll be watching.

That thought incenses me. I stand to get dressed and leave, but my cell ringing distracts me, and I shoot down the stairs, answering Dexter's call. "Hey."

"How are you doing?" he asks.

"Did you really call to ask that?"

"No, I called to beg you to come home. In an attempt to make himself feel better, he is now she, and Zinnea cries loudest of all."

My heart squeezes. I take no pleasure in Lawrence's despair. Or Dexter's exasperation. "How were things after I left the hospital?" I ask, wincing as I do.

"Dreadful. Your father demanded I arrest James, Ollie swore to kill him, and Lawrence declared retirement."

Basically, a fucking mess. And things haven't exactly been rosy for me here. "I'm coming home."

"Oh?"

The curiosity in his voice is undeniable. "No questions, but I'm coming home."

"Okay," he agrees, and I smile. He never presses. "I'm leaving now." Another call comes in, and I glance down to see Nath trying to get through. "I'll see you soon," I say to Dexter, accepting Nath's call. "Are you trying to kill me with stress?" I blurt, unable to hold back my exasperation. "Where have you been?"

"Don't ask," he mutters, sounding out of breath, completely harassed. "It's been the worst twenty-four hours of my career."

"You were supposed to meet me at your place. I've been so worried."

"The dead men send their apologies," he retorts sardonically. "All three of them."

Three? "What happened?"

"Who the fuck knows. I have dead bodies turning up all over town."

"Connected?"

"Well, they're all criminals," he says, sighing. "And to top it off, a shooting at a club."

"What?"

"Intended to take out Danny Black's cousin and ex-right-hand man."

"Proof that you can never get away from that life," I murmur walking over to the couch and lowering.

"Funny. He said the same. But more importantly, what the hell has been going on with you?"

I look down at my arm. "So Lawrence has been blabbing his mouth off?"

"No."

I frown. And then . . . "Ollie."

"No. Dexter, actually. He's worried. He swung by to see me. Lawrence is a mess. He's worried about him too. Where are you?"

I glance around James's apartment. "Not home," I say quietly, giving him an answer without actually answering.

"Who is this guy, Beau?"

What can I say? *An escape.* I can't tell Nath I have no idea who James is. He'll think I'm certifiable. I'm pretty sure Lawrence is a whisper away from helping my father send me back to that hell-hole they call a hospital. "He's my business," I retort with conviction I'm not feeling.

"Sure." Nath murmurs. "Coffee? We need to talk."

I'm up from the couch in a beat. "Mom," I breathe. "What did you find out?"

"Just tell me where you are. I'll pick you up."

Once again, I glance around James's apartment, my mind working fast, refusing to divulge that information to my friend. "I'll meet you. Where are you?"

"Ziff Ballet Opera House."

"What are you doing there?"

"Dead judge."

"At the opera house?"

"No, at the apartment block opposite. Like I said, dead bodies everywhere. Meet me at our usual place. Half an hour." He hangs up, and I stare at the city through the glass, my head set to explode. And I inhale, things seeming to click in my brain as my cell falls from my hand, hitting the floor at my feet with a loud clatter. Visions. Visions of James, of the opera house, of me restrained to the chair while he disappeared for twenty minutes. Of Goldie carrying the black case and slipping through a restricted access door. Of the shell casing under the chair.

"Oh my God," I whisper, the onslaught attacking me hard, rolling through my head relentlessly, making it spin. I lower down to the couch. Glance over my shoulder to the stairs. My head pushes the shell casing to the forefront.

If you leave, I'll hunt you down and bring you back here.

I look down my front, to my body still in James's clothes. Then to the door. And my arm. I can't drive. Perhaps an automatic, but not a stick shift. "Fucking hell," I curse, standing, swiping up my cell from the floor and heading upstairs. I find my clothes on the bathroom floor. Still wet. The universe seriously doesn't want me to leave James's glass box. My cell rings, and I look at James's name dominating my screen. I answer. Say nothing.

"Don't leave, Beau," he warns quietly, and I look up and around, searching for the cameras.

"Tell me who you are."

"Tell me you won't leave."

"I'm not bargaining for the identity of the man I'm fucking." I go to the bed, perch on the side, and remove my sling, awkwardly stripping with only one hand. I draw my jeans up my legs inch by inch, alternating between each leg, falling to my back and wriggling to help me get them up to my waist. The button fly is impossible, but the wet denim is tight around my ass, keeping them up. I slip my arms through the sleeves of my shirt and spend too long fastening a couple of buttons, hissing each time I twist my arm, before replacing the sling. Just looking at it angers me. The restriction. The pain.

My cell rings again and I ignore it, fetching my shoes and keys and leaving, my heart in my throat. The ride down in the elevator feels like it takes years, plenty of time for me to click the fucked-up puzzle into place. "Jesus Christ," I whisper, my head bombarded with every tiny detail I need to reach an unthinkable conclusion.

The moment the elevator doors open, I'm greeted by Otto, his wide frame filling the double glass doors onto the street. He gives me a look to suggest he's not up for any fun and games. "Be wise, Beau," he says, his voice full of warning. I keep my eyes on him as I stand on the threshold of the elevator, my memory providing me details of every inch of this lobby. Where the desk is. The mirrors on the wall. The lights on the ceiling. The chairs and how they're positioned.

And the fire escape door to the left.

I bolt, running as fast as my legs will carry me to the fire door and pushing my way through, ignoring the searing pain in my arm from moving so fast and abruptly.

"Beau!" he bellows, his big feet stomping after me. I stop, just for a moment to assess my options. There's only one.

Down.

I take the steps fast down one flight and burst into an underground parking garage. An underground parking garage with only two cars in it. One is Dolly. This whole block, over thirty floors, and just two cars? Two cars and no way through the metal gates keeping them retained. "Shit." I hear Otto's charging feet getting louder, closer, and all out of options, I get behind the door, plastering my back to the wall, holding my breath. The moment he bulldozes through, I slip around the wood and sprint back up the stairs to the lobby, my heart smashing dangerously, my speed fueled only by adrenalin.

I make it out onto the street. It's the middle of the day. Busy. People everywhere. My adrenalin subsides and makes way for panic. "No," I say sternly, looking back over my shoulder, seeing Otto run back into the lobby. His eyes fall onto me. His furious expression is the biggest kick up the ass I need to get me moving.

I jog to the end of the street and dip around the corner, crossing the road and disappearing down an alley. My cell is ringing off the hook.

And something comes to me.

I stop and look down at the screen.

And turn it off.

52

JAMES

"I lost her," Otto pants down the line. "I'm getting too old to play chase."

"Fuck!" I swing around and smash my fist into the brick wall, splitting my knuckles. *Fuck, fuck, fuck.* "Watch Butler." I shake my hand off and cut the call, pulling up my tracking app. She's turned off her phone. The rage. Oh, the fucking rage. It puts all other previous fury to shame. I stuff my phone in my back pocket and go to the boot of my car as I yank my gloves on and pull my balaclava over my head, before swiping up the rifle. I load it as I pace through the derelict factory, my jaw going into spasm, my pores sweating . . . fear. It's fear.

I lost her. Otto fucking lost her. Impossible. Laughable. But I'm not laughing. I'm in no mood for the intended, stealth approach. These men will die. Now. *No mercy.* I kick the iron door open, aim and fire, putting a bullet clean between the eyes of my first target. It's not the slow, painful death I had planned. But it'll have to do. I have more important matters to deal with. I move my aim, passing the down-and-out who's in the corner, his arms in the air, one of my Marlboros hanging off his bottom lip. Three more goons scramble for cover, their amateur shooting skills having them blasting bullets randomly.

Fucking Russian dickheads.

I pick each of them off one by one without moving a foot.

And I am done.

I turn and walk away, pulling my balaclava off to get some air. I need air. I need to breathe.

But that won't happen until Beau is back with me.

53

BEAU

By the time the cab has battled its way through midday traffic, an hour has passed and I'm late. I see Nath sitting outside, focused on his phone. I pay the driver and hurry to him. "Hey," I puff, still short of breath after dodging Otto. I take a seat and Nath exhales heavily.

"I was worried." He flashes his cell. "I've been trying to call you."

"I'm a half hour late," I point out, raising an eyebrow as I collect the water he's ordered me, absolutely parched. I swig and gasp. "*You* went radio silent for hours."

"What's going on?" He looks across the table at me in alarm as I guzzle the rest of the water down ravenously. "Did you run here?"

I shake my head, still drinking, unable to get enough.

"And are your clothes wet?" His eyes drop down my shirt. "Your buttons are undone."

I place the bottle on the table and start fastening the buttons I missed in my haste, awkwardly trying to sort myself out with one hand. "I'm fine. Everything is fine."

Doubtful eyes fall to the sling holding up my newly broken wrist.

"Don't even think what I think you're thinking," I warn.

"What am I thinking?" he fires, settling back in his chair.

"Tell me what you found out about Mom."

"Nothing."

I recoil. "Then why the hell am I here?" I look past Nath when someone approaches behind him, and my heart starts to beat double time. "What's Ollie doing here, Nath?" I ask, my hackles rising, every hair standing on end. I don't like the look on either of their faces.

"Did he do that to you, Beau?" Nath asks, and it all becomes clear. Is that what his call was all about? He left me thinking, hoping, praying he'd found out something about Mom's car being at the dealership, and the whole fucking time he was planning an intervention? All I need is for Dad, Lawrence, and Dexter to show up, and we'll have a full house.

"Are you for real?" I ask, standing abruptly, sending the metal chair flying back. "You've dragged me here to ask if my boyfriend broke my fucking arm? Is that what you think I've become? That weak? That desperate?"

"I looked into him, Beau." Ollie stops at the edge of the table, looking down at me. My heart goes from double time to triple time. "James Kelly didn't exist until five years ago."

I stare at my ex, flummoxed. "You had no right to do that." I'm not shocked by his declaration. I'm simply pissed off that they've taken it upon themselves to pry. Deep down, I had a feeling their search would either turn up nothing or turn up a record longer than my broken fucking arm.

"You were born in England."

"Yes."

"How long have you been in the States?"

"Five years."

Five years. And his company has probably only been in existence that long too.

"He's not who he says he is," Nath continues. "He's deceiving you, Beau. Lying to you. Why would he do that?"

"Then who is he?" I spit, furious, my mouth firing words before my brain can engage. "If he's not who he says he is, who the fuck is he?" I need to shut the hell up.

"Probably a guy who got sent down for domestic abuse and legally changed his name when he got out."

I drop my head back, looking at the sky, gathering patience. How many times have I got to tell them? "James did not break my arm." I breathe in deeply, all out of patience, and calmly push my chair in. Nath won't find anything on my mom. I know that now. And Ollie? He's just pushed me too far. "I don't want to see you again." I look at Ollie. "Either of you."

"Beau, come on," Ollie pleads, reaching for me. "We're just looking out for you. You're vulnerable."

"No!" I yell, shrugging him off and storming away. "Just leave me alone." I'm dizzy with rage, confusion, my head about to detonate.

When I round the corner, I come to a stop, resting against the wall, trying to get my labored breathing under control. I turn on my phone. Endless missed calls and a text from Dexter, asking where I am. I close my eyes. "I don't know where I am," I say to myself. "Or where the fuck I'm going."

I exhale. It's long and defeated, as my thumb works across the screen, telling him I'm okay. That I'm on my way. Then I turn it off again.

There are no records on James. He didn't exist until five years ago.

Excessive security.

His other name.

The opera house.

In too deep.

Enigma.

54

JAMES

Goldie can't find her. Otto can't find her.

I can't fucking find her.

Goldie is watching Beau's uncle's place. Nothing. I've wandered the supermarket for an hour. Nothing.

I pace my office, up and down, the screens drowning the space with a bright rainbow of lights. I haven't even the will to amend the status of my latest hits.

"Fuck, Beau, where the fuck are you, baby?" I rake a hand through my hair as I slump into my chair and close my eyes, wracking my brain. I see her mother. The sheer determination on her face. Her voice down the line whenever we spoke. Her words, words of conviction.

I will find you. I will finish you.

I snap my eyes open quickly, and I'm out of my chair like a rocket, sprinting down to get my keys. I'm out the door fast and soon speeding toward the old church.

. . .

When I pull up in the lay-by on the lane toward the church, the biggest, blackest cloud is creeping over, casting a shadow over the graveyard. The sky looks like it could open at any moment. I see a cab sitting in the lane, the driver reading a paper. My phone pings an alert, and I open it, seeing Beau's turned her phone back on. She wants me to find her. "Already did, baby," I murmur, getting out, not bothering to check her exact location. I can smell her, her fragrance mixing with the heavy, clean scent of the impending rain. I make my way down the paved pathway, the ancient slabs cracked and uneven, not a single stone in one piece. The metal gate into the graveyard is twisted and rusty. It's sad and dreary. Everything a graveyard should be.

I let myself through and find her immediately, sitting before a gray marble headstone, her arm wrapped around her knees, hugging them. Weaving around the graves, crushing the long grass with my boots as I go, I keep my eyes on the blurry words of Beau's mother's headstone until the inscription is clear. I come to a stop and read it. Three times. And that day two years ago is as real now.

"Tell me who you are," Beau says quietly, not looking back.

"To you or them?"

"To me."

To her. Most importantly, who am I to her? I move in and lower behind her, framing her seated form with my thighs. I wrap my arms around her upper body and pull her into me, placing my mouth at her ear. She doesn't resist. "To you, I'm freedom."

"Hello, freedom," she whispers, and I swallow, relaxing, as she starts to turn in my arms. I release her, just enough to let her, and she kneels before me, taking my arms from around her back one at a time. Her eyes meet mine. Resolute. "I'm ready to know who you are. Are you ready to tell me?"

I nod, even though I know and accept that I can't tell her everything. "Will you leave?" It's an unfair question, and, crazily, it feels like telling her I'm a killer will be the easy part. Because she's worked that out for herself. And, whether I wanted to or not, I helped her along the way to enlightenment. I'm still unsure why. Maybe because I see life beyond death and revenge with this woman. Am I capable of that? And do I deserve it?

"I don't want to," she whispers.

I guess that's all I can ask for. "Let me take you home."

"You mean to your home," she says, staring at me with so much acceptance in her eyes, I honestly don't know what to do with it.

"My home."

She nods and stands, looking at me and offering her good hand. I take it tentatively and she tugs, as if her small frame and strength actually contributes to pulling me up.

I tuck her into my side and walk us out of the graveyard. "The cab," she says, pointing. "I told him to leave the meter running."

"I'll sort it." I deposit her in the passenger seat of my car before wandering over to the cab, pulling off some notes and handing them over.

"There's a bag on the back seat," he says, motioning over his shoulder.

I frown and look back to Beau. She's daydreaming, staring out of the window. I reach for the paper bag, open it, and freeze. "What the—?" I stare at the box for an eternity, trying to turn it into something else. *Anything* else. A minute later, I'm still gazing at a pregnancy test. "Oh Jesus," I whisper, my mind not telling me what the fuck to do. I pull it out of the bag and stuff it in the back of my jeans, slamming the door of the cab and pacing back to my car, my head fucking bent.

I slip in beside her. Regard her closely. She's despondent. Distant. "Where did you go?" I ask, starting the car and crawling along the gravel lane. A fucking pregnancy test?

"Nath," she says quietly, looking out of the window. Which means she doesn't see my unstoppable widening eyes. "A friend."

Fuck me, she was with that corrupt shit? When? I've got eyes on him.

"And my ex." Now, she does look at me. For a reaction? I know my tight jaw is giving her one. When was the last time she slept with her ex? "They're both FBI," she adds.

"And they've looked me up," I say, feeling the tightening of my grip on the wheel.

"They didn't find a thing past five years."

"That's because I didn't exist, Beau."

She says nothing. She doesn't need to.

I return my eyes to the road. "But I exist to you." I take her hand from her lap and squeeze. "To everyone else, I'm illusive." Such a statement should earn a gasp. A cry of realization. The retraction of her hand from mine.

Not Beau. She slowly looks away and gazes out of the window, processing what she's learned about me.

She doesn't look like she wants to bolt. But there is one thing that'll have her walking away from me, so I have to ensure she doesn't find out. Beau's mom was relentless. Frustrating as fuck. Always there in the background ready to fuck everything up. One way or another, I knew she would end up dead. She pissed off too many people with her hunger and persistence, started to uncover too many truths. I don't want Beau to follow the same path.

I pull to a stop at the junction, and a fleeting look at my rearview mirror has me stalling from indicating. A BMW in the distance, the nose of the car just jutting out of a dirt track we passed. I flick my eyes to Beau. She's oblivious, still gazing out of the window. I slowly return my eyes to the mirror, pushing down the lever for my indicator as I do, edging forward a few feet, waiting. The car appears.

I pull away, smooth and calm, glancing at my mirror constantly.

I'm at least three hundred yards down the road before it gets to the junction, keeping a safe distance. Not safe enough. And way too close for comfort. My fingers start drumming the wheel, my mind strategizing. God damn state laws in Florida. No fucking front license plate. But it's a BMW. Butler drives a BMW. I look across to Beau, finding her still gazing out of the window. Still oblivious. I pull my phone out and text Otto.

Butler?

His reply is instant.

Can't find the fucker anywhere.

Motherfucker. My teeth grate as I keep eyes on three things. Beau, the road, and my mobile.

He's tailing me. I've got Beau. He was following her.

A bend in the road ahead gives me the opportunity I need, I just hope there's a turning off the main road soon after. Another look at the mirror. I need more distance, so I discreetly build up speed as we approach the curve ahead, just enough to gain more space, but not enough to rouse suspicion in Beau. The moment I take the bend, I look up, seeing the BMW out of sight. And ahead, the turn I need. I indicate, all rather considerately, considering the circumstances, and take the turn onto a small dirt track, stopping a few yards down. I look up at the rearview mirror.

"What are we doing here?" Beau asks, knocked from her quiet daydreaming.

My eyes remain on the mirror, and the second I see the BMW fly past, I turn into her and take her cheeks, kissing her hard, deep, and long. Her tongue surrenders to mine in an instant, swirling and rolling, her good hand in my hair. Thank God for her inability to resist me. I'm banking on it going forward. "Just in case you forgot what it feels like," I say, my throat hoarse, slowing our kiss until our lips are merely touching and our breaths clashing. Her eyes are glassy. Her expression blank. "Don't look at me like that, Beau. Don't look at me like you can't decide whether I'm worth staying for."

She inhales, and thoughts run amok in my brain. What she's been thinking. How she's feeling. *The pregnancy test.* She seemed so accepting back at the graveyard, and now that look? It says too much. I need to get her home.

I slam the car into gear and reverse out of the track, pulling off fast.

If I was in the right mood, I'd be forced to hold back a smile when Otto's face wrinkles in annoyance as we enter the lobby. Naturally, he was mortified he was given the slip. Naturally, he was worried I would turn psycho on him.

Naturally, I very nearly did.

I get Beau into the elevator, smacking the code in with a heavy touch. The doors close. She looks at me in the reflection of the mirror, so impassive. It's killing me. She's shutting down. Thinking too much. I shake my head mildly, silently warning her away from where her mind is going. She looks away. It's not what I need right now.

The doors open, and I pull her out, leading her upstairs with a firm hold. I get her in my bedroom, place her before the frame, and start stripping her out of her clothes. She doesn't stop me. But she also doesn't help. Neither does she show any signs of being turned on. What the fuck has happened? Has her conscience found her? Her morals? I look down at her arm. I can't restrain her. Hold her in place. *Fuck.*

I remove the sling and ease her shirt off before pulling her jeans down and casting them aside with her shoes. "Kneel," I order, desperation getting the better of me. Docile and subservient, she lowers to her knees before me and looks up with vacant eyes, waiting for her next order. Shutting down.

I want escape, and I don't want to be forced to explain why.

Fuck, no.

I could still restrain her. I could deprive her of release, make her beg and cry. I could shove endless objects in her arse and fuck her black and blue. But . . .

Not today.

I pull my T-shirt up over my head as she watches, unbutton my jeans and kick them off, and then fall to my knees in front of her. I'm surrendering. Giving in to this crazy. And by the fleeting look of surprise that passes across her expressionless, hauntingly beautiful face, she sees that. I take her hand and place it on my scarred shoulder.

She's toxic. But to me, she's a balm.

And I'm fatal. But to her, I'm life.

She takes in the damage under her fingers, flexing them into the shiny, pitted flesh. My skin sizzles. "You think you can fix me," she says to her hand, her head tilting in thought, like she's pondering that notion.

"I don't want to fix you. I just want to love you."

Her eyes turn to mine quickly, her fingers stilling.

"I've fought for power, Beau," I whisper. "I've fought for freedom. For revenge. For hatred. But I've never fought for love." And it's the toughest fucking battle yet. "Can I win?" I ask, and she slowly lowers her arse to her heels, silent. Stunned. "Answer me," I grate. "Because everything is fucking irrelevant otherwise." I join her, settling my arse on my heels too. "So, can I win?"

"Can I?" she counters quietly.

"Yes." It's an easy answer. I will make her a conqueror. "No more losses, Beau. Not for either of us. Tell me you understand. Tell me you agree." I take her cheeks harshly. "Do it."

Her eyes dart across my face, her swallows hard and constant. Then she slowly reaches for my boxers, encouraging me to lift, and she draws them down my thighs. My cock twitches, coming to life, and she circles it gently at the base and watches herself draw a long stroke down the shaft. I close my eyes, reaching for her shoulders for an anchor. I'm weeping. On the inside and out. "Beau," I whisper.

"I understand." She calmly pushes me to my back and rids my legs of the material before straddling me, one hand sunk into my chest, the other resting lightly on her stomach. I look at her with all the respect I feel. Respect that's undoubtedly misplaced until she knows every dirty detail. Until she knows how guilty I really am.

I calmly slip a thumb into each side of her knickers and yank, ripping them down each seam. She lifts and I pull them out of my way before taking hold of myself, my eyes glued there, watching as she lazily lowers onto me. Every inch I sink into her, I lose a little more breath until my lungs are ballooned and I'm submerged balls deep, every throbbing piece of me surrounded by the hot, pulsing walls of her pussy.

"Breathe, James," she whispers, rolling her hips. My fingers claw into her flesh, my growl carnal, and she inhales sharply, her jaw tight. She brings her legs out from under her, placing a foot by each side of my head, and my palms wrap around her ankles, my knees coming up so she can rest back on them. The vision of her sitting on me, riding me, of her rolling in circles, grinding down. It will never leave me. Of her breasts bobbing lightly, her lip being bitten harshly, her eyes alive with fortitude. She doesn't think she's strong. But there is nothing but strength staring back at me. Strength and mercy. I can't take my eyes off her. I just hope she holds on to both. I need her strength. But more, I need her mercy.

Her hoarse whimpers become throaty moans, her rolls turning into grinds. Her hand pushes more into my chest, her mouth lax, her eyes glazing. “Feel me, Beau,” I choke, biting down on my back teeth, my dick pounding within her, blood rushing in my veins.

“I feel you,” she murmurs, her head dropping back, lengthening her throat. “Fuck, I feel you.”

I ram upwards, and she cries out as I bark my pleasure. “More?” I ask.

“More,” she whispers, and I flex upward harshly again, the slap of her arse on my flesh deafening. I drop my legs, sending me deeper. And Beau louder. “More!” she screams.

The sound of her hunger sends me into orbit, and my hips begin to piston out of control as I pound into her repeatedly. She bounces on my lap, her hand in her hair, grabbing, pulling, her face a picture of pained ecstasy, mine cut with ruthless pleasure. Her chest expands, and she drops her eyes to mine. Clear eyes. Eyes so crystal, I can see every word she’s saying to me. Amid the chaotic, loud crashing of our bodies together, there is silence. Her eyes. My eyes. Her thoughts. My thoughts. Her heart. My heart.

Her darkness. My darkness.

Her demons diluted by mine.

And mine by hers.

Our releases arrive together, and they arrive calmly, slithering through us steadily as our motions slow and our bodies tremble.

Our eye contact never falters.

But my heart misses endless beats.

Beats that are filled by Beau’s.

Making us one.

She lowers her front to my chest, her nose touching mine, her uninjured arm framing my head. “You found me.”

“Always will, Beau.” I couldn’t have waited until she returned this time. *Always. Until death.*

“You’re The Enigma,” she whispers, her eyes searching mine.

I circle my arms around her back, carefully holding her to me. Not because I'm afraid she'll pull away, but because I'm afraid she won't. I take a breath. "And you're now the darkness within me."

"And you in me." She puts her face deep into my neck, as if she could crawl inside of me. "I love you," she whispers, as if it's forbidden.

It is.

55

BEAU

I'm more morbid than I ever imagined. But broken? No. Nothing broken could withstand this truth. I know little about The Enigma. I know my mother tracked him for three years. I know he's killed many people. I know he disappeared off the face of the earth for a time. But now I know he's back.

And I know I'm in love with him.

Is it the connection to my mother? Is it the warped sense of freedom he makes me feel? Or is it simply that he made it impossible not to love him?

As I lie on top of James, letting my breathing settle, my fingertip circling his nipple slowly, I try with everything I have to make sense of this. Of him, and of me. Of us. There are a million reasons why I shouldn't be here. And just one reason why I should.

Peace.

And peace in me trumps all the things. It's been years since I've felt anything other than hate or grief. Years since I've recognized myself. "You were top on Mom's list," I say, still rising and falling with each expansion of his chest while he works to get his breathing steady.

"I know," he says, almost sadly. "She said she'd never stop until she had me behind bars. And I knew she wouldn't."

I turn my face up to his "How did you know?"

"Because I was looking into her eyes when she said it."

I gasp, scrambling up on his chest, wincing when I jar my arm.

"Be careful," he warns.

"She saw you?"

"She never saw me." He reaches behind him, stretching to get my sling. "No one ever sees me, Beau." He loops it over my head and gently lifts my arm, easing it into the material.

"Not true," I whisper, my eyes flitting over every inch of his face. I see him. I see him so clearly. "You kill people," I say, not accusingly. I'm simply saying it out loud. Saying it and wondering if hearing it will make it any more real. Something has to click soon. My ethics have got to appear and ask me what the fuck I'm doing here with him.

He reaches up and cups my cheek. "I do."

"Why?" I ask, and his hold moves back to my waist. It's firm. "Why are you holding me tightly?" I ask, and he loosens his grip. But only a bit.

"I kill them because they deserve to die."

"According to whom?" I press. "Murder is murder."

"But justice isn't always justice," he fires back quietly, making me pause for a beat. He's right. Where is justice for my mom? For me? I would happily kill whoever is responsible for her death. Slowly. And, sickly, I know I would take the greatest of pleasure from it. I know I'd feel like a weight was lifted. I know it would bring me peace. More peace than James could ever give me. "I wasn't born a killer, Beau."

"Then who were you?"

He looks away, and it's so painfully obvious how difficult he's finding this. "I was a son. A brother." He winces, shying away from the memory. "I had everything until he took it away."

He.

James frowns, and his head shakes mildly, as if he can physically toss those memories away. Which makes me feel plain awful for needing to know more. And I do need. Really *need*. I'm in love with an assassin. A vigilante. Anything I can find to justify that, I will gladly take. "Who?"

"The Bear."

My mouth falls open. The drug smuggler. Human trafficker. Arms dealer. Bomb supplier to endless terrorist organizations. He moved his men in on London to take out the mob kingpin Spencer James. Blew his estate to smithereens. And as soon as The Brit died, he moved in on Miami. I'll never forget Mom's face when The Bear first made his presence known in town.

Clarity seems to smack me in the face, and I breathe in, my attention falling to James's scarred shoulder. British. Explosion. He got caught up in an explosion. *Oh my God.* His entire family wiped out. I stare at him, stunned. "Your dad was Spencer James," I murmur, everything clicking into place. "You're Kellen James." I go to stand, needing to walk and think, but James locks his hold down on my thighs, keeping me close. "That's your other name."

He nods, and the sadness mixed with vengeance is potent. "Everyone's demons are relative, Beau," he says, sitting up and circling my waist. "I'm dead."

"Does The Bear know it's you who's killing all of his men?" Jesus, all these bodies that are cropping up all over town is James's doing? *Fucking hell, what madness am I in?*

"No. No one knows who I am."

"Your accent. He's not connected the dots?"

"Do you know how many people he wiped out along with my father?" He rubs his nose with mine. "You need a bath."

I need many things. A bath isn't one of those things. For a start, I could do with someone pinching me, because this has to be some kind of twisted nightmare. I also need a drink, because I'm feeling slightly unstable, but before I can voice my needs, I'm lifted to my feet and being led to the bathroom. "James," I say, staring at his back, his scars suddenly bigger. Redder. Angrier.

We arrive in the bathroom, and he glances at me, waiting for what I might say. *James, what?* What do I want to say? I have no idea, my brain failing me, so I remain mute. Blank. He starts to draw a bath, adding lavender oil, and I stand behind him, motionless, naked, and utterly absorbed by his scarred skin. I'm not aching. I'm not sore. I don't need to soak myself or soothe my muscles. Perhaps my brain, but not my body. And yet I can't bring myself to challenge him. Not after he's spilled his tragic history.

I was a son. A brother. I had everything until he took it away.

Utterly alone. *An orphan.*

So when the tub is full and he removes my sling, I do as I'm bid and step in, letting him do what he needs to do in this moment. "Here," he says, collecting something from the side and holding it up. A waterproof arm protector. He's got me covered. I let him slip it over my cast before I sink into the water as he climbs in the other end and slides down, submerging himself. He cups his hands and collects some water, splashing his face and pushing his hair back. "I need you to make a few promises," he declares.

"I need you to make me a few too."

His eyebrow quirks in amusement, and it's so out of place for this moment. And yet completely us. "Is that right?" he asks.

"It is."

"And what might those promises be?" His hands spread around my ankles under the water, and the water ripples with the subtle jerk of my body.

"You first," I virtually pant, and he smiles.

"You be patient with me," he says quietly.

"Why?"

"Because I have a lot more men to kill."

I swallow, silently alarmed. "Do they all deserve to die?"

"They're all in The Bear's fold."

Then they deserve to die. Simple. "Okay," I say, not quite believing I'm having this conversation. Perhaps I do need to be committed because I seriously can't be sane. "Anything else?"

"You stay here."

"What?" I reply, quiet and unsure, and his hands clamp down further. "All the time?"

"Yes."

"Why?"

"Because I want you here."

"To wind down after a kill?" I retort, staggered. And it hits me for the first time. The worry. The nerves. Every time he leaves, I'll be a wreck, wondering if he'll be coming back. Who he'll be killing.

James scowls, unimpressed. "Stow away that sarcasm, Beau. Now isn't the time."

"Now's the perfect time," I say, half laughing. "When you've left me here, when you've disappeared, had errands to run, you were killing men, weren't you?"

"I was working toward justice," he grates.

"And the opera house? You left me handcuffed to a chair while you murdered someone. Why the hell did you take me?"

"It would look a bit suspicious if a man was alone at an opera."

He's right. Especially a man as good-looking as James. "So I was an alibi?"

"No, you were my date."

"It wasn't much of a date," I retort, indignant. "I didn't see all the performance, my *date* disappeared for twenty minutes to commit murder, and I was restrained."

His smirk is faint but filthy. "You didn't enjoy me eating your pussy?"

My mouth snaps shut and the elevator dings in the distance. We both look toward the bathroom door. "Details of your next kill, I expect," I say quietly as he rises, the water pouring down his hard physique like it could be tumbling down solid, perfectly cut rocks. He steps out and leans over, slamming a hard kiss on my lips. "Make sure you soak."

"I don't need to soak."

"You do. You also need to start doing as you're told."

"Fuck you."

He smirks. Another hard kiss, and I stubbornly yank my face away. "You're even more beautiful when you're insolent."

I look out the corner of my eye at him. Damn that cute half-grin. It's about as much as I've ever had out of James Kelly. And then he places a hand on my head and dunks me. He actually dunks me! The coldblooded assassin, The Enigma, the silent, invisible killer, just fucking dunked me.

"James!" I gasp when I break the surface, using my one good hand to wipe the water from my face. "You asshole."

He strides out of the bathroom. "Soak," he calls back.

I snort, outraged.

But I smile the brightest I've smiled in years.

And I wonder . . .

Could James find who killed my mother and put an end to them too?

56

JAMES

Relief. God, it feels good. But I have to remember I'm getting ahead of myself. She knows. But she doesn't know.

With a towel wrapped around my waist, I walk to the kitchen to greet Goldie, and the second I clap eyes on her, my relief falls. "What is it?" I ask as she reaches into her pocket and slaps something on the table. Photographs.

Photographs of this building.

Of me.

And of Beau.

What the fuck? My heart jumps, and I turn on my heel and race back up the stairs, bursting into the bathroom. The tub is empty. "No," I breathe, backing up, going to my office. No Beau.

"Where was she?" Goldie asks, joining me on the landing.

I march into my bedroom. "In the tub." No Beau. "Fuck!"

"What?" Beau appears in the doorway to my dressing room,

looking on in alarm. Even more so when she sees Goldie behind me. "What's up?"

What is that leaving my body? It feels like ten tons of fear. *Fuck...me.* But, shit, I need to play this down. "Nothing's up," I say, adjusting my towel, cringing. Beau's not stupid, and here I am treating her like she's stupid. I peek at her and see what I knew I would. Disbelief. "You didn't soak for very long."

I hear Goldie sigh from behind me and Beau's eyes dart to her too. "I'll wait downstairs," she says, backing out of my bedroom. "Don't be long."

"I won't." I'll be right along just as soon as I've pacified a woman who looks nowhere near close to being pacified.

"What's going on?" Beau asks, awkwardly pulling in her towel tighter with one hand, trying to hold one side by clamping her arm to her hip. I can't watch her struggle like that.

"Here." I go to her, pulling it open and evening up each side before wrapping her up neatly and securely. Her eyes burn holes in me the entire time.

"What's Goldie doing here?"

"Delivering the details of my next kill," I quip, buying myself some time, quickly walking through my options. I have only one.

I grab a robe, help her into it, and take her hand, leading her out of my bedroom, down the stairs, unwilling to leave her alone, even in my own apartment. I place her on the couch, drape a throw over her, and hand her the remote control for the TV. "Give me five minutes." I kiss her and leave her still looking stunned.

When I make it to Goldie at the island, she gives me a nod to confirm she's scoped the place. I take my phone from my pocket and load my security app multi-view screen, placing it down before us, my eyes darting across each camera view. Nothing. No one here except us.

"Otto's watching the rest of the cameras," Goldie says quietly as I turn all the frosted glass inside my apartment to clear glass with one click of a button on my mobile, and make sure all the external glass is opaque so no one can see in. "There's no one in the building."

"How the fuck?" I whisper, perching on a stool, trying to keep my concern from my face, knowing Beau's not too far away and she's riddled with curiosity.

"You missed this picture." Goldie spreads the photos and pushes one toward me, and I inhale when my twisted mind computes what I'm looking at.

Me.

A rifle in one hand, my balaclava hanging from the other, stalking out of a factory with murder etched all over my face. Not because I'd just committed it. But because Beau was missing.

"You fucked up," Goldie murmurs, as I stare at the condemning image, wondering how I could have been so fucking stupid. I look over my shoulder to Beau, to the woman who's made me stupid. She's watching us closely. I don't force a reassuring smile. It would be insulting her.

"I know," I whisper, returning my attention forward. "I fucking know."

"So what now?"

"Now I wait." I get up and get two beers from the fridge, twisting the caps off each in turn before taking one to Beau. She looks up at me as she accepts, her expression screaming questions. Questions I can't answer, because the truths will have her running. I tear my eyes away from hers and return to Goldie.

"Wait for what?" she asks.

"His call." I take a slurp of my beer, wondering where *he* is. Plotting. Planning my demise. Because now he knows where to find me. What I look like. He's played the game, and he's played it well. "Be ready," I tell her. "And I need you to pick some things up from Beau's place."

"Like what?"

"Her passport."

"How the hell will I know where to find her passport."

"Because Beau's going to tell me." I look to my side and find confusion that doesn't suit Goldie plastered all over her face.

"She's just going to jump on a private plane with you and go wherever the hell you say, is she?"

"Yes," I answer surely, even if I feel anything but. "She knows who I am."

"What?"

I smile on the inside. "She figured it out."

Goldie laughs, and it's one hundred percent sarcastic. "Did she figure out you were involved in her mother's murder?"

My secret smile falls.

"Didn't think so. What the fuck, Kel? Have you lost your fucking mind?"

"Without question."

"Then let me help you find it," she hisses. "On your couch is a woman who is a sure-fire way to get yourself killed." Her arm shoots toward the table where the photos lay. "I give you exhibit C."

"What's exhibit A and B?"

"Your dick and your fucking heart, my friend." She stomps away, and my teeth naturally clench. But she won't go far. Never will. Because Goldie couldn't repay me in a thousand lifetimes for finding her and giving her a new purpose.

"James?" Beau calls from the couch, pulling my attention her way. *Just tell her. Spill it all.*

And then what?

She leaves.

And if she leaves, she's dead.

And if Beau's dead, I may as well be too.

My foot lifts from the floor to take the first step to her, but I'm halted by the sound of my phone vibrating behind me. I look back.

"I've got to take that," I say, swapping my beer for my phone and wandering away, feeling Beau's eyes on my back as I go. As soon as I'm out of earshot, I answer. And as always, I remain silent, unwilling to kick off the conversation or the threats. Him, though? He's straight in.

"All these years I was sure I would know your face when I saw it."

I smile, and it's as salacious as fuck. My father was a showman, yes. But he kept me, Mum, and my sister well away from the spotlight. I'd love nothing more than to tell him who I am. Why I've hunted him and his men for so long. Unfortunately, I can't do that until I can look him in the eye. Right before I kill him. I'm dead. *Otto made sure of that.* I need to remain that way after this is over. "Annoyed?" I ask.

"Mildly. I lost a few good men for the cause. But whether I recognize you is irrelevant now. I know what you look like and where you are. So I'm one step ahead of you, yes?"

For the first time, yes. He's one step ahead. But not for long. "Seems we're both being enlightened these days."

"Oh?"

"Nathan Butler," I say simply, but I get no reaction. Not that I expected one.

"Beau Hayley," he says instead and, fuck me, I react.

"She stays out of this."

"You've put her in the center. That was very stupid if you want her to be safe."

"She's innocent."

"She's digging like her mother."

My jaw feels like it could break. "She knows her mother's death wasn't an accident."

He laughs. "Then perhaps you should convince her. If you want her to live, that is."

"Do not push me."

"Back off, and so will I."

It should be an easy deal. Should be. "Never."

"Every time you kill one of my men, I lose money. *And* patience."

"I bleed for you," I seethe, my blood burning my veins.

"Who are you?" His voice is suddenly lacking the lightness he kicked off with. "James Kelly, who the fuck are you and what do you want?"

"I'm your end," I promise, hanging up and bracing my hands into the wall, breathing through my fury. And my fear. Because the bomb has started ticking. I'm running out of time, and it isn't only me I need to worry about now.

I flinch when I feel a hand slide onto my shoulder. "Your whose end?" Beau asks quietly.

"Yours. Mine. His." I clench my eyes closed and push away from the wall, turning to face her. I'm shaken. For the first time, my nemesis has me shook. And so has the woman before me. The pregnancy test flashes through my mind. It has to be playing on hers too. "Maybe your ex's," I add.

She retracts her hand like I could have burst into flames. "What?" she whispers.

"When were you last with him?" I ask, sounding harsher than I meant to. But, again, The Bear and his bombshell isn't the only blow I'm dealing with.

Her round eyes stare at me in disbelief. "I assume you mean intimately."

"Yes, I mean intimately." She was at his place. Did he talk her into his bed? My gaze falls to her stomach, and I stare hard, my eyes burning. "When?"

"That's none of your fucking business," she retorts, stepping away.

I finally blink, dampening my dry eyes, trying to see straight. "None of my business?" I ask, stunned. "None of my fucking business?" I grab her uninjured hand, and all but manhandle her up the stairs.

"What the fuck, James?" she yells, unable to even try and pry my grip away. So she yanks and pulls instead.

"Shut up, Beau." I turn and dip, getting her gently on my shoulder. "Don't wriggle or you'll hurt yourself.

"James!" she shouts as I cart her the rest of the way, taking her into the bathroom. "I'm not having another bath."

"I didn't say you were," I place her down. "Wait," I order, marching out of the bathroom. I go to my room, find the pregnancy test buried in my pile of clothes, and stomp back. "You're doing this." I hold it up and watch as her face falls and she retreats. But she's silent, just staring at the harmless box. Harmless? Good God, this box could finish us both.

Enraged by that thought, I tear it open and slam it on the vanity unit. "So I'll ask again." I fold my arms over my chest like some kind of idiotic, proud twat. "When were you last intimate with your ex? Or any other man, for that matter?"

She backs up, her eyes still rooted on the test, until she meets the wall. Then she slowly slides down the tile until she's a small bundle on the floor. "Nearly two years," she says quietly, refusing to look at me. "I haven't been with any men since Ollie."

Something inside lifts. Stress. And doesn't that speak volumes?

"Only you." Her eyes drop to her feet, ashamed. She's not refusing to look at me now. She simply can't face me. "I'm sorry," she whispers.

Sorry? She's sorry? I look at the ceiling, my cheeks ballooning. Maybe she is, but never as sorry as me. "I thought we were protected."

"I didn't take the pill for protection. I took it to stabilize my periods. I only missed one," she whispers. "And I'm not due until tomorrow, but since the doctor mentioned it, it's all I can think of."

"Fuck me," I breathe, lowering to my arse and moving in close to her, my knees bent and framing her curled up body. "Look at me." I take her chin and pull her face from its hiding place. Tears are bursting from her eyes, and it's the most painful thing I've seen. "It'll be okay."

She chokes on a sob. Or was it a laugh? "You're a murderer."

It was a laugh. And, yes, okay, it's quite fucking laughable. If it wasn't so fucking tragic. "Not by nature," I say, and then frown at myself. Am I going to just keep saying stupid shit? "I mean it's not something I *want* to do."

"Then why do you do it?"

"Because there was nothing else but that need."

"And now?"

"Now there's you." I reach blindly for the vanity unit and pull down the test, holding it between us. She looks at it. "And maybe someone else," I add.

Her shoulders jerk, her eyes round and surprised. But not happy. Not relieved. "I'm not mother material." She hiccups over each word, and it shocks me that I feel hurt by that statement. And annoyed. "I can't do it." She's suddenly up, standing over me.

"Do what, Beau?" I stand too, making sure she can't get past me.

She points at the test in my hand, and I take the tops of her arms, moving her to the toilet and sitting her down on the lid. I crouch, holding the test up. She's looking at it like it could be her end. "You don't have a choice this time, Beau. No running." I take her hand and put the test in her grasp, squeezing her fist around it. "I can stay, or I can wait outside. What's it to be?" I know what I want to do, but what I want has to take a back seat for the time being.

"Stay. No, go. Stay." She growls and stands, nearly knocking me back to my arse. "Go," she says, resolute. "I need to be on my own."

I don't like it, but I give her what she thinks she wants and leave the bathroom, shutting the door behind me. I turn around and find her on the other side, the now clear glass not giving her the privacy she's requested. She shows the ceiling her palms, and I reluctantly switch this pane of glass, and this one only, back to frosted. The lock engages, telling me she'll only let me back in when she's ready. It doesn't matter that one shoulder barge could put me back in the bathroom. Or that with another press of a button, I would be able to see her. I'll give her space.

I start to pace outside the door, walking in circles for what feels like forever, intermittently checking the security cameras while my head tangles more with every circuit.

Ten minutes pass, and there's not been one sound from beyond the door. Nothing. How long do these things take? I lift my fist to knock but withdraw again when movement on one of the cameras catches my eye. I tap on the screen, bringing up that one camera's live footage. My blood runs cold. "Fuck," I hiss quietly, looking at the bathroom door, torn between speaking up or not. But I know Beau, and if I tell her to keep the door locked and stay put, she'll do the exact opposite. So I mentally beg her to stay in the bathroom for another few minutes. Just a few minutes.

Because that's all I need.

I haven't got time to arm myself fully. Or even fucking dress myself. I take the stairs silently, three at a time, and sprint to the kitchen, pulling open a cupboard and feeling around the back of some books. I pull out the Heckler, grab the biggest kitchen knife I have, and head for the lift. I look down at the screen of my phone as I go, wondering how the fuck they got past Otto and Goldie. *Where the fuck are they?*

I pull up the rest of the cameras and scan them all. Nothing, except for the fucker in the stairwell. I board the elevator and smack the button for the next floor down.

And as the cart starts moving, something sounds above me.

I look up to the ceiling.

"You fucker," I growl.

57

BEAU

My eyes won't move from the white stick. My mind won't stop praying for one line. It feels like I've been standing here for years, waiting and praying. He's outside the door. Close but giving me space. I can feel him there. Tense. Stressed.

He has nothing on me.

I'm staring at the test on the back of the toilet so hard, my eyes are burning. *One line. Please, just one line. One little li—*

I hear a thud and dart my eyes to the door. I wouldn't be surprised if that was James's big body hitting the floor after passing out from stress. I laugh nervously. And stop in a heartbeat when I realize that could be a very real possibility.

I rush to the door and unlock it, swinging it open. He's not there.

Another thud.

"James?" I take small, tentative steps to the top of the stairs, and when I make it there, it's me who nearly passes out. "Jesus," I gasp, grabbing at the rail to hold myself up.

James looks up at me, his eyes filled with a wildness I've never seen before. Not in any man. Not in any criminal or crazy bastard I've dealt with while in uniform. His naked body is covered in blood, the knife in his hand glistening, the towel that was covering him nearby on the floor.

"Stay exactly where you are," he says quietly, going to his phone and staring at the screen for an eternity. I lower to the top step, not challenging him, not daring. There are times when you simply trust in the skill of your partner. And, strangely, I know to completely trust James now. My gaze drops to the body at his feet. To the gun in the man's limp, dead hand. I've lost the power of speech. I can't ask who it is or what the hell is happening. I'm numb. Shocked.

James's phone rings and he's quick to answer, splitting his attention between the open elevator doors and me. "One in the stairwell. One dead on my apartment floor." He paces to the elevator and steps inside, smacking a few buttons and looking up before stepping out. The doors close. "The elevator's coming down." He goes back to the man, crouching down by his body and patting at his pockets. He pulls out a cell and hits a few buttons before setting it aside and rising to his full height. He casts his eyes my way. The wildness has subsided. But it doesn't ease me, because in its place is worry.

"What's going on?" It feels like a crazy thing to ask. I know what's going on. An ambush. A murder. But why? And who?

James says nothing, just raises his finger to his lips in a silent sign to quieten me. Then he mouths, "It's okay."

Okay? Am I not staring at a dead body at his feet? Am I imagining the blood covering him?

I startle when the elevator dings, jumping out of my skin, and James flies around, his naked body poised and ready as the doors slide open. Goldie appears, and he relaxes. I don't know why. She looks fucking murderous, and above her eyebrow, a nasty gash. "Otto took care of the stairwell," she grates, reaching up and wiping the blood with the cuff of her suit jacket. "The building is clear."

At those words, James drops the knife and collects the towel, covering himself before pulling up one corner and wiping his hands. "Find out who it is," he orders shortly, looking at the corpse like he wants to kill him all over again. Goldie approaches and pulls out her phone, taking a picture of the man's face and tapping out a message.

Within a few seconds, she looks at James and shakes her head, and he curses, turning and stalking toward the stairs. I slowly rise as he climbs the steps, his eyes drilling into me. "Do you have a passport?" he asks, and while I'm scared, concerned, and many other emotions that I'm trying to contain, I know it wouldn't be wise right now to question him.

"Yes."

"Where?"

"In my nightstand at home," I answer as he takes my hand and pulls me toward the bathroom.

He closes the door behind us and goes to the shower, flipping it on. And I just stand like an idiot, my mind twisting painfully. He doesn't look like he's in the mood for questions or talking. So I'm expected to see what I saw, hear what I heard, and say nothing? He pulls his towel from his waist and tosses it in the tub before going to the sink and washing his hands thoroughly. Then he braces them on the edge of the vanity unit, leaning in, staring into his own eyes in the mirror. I don't wonder what he's thinking. Vengeance is thick in the air. His naked body looks lethal, every muscle pulsing, like he's preparing for another attack.

This now, the man before me, the man with murder etched on every inch of his skin.

He's The Enigma.

"Was it positive?" His eyes turn to me, and I frown, momentarily lost. Then it hits me like a sledgehammer square in the face, and my gaze falls onto the test still on the back of the toilet. My blood turns to ice. My heart starts racing. "Why are you panicking?" James asks, turning at the sink to face me.

"Why?" I motion to his blood-drenched torso. His beautiful torso that's now as ruined as his back. Although it can be washed away, there is nothing that could clean my mind. "I'm an ex-cop, and I'm potentially pregnant by a murderer."

He smiles a little, and it's wholly inapt. "Potentially?" His ass rests on the vanity, his palms wedged on the edge.

I look at the back of the toilet again, to the white stick that could ruin us. And I laugh on the inside. We're both ruined already. But that little stick and the potential lines on it could tip us. And there's another thing. Us? For God's sake, I barely know the man. I look at James. His eyebrows are high. Waiting. "I didn't see the result," I answer, fiddling with my towel, refastening it. "I was distracted by my boyfriend murdering someone."

"Boyfriend?" he asks over a laugh, and I feel my cheeks heating. It's fucking ridiculous.

"What the hell do you want me to call you?" I ask, as indignant as could be. "Lover? Better half? Murderer?" I am completely and utterly exasperated by the whole situation. I walk over to the tub and rest my ass on the edge, ignoring the blood-soaked towel behind me. I feel lightheaded all of a sudden. And hot. My skin is clammy, and it has nothing to do with the steaming shower running.

"So we still don't know?' he asks, looking over to the toilet. I follow his gaze and narrow my eyes on the white stick.

"No."

"Are you going to look?"

"You do it," I murmur, back to being plain terrified, the bludgeoning of a man downstairs long forgotten. My boyfriend's true identity forgotten. This somehow feels more serious. Why doesn't James seem as worried as I am? He's standing there stark naked, his solid arms braced and splendid, all casual, appearing as impassive as I know he can be.

"Fine." He pushes himself off the unit and takes his sweet time wandering over to the toilet. I don't think he's nervous or stalling. I feel like he's simply drawing out my torture and enjoying it. I scowl at him as he stares at me, blindly reaching for the stick. Then he looks down, and I hold my breath. His face is blank. I can't read it at all. *God damn, what is it?*

But I can't ask; I'm too scared of the answer. My lungs are screeching for some oxygen, my heart begging for some respite. "Negative," he says quietly, and all the air leaves me loudly, my entire being deflating.

"Oh thank God," I breathe, reaching for my chest and massaging the lingering pain away. I look to the ceiling, and I smile, so fucking happy. I will *not* let that happen again. No fucking way. How could I have been so careless? James drops the stick in the trash can by the toilet. "I'm sorry for putting you through that."

He nods, stepping into the shower stall, letting the hot flow wash away the blood all over his hands and chest. He doesn't ask me to join him, doesn't talk, but his eyes hardly stray from me the whole time he cleans himself.

My ass starts to numb on the edge of the tub, and I stand, moving across to the toilet and lowering to the seat. "Did The Bear send that man?" I ask.

"Yes." He reaches for a towel and steps out, drying.

"How did they know where to find you?"

"I fucked up."

"Am I in danger?" It's a crazy thing to ask when I'm sleeping with one of the country's most wanted men. Utterly crazy, and yet look at all this crazy going on.

"You're the safest woman in this world, Beau Hayley." He secures the towel around his waist. "Nothing can harm you."

"You can," I whisper.

His movements falter, and he glances up at me. But he doesn't say anything, doesn't correct me, and that terrifies me more than any truths he could share.

I wake to the sound of my cell ringing. The feel of it vibrating registers, and I pat around my body until I lay my hands on it. I hold it up and squint at the screen until Dexter's name forms. My hand plummets back to the mattress with my phone. I can't talk to him now. Not only because I'm still half asleep.

I roll onto my side and find the space next to me is empty. The room is dusky. The morning sky in the distance is red. *Red at night, sailor's delight*.

But it's morning.

I grab my sling off the nightstand and edge to the side as I get it on, before following my feet to the stairs. The first thing I see are the bags by the door. Travel bags. And any signs of murder have vanished. No dead guy. No blood.

I see James below on the couch in his boxers, sitting forward, a candle burning on the table before him. He's watching the flame intently. Studying it. Mesmerized by it. He takes his hand and glides it through the air above the glass, back and forth slowly, over and again. Heat. Burn.

His scarred body.

He eventually stops directly above the flame and holds it there, his torso tensing. He's hurting.

I don't call out, don't disturb him. I'm rapt, watching him withstand the heat. Then suddenly he pulls away and looks down at the center of his palm. "When you've been burned alive," he whispers, looking up at me, "nothing can hurt as much." He rests back and gives me a look that suggests I should go to him. So I do.

The moment I'm close enough, he takes my hand and pulls me onto his lap, positioning me just so, my back to his front. My eyes root to the flickering flame as he takes my arm. "Nothing will ever hurt you like this hurt you." He draws faint lines up and down the scar tissue. "Not physically or mentally."

"I'm in a mindfuck that hurts quite bad right now."

"Your mindfuck has nothing on this," he says, holding up my deformed arm in front of us before sliding his palm down to my hand and lacing our fingers. "That's why you're here."

"That's why I'm here," I reply on a whisper. "And because I love you."

"And because you love me." He brings our entwined hands to his mouth and kisses them. "And I'm hurting now more than I thought possible again, because I love you too."

I swallow, the flame swaying rhythmically. I keep asking myself how I can love James. It's a mental battle I'm having every minute. Sensibility is yelling at me to break away before my love kills me. Logic is demanding I stay before something else kills me. *Don't break the bond.* "How can you love me?" I ask, and the moment the question is out there, he stills beneath me. Even his heart beating into my back slows.

"Turn around," he orders, helping me to shift on his lap until I'm facing him. I spend some needed time taking in every inch of his face. From his mussed-up hair to his rough stubble. From his soulful eyes, to his beautifully shaped lips. From his defined jaw to his perfectly crooked nose. Every inch of this man is breathtaking. Every part of him sends my senses into meltdown. His rough, gravelly voice. The words he says. The feel of his touch on my skin. His scent. Manly but soft. His tongue in my mouth. The taste of him.

Flattening my palm, he places it on his shoulder. "I can love you because you're as merciless as I am." He moves my fingers across the bumpy flesh of his shoulder, and my eyes fall there, seeing my scars blend with his. "I can love you because you're crippled by hatred and a sense of injustice." My eyes bolt back to his, and I lose myself in their blazing depths. "Your love for me walks hand in hand with your hate for the world." Bringing my hand to his lips, he presses a kiss in the center of my palm. "They are equals. Passion fueled. Your love and your hate are what makes you, Beau, and mine is what makes me." His hands land on my hips, and my traitorous lip wobbles. Love and hate. I couldn't stop loving this man if I tried, no matter who he is. And I couldn't stop hating the world if my life depended on it. But I can do both. Love and hate. "I will treasure your love, and I'll nurture your hate. Because without your hate, you're not the woman I love."

"That's so fucked up," I whisper, my voice breaking.

"That's so us," he replies, taking my nape and holding me firmly. "We understand each other. Feel each other's pain. See each other's struggles. I've searched for one reason not to love you, and yet all I can find are a million reason *to* love you."

I'm not sure if a weight has been lifted or lowered onto my shoulders. I feel heavy but light. Hopeful but full of dread. "That's quite swoony for an assassin," I say, and he smiles a little.

"It's not swoony. It's the truth." His eyes lower to my exposed chest, and he leans forward, peppering kisses over each boob before finishing on my tummy. "We should eat." Cupping my ass, he stands effortlessly and takes me to the kitchen area, placing me on the counter by the sink.

"Shouldn't we be leaving?" I ask, glancing around, now noticing all of the windows are no longer clear. No one can see in. Protection.

"He thinks the job's done," he says, going to a cupboard.

"Well, it's not," I say, motioning to his beast of a body, like he could have missed the fact that he's still breathing. *Thank God.*

"Surely when he doesn't get word from those men, he'll know you're still here."

"He *has* got word from his men," James says, and I withdraw. Did one of them get—

It clicks. He's used the cell he found on the body to check in. "We have some breathing space," he says.

I don't like the sound of that. Breathing space. He's plotting something. I hear my cell in the distance as James reaches into the fridge, peering back at me.

"I should get that." I slip down. "It'll be Dexter. They're worried."

I get a small, accepting nod, but I can see his concern. "Will they try to talk you out of this?"

"You mean me and you?" I ask, and he nods, lowering some milk to the counter. "You're a killer, James." It sounds as crazy as it is. And yet here I am, in love with a killer. I can sugarcoat it all I like. Plead justice. Claim every life ended was warranted. That every man James has killed deserved to die. None of those things change the fact that James is a cold-blooded murderer.

"They don't know what I do," he says, leaning against the counter, casual and cool.

"Then they clearly just get a bad vibe from you."

He pouts, and it's quite adorable. "Go answer your phone," he orders, continuing to make whatever it is he's making.

I do as I'm bid and find my cell nestled in the sheets, but I falter answering when I see it's Nath calling again, not Dexter. I don't want to argue with him. I'm not interested in hearing what he has to say. There's nothing to be gained from answering, so I don't. He tries again immediately. And again. Then the messages start landing, one after the other, all urgent words begging me to take his call. Something about my mother. He's done this before. Lured me in with false promises of information. But what if . . .

My heart constricts in my chest, and I answer, lowering to the bed as I do.

"Beau," Nath blurts urgently. "You have to leave."

"You said you had information on my mother," I whisper lowly, my tone loaded with warning. "Don't tell me you've lied again, just so you can tell me to leave James."

"Beau, you have to listen to me."

"I don't have to listen to anyone," I seethe, slamming my fist down on the bed with my phone so hard, it jolts my other arm. I hiss as a wicked pain shoots up my limb. How could he?

I head to the bathroom to splash my burning face, but another message halts my tracks. I look down at the screen as it pings, one message after the other.

You're in danger.

He's not who you think he is.

I don't know who the fuck he is, but he's not James Kelly.

He was involved in your mom's death.

My inhale is so sharp, so abrupt, it has me reaching into thin air to grab something for support. My thoughts chase in circles, my mind trying to process what I'm reading. I look up at the glass, seeing through to the top of the stairs. *Transparent.*

Another ding from my phone pulls my attention back there.

Watch this. I'm sorry, Beau. GET OUT.

The shakes come on strong, unstoppable and relentless, making my thumb uncoordinated and clumsy as it hits the play icon of the video attachment. A computer comes into view, and on the screen, footage of a place I recognize. I lower to the bed, seeing the comings and goings of the store parking lot. My eyes drop to the bottom corner. To the time and date. "Oh my God." That date, that time, they're etched in my memory. And then I see us. Me and Mom. She pulls into the parking lot and zips into a space, and the car sits there for a while. I remember the conversation. I remember pulling on my boots. I remember her face when her cell rang.

I watch as I get out and shut the door, wandering through the automatic doors of the store, and the whole time I'm in there getting our wine, I stare at her car, looking, searching, waiting, watching.

Ten minutes later, I emerge from the store.

My heart starts to pound.

I wander across the parking lot.

My throat clogs.

I approach Mom's car.

I hold my breath, unable to look away from the carnage about to happen. Then the screen changes. Another angle of the store.

And a man.

There's no mistaking his frame. His build. His height. And if that wasn't enough for me, his face. I inhale, checking the digits in the corner. Same day. Same time.

"No," I whisper, as James moves out of the shot. I only see a spark. Not the full explosion. Not me being flung skyward and landing in a broken, burned heap. I drop my phone. Numb. Dazed. I look around James's bedroom. See a black T-shirt hanging over the chair. I get up and walk on surprisingly steady legs to fetch it, pulling it over my head and down my body.

Then I go to his office and pull open drawer after drawer. I find burner phones. Lots of them. Then a drawer with a laptop. And under it . . .

58

JAMES

I scrape some peeled mango from the chopping board into the blender, checking the cameras on my phone where it's propped against the coffee machine. I see Beau in my bedroom pulling on one of my T-shirts. Naturally, I wonder how the conversation with her uncle went. And, naturally, I growl under my breath.

I watch her leave my bedroom and enter my office. She goes to my desk and starts rummaging through the drawers where I keep my phones and laptop. I lay down the knife. What is she doing? Or looking for? She pulls something out and rushes to the door, and I collect my phone to zoom in, but she's out of my office fast. I turn my stare from my mobile to the top of the stairs.

And freeze.

My eyes travel from Beau's empty, emotionless eyes, down her scarred arm to her hand.

Where I find a gun.

And I know the fucker is loaded. "What the fuck?" I ask, watching as she takes the stairs, her arm extended, the gun aimed my way. If I didn't know her, if Beau was any other woman, I'd say her chance of hitting me from that distance was minimal. But I know Beau. I know she aced the Phase 1. I know she breezed through target practice and rarely missed the fucking bullseye. And here I am. The bullseye.

"You killed my mother," she says, reaching the bottom of the stairs and edging around the room carefully, her aim never wavering. My world narrows and tunnels, every vision from that night charging forward. And my heart? That fucker slows until it feels like it could stop.

"Put the gun down, Beau," I order, turning on the spot so I remain facing her, keeping her target in range.

"You lied to me. I saw you on the footage." Her face is scarily impassive. Her voice worryingly steady. Her body free from shakes.

"The gun, Beau," I say calmly as she comes to a stop by the window. "Please, put the gun down."

Her arm jolts, the gun jarring threateningly, and I retreat a step, wary. "My mom was hunting you for years. Did she get too close for comfort?"

"No," I say, shaking my head to reinforce it, but I really can't deny that Jaz Hayley got too close too many times. The woman's capabilities were frightening. I often thought it was right place, right time. But I soon learned she had a kind of sixth sense, and it was that sixth sense that earned her the respect she demanded from both her peers and the criminals she hunted down. But . . . what footage is Beau talking about, where the hell has it come from, and why only now, two years later?

"Yes," she says calmly.

"What fucking footage, Beau?"

"Outside the store. The night my mom was killed. You're there."

Oh Jesus. "It's not what you think."

"Don't lie to me!" Beau screams, her composure gone, her arm starting to shake. I watch as she lifts her cast to try and support her other arm. She's aching. She won't be able to hold her position for much longer.

I step forward slowly, my hands up in surrender. "Let me explain." The elevator dings, and Beau swings her aim toward it as the doors open, revealing Goldie. It takes her a second to take in the scene and draw her gun, aiming it at Beau.

"No," I yell, torn between getting between them or backing off. Beau's gun redirects to me, and Goldie looks between us, her face a picture of *What the fuck?*

"Put the fucking gun down, Beau," I demand, raising my hand in indication for Goldie to do the same.

"Take it easy," Goldie says quietly. I know she doesn't like it, but she slowly lowers her weapon to the floor.

"Don't fucking tell me to take it easy," Beau shouts, her eyes pooling, the gun shaking. "It was you in the footage. Say it was you."

God damn it, this is not how this was supposed to go. "It was me," I admit, my options limited.

She moves fast and fires a shot, and I flinch, ducking, the bullet sinking into a cupboard behind me.

"Beau!" Goldie barks.

"What the fuck?" I murmur, all hell breaking loose across the room. I gather myself, just as Goldie moves in, tackling Beau to the floor. "Goldie, no!" I roar, sprinting toward them as Beau lands with a thud, crying out as her arm smacks the floor. It doesn't stop her. A second later, she has Goldie at her mercy in a choke hold and her eyes bulge, her legs flailing, as her hands wrap around Beau's arm and cast to try and free herself. *Jesus Christ.*

I see it happen before Goldie has even engaged, her head flying back and cracking Beau on the cheek. It gives her the moment she needs to free herself, and she spins, pulling back her fist, ready to sink it into Beau's face. But Beau moves fast, flipping herself over, and Goldie's fist lands in Beau's side, winding her. "Goldie, stop!" I bellow, grabbing her from behind and yanking her back. "For fuck's sake, stop!" I've seen Goldie lose it only once. Only once has the red mist descended and sent her psycho. When that happens, she's unmoving. Unstoppable. She won't quit until her victim is unconscious or even dead.

"She's pregnant!" I yell, shoving Goldie away. "For fuck's sake, she's fucking pregnant." I go to Beau on the floor and start to gather her up, but I'm met with force, her hands batting me away.

She scrambles up, moving back, retreating. "What are you talking about?" she wheezes, eyes darting wildly. And it hits me. What I've said. *Fuck.*

"You're pregnant." I exhale, wishing for a clean outcome to this shitshow.

"You said negative." Beau points up the stairs, as if I could have forgotten the scene in the bathroom after my apartment got ambushed. "You said it was negative."

I did. I don't know what came over me. Maybe it was seeing the absolute terror in her eyes. Maybe I wanted to test just how relieved I thought she'd be. How much she *didn't* want it. I never anticipated the level of her appreciation. How happy she was. Her smile. And then I couldn't bring myself to utter the words that would send her relief spiraling into regret. And the truth is, I was gutted. Stunned. Not only by Beau's reaction, but by my disappointment. Because in that moment, I saw a glimmer of hope for us both. Something to turn us both around. Something to tear us away from vengeance and bring us peace. Something other than each other, for there is nothing to save us from ourselves. Except, perhaps, a new life. Not death, not blood, not pain, not revenge.

Peace in its purest form and purpose of the most promising kind. It's something I never considered finding, and in that moment, it was mine.

"You were so relieved." I look away, forcing back any signs of hurt. "I didn't want to take that away from you."

Beau coughs over a laugh, and I flick my eyes to Goldie who's standing quietly by the elevator. She shakes her head at me. It's understandable. She sees the hidden hope. I'm a fucking joke. Do I honestly think there's anything that can save me? No. But without hope that there's something that can save Beau, what's the fucking point in me being here?

I drag my eyes back to the woman who has taken everything I thought I understood and blew it apart. I'm not the man I was when she walked into my apartment only a few weeks ago. Unfeeling. Unrepentant. *Unseen*. Problem is, I'm not sure who I've become in that short time. Or if I can keep him alive.

Beau looks spaced out. It's not sunk in yet. I can relate. I've thought of nothing since I saw two little lines. "Beau?" I say, moving forward.

Her hand comes up, halting me. "Don't touch me," she orders, her chest pulsing. "Just do not touch me."

"We need to talk about this."

The elevator doors open, and Goldie enters it silently, leaving us alone. She gives me another shake of her head before I lose sight of her.

Beau moves across to the kitchen and opens the fridge. She reaches for a bottle of beer, and I feel every muscle in me tense, ready to go over and fight her for it. But she diverts her reaching hand to a water before I'm forced to intervene, swigging half the bottle down in one long gulp. Then she turns and paces to the stairs, taking them two at a time, fast and determined. I grab my phone and follow her, checking the cameras as I do. There's a message from Goldie.

I've never in my life known such a stupid fucking man.

"Me neither," I say to myself, calling her. "Are you okay?" I ask when she answers.

"I'm fine. For fuck's sake. I don't even know what to say to you."

Nothing. Say nothing about *that*. "Do we know how they got in yet?"

"The sensor on the roof failed. Or was cut."

"Fix it. Add more backups." I hang up and realign my focus, finding Beau in the bathroom sitting on the toilet seat rifling through the bin. She pulls out the stick. Looks at it. Then she hiccups over a sob, dropping it to the tile and burying her face in her palm. My heart twists in my chest as I stand on the threshold, wanting to go to her but knowing I'm walking on dangerous ground. We still haven't cleared up the matter that had her pointing a fucking 9mm at me. I don't know who told her I was there, or where the fuck this footage has come from. I can't bear watching her fall apart like this. I should be on my knees before her, holding her, telling her it's all going to be okay.

But . . . is it?

Can it be okay?

She snivels and brushes at her wet cheeks angrily, finding me by the door. "I don't want a baby."

"You don't have a choice," I say without thinking, my instinct taking over.

She glares at me, steely faced. "Don't I?"

I recoil, unable to wipe the disgust away. Is she suggesting . . .? "I've killed many men, Beau. I've tortured them and felt not a shred of remorse. You expect me to let you kill my flesh and blood?" My protectiveness surprises me. I've not had a moment to digest what's happening. Beau even less time. But something deep and unyielding will not tolerate nor entertain what she is suggesting. This is a life she's talking about. A life we made together. Not a tarnished, ugly, blood-bathed existence. It's a fucking child. I slump against the doorframe and slide down to my arse, my legs hollow and weak, my heart hurting.

She looks away and shame engulfs every inch of her. It's a mild consolation. "This wasn't supposed to happen."

"And yet it has. So we fucking deal with it."

"How are you being so stable?" she asks, looking at me for an answer. "This is the worst thing that could have happened."

Stable? I'm far from stable. I've got someone trying to turn Beau against me, she's pregnant with my fucking child, The Bear has sent two killers into my home, and she thinks I murdered her mother. Stable? I should be in a straitjacket. But to keep my life—Beau's life, our fucking baby's life, I need to keep my head. "The worst thing that could happen is you believing I killed your mother."

Her head snaps up. "I saw you on the footage."

"What footage? Who sent you this footage?"

"Nath sent it. And you're there. Watching. Making sure you got the job done." She frowns. "But Nath's never met you. So how did he know it was you in the footage?" Her hand goes to her head, like she can't cope with the information overload.

Nath. Her *friend*. That fucker is as dirty as they come. "He knew what I looked like because he saw me at your mum's grave." I can feel my nostrils flaring, the rage threatening. "He was following you." Her face is a picture of disbelief. Jesus, she *has* to believe me. "Show me the footage."

"I dropped my cell in your bedroom."

I drag myself up and go find it, returning quickly and handing it over. Her lips straight, she taps her screen and thrusts it in my face, and I watch the footage while Beau watches me. Jaz's car. Beau getting out. Me in another shot.

It cuts before the end. It's condemning. It's exactly how Nathan Butler wants it to be.

Manipulated.

"Yes, I was there the night your mum died, Beau. But I was trying to stop it." I turn away from her, giving her my back, which feels like it could be burning all over again. "This didn't happen in the explosion that killed my family. I wasn't in the house, I was at the back of the grounds playing golf with Otto. This happened the night your mum died. This happened when I pulled you away from the car. This fucking happened when I tried to get your mother out." I swallow and clench my eyes closed. The silence behind me is unbearable. The feel of her eyes, new eyes, taking in the damage on my back is as painful as the night I sustained the burns. "Your mother didn't deserve to die, so I tried to save her."

I escape her scrutiny, walking away, heading for my office. The drinks cabinet calls, and I make fast work of unscrewing the cap off a bottle of Black Label and swigging a good dose. The bottle hitting the cabinet masks my gasp. The burn on my back masks the burn in my throat. What the fuck is this mess? And the footage? The Bear would've seen it two years ago. Seen *me*. Wondered who the fuck I was. He wouldn't have connected the man in the footage to The Enigma, because why the fuck would the man killing off his army want to save an FBI agent? But now? Now he's connected the dots. Now he knows the man who tried to save Jaz Hayley is the man killing his men. I can only imagine the mindfuck that's got him in. I'm mildly satisfied. For the most part, I'm frustrated. He has my face, thanks to that footage and the photographs from the factory. One of my names, thanks to Butler. My location, thanks to my stupidity. It's a fuck load more than I have on him.

My fingers claw around the bottle, my breathing shallow and erratic. "Fuck." I swing around and hurl the bottle at the wall, taking out one of the screens. Ironically, it's the screen where The Bear's face should be. Is it a sign? A sign that I'll never find him? Never kill him? Never get the justice I need?

Beau appears in the doorway, taking in the mess of glass shards all over the floor. "Talk," she orders, closing the door, a silent sign that neither of us is leaving until this is sorted out. Will it ever be? I've delved into the deep, and I'm fighting to keep my head above water.

My body as heavy as fuck, I go to the chair at my desk and drop into it with a thud, rubbing at my eye sockets. "The night your mum was killed, I found a phone on the body of an associate of The Bear. A message was sent confirming the hit on your mum." I look up at Beau and find no reaction. Nothing. "I tracked where the message came from. Another burner. It's been off since. Untraceable. Until a few days ago." She still shows no reaction, and it's beginning to fuck me off. What the hell do I need to say to penetrate her? She's found out the man who ordered the death of my family also ordered the death of her mother. Where's her fucking shock? "It was tracked to Nathan Butler's flat." And there it is. A recoil. "Your mother hunted me relentlessly, but she and I were after the same people, Beau. We just had different ideas of justice. I killed them before Jaz could cuff them. It pissed her off." Beau's reinstated her impassiveness. Shutting down? "I was tailing your mum the night she was killed. I called her. Warned her. She told me to fuck off and die." If I could, I'd smile. How Jaz would have loved me to fuck off and die. "By the time she realized I wasn't fucking with her, it was too late." I see balls of fire in my memories. Hear screams. Feel the heat. Butler must have burst a blood vessel when he saw me at the graveyard with Beau. James Kelly—Beau's boyfriend—is the man in the footage. The footage that's been missing for two years. The footage that's missing from the police report. The footage that, if complete, would have proved Beau's mother's death wasn't an accident. But also would have put my face on the FBI's radar as a person of interest. I laugh under my breath. *Interest?* They'd have no fucking idea.

Beau steps back. "It was you on the phone to her," she says, and I nod. "Why did you contact me? Why did you bring me here?"

"Because your relentlessness would have got you killed too. The investigation you want won't happen. You won't get justice, Beau." I eye her carefully. She looks about ready to bolt. "Not if you play by the rules," I add gently.

She inhales. Swallows. "But if I play by your rules?"

"I have only one rule."

"What?"

"No mercy." Who I really am is still unknown. My motives are a mystery. But the game is nearly over, and it'll be me who wins.

Her eyes drop to her bare feet. I would give anything to know what she's thinking. "Are you saying Nath had my mom killed?"

"He's dirty, Beau. Your mother figured that out."

"No."

"Yes." I get up, resting my hands on the edge of the desk, leaning in. "The Bear's got an inside man. Nathan Butler. Your mum was a clever woman, Beau. She figured that out. That's why she's dead. You want justice? Let me get you justice."

She shoots her eyes my way, and I fucking detest the pain in them. "You want to kill Nath?"

"I want to kill them all."

Her chest expands, her eyes darting across the glass of my desk. "And what about us?"

"*Us*, me and you?" I ask. "Or *us*, you and my baby?"

She quickly steps back, her eyes wide, her lip wobbling. "I don't know," she admits, and it's crushing. I understand her doubt. Hate it, but I understand it. "What if you're wrong?"

She's clinging to hope. I wish it wasn't so wasted.

"He's hidden that footage for years, Beau. Why hasn't he shown you it before now? He knew all along your mother was murdered because he played a part in it. He's cornered."

"I've trusted Nath with . . . everything."

I can't stand the devastation on her face. "I tried so hard to save her, Beau. And I'm so fucking sorry I failed." I collapse back to the chair, exhausted, wedging my elbows on the glass and burying my face in my hands. My head feels heavy. Heavy with regret, with sorrow, and with fury. And yet I can't regret stepping in and bringing Beau here. I can't entertain the thought of what might have happened if I'd left her alone. She would have kept digging. And she would have ended up dead.

I flinch when I feel her touch on my shoulder. "I want justice." She takes my hand and places it on her stomach, and I look up at her. "I can't move on until then. I know it's fucked up, but I have to prove for my own sanity that Mom's death wasn't an accident."

Fucked up? She's pretty fucking perfect in her own fucked-up way. I yank her onto my lap and hug her to my chest. "I want justice for your mum too. But by digging, I'm risking exposing myself."

She frowns. "How?"

"Your mum figured out who I was," I whisper. "She said she was keeping my identity as security. You pushing an appeal into the circumstances of her death wasn't only bad news for The Bear and Butler, it was bad news for me too." The video footage case in point.

"So why show me the CCTV footage now? They're risking exposing themselves too."

"No one will see that footage."

"I have a copy."

"It's a cut version, Beau." And even if it wasn't, she'd be dead before she could share it.

She closes her eyes, shaking her head, as if trying to let the information settle. "So you found me," she whispers, looking at me.

"And I wanted to kill you," I admit quietly, hoping she'll forgive me, since she just shot at me herself. "But only because I wanted to physically get rid of you to stop the crazy in my head every time I saw you. And because I knew you'd be the end of me. And you are."

"The end of you?"

"The end of *this* me."

"I kind of like this you," she whispers, almost reluctantly. I smile. Perfectly fucked up. Both of us.

"I need to ask you something."

She stills. "What?"

"Did your mum leave you anything?"

"Like what?"

"Like a safety deposit box key?"

"That's very specific." She leans back, eyeing me with suspicion. "And also the reason, I expect, why you conveniently brought up a conversation about safety deposit boxes the other day."

I shrug. "I found a record for an account held by Dolly Daydream." I raise a brow when Beau's eyes widen. "Knowing your mum as I knew her, she would always cover her arse. Put security measures in place."

"You think she's put your identity in there?"

"It's a possibility. Along with other information that might be of use to me."

"Is that the only reason you hunted me down?"

I inwardly roll my eyes at her indignant face. "If I hunted you, you'd know about it." I lean forward until our noses meet. "I'm hoping now that you're carrying my baby, you might help me find the key to that safety deposit box to eliminate any possibility of your child's father being murdered or put behind bars for thirty life sentences."

"Thirty?" she blurts. "Fuck me, is that how many men you've killed?"

My lips straighten, and she pouts.

"I don't know about any safety deposit box. Or key." She looks truly sorry about that. "So what now?"

I pull her in, smoothing her hair from her face. "I find another way."

"You kill more men," she says quietly. "Before they kill you."

Basically, yes. All while keeping Beau safe too.

59

BEAU

I sink my teeth into the toast and chew slowly, staring at the kitchen window. There's no view today, the glass still frosted, closing me in. Keeping us safe. On one hand, I feel like a weight has been lifted from my shoulders. On the other, I feel even heavier than before. A key. A box. It's driving me insane.

And Nath.

I don't want to believe it's true, and yet it makes sense. His reluctance to help me. His evasiveness. His weird behavior recently. His dislike for James—a man he's never even met. I need to know what the hell happened to get him in up to his eyeballs. And, maybe, convince James to let him live. I'm not a monster, after all. But James . . .

My cell starts dancing across the counter. "Oh no," I mumble around my toast, leaning back.

"Who is it?"

I twirl around and find James coming down the stairs. He's still in his boxers. I'm still in his T-shirt. All morning, he's not let me leave his sight, except for just now, when he used the bathroom. But I know he had the cameras up on his phone the whole time.

"My uncle." I brush my hands off, not only to get rid of the crumbs. "I need to build up to that conversation."

"What conversation?" James asks, giving my thigh a squeeze as he passes me to the fridge. "That I'm a cold-blooded killer?"

"Stop it." I roll my eyes and turn on my stool to face him across the island. "You're not cold-blooded."

"Hot-blooded?" He gives me high brows, downing some water, and I laugh. Then James stills, the water in midair. "What?" I ask, suddenly worried. Did he hear something? See something? I glance around his apartment.

"I've never seen you laugh before," he says quietly. And it occurs to me. I've never seen him laugh either. Nor have I heard him. "Do it again."

"What, laugh?" I ask, and he nods. "I can't just laugh on demand."

He pouts and sets his bottle of water aside, and I see something in James that's new. Mischief. "Laugh," he orders, leaning across the island, his eyes glimmering.

"I can't just laugh."

He hums, drumming his fingers, his mischief growing.

"Whatever you're planning on doing," I say, tilting my head, "don't do it."

He tilts his right back, and just as I'm bracing myself to run, his arm shoots across the island at lightning speed and seizes me. I gasp. James grins. "I saw you moving before you thought to move yourself," he says, far too smugly, staring me down across the island, his hold of my wrist solid. I'm not concerned.

"You'll have to release me to get around the island to me," I point out haughtily. "And *then* I'll run."

"Who says I have to release you?"

"Oh." I nod, looking as sarcastic as could be. "Do they call you Mr. Tickle, as well as The Enigma?"

He can't restrain his smile. Neither can I. "Tickle," he muses, and I solidify on my stool. No. No tickling. I can't stand it. He needs to release me to get to me, and as soon as he does, I'm out of here. I'll lock myself in his bathroom. Just as I think that, James braces a hand into the counter and launches himself up.

"Oh," I murmur as he flies across the island. Literally. He didn't even jolt my arm. One swift swivel and drop has him on the stool next to me, my wrist still in his hold. Fuck it. I lift my cast. "This is a white flag."

And there it is. A laugh. It's rich and deep and like a balm to my broken heart. And that's just the sound. The sight makes me fall a little harder. I sit, admiring him, lost, dazed. Stunning.

Once he's gathered himself, James stands me up and walks me back to the rug by the window. He silently lowers me to my back and sits over my thighs. Not my stomach, but my thighs.

I'm rigid beneath him, unable to appreciate his gorgeous form or his twinkling eyes. "Please don't," I beg.

"Then laugh," he whispers, and I tilt my head back, clenching my eyes closed.

"I can't just laugh."

"Try."

"Ha!" I blurt like a fool. "Hahahahaha!"

"Lame." He digs me under my arm, and I burst into a fit of hysterics.

"No!" Oh my Jesus, torture! "Stop," I splutter over my laugh. "Please, stop."

He does, and I'm surprised. Then he shoots up, and I'm worried. "What is it?" I ask.

"The sensor on the front entrance," he says, going to his cell and checking a few things before taking it to his ear. "Visitors? Who?" he asks, coming back to me, his pace faltering. "Oh?" He holds his hand out for me, and I take it and let him pull me to my feet. I'm not grateful I got off lightly. I'm too concerned by these *visitors*.

He hangs up, his lips straightening. "You have visitors."

"Oh no," I breathe, pacing to the kitchen and getting my cell. I find three missed calls and a message threatening to come here. "Shit." I slam it down. "Time to be roasted."

"That's not fucking funny, Beau," James mutters, collecting me and guiding me to the stairs.

I don't have the mental capacity to be remorseful of my choice of words. "I think it's best I see him alone."

"Forget it," he snaps.

I grimace at the space before me. "Don't be so unreasonable."

James releases me from his hold when we make it to the bedroom and goes into his dressing room, while I scratch around for something to throw on. He comes out moments later in his jeans, dragging a T-shirt over his head. He's grouchy, and my inappropriate comment isn't the only reason. He has bigger issues than my family politics.

"Worried I'll let them convince me to walk away?" I ask, removing my T-shirt.

James laughs under his breath, then falters, his eyes climbing my body to my face. He scowls. "No."

I sigh. "Can we agree on one thing?"

"Depends what it is."

"Oh, for God's sake, what's got into you? You're behaving like a petulant school boy." It's actually quite hilarious, this heartless killer sulking like a brat. I pull my shirt on and start buttoning it with one hand. "I'm not telling them about this." I take my index fingers and point them at my stomach. "Not yet."

James stalks toward me and stops, dropping a kiss on my cheek. "Agreed." He heads toward the bathroom, leaving me a little shell-shocked in the middle of his room.

"Oh," I say to myself, going to the bed and sitting on the edge. That was easier than I thought it would be.

"You ready?" he asks, coming toward me with his hands in his hair, coaxing it into place. I smile, and he stops. "What?"

"Trying to make a good impression?"

"No, I'm trying to keep busy to stop myself thinking about all the things I should say to your uncles."

"Like what?"

"Fuck off."

I press my lips together to stop my laugh. He seems so tense. Could it be nerves?

"You can laugh," he mutters, and I fall back on the bed, clenching my stomach. Am I going crazy? I shouldn't be laughing. Not after the shitstorm and avalanche of information I've been hit with. I should be rocking back and forth in the corner. Crying. Screaming. Booking a lifetime's worth of therapy sessions, but, instead, I'm laughing.

My body jerks, and I sigh, laugh, sigh, laugh, unable to get a hold of myself. Wiping at my wet eyes, I open them and come face to face with James. He's bemused, his forehead a map of lines. "You done?"

And then I burst into tears. What the fuck is wrong with me? My sobs rack my body as much as my laughing fit, and I cover my face, hiding. "I don't want to do it. I just want to disappear."

"We can do that." He lays himself all over me, not resting his entire weight, cupping my cheeks with his big hands. "Disappear. I'm a master at it."

I laugh over my sob, and James dips and kisses the wetness away from my cheeks. "I'm just fed up with fighting everyone. Why can't they just leave me be? Ollie calling Nath, Lawrence calling everyone, Dexter turning up at Nath's—all to deal with me. I'm fine."

He's quiet for a while, looking at me in a way that suggests he feels as sorry for me as I feel for myself. "What do you want to do?"

I know what I want to do, but I can't do it. Lawrence would have a breakdown if I disappeared. I have to clear the air with him. Make him see James is good for me. It shouldn't be too hard. After all, to Lawrence, James is just a regular man with a regular job, living in a not-too regular glass box. *For fuck's sake*. "I should see him."

He nods and stands, pulling me to my feet and handing me my jeans. "It'll be okay."

I pull them on, and James reclaims me. I wish I could believe him. I don't know what happens after today. After Lawrence. After Nath. My father doesn't matter, and neither does Ollie. All I know is we can't stay here, and James must already have plans in place because he's asked if I have a passport and those bags are still by the door.

The sound of the elevator opening has my hand squeezing around James's tighter, and when we make it to the top of the stairs, I see him. My uncle. *And* Dexter. Neither man can hide their awe as they step off, gazing around. "Makes sense now," Dexter says quietly, grunting when Lawrence's elbow sinks into his side.

They both see us coming down the stairs at the same time. "Oh God," I breathe, feeling James's thumb stroking over the top of my hand.

"It's fine."

Is it? Not judging by the look on my uncle's face. "Hi," I say as we reach the bottom, letting James guide me to a stool at the island. Lawrence doesn't reply, his eyes following us the entire way. The silence is so awkward.

"Can I get you a drink?" James asks, going to the fridge.

"We're not staying." Lawrence appears to roll his shoulders. "Would you mind giving us some privacy?"

James's motions falter, his hand on the door, two bottles of water in his other hand. He slowly shuts the fridge, nodding mildly to himself. "Beau?"

"Maybe it's best," I say, needing to be rid of this awful atmosphere.

"For whom?" James counters, sliding one of the bottles across to me. "Not for me. And not for you."

"James," I plead, looking at him with imploring eyes. "Please."

"Are you worried we'll make her see sense?" my uncle asks.

"Lawrence," Dexter pipes in warningly.

"Listen to your lover." James grinds the words out, not looking at either of them, his focus set on me. "This doesn't have to be difficult."

"Why, what will you do?" Lawrence steps forward, and I stand, ready to stop him getting into something that he really isn't equipped to deal with.

"Stop this madness," I snap. "Why can't you be happy for me?"

"Happy?" He laughs sardonically. "Beau, you hardly know this man. And since you have, you've sustained more injuries in a few weeks than you have in your entire life." My guess is he's now focused on the bruise forming on my cheek, courtesy of Goldie. I look to Dexter, willing him to step in and reason with Lawrence. But he doesn't, his loyalty to my uncle preventing him.

"Stop dreaming up issues." James rounds the island and takes a stool next to me, showing his position. Unmoving.

"I thought you were leaving," Lawrence spits.

"I'm exactly where I should be." James takes my hand, and the look Lawrence throws his way as a result is pure filth.

"You will know when I talk to you because I'll look at you."

I recoil, stunned. Who is this man? "Lawrence," I whisper, stung on James's behalf.

"And why are you so quiet?" My uncle swings toward Dexter. "We agreed. Beau needs to come home."

"And maybe there's a better way to make that happen," Dexter says, reaching for his brow and rubbing into the creases. "Force obviously isn't it."

"Force?" James mimics, almost laughing. I can sense his body tensing beside me, his back straightening. "I've had enough of this shit. Get the fuck out of my apartment."

I fold in on myself, defeated, and yet I can't blame James for being at the end of his rope. Lawrence has walked into his home, thrown insults, and shown absolutely no willingness to reason. No acceptance. Only ignorance. He's more like my father than I thought.

"You're going to let him speak to me like that?" Lawrence asks me. I remain silent, so he turns to Dexter. "And you? You're happy about this? We need to get her away before it's too late."

"Too late for what?" I ask, completely exasperated. It's the most ironic situation. They know nothing, thank God. Their issues aren't even issues. And all I can think is, if only they did know . . .

"She's pregnant," James says, his voice quiet, but the words echo around the apartment loudly, banging off all the glass. My jaw falls open, and I look at him disbelievingly. "So it's already too late. Would be with or without my baby inside her."

Lawrence very nearly falls over, and Dexter looks like he's gone into shock, standing there, silent, staring. I can't believe he's done this. We agreed.

"Oh my Christ, this is a disaster," Lawrence wails, virtually staggering to a stool and collapsing onto it. He starts to hyperventilate. "I think I'm going to pass out."

I roll my eyes and unscrew the cap of my bottle, passing him the water. "Stop being so fucking dramatic."

I see James out the corner of my eye looking all too smug with himself, and I knee him, narrowing displeased eyes onto him when he turns my way. He's taking far too much pleasure from my uncle's shock.

"I'm done," he says, showing absolutely no remorse for throwing me under the bus.

"Pregnant?" Dexter finally splutters, blinking his way out of his trance. "You're pregnant?"

"I'm pregnant," I confirm, hearing myself say it for the first time. Odd doesn't cover it.

"But you're not fit to be a mother," Dexter blurts, and then quickly looks very sorry.

"Excuse me?" James's back straightens.

"I didn't mean that." He, too, staggers toward a stool and collapses onto it.

"Dexter?" I ask, deeply hurt, even if I can't really blame him for blurting something so unkind. But is that what they think? That I'm not fit? I feel myself shrinking on my stool, feeling so small. Unfit. Unstable. Unprepared. It's all true. Look at me. Look at my history. And the father?

I peek across to James, my eyes welling with unstoppable tears, but I still see the unbridled fury brewing. "Enough," he snaps, standing from the stool. "Get out."

I will Lawrence and Dexter to leave before James *really* loses it. This has all been so very unpleasant. I'm done. They won't support me. It hurts so deeply, but I refuse to let their contempt add any more weight to my shoulders. "You should go," I say, standing and walking away. "I'm sorry it had to be like this."

I feel so heavy as I climb the stairs, needing the handrail to help pull me up each step. I make it to James's bedroom and collapse on the bed, defeated. Tearful. Absolutely gutted. It feels eerily similar to when Mom died. That desolate, heart-wrenching pain, with nothing tethering me to life. Although, I guess this time, that's not quite true. But I am losing my biological family, one by one. Lawrence is more like my father than I ever thought possible. Judgmental. Stubborn.

I roll over and snuggle into the sheets, at the same time

listening for any signs that James has been forced to get physical. I just want this day to be over. The men in my life, Lawrence, Dexter, Ollie, Nath—especially Nath, if what James says is true—have annihilated any trust I had for them. Ripped the love for them from my chest.

"That went well." James's voice comes from the doorway, and I roll onto my back and find him filling it with his big body. His temper looks like it's been stowed away.

"You shouldn't have told them. We agreed."

"It wasn't exactly going swimmingly before my little bombshell."

"It's my bombshell too. I should have broken the news."

"You're right." He wanders over and sits on the edge of the bed. "I'm sorry. I was pissed off. But it was that or kill them both for being so narrow-fucking-minded."

I look away, tears pinching the backs of my eyes. *You're not fit to be a mother.*

"Don't cry, Beau." Taking my hand, he helps me up from the bed, wiping away the stray tears, his lips straight. He leads us out of his room.

"What are you doing?"

"I'm going to make us both feel better." Taking us into his office, he sits down in his big swivel chair and pulls me onto his lap. He slides the remote control from the desk and points it at the screens, and they all come to life at the same time. I expect to see footage from various rooms of his apartment. I don't. Instead, I see mug shots of men, one on every screen.

"Who are they?" I ask, a chill licking down the length of my spine.

"Those are all the men I have killed." He snakes a hand onto my tummy and pulls me back, resting his chin on my shoulder.

I swallow, my eyes gliding across the screens slowly, taking in each and every face. All associates of The Bear. I arrive at the final two screens. They're blank.

"One of them was reserved for the man who covered up your mum's death." James clicks a button, and the blank screen is filled.

"Nath," I breathe, my skin suddenly freezing. "And the other?"

"The other is for the man who ordered it."

The Bear. James won't only be getting justice for me—for my mom—he'll be getting justice for himself. "But no one knows what he looks like," I say.

"I will soon."

"What are you going to do, James?"

"I'm going to end this story."

60

JAMES

Having a private conversation when I'm determined to keep Beau in my sights is tricky. I've put her on the couch on the far side of the room and turned on the TV, making sure the surround sound is as loud as can be without raising suspicion. I'm a fool. A total, first-class prick. I accepted that some days ago. I can see by the way she keeps flicking looks across to me where I am in the kitchen that she knows something is about to go down. Plus, I told her I'm about to end this. I need to learn to control my mouth around Beau. But I'm keeping her well out of it. Especially now. *While keeping her close, Kel?*

My brain spasms as I put in the call, turning my back on Beau so she can't read my lips, because I know she'll try. A cop. Of all the women I could fall in love with, I fall in love with a fucking cop. A talented cop. A cop who was destined to become an FBI agent most criminals should fear. And here I am, a criminal, fucking terrified.

He answers, sounding as wary as he should. "Where did that footage come from?" I get straight to the point.

"Fuck you." And so does he.

I blink slowly, inhaling some patience. "You're in The Bear's pocket."

"Is that what you're trying to make Beau believe?"

"I didn't have to try very hard." I cast my eyes over my shoulder, checking on her. Of course, her eyes are nailed on me. "She trusts me."

"It's you who's in the footage. Fuck, man, are you on another planet?"

Another planet? He's not far wrong. I feel like I'm in orbit. "I'm in the fucking footage, you moron, because I was trying to fucking save them." I have to take a few breaths or risk destroying my kitchen in a temper. "But you made sure she didn't see that bit, didn't you? I'm coming for you," I hiss, threat dripping from every word. "Harder than I've come for anyone before." My mind's reeling, and I slam my phone down harder than I mean to. I turn around and find Beau blinking rapidly. I'd smile, if my face wasn't straining with fury.

She pops a grape in her mouth, chewing slowly while she regards me. "The end's going well, then," she says, looking at me in question. Christ alive, her lightness would be welcome if I didn't feel so fucking heavy. "Can I help?" she asks, and an unstoppable burst of laughter erupts. But I soon shut my big gob when she looks at me offended. "What's so funny?" she asks, insulted.

I exhale and stroll over, crouching before her and laying my hand on her tummy. I smile fondly at the flat plane and look up at her. She's smiling too, and it's precious. "No," I say sternly, dropping my smile and stalking back to the kitchen, hearing her huffing as I go. Help me? Someone needs to, but not Beau. "Fuck it," I whisper. I'm out of options. "Fancy a bath?" I ask.

"Depends if it's with you."

"It's not."

"Then no." She turns her attention to the TV and continues popping grapes in her mouth. "You're not locking me in your glass bathroom in your glass house so you can go on a killing spree, Mr. Glass."

I scowl at her profile. If anyone could hear us. "Then I'll have Goldie watch you," I mutter, just loud enough for her to hear, going to my mobile. I'm about to have two pissed-off women on my back.

"No," Beau yells, scrambling up from the couch and making her way to the kitchen.

I ignore her and return to my call when I hear Goldie's voice. "I need you to watch Beau."

"No," she says over a laugh.

Beau's smug face is perfectly slappable. "See?" she says. "Even Goldie thinks it's a terrible idea."

So they're allies now? Typical. "Fine, I'll ask Otto."

"No," Otto says, stepping off the elevator with Goldie.

I growl, pointing my mobile at them. "One of you is watching her. I'll give you ten minutes to decide who." I turn and stalk away. I've got shit to do, and here I am arguing with people who are supposed to work for me about who's going to babysit my girlfriend while I go on a killing spree. Why can't she be a regular woman? One who wants to stand behind me and be protected.

Because then you wouldn't have fallen in love with her, you dickhead.

I shake my head and take the stairs fast, going to my dressing room, hearing Beau running after me. "I'm coming with you," she declares, and I laugh my way into a pair of trousers. "I fucking am," she says, underpinning her defiance.

I approach her as I zip my fly, bending and getting my face up close to hers. "You're. Fucking. Not." I slam a kiss on her lips and feel her body folding, but her arm remains at her side, defiantly refusing to seize me.

"I don't want you to go," she murmurs into my mouth, sounding truly worried. I pull back, thrown, and see pure fear. This is new. I study her closely, and she drops her eyes, as if trying to hide her uncertainty. "I think it's my hormones or something," she murmurs. "I'm feeling weirdly scared."

I pull on a shirt and start buttoning it up. "Your boyfriend's The Enigma."

"Not anymore, are you?" she retorts. "Because someone knows who you fucking are, so we need to think of another name to scare the shit out of the people you're going to hunt down."

"You're so cute."

"Fuck off."

"It's not safe, Beau."

"Exactly, which is why you should stay here."

I fasten a tie and pull on my jacket. For years, I've only ever had Otto and Goldie to worry about me. Not that they ever have. They know of my capabilities. My determination. "I'll be fine."

"Why are you wearing a suit?" she asks, looking me up and down, her confusion obvious. I go to the safe at the back of my wardrobe, punch in the code, and pull out my Beretta. "A suit and a gun."

I smile and check it over before slipping it into the back of my trousers. "Would you prefer a suit and no gun?"

With her jaw twitching, she swivels and marches to the bed, dropping to her back, and while I'd love to go and smother her with some reassurance, regrettably, I don't have time. I back out of the room, and she drops her head to the side, watching me go. Silent. But her hand falls to her stomach to remind me that it's not just her here waiting for my safe return.

I take two fingers to my lips and kiss them, holding them up.

And then I leave her. And it's one of the hardest things I've ever had to do.

I stop by my office to collect a few things, and when I make it to the top of the stairs, Goldie and Otto are in a full-blown row. "It's because I'm a woman, isn't it?" Goldie more or less growls, poking Otto in his shoulder. "You think I should stay here and be the babysitter because I'm a woman."

I fasten the button of my jacket, watching them.

"I'm not sexist," Otto mutters, stalking to the elevator.

"No? He who's buying a fucking villa and filling every room with women."

"I like variety."

"Good," Goldie barks, stomping after him. "Then you can stay and watch the pregnant girl."

"Pregnant?" Otto blurts.

"Oops."

"For fuck's sake," I mutter, taking the stairs. "You two done?"

They both turn, silenced for a few moments. "She's pregnant?" Otto asks. "Then you're definitely babysitting," He steps into the lift and pulls his gun, aiming it at Goldie. "I don't do hormonal women."

"Bastard," she seethes.

"Shut up and listen," I order, loading the security app on my iPad. "I want you in the lobby," I say, moving my gaze over both of them, since it's still not confirmed who's staying to watch the pregnant woman.

"Got it," Goldie replies. She's relented.

"I'll make sure everywhere is clear before we leave." I step into the elevator with them and hit the button for the ground floor. "Give me a lift."

Otto cups his hands and holds them out, but before I get a chance to use them as a launch pad, Goldie shoulder barges him out of the way. I laugh to myself and her need to prove a point as I step onto her hands and push through my knee to reach the elevator hatch. I pull my gun, pop the ceiling tile, and slide it across, peeking through. Nothing. "There's a remote camera in my bag. Pass me it."

"There's a good boy, Otto," Goldie says.

"Fuck off, witch."

For the love of God. I dip and get them both in my sights. "Shut the fuck up before I shut you the fuck up." Ironic. They both shut the fuck up. Otto passes me the camera, and I hoist myself up higher. The mechanics of the lift clank and whirl, carrying us down, and I stretch to reach the bare brick wall. I see an iron support bar nearing, and I activate the magnet on the camera. The moment it's in reach, I stretch farther and slip it onto the edge as the lift passes. Done.

I grunt as I drop back into the lift. "That gives you a three-sixty view of the shaft, up and down. Keep it on the screen." I tune in the live footage and hand Goldie a phone. "Keep the rest of the block on the screens in the foyer, and I want every room in my apartment on here. I hand her the iPad. "The glass is all clear. Do not let her out of your sight." I've never been concerned about security—my building is like Fort Knox—but since the breach, I'm twitchy, despite all the extra measures that have been put in place.

The doors open, and I stride out, Otto on my heels. "Dare I ask who you're going to kill?"

I don't answer.

61

BEAU

If I walk around this apartment one more time, I'm going to fall through the floor from the hole I've worn doing laps. I stop at the foot of the glass wall spanning one side of James's apartment, looking at the barrier between me and the view of Miami. The cars would be dots, if I could see them. The people mere specks.

Where is he? My stomach is constantly churning, my pulse thrumming. "God damn it," I mutter, heading for the stairs. I need a change of scenery.

I find myself in James's bathroom, and as I stare at the bin by the toilet, my pulse thrums harder, my tummy cartwheeling more. I rummage to the bottom and pull out the white stick. Except now, I don't see a disaster. I see hope. These two little lines could be a sign. A new start. A new attitude. There's never been anything other than my misery and anger to focus on. Then there was James. And now there are the lines on this white stick. *Hope. Purpose.*

Urgency takes over, and I rush downstairs to call James. To get him back here. To convince him we don't need anything other than this stick. No justice. No revenge. It could ruin everything, take away this unexpected opportunity of freedom and happiness.

I pull up his name, but before I have a chance to hit the dial icon, my cell rings in my hand. An unknown number illuminates the screen, and I stare at the digits for a lifetime, torn, not knowing if I should answer. My mind tangles, my eyes flit from my cell to the floor repeatedly. Answer. Don't answer.

I gulp back my uncertainty. "Hello?"

"It's Goldie."

My body relaxes, but my mind does not. "Hi."

"Would you please remain in one room? You're making me dizzy."

I lower to the couch. What can I say? I'm worried? Anxious? Is she? "Have you heard from him?"

She sighs. I can't figure out if it's sympathetic or tired. "Trust me, Beau. He will be okay."

"How do you know?"

"Because good shades evil," she says quietly, and I swallow. "Now stay in the living room, for God's sake." The line goes dead, and my shoulders drop, my anxiousness still firmly with me. *Good shades evil.* Then why is my mother dead? Why—

My phone rings again. Goldie. "I haven't moved," I say when I answer.

"I'm ordering a Starbucks. Do you want one?"

I blink back my surprise. "Is this your way of saying sorry for headbutting me?" I ask, reaching up to my cheek. It's still tender. That woman has one hard head.

"Do you want one?"

"Sure. A latte, please."

"You'll have to come down and fetch it. I can't leave the entrance."

"Okay." Another change of scenery. Perfect. "I'll keep you company."

"Whatever," she grunts. "I'll order now. Bye."

I bring my cell to my chest, my eyes drifting across the frosted glass before me. Call him. Don't call him. What if I disturb him? What if he's stalking his prey and my call blows his cover? What if I didn't have to think about that kind of crazy shit? And who's his prey? Nath?

My final thought has me pulling up his number and dialing as I head to the elevator. It rings and rings until it eventually goes to an automated message, telling me the person I'm trying to reach isn't available right now. "Come on," I murmur, stepping into the cart, dialing him again.

The doors close, and he answers. "James," I breathe, so relieved just to hear his voice. "You don't have to do it."

"Do what?"

"Whatever you're doing. Killing whoever you're killing. You don't have to do it."

There's silence, and I know he's probably wondering who's got a gun to my head. But clarity has arrived, and I need to keep it.

"Let's just go somewhere," I say. "Anywhere. Away from Miami. Away from America."

"Are you serious?" he asks, not sarcastic, more daunted.

"So serious. Let's just get on a plane and go."

"I . . . leave . . . people . . ." His words crackle and break. ". . . Beau."

"James?" I say, circling on the spot. "You're breaking up." I check my cell, seeing the service has dropped. "Shit. James?"

"Can you hear me?"

"Yes, but you're fuzzy." I look up at the screen above the door, watching the lights for the floors illuminate in turn as I'm carried down to the first floor.

"Where are you?"

"In the elevator."

There's a brief silence, and I wonder if I've lost service again. But then he speaks. "Beau, why are you in the elevator?"

"Goldie's having Starbucks delivered. She can't leave the foyer so I'm going to collect it from her."

"What?" he bellows.

I jump, pulling my phone away from my ear. "I—"

"I fucking told you not to leave the apartment," he seethes. I can literally feel the fire of his temper down the line.

"A coffee." That's all. He's overreacting.

"No. Beau, she'd never ask you down there. Stop the—"

"What?" I murmur, looking up at the screen above the doors again.

Five.

Four.

I look to the buttons on the panel, hitting anything and everything before me, glancing up at the screen.

Three.

Two.

"Beau, stop the fucking el—" James breaks up again, as I frantically smack at the buttons.

One.

"Shit." I try to hook my fingers around the locked service door to access the emergency buttons, but the damn stupid cast won't allow me to bend my fingers.

Ding!

I shoot back against the wall as the doors slide open, and I come face to face with Goldie.

And behind her, Nath.

With a gun aimed at her temple.

I reach for the wall of the elevator to steady myself, my throat clogging with fear and dread. "What are you doing, Nath?" I whisper, my eyes bouncing between them.

"Come with me," he says, looking stressed. Sweaty.

Guilty.

"Don't go," Goldie orders, her eyes daring me to defy her.

"Get out of the elevator, Beau." Nath jerks the gun in Goldie's temple, making her eyes shut, and I step out immediately, raising my hands in that pacifying way people do when there's a gun be brandished around.

"I'm getting out, Nath," I say calmly. "Think about what you're doing."

"What I'm doing?" He shoves Goldie away and grabs me, pulling me into his chest, backing out of the foyer. "This is fucking madness," he mutters. "All of it."

He's a man on the edge. "Where are we going?" I look out the corner of my eye, seeing the gun still aimed at Goldie.

"Get in the elevator," he says to Goldie, and I watch as she looks across to the floor where her gun lays on the ground, torn. We both know she won't make it to her weapon before Nath has a chance to pull the trigger. She's cornered. "Get in!"

She backs up, her expression cut with frustration.

"Press the button for the top floor."

She slowly reaches to her right and the beep of a button being pressed sounds. Moments later, the doors start closing, and the last thing I see are her nostrils flaring.

"Let's go," Nath says, releasing my back from his chest and taking my arm. I turn and come face to face with the hood of his car, the doors into James's building, or lack of, smashed to smithereens around us.

"What have you done?' I ask, my feet crunching across the shattered glass as he guides me into the passenger seat, shutting the door and rounding the front, dropping into the driver's seat. His gun is placed in his lap. The safety is engaged. Something's amiss here. I stare at his profile, my mind turning in circles, and

I'm jolted forward when he reverses fast, reaching up to wipe his brow.

He drives erratically, and half the journey is spent with me silent, trying to untangle the mindfuck going on, as well as ignoring my vibrating phone. "Nath, what's going on?" I eventually ask, and he looks across the car at me like I might have just stepped out of a circus.

"You're in danger, Beau." He returns his attention to the road. "Why didn't you answer my messages? Did you watch the footage I sent you?"

"Yes, I watched the footage."

"Then why didn't you answer me?"

"Because I was busy holding my boyfriend at gunpoint," I mutter. *And finding out I'm pregnant.*

"He was there, Beau. You were right all along. Jaz's death was covered up. Who the fuck is James Kelly, and why did he want your mom dead?"

I turn in my seat to face him, my head hurting. "Nath, James had nothing to do with Mom's death."

"Yes!" he yells, smacking the steering wheel. "You saw, Beau. He was there, and to cover his ass, he's trying to convince you I had something to do with it."

My head finds my hands. Things aren't adding up. None of it. "Are you telling me you had nothing to do with Mom's death?"

He laughs, and it gets right under my skin. "I don't believe this. You have the nerve to ask me that? *Me*, your friend, your mom's friend, but a man you've known mere weeks *and* who is seen clear as fucking day on the surveillance cameras isn't under suspicion at all? What the fuck was he doing there, then? Who the fuck is he? And how the fuck do you know him, Beau? How did you meet him?"

I begin to sweat. There's no reasonable explanation, nothing to justify my reasoning, except the truth. And if Nath is telling the truth, I can't tell *him* the truth. Who James really is. Why he was there. *Fuck.* "You didn't follow us from the graveyard?" I ask.

"What?"

"You had nothing to do with the two men sent to James's apartment to murder him?"

Nath starts laughing hysterically. "Are you serious?"

"Yes, I'm bloody serious!"

"Two men in James's apartment sent there to kill him?" He looks across to me, grave. "Then how the fuck is he still alive, Beau?"

I rest back in my seat, snapping my mouth closed. *Because he killed them instead. Shit.* "Is this some rescue attempt?" I divert quickly. He's ambushed James's apartment, held Goldie at gunpoint, because he thinks I need rescuing?

"Something's going on," he says to the road. "I looked into the car thing you mentioned. Checked the records. Nothing. But when I called the dealership, they confirmed Jaz's car *was* booked in that day. So I dug deeper. Visited a few people." He looks at me, and I hate the haunted glaze in his eyes.

"What?"

"A tattoo place over the road from the store. Cameras outside with a perfect view over the parking lot, but there was no CCTV footage in the case file. So I paid the owner a visit. Apparently, the night of Jaz's death, the police turned up and seized the footage."

The footage with James in it. "So how did you get it?"

"A few threats, a peek of my badge. The owner managed to salvage some. Not all, but enough to prove James was there."

But not enough to show him saving me. Trying to save Mom. The police seized the footage. *What the fuck is going on?* "When you saw the recording, how did you know it was James? You've never met him."

He looks at me out the corner of his eye. "Ollie," he mutters. "I showed it to Ollie."

My mouth falls open. "Ollie?" I breathe.

"Yes, Ollie."

So now Ollie knows James was at the scene of my mom's death too? "Oh Jesus, Nath, you've made this so much worse." I run my hand over my forehead, my brain heavy with a million questions, a million worries. If not Nath, then who? But by taking me, *rescuing* me, he's put himself in the frame even more.

"How have I made this worse?" he asks as he pulls a left at the lights.

"You need to take me back. Let me explain to James." It'll be okay. *I think.*

"No, Beau."

"Don't you think Goldie's going to tell him where I am? Don't you think he'll come find me?"

"I know nothing right now."

"And where the hell are you taking me?"

"I don't know, Beau!" he yells, looking up at his rearview mirror as we pull off the main street. "Fuck."

"What?"

"Cops."

I look over my shoulder. "You're driving like a dick. I'm not surprised you've been pulled."

Nath signals and starts to slow, pulling over at the side of the road. "I'll deal with it."

"And then what? Are you kidnapping me?" I ask, incredulous, smacking the door with my cast and immediately wincing in pain. The door slams, and my eyes follow Nath as he strides around the back of his BMW toward the cop car, pulling out his badge as he goes. I sink into my seat and look at my cell when it rings yet again. I can't even begin to imagine James's mental state. "I'm okay," I say when I answer. "And Nath isn't dirty, James."

"I know," he breathes. "I fucking know."

What? I look into the side mirror, seeing one of the cops

laughing with Nath, the other with his ass resting on the hood of his car. "How do you know, James?" I ask.

"It's not safe there, Beau," he says, ignoring me. "With Nath, it's not safe."

"He's FBI," I argue.

"Where are you?"

"We've been pulled over."

"Why?"

"Because . . ." I fade off, my eyes returning to the side mirror, my heart slowing, ice gliding through my veins.

"Because what, Beau?"

"He's been pulled over by the police," I whisper.

His inhale is loud and sharp. "Get the fuck out of there now!"

I sit frozen, my cell limp at my ear as James bellows his orders down the line, my stare rooted to the mirror.

"Beau!"

Nath lifts a hand in goodbye to the cops. Turns. Walks away, smiling, but I can still see the stress all over his face.

"Beau!" James roars. "For fuck's sake, get the fuck out of there."

I see the cop who's on the hood reach for his belt. "No," I murmur. "No, no, no."

"Beau!"

"Nath," I scream, startling at the sound of a gunshot. Nath drops like lead to the ground. "Oh my God." My hand goes over my mouth, suppressing my wretched cry. Panicked and hardly able to see through my tears, I scramble to get the door handle, hearing James still yelling. I get out of the car. Both cops look my way. Both look surprised to see me. And both reach for their belts.

I dive back in and clamber across the car to the driver's seat, starting the engine, looking at the mirror. They're heading toward me. "God, no."

I slam the car into reverse and hit the gas awkwardly, shooting back, one arm braced on the wheel. I crash into one of them and push his body a few feet back until it smashes into the cop car with an almighty bang. And when I look up to the mirror again, I see him trapped between the trunk of Nath's car and the hood of the cop car. A trail of blood seeps from the corner of his mouth. "Oh my God," I breathe, frozen. I'm woken up from my inert state when the other cop appears at the passenger side, and I push myself into the door, swinging my legs round and kicking aimlessly, catching him on the jaw, sending him flying back onto the sidewalk.

I can hear James yelling. Screaming. "Beau, talk to me!"

I frantically search for my cell and take it to my ear with a shaky hand, wedging it between my shoulder and my cheek. "I can't leave Nath."

"Drive, Beau. For the love of God, drive. Otto is coming up behind you."

I look up at the mirror and see a car pull over, Otto getting out.

"Drive!"

The tears come on thick and fast. The heartache. The pain. The anger. I screech away, wiping at my face, sniffing back the tears. "No," I sob, smacking the wheel repeatedly. "No, no, no."

"Beau, listen carefully. I need you to head for Midtown. Tell me what street you're on."

I carefully glance around, furiously brushing at my eyes to clear my sight. "On Northwest Nineteenth Avenue passing Northwest Sixteenth Street," I sob.

"Keep going until you get to Northwest North River Drive. Do a left and follow the road. There's a right turn just past the marina. Pull in there. Goldie's not far behind you," he says, just as I see the nose of her car poke out in the traffic before overtaking a few cars, speeding past them and pulling in behind me.

"I see her."

"Good girl. She'll bring you to me." He hangs up, and I grip the steering wheel harder, trying to drive sensibly, my vision foggy. When I reach the end of the road, I take a left as instructed, my eyes looking for the turning past the marina, my frayed nerves obliterated. I see it and peek at my mirror as I take it. Goldie is still close behind. I pull over and get out. My legs are wobbly, and I grab the top of the door to steady myself.

"You're not going to pass out, are you?" Goldie asks, seizing me and steadying me.

"Where's James?" I demand, hating having to depend on her to hold me up. "Tell me where the fuck he is."

Her lips press together. She won't tell me. She won't disobey a direct order. "Get in," she says, depositing me in her car. Then she goes to Nath's BMW and drives it further down the deserted lane, pulling in past some overgrowth. She's out of sight for all of ten seconds, and when she emerges, she walks toward me as cool as could be, fastening her jacket.

Then the sky lights up, a fire ball erupting behind her.

62

JAMES

I hear the explosion down the line and push my fist into the steering wheel. "Fuck," I curse, thumping it repeatedly, so fucking furious with myself for missing so many fucking clues. The moment I parked, clarity struck. Small moments kept coming back to me. Little things. Things that probably would have gone amiss to many. Fuck, I missed them myself. But now?

Now it's like a cloud of comprehensions has burst above my head. "Fuck, fuck, fuck." I slip my car into drive and pull out of the side street up the road from Butler's house. How could I have got it so wrong?

"All sorted," Goldie says.

"How's Beau?"

"In shock, I think."

"Take her back to mine. I'll meet you there." I drive home in a haze of fury mixed with worry, because what needs to happen next might be the end of Beau and me.

And no matter what, I can't let that happen.

I feel like my fucking hands are tied.

Powerless.

When I pull into the underground car park, Goldie is literally holding Beau up as she walks her to the stairwell. I hop out and hurry over, taking over and tucking her in close to my side. "She won't stop shaking," she says, opening the door for us. I nod and check Beau. She's vacant. Hollow.

"Beau, look at me," I demand, harsher than I should, truly worried.

Her eyes turn up. Expressionless eyes. She's looking straight through me. I have no idea how to handle this. "Bath," I say like a chump.

"Is that your answer for everything?" she asks, blinking and moving away. "Fuck me black and blue, have a bath. Get me pregnant, have a bath. My best friend is murdered, have a bath."

I recoil, injured. "Okay, no bath," I say quietly.

"I want a bath," she whimpers, her bottom lip wobbling, her eyes welling. "I want a fucking bath!" She flips out, screaming, and Goldie withdraws, shocked, while I stand like an idiot wondering what the fuck to do. *A bath. Give her what she wants, James.*

I scoop her up, my heart squeezing when she clings to me, and walk through the doorway. Goldie keeps her distance, trailing a few paces back. "Otto's boarded up the doors and swept the apartment and building."

I frown. "Boarded up?"

"Butler drove himself in."

For fuck's sake. Hardly a security breach, more a fucking ram raid. Regardless, we need to get out of here. "Get it repaired."

"Already on it."

When I get Beau into my apartment, I'm forced to hang back

while Goldie runs more checks, and the whole time, Beau cries shallowly, her shoulders jerking. Eventually, we're allowed to enter, and I take Beau straight to my bathroom and sit her on the toilet seat while I slip my gun on the vanity and run her a bath. She stares blankly at her feet.

"This is all my fault," she mumbles. "I should never have asked him to dig. I should have left it alone."

"This is not your fault."

"It is. All of it."

I growl and kneel before her. "Stop it."

"I killed him. And a cop." She looks at me with glassy, traumatized eyes. "I backed Nath's car into one of the cops. I'll be sent to prison." She shoots up, knocking me back, and starts pacing the bathroom, her hands in her hair. "Our baby will be born in prison." Swinging around, she finds me, and I see nothing but terror splashed all over her face. "We have to leave." She marches out of the bathroom, and I follow, my worry multiplying. "Pack your things, we have to go." She flies into my dressing room and starts pulling down my clothes with one hand, tossing them in a pile behind her. "Where's your passport?"

"Beau," I say gently, moving in slowly, warily. "We can't leave."

"Stop me." Drawers are yanked open, my boxers and socks tossed out. "I'll be dead before I bring my child into this world in a state penitentiary." She whirls around. "Why aren't you packing?"

"Because we're not leaving."

She laughs. "Of course we're leaving." Her arm swings out and points at nothing. "I just killed a cop and drove away."

"You killed no one." I go to her and pick her up, carrying her back to the bath. "Nath's car was hijacked and the felon shot him." I help her into the waterproof arm protector. "The police showed up, and the felon panicked, ramming Nath's car into the police vehicle. Later, the police found Nath's stolen car burned out in a disused yard." I pull her T-shirt off and lift her into the tub. "The end."

She blinks rapidly. "Are you forgetting the cop left alive at the scene?"

"What cop left alive at the scene?" I ask, and she inhales, withdrawing. "They were dirty, Beau," I say, placing my palms on her shoulders and pushing her down.

"You killed them."

"No. The carjackers killed them." I tilt my head, and she stares at me, stunned, as my phone rings. I dig it out of my pocket. "Otto," I say, as Beau listens, her heart visibly pounding.

"Butler's alive. An ambulance has taken him to the emergency room."

"What?" Beau asks, sitting up straight in the bath. "What is it?"

"Nath's alive," I tell her, and she deflates, her hands going over her face. He's alive. But he's far from okay. I turn away from her, returning to Otto's call. "Give me a minute, I'll call you back." I disconnect and place a towel on the edge for her arm. "Soak," I order, adding some lavender oil.

"You're not getting in?"

"I have things to do, Beau."

She's up in a heartbeat, water pouring from her body. "You're leaving me again?" she asks, snatching a towel down off the rail. "No, James. No way."

"Calm down," I say, pacifying her, not liking her looking truly fraught.

Indignant, she smacks my hands away, as I try to push her back into the tub. But she dips. Turns. And my palms slip right off her shoulders, sending me plummeting forward.

Face first.

Into the bath.

Fully clothed.

Splash!

I instinctively yell, getting a shitload of water down my throat and up my nose, making me choke and cough, my arms flailing to find an anchor to sit myself up. "Fuck," I bark, followed by a cough, as I emerge and push my hair from my face. I find Beau looking at me, her good hand over her mouth. And then . . .

Laughter.

Loud, belly-clenching, hysterical laughter. She sounds psychotic. And I feel it.

Fuck, she looks beautiful. I should be glad she's okay. Glad I didn't catch her or knock her stomach when I tumbled. But right now, I just want to strangle her.

Walk away, James. Walk away before you really do strangle her.

My jaw ticking, I rise, water pouring from me, my suit a sodden mess, sticking everywhere. I take one step out, reaching for a towel. And get yanked back.

I land with another splash, except this time on my arse, not going under. "I'm going to kill you," I seethe, not amused, not at fucking all.

She raises her eyebrows, lowering back into the water at the other end. "Don't bottle it this time, will you?"

I inhale, my eyes narrowing, as she stares me down, challenging me all the way. "I won't."

She lifts a little, exposing her wet boobs, and reaches for the vanity unit. With my gun in her grasp, she settles back in the tub, aiming it at my chest. "You know who killed my mom. You know who The Bear has on the inside. Tell me."

She's a fucking case. "No."

Bang!

I jump out of my fucking skin, instinctively slipping down into the water for cover. "What the fucking hell, Beau?" I yell, looking behind me to see a mirror shattered. Is this the woman who's been hiding under all that darkness and misery, because I'm not sure I can cope with her? Or is this just pregnancy?

"Tell me who it is," she orders.

Fuck me, I need to think before I speak. I can't tell her. Not until I have the proof I want and which Beau will need. But I can't get that if I'm fucking dead. Pacify her. Lure her in. "I need you to tell me a few things first."

Her eyebrow quirks. "Have you missed who has the gun here?"

Fuck, I love her. "You won't kill me." I pout. "Because you love me."

She swoons so hard, the gun sways, and she sighs, lowering it.

I get on my knees and crawl my way over to her, pushing my mouth to hers. She doesn't resist, returning my kiss, and I moan, blindly reaching for the gun and confiscating it. "How did you know it wasn't Nath?" I ask, freeing her of my lips.

Her cheeks blow out, and she settles back, letting me lie on her front. Still fully clothed. Reaching for my hair, she pushes it back from my face. "He got that footage from a tattoo place opposite the store. Apparently, a cop turned up there the night Mom was killed and flashed his badge. He took the footage. The owner kept a copy. He gave it to Nath." She takes a few breaths. "You said Nath knew what you looked like because he followed me to the graveyard. It couldn't have been him, James. He only knew what you looked like because he showed the footage to Ollie. So if it wasn't Nath, who was following me?"

"The cop who took the footage?"

Her jaw flexes, frustrated by my blatant diversion. "I didn't get that far in the conversation, James. I was too busy dodging bullets. My life kind of depended on it."

My blood runs cold just thinking about it. My question is, though, did they know Beau was in the car with Butler? Because if the answer to that question is yes, their death just got messier. I shake away the rage and focus on Beau. Just focus on Beau. She's here. Alive. Carrying my baby. But when the fog of fury dissipates, she's looking a bit stunned. "Beau?" I say, reaching for her cheek, stroking it. "Beau, baby, what's up?"

"Life or death," she breathes, her eyes turning onto me. "I'm not to go near it unless my life depends on it."

"What are you talking about?"

She jumps up, diving out of the bath, leaving me a pile of wet suited man sitting in the tub. "Life or death," she says, over and over, pacing up and down. Then she seems to shake her head to herself, walking calmly out of the bathroom.

What the fuck? "Beau!" I bellow, scrambling up and flopping out of the bath, going after her, my body feeling ten times heavier, dragging a saturated suit with me. I land in the dressing room and find her pulling on a pair of my pants and a T-shirt. "Will you tell me what the fuck is going on?"

"Our lives depend on it."

My God, I'm going to headbutt the fucking wall in a minute. "Depend on what?" I grab her and hold her still, not prepared to let her go until she clues me in on what the fuck she's talking about.

"I know where the key to Mom's safety deposit box is."

I recoil, dropping her, stepping back. "What?"

"The night of the explosion," she goes on. "I asked if we could open Mom's special bottle of Krug to celebrate my Phase One Test results. She said no. She said I mustn't go near that bottle unless my life depended on it."

She turns and leaves, and I stand there, stunned, coming to terms with the fact that I might finally have that mystery put to bed. Did Jaz Hayley know who The Bear is? My cheeks blow out. In that box are potentially the names of two men many would pay millions for. But now there's the footage to be rid of too. And the rest of The Bear's army.

And, the top prize, The Bear.

"I'm going to Uncle Lawrence's to check," she calls, and doesn't that snap me back to life.

"What?" I murmur, my mind playing catch-up. Going. Leaving. "Beau!" I yell, chasing after her. I'll chain her to the frame in my bedroom if I have to. She's not going anywhere.

I, however, have someone to kill.

63

BEAU

I smack the button of the elevator repeatedly, and as soon as the doors slide open, I walk in. I feel so calm. Resolute. Together. But as soon as I hit the button for the first floor, I'm dragged back out. "What are you doing?" I ask incredulously.

"Have you forgotten there's an army of murderers out there that want us both dead?" He carries me to the kitchen, placing me on a stool.

"Have you forgotten that the army of murderers know where you live?" I retort, and he scowls at me but doesn't come back with a counter. Because he doesn't know what to say. He's stumped. Doesn't know what move to make next. To me, it's easy. Go to Lawrence's, find the Krug, find the key, find the deposit box, and burn the contents. Then we walk away. Why isn't he seeing this? It's all obvious to me, and what's also obvious is the fact he's being held back. Because of me. He won't leave me, not now that his safe place has been compromised. Twice. I'm a problem, as well as a solution.

I look around his apartment, high and low. "Why all the glass?" I ask, settling my eyes back on him. I have so many questions, but this is the only one I know he'll answer at this moment in time.

Slumping down on his stool, he rubs at his forehead. I hate the pain I see. It's all over his face. "I was raised in a house with few windows, and what windows there were remained covered. My father worried about people seeing us. Knowing what we looked like." He smiles, and it's the saddest smile I've seen. "It was suffocating." He blows out a breath. "And then when Otto hid me, he literally hid me. My whole family was dead. I was dead. And where we stayed, where I grieved and mourned and became angrier and angrier, it was damp. Cold. Lightless. I yearned for light. For windows to see the light. For things to be . . . clear."

God damn my wobbly lip. I reach for his hand, and he turns his, clenching mine. "Let's get out of here," I plead. No more death. No more blood. No more darkness. I'm tired of hating. Seeking revenge is exhausting. Seeing this pain on James is crushing.

"I can't." He looks at me with a million apologies in his eyes. "Not until I find the man who killed my family."

My shoulders drop. "And what if you never find him? What if Mom didn't know who he is? Then what? I have to sit here waiting for you to finish the story?" I can't do it. "Don't make me walk away."

"Walk away?" He looks offended, leaning in, making sure he gets as close as possible, perhaps so I can appreciate just how pissed off he is. "We are one now, Beau. Which means the target on my back spreads onto yours." He slaps a palm down on the counter with force, and I flinch. "And that means I have to finish this."

His expression, not the anger but the pain, has me comprehending with frightening clarity that he will never let this go. And, really, there's no life for us constantly running. This has to end. "Then finish it," I murmur, reluctant but accepting.

He swallows, nods, and rises to his full height, dropping his mouth into my hair. "I need to get out of these wet clothes."

I get down off the stool, suddenly deplete of energy, knowing he'll be going nowhere without me. He collects me and guides me up the stairs, and I yawn, not once, but three times on our way.

"Take a nap," he orders, pulling back the sheets and physically placing me in the bed.

"And what are you going to do?"

He doesn't answer. Just looks at me in the way he does that tells me more than my tired brain can cope with. He pulls the covers over me, collects an iPad off the nightstand, and goes to the bathroom, yanking at his wet tie.

I don't want to sleep. I don't want to close my eyes. I don't want to shut off from a world I need to remain alert in.

But my eyes are heavy.

And James is watching over me.

I come around to the sound of whispers. I feel around for my phone and look at the time. *What?* I sit up, looking out of the window, seeing the frosted glass glowing. The sun is out. A new day.

And still, whispers.

I look at the door. It's no longer clear, and the low talking from beyond is sounding angry. I get up and creep over, coming to a stop and listening.

"That's the plan," James hisses. "The end."

"It's a fucking stupid plan," Otto mutters.

And then, silence. No comeback from James. Why is it a stupid plan?

"I can hear you breathing, Beau," James says clearly, and my nose wrinkles, my hand taking the door and pulling it open. They both step back.

"Don't let me interrupt you," I say, my eyes dropping down James's semi-naked torso to the gun in his hand. "Did something happen?"

"Yes, someone thought of a stupid plan," Otto mutters, stalking off, shaking his head in despair, which leaves me wondering what the hell this plan is.

James passes me, going to the dressing room, and I go after him, not liking the sense of foreboding I'm feeling. Otto doesn't like the plan, and if Goldie was here, I bet she'd hate it too, which means I'm going to despise it.

"What's the plan?" I ask, standing in the doorway while he pulls his jeans up his thighs, the gun still in his hand.

"The plan . . ." he says, buttoning his fly before snatching a T-shirt off the back of a chair and his boots off the floor. He drops a kiss on my cheek as he passes me back into the bedroom, ". . . is that Beau doesn't know the plan."

"What?" Is he out of his mind? "James," I say, going after him, following him into the bathroom. He's dumped his boots and T-shirt on the counter and is brushing his teeth. Still with the gun in his hand. "You can't do this to me."

"What?" he mumbles. "Protect you?"

"Yes. I mean, no," I growl and push my fist into my temple as he spits into the sink. "Don't do this. Don't treat me like glass because I'm pregnant."

"Whether you're pregnant or not is a moot point." He rinses his brush. "But you *are* pregnant."

"I knew it. This isn't only your war, James. I'm not—"

He's across the room like a rocket, his palm over my mouth. "Yesterday, you asked me to walk away. You accepted I can't." His head tilts expectantly. I know where he's going with this, and he can forget it.

"You don't get to do this." I remove his hand from my face, incensed. I will not be that woman. I refuse to be kept. Wrapped in cotton wool. "I don't need protecting. I don't need looking after."

"Beau, come on. Be reasonable."

"You wanted the real me. Now you have me, and you're suppressing me."

"You're fucking pregnant!"

"And I wish I wasn't," I retort, walking away.

"Hey!" He grabs my arm to stop me, and on complete reflex, I send my elbow sailing back.

Into his nose.

"Motherfucker," he chokes, staggering back, blinking, his free hand holding his face. "Control that fucking elbow of yours."

I wince. Shrink. *Shit*. I didn't mean to do that, but I'm not glass, and he's not making me glass so he can put me in his glass house with his glass things. I roll my shoulders back, standing my ground, refusing to apologize. Not out loud, anyway. Mentally, I'm throwing him apologies left and right.

Grabbing a towel, he wipes the blood from his face. "You . . ." he says on an exhale, his eyes raging, his bare chest vibrating. Fuck, he looks savage. But I will not back down. He slowly lifts the gun and aims it at me. What the fuck is he doing? Proving a point?

"The safety is on," I point out, and he releases it, jaw rolling. I step forward, my eyes narrowing, daring him. This is fucking ridiculous. "Do it," I push.

"Don't fucking tempt me."

He growls.

And I smile, stepping back.

Then perform a perfectly executed roundhouse kick, knocking the gun right out of his hand. I land softly on my feet, my arm safe, close to my chest, and the gun flies across the bathroom and hits the wall, dropping to the floor.

Bang!

The mirror above the sink shatters, I flinch, and James jumps, his eyes darting to me, checking me over. And he stares at me, stunned, his hand still in position, except now he's unarmed. I throw him a filthy look, turn, and walk away.

"*Not* glass," I call back.

With every minute that passes, James's mood declines more. I've asked him two questions and got no answers. Not because he's ignoring me. Not because he doesn't have the answers. He just can't hear me speak, his mind elsewhere.

I'm sitting on the bottom step, watching him pace up and down in front of the window, turning his phone over in his hand repeatedly. The air is thick with tension. No conversation. Hardly any breathing.

Hearing movement behind me, I look over my shoulder up the stairs. Otto appears, carrying two bags, which I know will literally be loaded. I shuffle to the side, giving him room to pass, my eyes glued to them until he sets them down on the floor by the elevator. He flicks eyes to me. I don't like the uncertainty I see.

The elevator doors open and Goldie appears, tossing a look I also don't like to James. She's fiddling with her suit jacket, fastening it and unfastening it, and Otto is spinning the piercing in his lip constantly.

James goes to the bags and crouches, pulling the zipper of each one open and checking inside. I get up from the stairs and go to him, slowing when my cell rings. The name on my screen has me rejecting the call without thought, and James slowly lifts his head, giving me his attention for the first time in an hour. Of course he would hear my cell. And very quickly, the bastard thing rings again.

"Who is it?" he asks. He knows damn well who it is. Who else would make me this uncomfortable?

"No one."

"Answer it."

"Why?"

"So you can say goodbye," he grunts, nothing but pure hatred marring his face. I've already said goodbye. Numerous times. "A final goodbye," he adds, and because I'm not completely stupid, I take the call. James looks like he could pull one of those guns at any moment and go on a shooting spree. Ollie's timing is the worst.

"Ollie," I answer, turning away, unable to see James looking like he's about to kill something, which is irony at its best. "Now's not a good time."

"You're pregnant," he says, his tone loaded with disgust. "And by the man who killed your mother?"

"Ollie," I whisper, stunned by the condemnation in his words. "James had nothing to do with Mom's death."

"Explain why he was there then, Beau. I saw him with my own eyes in that footage Nath had. Come on, you were a smart cop."

"I can't do this, Ollie." My shoulder rises to my earlobes, feeling three sets of eyes aimed at my back.

He sighs over a curse. "Beau, please, come to me. Let me help you. I can't sit back and watch this happen."

"Ollie—"

"Remember the good times, Beau. We can have that again. Jaz would want that. She'd turn in her grave if she could see this. Who the fuck is he, anyway?"

"Goodbye." I quickly hang up and turn off my phone, my hands shaking terribly. And suddenly they're not. Suddenly, James is holding them. I look up at him.

"We need to go," he says, motioning to the elevator. "Ready?"

Ready? For what? What's going to happen? What's his plan?

When I don't answer, he pulls me along behind him as Otto and Goldie lift the bags from the floor.

Those bags. How many weapons do they need?

And, more to the point, who's going to bear the brunt of James's mood?

James rides up front with Otto driving, and I get the pleasure of Goldie's company in the back. James remains glued to his phone, and numerous times Goldie catches me staring at her. "You never did tell me how you and James know each other."

She smiles, and I notice out the corner of my eye James moving for the first time since we got in the car. He looks up to the mirror in the sun visor, his eyes on Goldie. Waiting. Or is he warning?

"He saved me," she says, simple as that, no elaboration.

"How?"

James looks at me before returning to his cell. "Rape," he says, all too casually, almost detached. "She was being raped."

I turn my stunned eyes Goldie's way, and for the first time since I've known her, I see emotion on her face. Raped. I can't imagine any man would be crazy enough to take Goldie on. Frankly, she's frightening. "I'm sorry," I murmur, at a loss. What does a woman say to another woman who's faced that kind of horror?

"Don't be. He'll be dead before I leave this world."

"Amen," Otto pipes in, and my eyes turn onto him, finding his grip of the wheel turning his knuckles white. Goldie isn't a woman who needs protection. Not now, at least. But she's got it. I settle back in my seat and turn a small smile onto Goldie, but it falls when I find her still staring at my stomach.

And it hits me. *Oh God*. A baby? She must sense my change in persona, the increase of my sorrow, because she snaps out of her daydream and looks at me with sad eyes. My hand is on hers in a second without thought, squeezing, telling her I'm sorry again without words. She looks away, but her hand turns and accepts mine, squeezing in return. Abortion? Miscarriage?

"You ready for that ten-bedroom villa full of women?" she asks, but only after clearing her throat.

"Damn straight I am," Otto replies, pulling off the main road into a street. *My* street. "Beats ice cream in the park, you pussy."

I frown through my increasing anxiety, as Goldie laughs and drops my hand, reaching forward and smacking him over the head. "Fuck you, Dino Dick."

The car has stopped outside Lawrence and Dexter's house. I have to get out and face my uncles. I have to see if that bottle of Krug is hiding something. "I think I should go alone," I say, trying to sound assertive but only achieving a whisper.

Otto's laugh and Goldie's sympathetic smile don't bode well.

"Over my dead body," James grunts, swinging the door open and getting out. I watch as he looks up at the house, pulling his T-shirt out the back of his jeans.

Concealing his gun.

I hop out and join him on the sidewalk. "You don't need that."

"Don't tell me what I need, Beau." His dismissal riles me, and then he further insults me by walking away. "Wait in the car."

He's not fucking real. I go after him, and when he reaches the door, I muscle past him and plaster my back against it, craning my neck to look him in the eye. "I will handle this." I haven't come here to argue, and the hostility pouring off James is a recipe for exactly that. An argument. "I'll get the champagne and we'll leave."

"And your passport and some clothes."

"Fine." I turn to the door, pushing it open slowly, listening. If I'm lucky, Lawrence is out shopping and Dexter is on shift.

I'm not lucky.

Both appear in the kitchen doorway, Lawrence with puffy red eyes and Dexter looking utterly worn out. "I'm just collecting a few things," I say, motioning toward the stairs.

"You're moving out?" Lawrence blurts, his lip wobbling again as he backs up into the kitchen and lowers to a chair.

Moving out? I wish I was *only* moving out. I turn to James. "Give me a minute," I plead, wishing he'd lose the angry lines on his face. He doesn't respond, and I can see he won't. He's not moving.

I turn and go to the kitchen, passing Dexter on a small smile and settling down next to Lawrence, taking his hand. I can't leave him on bad terms. "I'm okay."

"Okay? My God, Beau, you are far from okay." He squeezes my hand, his hold begging.

"I'll make coffee." Dexter takes the coffee jug and empties the old filter, as James comes to the threshold, standing in the doorway. I motion for him to take a seat. He shakes his head.

"We can help you," Lawrence says, talking as if James isn't here.

"I don't need help."

His bottom lip slips between his teeth, and he gnaws on it, assessing me. Disagreeing with me. "You're throwing everything away, and for what?"

Freedom. Peace. A life I'd long accepted I'd lost. But Lawrence would never understand, and there is only so much I can share, which makes convincing him harder. Or, actually, easier. I don't think anyone could understand James and me. Only us. It kills me over and over, but I accept defeat and move my hand out of Lawrence's. I'm fighting a losing battle. And James is fighting a winning one.

I hope.

I have to be sensible with my time—it's not on our side, and sitting here attempting to break Lawrence down is wasting it. I give him a small, sad smile, a smile that tells him I'm hurting, and start to stand. I only manage to lift my ass off the chair a few inches when the door from the yard flies open, ricocheting off the wall with a bang.

Ollie appears.

Armed.

His weapon pointed at James behind me.

I fall back to the chair, Lawrence cries out, and Dexter drops the coffee pot. It smashes on the counter, the sound of breaking glass echoing around the kitchen. "Ollie?" I whisper, taking him in, noting his distressed state. He's . . . edgy. Sweaty. Shaky.

"Stay where you are," he says, his voice shaky too, as he moves farther into the kitchen, his eyes laser beams on James behind me. I look over my shoulder slowly, wary to make any sudden movements, keeping as calm as possible. It's a difficult task when my insides are in chaos—my heart pounding, my lungs shrinking, my stomach turning.

James is still and steady in the doorway, his focus unmoving. "Put the gun down," he warns Ollie, only his mouth moving.

"Shut up." He approaches James, edging closer warily, jerking the gun in gesture for James to raise his hands.

Wisely, James slowly lifts his arms, calm and collected, but I can see the monsters swirling in his eyes.

"Ollie, what on earth?" Lawrence breathes, and I slowly and blindly reach for his arm, settling him, telling him to be calm.

Ollie proceeds to pat at James's torso, feeling around his back while holding the gun to his chest. He pulls James's gun free from his jeans and tucks it in his own trousers, and the whole time, I'm waiting, tense, for James to make his move. Because he could. One swift, meticulous move could have Ollie disarmed and on the floor before I could draw another breath. Except he remains a statue. He lets Ollie take his gun.

And it hits me.

If not Nath, then who?

Ollie.

Oh my God.

I stand, shocked, and James's eyes turn onto me, silently warning me away, but if anyone can talk some sense into Ollie, it's me. I have to try. He looks so volatile. He looks ready to fire that gun. "Ollie, look at me," I order gently.

"Beau," James grates, his hands still in the air. "Sit the fuck down."

"Ollie, think about this," I plead.

"Beau, don't make me tell you again."

"Ollie," I go on, ignoring him. "Be wise."

"Beau!" James barks, and I flinch, the aggression and anger in him shocking me. "Sit. Down."

I feel Lawrence's hand take mine and pull, but I resist, unable and unwilling to let what's inevitably going to happen play out. "Ollie—"

"Do you hear how he talks to her?" Ollie asks over a salacious laugh.

"I want her out of the firing line." James flicks his eyes to mine, and I see something in them. Something I haven't seen before. Fear. And it makes me slowly lower to the chair.

"The gun's aimed at you." Ollie's grip flexes around the handle. I've seen him do that before when we took target practice together. Just a few seconds before he'd fire, he'd adjust his hold a fraction. My heartbeats accelerate. "Did you think I'd stand back and let you ruin her?" he asks James. "I don't know who you are or—"

James moves so fast, his big body is a blur, and Ollie is quickly disarmed, flying back into the counter. James reaches for his shoulder, pulling another gun, and I hear the safety disengage before he swiftly has his arms braced, the gun aimed.

But not at Ollie, who's unconscious on the floor, knocked out.

I slowly turn on the chair and find Dexter with his hands up in surrender.

My mind explodes. "James?" I question quietly, as Lawrence jumps up and shrieks. "James, what are you doing?"

He says nothing, leaving my head swinging back and forth between him and Dexter, who remains still and quiet.

"James! For fuck's sake, talk!" I grab Lawrence's hand and yank him back down to the chair as James lowers to his haunches and collects Ollie's gun from the floor. He rises, engaging the safety, and comes to me, but his eyes never leave Dexter.

"Take it," he orders me, and I do because I don't know what else to do except listen to him. Trust him. I release the safety again.

"What's going on?" Dexter asks, still backed up in the corner, his eyes darting around the room, looking for anyone to enlighten him. "What is this madness?"

"How did you know where I lived?" James asks calmly, his voice so composed, his body equally so, whereas everyone else in the room seems to be shaking with nerves, including me. "When you and Lawrence visited yesterday, how did you know where I lived?"

"Beau mentioned it," he blurts urgently.

My eyes drop to the table, my thoughts chasing in circles. I try desperately to slow them. To get things straight. It doesn't take me long. "No, I didn't." I look up at him in question. "I've never shared where James lives." Of that I'm certain. I made a point of it, in fact, because I knew any one of the men in my life, most in law enforcement, would dig. I made a conscious effort to keep everything about James a secret.

"You did," he argues. "Right here in the kitchen."

"What are you suggesting?" Lawrence barks, outraged. "Where the hell is all this leading?'

I shake my head. "I never shared anything about James, Dexter," I say quietly, wondering what the hell this means. I look at James. He has a million apologies in his eyes.

He swallows. "You paid Nathan Butler a visit."

"Yes, to discuss Beau. To talk about how toxic this relationship is."

Lawrence recoils, clearly shocked by this news. "When?"

Dexter's eyebrows become heavy, like he's wracking his brain, thinking. "I don't know, sometime last week."

Toxic. He's probably right. Poison. But James's poison has cured me. And now there's this poison threatening to send me plummeting into a dark pit of helplessness again.

"And while you were there," James goes on, "you turned on the burner phone I've been tracking since the night Jaz Hayley was killed."

"What?" I gasp.

"Rubbish!" Dexter screeches. "You're fabricating shit to clear your own ass."

"Why?" James asks, calmly. "Why would I do that?"

"Because you killed Jaz! You're there in the footage, it was you."

My eyes widen. "How do you know about that footage, Dexter?" I ask, unable to comprehend what's unfolding.

"Footage?" Lawrence asks. "What footage?"

"The footage Dexter had hidden for years. The footage that would have proven Mom's death wasn't an accident." I slump in my chair, stunned.

"The footage," James says, moving forward slowly, "that you obtained from the tattoo store by the car park before forensics moved in."

I stand, trying to get some feeling back in my limbs. "Beau, sit down," James warns.

"Dexter, what have you done?" I move toward him, trusting—hoping—that the years I've known this man will prove our suspicions wrong. *We had it wrong with Nath, so maybe—*

"Beau," James yells.

Dexter's face turns from the usual softness I've come to know and love, to a hardness that doesn't suit him.

"Beau!"

I'm grabbed and whirled around, being pulled back into Dexter's chest, and the gun in my hand is quickly gone. "Okay, let's all calm the fuck down," he says, backing up, taking me with him. James's nostril flare so hard. His body visibly tenses. I want to tell him not to worry, that Dexter won't hurt me. But I can't. Especially now. "I've spent years wondering who the man in that footage was. The man who dragged Beau away from the vehicle. The man who tried to save Jaz. Years!" He laughs, tightening his hold of me. "And then he shows up on my fucking doorstep trying to seduce my niece? Who the fuck are you?"

"Dexter?" Lawrence murmurs, crumbling before me. "Dexter, why?"

"Because I was told to!" he yells, starting to shake against me. "It was Jaz or me."

Him or my mom? "Jesus Christ, Dexter," I whisper, my throat tight.

"The Bear," James says, his voice ice. "Who the fuck is The Bear?"

"Back off," Dexter warns, jolting me. "No one knows who he is. I get information, I'm paid. I get an order, I do it, or I die."

"You're going to die anyway."

"Oh my God, Dexter!" Lawrence cries. "What have you done?"

I'm moving, being walked backward. He's heading for the door into the yard, the door that's still open from Ollie's grand entrance. "Why, Dexter?" I murmur.

"Because she figured it out. She knew I was—"

"Corrupt," James grates, his jaw pulsing.

"I was told to deal with it. So I did."

"No," Lawrence screeches, his hands in his hair, utter disbelief plastered all over his face. "No, no, no."

"By manipulating the service record of her car," James says. "Suggesting she was smoking. Manipulating all of the fucking evidence."

"I was in the car, Dexter," I whisper, a lump in my throat forming. It's suffocating me.

"I didn't know you would be!"

"But I was!" I yell, my heart cracking. This man has been a rock to me. Hugged me, talked me through endless panic attacks, calmed me. And he's the cause of my misery? I look at James, my eyes welling, knowing what this means.

And I see it. The look in his cold stare. Never have I been more thankful that our relationship has been so heavily based on talking without saying a word. One flick of his eyes to mine. The rage. The purpose.

I throw my head back and drop to the floor as soon as Dexter loosens his hold of me, and all hell breaks loose, guns firing, Lawrence screaming, James charging forward.

"Fuck!" The door slams, and I shoot up from the floor, seeing blood smeared all over the jamb, but there's no Dexter in sight.

"Beau," James barks, checking me over, his attention split between me and the door.

"I'm okay," I assure him, still patting myself everywhere, waiting for the pain to kick in. Two shots were fired. Only one of them hit Dexter. *James.* I look up, expecting to see red, but there's no blood.

He swings the door open, bracing himself to fire again, just as Goldie and Otto come charging into the kitchen, armed and ready.

"Over the back wall," James says, and they disappear as fast as they appeared, going after Dexter, while James hurries over to me, checking me over with panicked eyes, feeling everywhere, checking my legs, my chest, my face.

"I'm fine," I assure him, as he yanks my shirt up my body. And it hits me. The pain. The pain and dizziness.

"No," James whispers. "No, no, no, fuck, no!"

I slump against him, suddenly overwhelmed by the agony, feeling my body becoming light. Lawrence screams, and it is a scream of pure, raw agony.

The last thing I see is James's distraught face.

And the last thing I hear is his roar.

64

JAMES

I thought I'd known pain at its greatest. I thought I would live out my life immune to further hurt. Because surely there was nothing that could compete with losing my entire family. Or being burned alive. How wrong I was. But scarier than the pain is the anger. Anger that has taken on a frightening level. Anger that might not ever be sated.

My arse on the chair is numb, my eyes unmoving from the speck of dirt on the floor a few feet away. I don't know how much time has passed. It's an effort to turn my eyes to check. To lift my wrist to see my watch.

Save her. The two words circle my head persistently. I focus on only them, because letting my mind go elsewhere would be dangerous.

Save her. Save her. Save her.

I hear the door open, but my eyes remain locked on the speck of dirt. "I'm sorry, Kel," Goldie says, softer than I've ever heard her speak before. "We lost him. I got his license plate number."

"BMW?"

"Yeah."

"Leave me," I order, not needing to hear anymore. They didn't chase him down. They didn't catch the fucker so I could torture him until he passes out. But I'll find him. I refuse to die until I do. "And make sure Nathan Butler is still being watched."

The door closes, and I lean forward, resting my elbows on my knees, taking my head in my hands. God help the world if I lose her.

God. Fucking. Help. It.

I stand abruptly, starting to circle the room, forcing my breathing into steadiness, shaking the burn out of my twitching hands. Calm. Give me calm.

No calm.

I roar and upend a table, picking it up and launching it out of the window. It shatters, and glass sprays the room, pelting me with shards.

Still no calm.

The chairs follow the table.

My fist sinks into the wall.

I kick and punch anything is sight, completely unhinged, finding no peace in this fucked-up world.

"Mr. Kelly!"

I spin, heaving like a raging bull, the red mist thick.

"For fuck's sake, Kel." Otto appears next to the doctor by the door. I can just make them out through the fogginess of my vision, both of them taking in the carnage. "I'll ensure this is all taken care of," Otto assures the doctor. "My apologies."

"Miss Hayley is out of surgery," the doctor says, tentative and wary.

The fog clears. Hope has arrived.

I'm almost too scared to ask. "And . . ."

"We removed the bullet from Beau's abdomen. She's stable."

I fall back against the wall, my knees giving way. Stable. She's stable. I slide down the wall, the relief too much, but the doctor doesn't look as relieved as I feel. He doesn't look like a man delivering good news. I hold his eyes, once again scared to ask. "The baby?"

He swallows, backing out of the room. Getting out of my line of fire. "I'm afraid there was nothing we could do to save your baby, Mr. Kelly. I'm very sorry. The blood loss, the trauma. I'm afraid the pregnancy ended while Beau was in surgery."

I stare blankly at the doctor, my head bobbing mildly, nodding, agreeing.

Accepting?

Never.

"She's in recovery now," he goes on. "You can see her." He casts his eyes across the room, assessing the damage. There's nothing else for me to destroy in here. But out there?

"Kel," Otto says quietly, and I look at him blankly. "You should go to her."

"Worried what else I might do?" I ask, slowly dragging myself to my feet. "Because you should be." I pass him, heading for Beau, trying not to plot every move I'm going to make until I can make it. Until Beau is well. "I have some things I need you to do," I call back. There's nothing to stop me preparing.

I turn at the end of the corridor and see Lawrence and Beau's ex up ahead, both still looking like they've seen ghosts. "She's out of surgery," I say as I pass them. Lawrence, naturally, is on my tail, though Ollie, wisely, remains where he is, waiting for an invitation to visit her. He'll never get that invitation. "Are you okay?" I ask Lawrence over my shoulder as I walk, trying to be sensitive. The man looks like death warmed up, his face puffy, his eyes red.

"Don't worry about me," he says, his voice wobbly. "Beau is my priority right now."

"We've lost the baby." The words come from nowhere, and I slow at the door to Beau's room, staring at the wood.

"I'm very sorry." Lawrence has given up trying to keep his emotions in check, but I'm under no illusion that his sorrow is for me.

"I'm going to kill your husband," I vow, taking the handle, bracing myself, breathing deeply. "For what he's done to Beau, to her mother, to me. I'm going to kill him." Lawrence needs to know this isn't over. He needs to be prepared.

"Who are you, James?" he asks on a snivel. "Really, who are you? You tried to save Jaz. You turn up in her daughter's life years later. Tell me who you are."

I turn to face him, taking no pleasure from the mess of a man he is. "Just see me as the man who saves your niece, Lawrence. That's all you need to know."

He swallows and nods. "May I?" he asks, nodding to the door past me.

"Give me five minutes," I say, though he knows it's not a question. I'm simply maintaining some civility for the sake of Beau. He accepts without fuss, and I turn to the door, spending a good few minutes bracing myself again. Tamping down the threatening rage before I look at her. Look at her and see the damage that's been done because of me.

Pushing my way in, I stall when I see a nurse by her bed adjusting the line into Beau's arm. She looks up and smiles in that way I expect they do to all loved ones whose closest are so desperately ill. "You must be James," she says, taking a syringe to the cannula. "I'm Vera. I'll be looking after Beau while she's here in recovery."

I close the door and focus on the liquid in the syringe getting lower, hearing the constant, consistent beeps from the machinery. I can't bring myself to look at Beau, truly petrified of the further anger I will feel. "What's that?" I ask, standing motionless on the other side of the room, scared to even get closer.

"Morphine." She finishes up and drops the needle in a clinical waste bin. "It'll keep her comfortable." Pulling off her gloves, she makes a few notes before offering me a small smile. "I'll give you some privacy."

"Thanks," I say, my eyes now on my boots. I hear the door close gently, and I will myself to man the fuck up and look at her. Or even just get closer to her. It takes more mental preparation than anything has taken me before, and when I finally lift my burning eyes and see her, the heat inside rises to a full-blown inferno. It doesn't look like Beau. The woman on the bed, pasty in complexion, her skin gray and lifeless, does not look like the woman I've fallen in love with. And that just makes me angrier. I swallow down the fireball in my throat and lift my heavy feet, feeling like I'm trudging through thick mud as I cross the room and lower into the chair beside her bed. I gingerly reach for her hand. She's warm. It's the only thing I recognize. Her warmth. But there's no sizzling when our skin touches. She doesn't tense. Her eyes won't shimmer and her lips won't part with want.

Calm down, Kel.

"I won't rest until justice is served, baby," I promise quietly. "Justice *our* way." And it's going to be my bloodiest death yet. Lifting her hand to my mouth, I kiss the back, breathing her into me. But all I can smell is antibacterial liquid. Not Beau's light, sweet, fruity scent. As if I need anything more to increase my motivation to kill.

The sound of a throat clearing pulls my attention over my shoulder, and I find Goldie's at the door. She closes it softly and joins me by the bed. "Nathan Butler passed away ten minutes ago."

I exhale, closing my eyes. It's one more thing for Beau to be devastated about.

"And I found this." She lifts her hand without looking at me. Held between her thumb and index finger is a key. "Taped to the inside of the box." She tucks it into her inside pocket. "What do you want me to do?"

"For now, wait," I say quietly, my thoughts all over the place. It's silent for a while, but I can hear Goldie's mind turning as fast as mine. "Whatever you're thinking, just say it." I look up at her, and she peeks out the corner of her eye at me.

"Why do I get the feeling you're going to do something stupid?"

"What gives you that feeling?"

"The look in your eyes. The unrestrained rage."

"Killing the man who did this to Beau would be stupid?" I ask, reining in my temper. "The man who killed my unborn child?"

"I don't mean that."

"Then what the fuck do you mean?" I ask. "And choose your words wisely, Goldie."

"No one knows who you are."

"The Bear does."

"He knows what you look like. Where you live. He doesn't know *who* you are."

"And?"

"And, again, why do I get a bad feeling that soon every fucker in this town will know who you are?"

So what if they do? I can't deal with this right now. I place Beau's hand gently on the bed and stand. "I need a piss." And to splash my burning face. "Watch her." I open the door and locate Lawrence on the chair down the hall, giving him a gesture to suggest he's now welcome. He's in the room fast, probably worried I'll change my mind. Oliver Burrows, however, wisely stays back. "You can leave." I say to him, cold and brittle.

"Over my dead body."

I step toward him. "It can be arranged."

"Who are you? Where's Dexter?"

"Are you here as Beau's concerned ex, or an FBI agent?" I advance, getting threateningly close to him. "Forget about who I am or what I do. Dexter killed Jaz Hayley. Fuck off and investigate that." I turn to Goldie. "Do not leave this room."

"I'll come with you," Otto says, pushing his back from the wall.

"No, you'll watch the door."

"Fuck you, James. I'm coming with you."

My jaw goes into spasm. "Am I not making myself fucking clear? Watch the motherfucking door, Otto."

He's up in my face in a heartbeat and, fuck me, I'm caught off guard, which means he gets me against the wall with ease, his pierced face close to mine. "I've not spent years protecting your arse so you can go to the fucking toilet in a fucking hospital and be taken the fuck out. You hearing me? Goldie's in there. The girl is safe. I'm coming to the God damn toilet with you, and if I say I want to hold your fucking dick while you take a piss because it's safer that way, you will God damn let me. Am I making myself clear?"

Well, fuck me. "Crystal," I say quietly, and he shoves me as he releases me, straightening himself out. He's stressed. I've never been on the receiving end of Otto's temper, and I know I'll avoid it in future.

"Good." He nods. "Let's go."

"Who the hell are you people?" Beau's ex backs up the corridor, his eyes wide as he makes his escape.

"Fools," Otto grunts, striding away, leaving me to follow. I tail him a few paces behind, giving him space. "Hurry the fuck up," he mutters, edgy.

Opening the door for me, he ushers me inside and loiters while I take a piss. I pull my dick out, my body heavy with stress. "Want to hold it?" I ask, my eyebrows high. He stops pacing and throws a scowl at me, and for the first time in what feels like forever, I'm amused.

I finish up, wash my hands, and we head back, silent, our boots creating rhythmic thumps as we walk the corridor. I feel the tension leave me the closer I get back to Beau, but before I get to her door, my mobile rings. I pull it out of my pocket, looking down at the screen. "I need to take this," I say, taking a seat in one of the uncomfortable plastic chairs outside her room. "Spittle."

"Beau Hayley."

"What about her?"

"She was seen driving away from the scene of Agent Nathan Butler's and two cops' murders in Butler's car. It's been found burnt out. Care to enlighten me?"

"You're rather close to the latest police news considering you're retired, Spittle."

He laughs. "Fuck my life. Did you get my message?"

"The one involving me meeting you?" I find my fists clenching. "What part of *enigma* don't you understand?" What's his goal here? I don't know, but one thing I've learned about Spittle is that he can't be trusted. But he's still useful. Until I kill him.

I hang up and push my hands into my knees, using energy I shouldn't be wasting to stand, and push my way into the room, coming to a screaming halt when I see a man by Beau's bedside. Tom Hayley.

"How the hell did this happen?" Beau's father directs his question at me and me alone, his chest puffy. He's lucky I'm conserving energy, or I'd put his head through the nearest window. Getting no answer from me, he looks at Lawrence, who only shakes his head, losing control of his lip again. "I want answers," he bellows, yanking out his phone and dialing. He paces up and down a few times before cursing and hanging up. "What's the fucking use having a cop in the family if you can't get hold of them in an emergency? Where the hell is Dexter?"

I laugh out loud. I don't mean to, but the prick is comical. "I suggest you get yourself a coffee and calm the fuck down," I warn, and he recoils.

"Excuse me?"

I pace forward slowly, and he starts to back up. I need an outlet for this unrestrained wrath, and it looks like it's just arrived. Goldie steps in front of me. She doesn't need to say anything. Her look says it all. Not here. Not now.

"Get a coffee," I order again, as I look into Goldie's eyes.

"Who the hell do you think you're talking to?"

I turn my death stare his way. "Get a fucking coffee, Mr. Hayley."

He withdraws, obviously seeing the murder etched on my face, casting his eyes across Goldie and Otto too. "I'll be back," he declares, his chest swelling in fake confidence before he exits, slamming the door behind him.

"Don't let him back in or I'll kill him."

Goldie nods, flicking her eyes to Otto behind me, who swiftly leaves to keep my prey at a safe distance. I move toward the bed and sit down, reclaiming Beau's hand. "Leave me," I murmur quietly, lowering my head to the mattress and closing my eyes. I'm beat. Exhausted. I just need quiet for a moment. Quiet and calm.

I doze off to the hypnotic sound of Beau's heart monitor.

And vivid images of death and blood.

I jump and look back when the door closes, finding a nurse in the room. She raises her hand in apology for waking me. "Time for some pain meds." She moves to the other side of the bed and starts fiddling with Beau's cannula as I look down at my watch. I've been out for only ten minutes.

"Russian?" I ask, detecting the remnants of an accent.

She smiles. "I've been in the States for twenty years, and I still can't hide it."

I watch as she tries to unscrew the cap, fiddling terribly, her hands shaking. I rewind back only half an hour, to when the other nurse pumped some morphine into Beau's veins. I look up at the nurse. "Where's Vera?"

She falters in her moves and doesn't look at me to answer. "On her break."

My eyes fall to her working hands again. "You okay there?"

She laughs. "Yes, they're so fiddly."

"Probably because you have no fucking idea what you're doing." I drop Beau's hand and stand fast, pulling my gun and aiming it across the bed. "Put the syringe down."

She drops it fast, eyes round, and backs up against the wall, her hands in the air. "Sir, please," she cries, alarmed, shaking more now than before.

"Who the fuck are you?"

"I'm a nurse." She points to her name badge and quickly raises her hands again. "Please, sir, I'm just here to do my job."

The door behind me bursts open, and Otto and Goldie appear, taking in the scene, both stunned. "What the fuck, Kel?" Otto says, his hand twitching, like he's unsure whether he needs to draw or not. Truth be told, I don't know either. My head is fucked, my eye off the ball, exhaustion still clouding my brain.

"I'll show you my papers," the nurse nods jerkily.

I blink, swallowing, trying to straighten out my mind. "Show me."

"Okay, yes, I'll show you." She reaches for her pocket, and I start to relax. But then I see something turn in her eyes, and her stance changes, her hand going to her back rather than her trousers.

"Kel!" Otto bellows.

I close one eye, getting my aim straight, and squeeze the trigger, and she flies back into the wall before falling to the floor in a heap, wailing and crying, speaking a load of Russian shit I don't understand.

"What the fuck?" I breathe, rounding the bed and going to her, grabbing the front of her uniform and yanking her up close to my face. "Who the fuck sent you?"

She snarls and spits in my face.

So I put a bullet between her eyes, and the echo seems to drag on forever. I slowly rise and look across to Goldie, who's up against the door, stopping anyone from coming in. And Otto is staring. Just staring at the dead woman on the floor. "Place your bets on who sent her," I say quietly. So maybe Sandy *wasn't* in that factory when I popped off half a dozen Russians.

"I let her in," Otto murmurs. "I fucking let her in." His hands go into his hair. "Fuck!"

That's it.

My time thinking is up. I get my mobile out and dial.

"What are you doing, Kel?" Goldie asks.

"I'm getting Beau out of here." I go to her bed and gaze at her unconscious, oblivious face. And I realize now why the woman in this bed is unrecognizable to me. It's not only because she looks sallow. It's because she looks peaceful. I would do anything to maintain this look on her, but through my turmoil, my agony, I appreciate one thing. I can't do that. I can't take care of her *and* kill the enemy. I can't even do it with Otto and Goldie by my side. It's too much of a risk.

For the first time, I need to do things differently.

Which means revealing who I am.

The call connects, and Spittle gives me a wary hello. "Find me a doctor. The best," I order.

"And what do I get in return?" he asks, sending my jaw into spasm. But . . . Beau.

"What do you want?"

He's silent for a time, telling me that whatever he wants is pretty fucking colossal.

"Talk, Spittle."

He inhales, building himself up to say it.

"I want you to kill Brad Black."

65

BEAU

Rainbows and sunshine, smiles and contentment. I don't know where I am, but I never want to leave.

No pain, no darkness, no fear, and no anger.

But also . . . no James.

That alone is enough for me to back away from the enticing light. And as I do, the pain starts to build deep in my tummy. The darkness begins to shroud the light. My smile starts to fall.

My eyes snap open, and I inhale, the air hitting my lungs and burning them. I can't see. Can't focus. Can't breathe. Can't move. Nothing will move.

"Beau?" My name is being spoken repeatedly, over and over. "Beau. Beau. Beau."

My cheeks are suddenly encased. My wild, darting eyes still.

"Beau, baby, look at me. See me."

I blink the blurriness from my vision, trying so fucking hard to do that. To see him. But where is he? I can hear him. I can feel him.

But I can't see him. "James?" I croak, willing life into my muscles. "I can't move. I can't see you." Panic takes hold, my body not listening to me, not taking the instruction.

"I'm here."

"Where?" I yell, my throat raw. "Where are you?" Take me back to the light. Take me back to rainbows and sunshine. The pain and darkness are only worth bearing if he's here, and he's not here. "James!"

I jolt on the bed, and I still, a tidal wave of pain ripping through me. I cry out, trying desperately to curb the agony by making myself small, by curling into a ball. But I can't move. "I can't fucking move!"

"Hey, hey, hey."

There he is again. Speaking but not showing himself.

Enigma.

66

JAMES

I give the doctor a nod, and he moves in, putting more meds in her arm to calm her. I don't know how many times I can let him do that. Knock her out. Stall her waking. Delay having to tell her we've lost our baby. That Dexter disappeared without a trace. That the man responsible for her mother's death is still out there. That Nathan Butler is dead.

Beau settles immediately, and I rest her hand by her side, tucking in the sheets around her. I go back to the message on my screen.

Ready when you are.

"You cool?" I ask Goldie, and she nods her agreement, resting back in the chair, her eyes lasers on Beau's sleeping form. "Call me if anything changes."

"She's perfectly stable, Mr. Kelly," the doctor says, a refined looking fellow who happily came out of retirement to help. "Keeping her still and peaceful will only aid her recovery."

"Thanks, Doc." I breathe in and turn, making my way to the door of the hotel room. A fucking hotel room. I meet Otto outside.

"Kel," he says, grumpy as hell, falling into stride next to me. "Why the fuck are you being so cagey?"

If Otto knew what we're doing, where we're going, I'd be staring down the barrel of his Glock before I got to the finer details. "Because you won't like it," I answer, staring forward, my pace determined.

"I don't like any of this shit, and it only started because you couldn't keep your curiosity contained."

"Fuck you, Otto. You know as well as I do that Beau was the key to ending this." Literally.

"So where are we going?"

"To hell."

He laughs. "I'm an honorary fucking resident, you dick."

The Viking of a doorman pulls back the velvet rope, letting us pass, and the pumping music gets louder and louder until we're in the thick of it, *Fired Up* filling the club. I look around the vast, dark space, strobe lighting bouncing off all the bare brick walls, the dance floor packed, the bar five deep.

And on a stage in the center, strippers.

"Now this is a bit of me," Otto says, his eyes set on that center stage. "This ain't hell, brother."

"Enjoy, you tart," I mutter, heading for the industrial metal stairs to the right, taking them two at a time to the top. I make my way to the edge and lean on the balustrade, looking down on the club. Brad Black's club.

"What the fuck are you playing at?" Otto says, joining me, taking in the view. "Don't just fuck off like that."

"How long did it take you to notice I was gone?"

"Two spins of the pole and a grind."

I laugh under my breath, my eyes casting back and forth across the space. "This is Brad Black's place."

He groans. "So you really have brought me to hell, you twisted fuck. What the fuck are we doing here?"

"I've been sent to kill him."

He swings stunned eyes my way. "By who?"

"Spittle."

"Why?"

Good fucking question. "I'm working on it. Go make yourself busy," I order, gazing around the space, and because Otto knows I prefer to kill alone, he moves away, but he can't hide his displeasure. And I know he won't be far.

I push my body up from the balustrade, my eyes high and low. "Drink, sir?" someone says, and I look to my left, where a tray hovers before me. The waitress holding it smiles. "Courtesy of management."

I exhale my amusement and accept the tumbler, sipping and looking around. *So where are you?*

He doesn't show himself, so I lean back on the balustrade, waiting. Patient. I have to be patient now, think things through, make wise moves.

A man eventually appears beside me, leaning on the railing, looking out at the club. *His* club. He's a good-looking bloke, his dark hair well-kept, his suit expensive. He takes a sip, all casual, not looking at me. "I've not seen you around here," he says, turning a blank look my way.

I look past him, seeing various men in suits loitering around. "On your guard?"

He glances over his shoulder, but he doesn't acknowledge my question. "So, who are you and why are you in my club?"

"You don't need my name."

"And why you're here?"

"To kill you."

His eyes undeniably widen somewhat, his body becoming alert. "Then why am I still breathing?"

"Because you have something I want."

"What's that?"

I cast my eye over each of the six men in the vicinity, and Brad Black notes the direction of my stare.

"I'm out of that game now." He motions with his Scotch to the club surrounding us.

"Someone's put you back in it."

He stalls a beat, watching me closely. "And I should listen to you, why?"

"Because you want to keep breathing," I say quietly, although he still hears, despite the pumping music.

He nods, and it's slow. Wary. "My office," he says, dragging his eyes off me and striding away, his men following.

I look across the club, seeing Otto at the end of a bar, watching. His displeasure hasn't improved. I give him a nod, following Brad Black. His men don't enter his space, but rather wait outside, leaving me to walk through the middle of them, curious eyes following me. I close the door, and Brad goes to a cabinet, topping up his Scotch.

"Take a seat," he says, settling behind his desk as I lower to the chair, setting my untouched glass on the desk. "You don't drink?"

"Not today."

He nods mildly, taking more of his own. "So who sent you to kill me?"

"A mutual friend," I say, getting comfortable, smiling at Brad's raised brows. "Spittle."

"The fuck?" he says quietly over a laugh. "And you refused?"

"No, I agreed. Refusing would have had that slimy fuck slithering under a rock. Plus I needed something from him urgently."

"What?"

"A doctor."

"You ill?"

"No, my girlfriend was shot."

His drink pauses at his mouth. "You have a girlfriend?" he asks, an irritating smile threatening. "Why the fuck would you go and get yourself one of those when . . ." He fades off, and I exhale, waiting for it. "Fuck me, you're here because of her." He laughs, wiping at his forehead. "You know, my uncle always told us never to let a woman into your heart. Only ever your bed." He toasts the air, like it's something to celebrate. "His own son didn't listen to him, and now he's dead. Because of a woman. Cheers." He downs his drink and slams it on the table.

"The Brit," I say quietly, studying Brad carefully. "Danny Black. The Angel-faced Assassin."

"Dead because of a woman. Looks like you're heading the same way, my friend."

"The only place I'm heading to is out of town once I've killed The Bear and every single one of his men."

"And you need me because . . .?"

"Refuge."

"Somewhere safe to keep your girlfriend while you go on a killing rampage?" He smirks.

"Something like that."

He nods, his eyes thoughtful slits. "As it goes, I have just the place you need."

"I'd hope so, since my killing spree benefits us all." I stand slowly from my chair, and Brad smiles. He must feel like all his prayers have been answered. Every potential threat to him gone. Spittle gone. "We have a deal?"

He offers his hand across the desk, and I lean over accepting. "What do I call you?" he asks, shaking mildly. He knows. Of course he fucking knows. And, wisely, he wants me as an ally, not an enemy.

"Depends. Friend or foe?"

"Friend."

"James."

"And foe?" He wants me to say it. To confirm it.

"You'd have to be stupid." I drop his hand. "I know you're not stupid." I tilt my head, and his wry smile widens. "I'll be in touch." I stride to the door, coming to a slow stop before it. "You can tell The Brit he's welcome."

I look back, finding wide eyes and a lax jaw. "What the fuck are you talking about? The Brit's dead."

"Is he?"

Black's face strains, his cheeks pulsing. "He's. Dead."

I nod, thoughtful, watching his eyes rage. "But is he?" I ask quietly, swinging the door open, turning away.

"Shut the fucking door."

I hear the undeniable sound of the safety of a gun disengaging, and I still, a sick smile creeping across my lips. I slowly shut the door and turn to face him. He's standing now, his arms braced. "What do you know?" he asks.

"I know Spittle talks too much."

"And what has he said?"

"Small things here and there that built a rather vivid picture."

"Like?"

"Tenses. Past and present. Spittle seems to get clumsy with those. So if I were you, I'd ask myself who else he's got clumsy with and why he'd want you dead."

I take the door handle and back out, leaving Brad Black with my bombshell. "You can text me the address of where I'm taking my girlfriend."

"I don't have your number," he says, just as his phone rings in his pocket. He reaches in, looking at the screen as he pulls it out. His eyes fly to mine, his face screaming disbelief.

"Good to meet you, Brad." I pull the door closed and stalk through the club, and Otto is by my side in a beat, his eyes watchful.

"What the fuck's going on?" he asks, flanking me.

I keep my eyes forward. Always forward, because if I look back at this point, I'll lose my focus. I *need* my focus.

"I've just resurrected the dead."

67

JAMES

The address is a mansion in Miami. She's still settled. No more episodes, no restlessness, no extra medication needed. I made sure Doc is aware that this is a full-time position until Beau's fully recovered, and he didn't argue. I'm doing him a favor, both in time and cash.

I leave the swanky, over-the-top room and pull the heavily engraved wooden door shut behind me, backing into the corridor, where abstract art hangs between every one of the dozens of doors. Goldie and Otto are waiting for me.

"I don't like it here," Otto mutters.

"Why? Because your pierced, bearded mug looks out of place surrounded by all this fancy shit?" Goldie asks on a laugh.

He grimaces and glances up and down the corridor. "Where the fuck are we, anyway?"

I head off, nodding to Ringo, the guy who was here to meet us a few hours ago. He's an ugly fucker with a nose bigger than my apartment block and skin with more craters than the moon. He grunts and nods in return, and Goldie gives him a sideways glance.

"You could fit Miami up one of those nostrils," she mutters as we take the marble staircase down to the foyer.

"I'll let that slide because you're a girl," Ringo calls, his face poker straight.

Goldie comes to a grinding halt on the stairs, her face murderous as she glares at him, her nostrils flaring. He winks at her. It's the worst thing he could do.

"Who are all these men?" she asks, stomping on, taking in numerous men in various positions.

Men. That's exactly what they are. Men we need. Surviving the deadly world I've put myself in with only Goldie and Otto at my back was easy when it was just us. Now there are too many enemies. Now, there isn't only us three. I need an army to win this war. And I've found one.

"Where's Lawrence?" I ask, knowing Beau will ask after him as soon as she comes round. I had to bring him, not only because he's an utter mess, but for Beau.

"Unpacking in his room."

I head to the right at the bottom of the stairs as instructed and approach the double doors. More heavily carved wood. *And here we are.*

I do what's right and knock before I push my way in, but I don't find who I'm expecting. Spittle looks up fast, his eyes rooting to my face, taking in every bit of me. "Who the fuck are you?"

I can only smile. "Be careful," I murmur. "Haven't you heard that looking me in the eye turns you to dust on the spot?"

He frowns. Then every muscle in his face seems to give up, his expression falling. "Fuck, no."

I take myself to the sofa and lower as Otto closes the door and takes up position with Goldie. "Isn't it nice to put a face to the name?" I ask. He takes a sip of his drink—a big sip—as I cock my head. "Are you nervous, Spittle?"

He laughs, uneasy. "Christ alive, I'm sitting in The Brit's old mansion with another deadly Brit. What do you think?" He gets up and starts pacing, taking regular swigs of his Scotch.

I can feel Otto staring at my profile, and I turn my eyes onto him, my lips straight. He shakes his head in disbelief. "What the fuck are we doing in a dead mob boss's mansion?" he asks.

I don't answer him. He'll find out soon enough. Returning my attention to a pacing Spittle, I follow him up and down by the window a few times before I get bored of watching him go back and forth. "Will you sit the fuck down?" I say curtly. He's across the room in a heartbeat, his arse on the couch.

"Did you . . ." he stutters. "Have you . . ."

"Killed Brad Black?" I ask. "Yes. He's about as dead as The Brit."

Eyes like saucers, Spittle struggles to his feet. "I think it's time for me to go."

"Sit the fuck down," I shout, my fingers clawing into the arm of the couch to restrain myself. He drops like a stone to his arse, just as the door swings open and a guy appears, a young bloke, with dark eyes that contradict his pale blond hair. "Nolan," Spittle says, rising from the couch again, out of respect I expect, since I've just told him to sit the fuck down.

"Thanks for coming, Spittle." The guy, Nolan, grins at him, before takes me in, his broad chest lifting ever so slightly. "So what do we call you?" he asks, a sardonic smile on his face. I hear Otto huff his displeasure, and I roll my eyes.

I stand and, again, do what's right. This guy, albeit young, maybe mid-twenties, works for Brad Black. There's a reason for that. "James," I answer, offering my hand.

He strides over and takes it, his assessment of me never wavering. "And everything meets your expectations?" he asks, motioning in the general direction of the house.

"Yes, thanks."

"Your woman will be safe." As he utters the words, a couple more men appear at the door, Ringo and another, who I'm yet to officially meet. And someone else emerges between them. A woman. A middle-aged lady with a friendly face and warm smile. "And cared for," Nolan adds, smiling fondly at the woman. "This is Esther."

She approaches and offers her hand. "Danny Black was my son." Her British accent is as soft as her features. *Was* my son. "Anything you need, please, just ask."

"Thank you."

"British," she says, smiling, truly pleased. "We're taking over Miami, it seems."

"We?"

Her lips purse, though she's still smiling. "And what do I call you?"

"The Enigma," Spittle calls, and we all cast interested looks his way. "Why's everyone so fucking cool about the company we're in?"

"Found your way around again soon enough, didn't you?" Nolan says, looking at him like the piece of shit we all know him to be. "Bet you thought I'd asked you here for some help to find Brad's killer."

Spittle raises his drink and finishes it on a gasp. "Jackpot." He slumps back down on the couch, waving his glass in the air before him. "As you were."

Esther backs up. "I'll go check on your lady."

Lady. I smile to myself. Not Beau. "Thank you." I don't think I've shown so much appreciation in such a short space of time.

"What the fuck is going on?" Otto whispers, moving into my side.

"Yes, please do share," Goldie pipes in. "I feel like I've stepped onto the set of The Addams Family."

Brad Black strolls in and stops abruptly when he clocks Spittle on the couch. His arms come up, all welcoming. "Spittle, my friend, guess what?"

"What?"

He grins, and it's fucking wicked. "I'm not dead."

Spittle sags. "So you lured me here to kill me, I expect."

Brad heads for the desk across the room, but rather than taking the chair behind it, he pulls another out from this side of the room, turning it and lowering. He catches my interested expression, but his face remains deadpan as he gives Spittle his attention. "So you sent The Enigma to kill me? I'm deeply hurt, Spittle. After everything I've done for you."

"You've made my life a fucking misery, that's what you've done."

"I expected way more begging than this," Brad says over a laugh. "So, The Bear?"

"What about him?"

"How friendly are you?"

"No one gets friendly with bears."

"Well, that depends," Brad muses, kicking his ankle up onto his knee, "on the bear." He pouts. "But if you're gonna be a bear, then be a grisly, eh?" He beams at Spittle, who is suddenly twitching. Actually twitching. His eyes start to roll, and his face starts pulling some pretty fucked-up expressions. Then, quite dramatically, he plummets forward and hits the carpet face first, his body thrashing around.

I stare at him, as does everyone else in the room, and for a few minutes, no one says a word, just watches him convulse. I cannot believe what I'm seeing.

"Take him," Brad orders, and Nolan moves in, his muscly form preparing to drag Spittle's short, sturdy frame out of the office. "I'll decide what to do with him another time."

Nolan doesn't take Spittle's legs. He takes his head, and starts yanking it, tugging him along in short sharp bursts. "For fuck's sake!" Spittle cries, rolling onto his back. "Don't you men have any humanity in you? I was having a fucking seizure."

"You were having a brain malfunction, Spittle," Brad seethes, standing from his chair. "A bit like when you ordered The Enigma to kill me."

"I was cornered," he argues. "For fuck's sake, what was I supposed to do?"

"You cornered yourself when you opened your big, fat fucking mouth."

"I've got murderers coming at me from all fucking directions."

"You were trying to cover your corrupt, stupid fucking ass, you piece of shit." Brad waves an impatient hand. "Get him the fuck out of here before I stab the fucker in the throat."

I smile. Brad won't kill him. He hasn't had the order.

Flicking my eyes across to Goldie and Otto, I see they're both looking like fish out of water, confused as fuck, their stares following Spittle's fat body as it's dragged with little effort out of the office. I'm a fish out of water too. How I do things. My ways. I'm no showman. I get the job done and move out.

I stall for a moment, thinking. I'm lying to myself. I'm really no different to Brad Black. I'm the biggest showman of them all. How I kill. How I taunt them. How I maintain my illusiveness until that very last second before I end them. The pleasure I take when they realize who I am.

Brad pours himself another drink and sits on the edge of the desk. "So what's your plan?"

"Kill."

"What do you need from me? Men?" Brad cocks an eyebrow at Goldie, and she growls.

"Say one word," she warns lowly, threateningly. "I'll break your dick off and floss with it."

"Ooh, she's a feisty one. Does she bite?"

"She doesn't bite, she eats whole."

He smiles, and it's a smile that could tip Goldie over the edge. "For now, I just need a safe place for Beau to recuperate." *While I plot.* "And we need to find this guy," I say, as Otto slaps a photo of Dexter in front of Brad.

"Dexter Haynes. MPD. His license plate number is on the back."

Brad nods, and I leave the office, heading back upstairs to Beau. The doctor is still watching her closely, and Esther is changing her sheets. "You don't have to do that," I say, approaching, giving Beau a quick look over. She looks no different. No worse, but no better either. My heart sinks. I'm not going anywhere until she's on her feet, so death will elude The Bear for a little while longer.

"It's my thing," Esther says, pulling on a new pillowcase.

"Changing sheets?"

"Faffing." She smiles and gently lifts Beau's head, slipping the pillow under, getting her comfortable. "There." She collects a few things. "Come on, Doctor, I have a few scones in the oven."

They leave together, and I smile my thanks, settling on the edge of Beau's bed. I pull the sheets from her legs and take her foot, cupping the back with my spare hand to support it. "Time for your exercises, baby," I say quietly, slowly starting to bend her leg at the knee and elevate her lower leg in slow, smooth motions, circulating the blood. Up, extend, tuck in, back down. Over and over, at least half hour on each leg. And the whole time, I watch her face.

Waiting.

Hoping.

Praying.

68

BEAU

Walk away from the light. Walk away from the light. Walk away from the light.

There will be no freedom. There will be no happiness. If I walk into the light, there will be no James.

I still and listen, waiting for his touch again, my skin begging for the heat. The only heat I can tolerate. I breathe in through my nose, searching for his unique scent. There it is.

And a heat I've come to recognize meets my ankle. My leg rises. Extends. Lowers.

Over and over.

I open my eyes and let out a shallow sob when I see his beautiful, traumatized face above mine. The mere sight injects my useless body with strength. The pain has gone. I can breathe easy. I can see clearly. "I couldn't find you," I murmur.

He sighs, coming as close as he can, letting me hug him with one weak arm. My tears are unstoppable, seeping into the threads of his T-shirt. "I'm here," he whispers. His voice. That in itself is a medicine. "I'm here." He gently pulls away and spends an age gazing at me, wiping away the tears. He looks so troubled. "Do you remember what happened, Beau?"

I divert my eyes, shying away from the memories his question spikes. "Dexter," I say quietly, seeing a vivid image of his hostile expression the moment before he disappeared out of the door. I haven't the capacity or strength to try and unravel it all. Not now.

I suddenly feel empty, but the emptiness feels deeper. More profound. I look at my stomach. *Empty*. "I'm not pregnant anymore," I say quietly, looking up at James. "Am I?"

He can only shake his head, his throat swelling. The emptiness multiplies, and I rest my head back on the pillow, looking at the ceiling. James may appear as sad as I feel, but I can sense his need for justice. "Where's Lawrence?"

"He's safe."

"And Nath?" I look at him and know immediately that Nath is gone. I inhale, breathing out shakily, flinching at the pain that simply breathing brings. "Is Dexter still out there?"

"Yes."

"What are you going to do?"

"Kill him."

I nod, accepting, because what else can I do? Stop James? Nature's strongest force wouldn't be able to stop him. My own uncle. A man I've looked up to for years. He's watched me suffer. Held endless paper bags over my mouth when I've fallen into one of my merciless meltdowns. Held my hand. Spoken encouraging words. He fooled me. I feel myself begin to shake with the anger building, and I roughly wipe at my eyes, forcing myself to settle. Anger is pointless now. I'm helpless. Useless. It'll only fuel James, and he looks like he needs no fuel.

Breathe, Beau. I take a moment to gather myself and gather my bearings, looking around. I expect to see medical machinery everywhere. I see only one piece next to my bed, a line into my arm. I expect to see harsh, tubular lighting above me. I see an elaborate gold chandelier. I expect clinical bed sheets. I see a sumptuous spread in rich autumnal colors. I gaze around the room, an extravagant, plush bedroom, and finish at the French doors onto a terrace.

"Where am I?" I ask, finding James on the edge of the giant bed.

"We're safe."

"That wasn't my question." I try to sit up, hissing as I do.

"Beau, for fuck's sake, take it easy." His palms gently press into my shoulders and push me back down.

"I'm fine."

"God help me, woman, lie the fuck down."

I relent, but only because the pain is too intense. "How long have I been out?

"A week."

"A week?" I blurt, panicked. A whole week? I know what James is capable of in an hour. He's had a whole week to rain holy hell on the world? "And where have you been?" I ask. Looking for Dexter? Oh God, what about Lawrence? He'll be out of his mind.

"Here. Always here."

I stare at him, stunned, but I see only sincerity in his expression. It's a stark contrast to the man I first met. "A whole week has passed, and you've not killed one person?"

His smile is small and ironic. "I've killed more people in this one week than in my lifetime."

Plotting. He's been plotting. "Where are we, James?" I ask, gazing around again.

"Don't worry about that for now." He gets up and goes to the door, swinging it open. "Get the doctor," he orders, and I see Goldie craning her neck, looking into the room. Searching for me.

She looks worried, until she sees me on the bed, awake. And she smiles. But only through her eyes.

"Good to have you back, Beau," she says gruffly. I'd call *that* affection, but I can only smile, and it's weak.

James comes back and starts fussing around the sheets. He's stalling. Diverting. Distracting. I reach for his hand and stop him. "Where are we?"

"Somewhere safe."

"Where is somewhere safe?"

"You have a lot of questions for someone who's just come out of a week-long coma."

"I've not even started," I assure him. "Where—" The door knocks, and an older man walks in, his suit tweed, his beard gray. "Who are you?" I exclaim, looking to James for an answer.

"Beau, this is Doc," he says, dismissing me, giving his attention to the elderly man. "Check her over."

"I'm fine."

"Shut up, Beau," James snaps, and the doctor looks between us, a little alarmed. "Listen to *me*," he warns the doctor, and he gets straight to it, checking me over. He reaches my stomach and presses lightly. I hiss.

"Fine," James grunts, going to the stand where a bag of fluids hangs, pulling it closer as the doctor checks my pulse.

"I just need to empty your catheter," the doctor says.

Catheter? I look at the ceiling, despairing, and close my eyes, hiding from my mortification. "Remove it," I order, and the next thing I know, he's poking around in a place he shouldn't be. I breathe in and hold my breath, feeling the uncomfortable pull on my bladder. And when I open my eyes, he's brandishing a bag of pee in the air. "Oh my God," I murmur, looking at James to save me from this humiliation.

"Thanks, Doctor, I've got it," he says, smiling softly. "She's *fine*."

The doctor nods and leaves with my bag of pee, and I sigh, lifting my heavy arm, seeing a new cast.

"You upset your break when you fell," James says.

"How long will I be useless?"

He smiles, full of pity, and pours some water, sitting on the edge of the bed. "Here." He directs a straw to my mouth, but I try to take the glass instead. It's pulled back out of my reach. "Let me."

"I can feed myself, James." I am not depending on him to care for me. Never.

"Beau," he breathes, his patience wearing. I don't care. This is not how I'm wired. He knows that. "You've been shot. You've lost . . ." He fades off, his nostrils flaring. "Just let me look after you, for fuck's sake."

I swallow, wary of the monsters in his eyes, and drop my mouth open for him. I need to pull my head out of my ass and let him do whatever he needs to do to deal with this. Take care of me. And kill. But what about me? What will get *me* through this? The weight of the world feels heavy again. It lightened when I met James. He provided a relief. Now, there are more secrets. There's more danger. More hatred. And on top of that, my body is broken along with my spirit. So there will be no walking that path of nothingness with James for a while. No ecstasy. No mind-numbing bliss.

I suck on the straw and swallow, blinking back the tears. No more tears. I will not cry. *God, I want to cry.*

"Want some sunshine on your face?" James asks, setting the glass back on the nightstand.

No darkness.

I nod, tearful, and he helps me negotiate my stiff body to the edge of the bed. The whole time, my teeth are clenched, my muscles tense, trying to stem the pain. The soles of my feet meet the soft carpet. That hurts too. And I get a little head rush, just from sitting up.

"Whoa," I whisper, swaying.

"Okay, bad idea."

"No." I grab his arm. "I'm not lying in that bed feeling sorry for myself." Thinking about what we've lost. What's happened. How it happened. Who did it. "I need sunshine on my face. I need rainbows, James." My voice, infuriatingly, quivers. Rainbows are a long way away. I realize that.

He nods, understanding, and helps me to my feet, watching me closely, waiting for any signs that I might pass out. "I'm okay," I assure him, lifting one foot and placing it down, leaning into his big body as he holds me around the waist with one arm and pushes the metal stand holding the bag of fluids along with the other. I look to the French doors, to the gorgeous, green, vibrant garden beyond. "It's beautiful."

"Isn't it?" he says, taking it in himself. "Beauty amid so much ugly."

I look up at him. I couldn't agree more. He is beauty amid the ugly. We make it out onto the terrace, where there are sun loungers and another terrace directly next door. It's a hotel. A lovely mansion hotel.

"Here." He lowers me to a lounger and positions himself behind me, moving back and letting me rest on his front. I exhale, close my eyes, and feel the warmth of the sun on my face and the warmth of James on my back. "Good?"

"Perfect," I say. This is perfect. Wherever we are, wherever he's brought me, it's perfect.

Paradise.

No evil. No hell.

But I know it can't be sustained, because despite being in a place that looks like paradise, all I can think about is the loss.

Our baby's gone. Nath's gone. Dexter killed my mom. Lawrence must also be beside himself with grief. I'd thought I'd grieved enough already in my life, but the hits just keep coming. I feel like

I'm slowly losing my mind. I need some facts. Something to stop all these thoughts of loss and pain that are barricading my brain from good sense. Something to show me we have some hope. "Tell me where we are," I demand softly.

"No. Just enjoy it."

69

JAMES

Fuck, I'm going to have to share eventually. But revealing where we are will lead to other questions I'm not sure I can answer yet. "How's the sunshine on your face?"

I don't like the long silence that comes. Neither do I like it when she starts to try and turn over, so I lock my arms down around her upper body, mindful of her cast and cannula. Even broken, she's difficult. "James," she says, her voice threatening.

"Stay still. You'll hurt yourself."

"I'm fucking fine."

Anger. She's full of it, and I know my evasiveness is only a small factor. I close my eyes and search for calm, try to push back my own fury. Fury with myself, because while trying to tame the demons in us, I've created more. "We're at Danny Black's mansion," I say quietly, and she stills.

"What?" she whispers. "Why the hell are we at a dead mafia boss's home?"

"Because I can't do what I need to do while looking after you."

"I don't need looking after," she says, tensing, like she's intending to move. She jerks, not intentionally, but in pain, and the line in her arm pops out, blood starting to piss everywhere.

"For fuck's sake," I mutter, slipping out from behind her and crouching by the lounger, taking a towel from the table and applying pressure on the inside of her elbow. She stares at the towel, her breathing labored. "Just give in, Beau," I say, looking up at her. "You have to give in and let me help you." A fat teardrop slips off her cheek and splashes onto the towel. "Stop trying to be strong. You don't need to be." I reach for her face and wipe under her eyes. "I've got this," I assure her. "And once it's done, we go wherever you want to go."

She looks up at me, and I fucking hate the sadness I see. Not anger. Not need. It's pure, heavy sadness. "Will it ever be done?" she asks. "Do you know who The Bear is? Where Dexter is? You could spend years chasing your tail."

"You don't want this to end?"

"Yes. End it now. Let's just go. Me and you and . . ." Her words fade off and her hand lands on her stomach. *And our baby.*

Fuck.

"Do you want to spend the rest of our lives looking over our shoulders? Worrying about me. People know who I am, Beau. They know James Kelly is The Enigma. I have to end this."

She swallows, her eyes dropping. She knows. And she has to accept. "Is that why I'm here? Protection while you go on a mercy mission? What if you don't come back?" she asks, looking up at me. More sadness. "Then what happens to me?"

"He'll come back," a voice from behind me says, and every muscle I possess firms up as I look at Beau. She's frowning through her tears, her neck craning to see past me. I don't need to look. His British accent tells me everything I need to know. Not to mention the thick, deadly air that's arrived.

Beau's jaw drops, her eyes expanding. She knows who she's looking at. I squeeze her hand, take a breath, and rise to my feet, slowly turning to face him.

The Brit.

His impassive expression doesn't crack, the scar on his face silver, his skin tan, his eyes sharp. He turns his suited form slowly and leans on the railings, looking out over his gardens. "I think we need to have a little chat," he says quietly, slipping a cigarette between his lips and lighting it.

I knew. I slowly put the puzzle together with the scrap pieces unwittingly thrown my way, and yet still, seeing him in the flesh, I'm surprised.

Surprised he's here. Surprised he's revealed himself to me.

I turn to Beau, who literally looks like she's seen a ghost, and lean down to help her up. She comes with ease, and I'm grateful, despite knowing her compliance is fueled solely by shock and not willingness. "Here, hold this," I say, picking up the metal stand and placing it in her hand. She grips it, eyes still on Danny Black behind me, and I scoop her up and carry her back into the bedroom, laying her on the bed. She looks at me in question. "I've got this," I say again, pushing my lips to hers.

I make sure her arm has stopped bleeding before I text Otto to get Doc up here. Then I leave her, heading back out onto the terrace, pulling the door closed behind me. "How is she?" he asks, exhaling a plume of smoke.

"Difficult."

His scar dents slightly, the sign of a small smile. "I get it. Smoke?"

"I'm trying to quit."

He pushes from the balustrade and flicks his cigarette butt away. "Me too," he mutters, his hand coming out, extending toward me. "Danny Black."

Like he needed to introduce himself. "James Kelly."

His smile breaks. "I prefer The Enigma."

"He'll soon be dead."

He laughs under his breath. "Take it from me, not even death gets you away from this world." He motions to a chair and takes one himself on the other terrace. "Talk to me."

"What do you want to know?"

"I want to know who you are, where you came from, and how *you* know The Bear knows I'm alive. Because I've no interest in being resurrected unless I have to be." The side of his finger brushes across his Cupid's bow, his eyes watchful. "I have a wife. My chances of survival are zero if I have to go home to St. Lucia and tell her we're coming back to Miami."

I'm amused, but I don't smile. The Angel-faced Assassin is wary of a woman. I can relate. "Spittle was taking backhanders from someone connected to The Bear," I tell him. "I killed the connection, had Spittle looked up, and gave him a courtesy call. He took an instant dislike to me. I think he has a thing against British."

Black smiles, amused.

"Spittle knows he's fucked up," I continue. "He's said things he shouldn't have said to people he shouldn't have said them to."

"Like?"

"Like hints that The Brit isn't dead. And when he realized he'd let on you're alive, he tried to kill Brad to cover his arse and came to me when he failed. So I asked myself, why wouldn't he just wait for The Bear to kill Brad?"

"Because The Bear won't kill Brad." Black shakes his head, his lip close to curling. "Because he wants Brad to lead him to me."

"And then you'd find out Spittle's blown your cover and kill him."

"So he didn't expose me intentionally."

"No," I say, forcing my body into relaxing. "Does that mean you're *not* going to kill him?"

"All in good time," he muses, looking like he's already plotting Spittle's demise.

"Like when? He's stupid, and stupid people can be dangerous." That's been proven.

"Are you stupid, James?"

"I'm sitting here. Of course I'm fucking stupid. But I'm owning it."

He laughs lightly. "I've not met many men I've liked instantly."

"I've met none," I reply, and he regards me coolly, nodding. Understanding.

"Tell me why I shouldn't end you now, turn Spittle inside out, and kill The Bear myself."

"You don't know who the Bear is. No one does."

"And you do?"

"No." I lean forward, making sure he hears what I'm about to say clearly. "But I have a personal investment." My head tilts. "He killed my family. He ordered the death of my girlfriend's mother. So I know you hear me when I say I'd be fucked right off if I don't get to look that motherfucker in the eye before I end him. For him to see me. To know who I am. To know why he's dying." I have to pause to take a breath, my skin sizzling with that unrelenting need again. Danny Black sits quietly, observant, watching me fighting to control my rage. And something deep and potent tells me he gets it. He comprehends. But just in case . . .

I stand and turn, pulling my T-shirt up, exposing my back. "I will burn him alive. Listen to him squeal like a pig. I need vengeance. But more than that, Beau needs it. And I *will* bring her peace." Dropping my T-shirt, I turn to face him. "Are we clear?"

His face is poker straight, but I see the respect looking back at me. "Meet me in my office," he says, his eyes stuck to mine, his mind obviously spinning.

I nod, leaving Danny Black on the balcony, undoubtedly considering his options. He knows he only has one.

Come back to life.

Beau is still looking dazed in bed when I enter the room, and in an attempt to distract myself from the burn inside, I go to her, taking one of her legs and starting her physio routine. I can feel her studying me. Hear her silent questions.

But she says nothing. Nothing except, "I love you."

My working hands falter, and I look up. Her eyes shine, life in them somewhere. I'll bring it back to the surface, I swear it, and if I'm going to have to leave her while I hunt, I have to know something . . .

I lower her leg to the bed and round the side, settling on the mattress and taking her hand. "If I asked you to marry me, would you accept?"

"No," she says, straight up, no fucking about. And she's smiling.

"Why?"

"I was a cop. I can't marry an assassin."

"But you can fuck one? Kill with one?" *Have a baby with one?*

Her tiny scowl is cute. "We don't need to get married."

"Maybe I do."

"Why?"

"I don't know." I shrug. "Validation."

"That's exactly why I *don't* need it." She laughs lightly, looking over to the French doors. "I can't believe he's alive."

I balk, taking her chin and redirecting her face to mine. "Answer me."

"I already did."

"A different answer."

"No. I'm not marrying you." Her head tilts, her expression firm, as are her words. "The end."

"I'm about to go to war, Beau."

"Then don't."

"I—" There's a knock at the door, and I growl, getting up. "We're not done," I call back.

"Incorrect," she says as I swing it open. Danny Black stands before me, and Goldie and Otto are behind him, looking every bit as stunned as Beau did.

"You should get used to that," I say, motioning behind him.

He looks over his shoulder, interested. "I was just heading down to my office," he says, and I nod, thoughtful. He didn't need much time to weigh up his only option.

"Give me five." I shut the door and turn around, puffy chested. I'm injured. "I want a valid reason why."

Her weak body visibly sags. "I don't have much faith in vows." Her nose wrinkles, and I'm not sure whether it's in discomfort or simply speaking of marriage. Both? Her parents. Her father cheated. Betrayed. That's not me, but I haven't got time to convince her of that right now. I stride over, drop a kiss on her forehead. "We're still not done."

I walk away and swing open the door, finding Goldie and Otto whispering. They quickly stop, and I quickly hedge my bets on who will hit me first with their *what the fucks*?

"What the fuck?" they say in unison, both of them pointing limp hands down the corridor, where I expect Danny Black has just wandered away.

"I'll explain."

"We're definitely done," Beau calls. "I'm not marrying you."

I show the ceiling my palms and Goldie and Otto my despair. "She's just playing," I say to their stunned faces, making tracks down the corridor.

"Where are you going?" they ask as I go.

"To make a deal with a dead man," I murmur, rolling my shoulders, every inch of my back tingling.

The door to his office is open when I get there, and Danny Black is sitting at the helm.

Behind his desk.

In the chair Brad wouldn't take.

Because it was still his boss's seat.

He motions to the chair opposite, and I take it while he pours two Scotches. "How is she?"

"Still difficult." I accept the glass he hands me and hit the side of his.

"Cheers," he replies, smiling around the rim. "You should take her away," he suggests, waving a hand indifferently. "Give her some attention." He quirks an eyebrow. "I have a place, just say the word. Look at it as a welcome gift."

"A welcome to what?"

"My home," he says, although I expect there's more to it than that. "And speaking of gifts . . ." He nods at the door, and I turn, just as it opens.

I slowly lower the glass to the table, the heat rising from my toes to my head.

Dexter falls into the room.

"Where did you find him?" I ask, unbending my body from the chair, taking in the pathetic, disheveled piece of shit.

"One of my men got lucky," Black says, simple as that. There was no luck. I imagine there was blackmail, threats, but no luck.

He's crying, snot everywhere, his complexion gray, blood staining his thigh. Fuck, hold me back.

Or . . . don't.

I see Beau in hospital. I see her circling her stomach in her sleep. I see all the things Dexter really shouldn't want me to see.

The red mist can't be held back.

I lose my head and fly across the room, charging at him, swiping him clean out of the hands of Ringo and smashing him into the wall. I'm all out of control. This won't be quick and clean. "You killed my unborn child, you lanky, cocksucking fucker."

God help him.

No. The devil can have him instead.

He dribbles and moans as I drop my hold and back away,

reaching for my ankle and pulling out a switchblade. "Listen to me," he pants, eyes darting around the room.

"Shut the fuck up."

"I can tell you who The Bear is."

That just enrages me more, and I lunge forward, plunging my knife into his eye socket. He drops, the squeals of pain blood-curdling, the shrieks mixed with pleas irritating as fuck. I get up behind him, take a hold of his head, and tilt it back. I wrestle his tongue out of his mouth and slice the fucker off, then take the blade and sink it into his ear.

Instant silence.

Blood everywhere.

I step back, shaking. I've never seen red so vividly. Never shook so much when I've ended someone. I cast my eyes across the blood-soaked carpet. "Beau doesn't hear of this," I say clearly.

"Received loud and clear," Black replies quietly, as I turn to face him. He takes in my blood-stained form while casually sipping his Scotch. "He said he knew who The Bear is."

"He was lying. No one knows who he is."

"He'll be coming for me, assuming he really does know I'm alive."

Exactly. And Danny Black isn't the kind of man to wait around to be killed. And thanks to Dexter, The Bear knows who I am too. "He knows you're alive," I assure him. "You have Spittle to thank for that. So, are you ready to be my bait?" I ask, and he regards me for a while, as I stand before him, dripping in blood. Yes, I'm sick. But so is he.

His smile now, dark and moody, proves it.

He raises his tumbler. "To my resurrection." He takes a long slurp and slams his glass down. "You'll hold my fucking hand when I break the news to my wife."

EPILOGUE

St. Lucia – a week later

BEAU

The wheels hit the runway, and I jolt in my seat, feeling James's keen eyes on me. I try my hardest not to flinch, but the pain, albeit milder now, still gets me. I press my lips together and close my eyes, mentally calculating the last time I had any pain meds. I must be due some more soon.

I hear James's cell come to life, pinging and singing the arrival of texts and missed calls. I open my eyes. "Lawrence?" I ask, circling my stomach with my palm, sounding hopeful.

James shakes his head, and I try so hard to keep my disappointment from my face, closing my eyes again. He's not left his room since James took us to Black's mansion. Not spoken. Hardly eaten. Esther, Danny Black's mother, a lovely, gentle lady, has promised to send me daily updates while we're away. But I need to hear from him. I need to know he's okay. Or that he'll be okay eventually.

The brakes kick in, and I'm pulled back in the plush seat, breathing through the discomfort. I can feel James watching me. Has been the entire flight. Assessing me. "I'm fine," I say for the thousandth time, and I so desperately want to be fine, but no matter how many times I try and convince myself of that, I return to the same circle of worry. This here, where we've just landed, is a temporary respite. A vacation from our real life, where James is a cold-blooded killer, and I am a broken ex-cop. We'll need to return to Miami. James will need to kill. I will need closure.

Closure.

It seems like a pathetic word to use in such a life-or-death situation. Which brings me to something else. Something I've been afraid to ask. "Did you find a key?"

He unclips his belt, despite the jet still cruising down the runway at some speed, and pulls one of his bags onto his lap. "No."

I eye him with suspicion. "You're lying."

"Okay." He looks up and smiles. It's sarcastic. "I'm lying."

"Why are you doing that?" I ask, unclipping my belt and slowly standing, trying to get some life back into my limbs.

"The less you know the better. Sit down."

The brakes kick in harder, and I'm knocked back into my seat. "Fuck," I hiss, my face screwing up.

"God help me, Beau," James seethes, leaving his seat to refasten my belt. "Stay."

"The less I know the better?" Does he seriously think that'll wash?

"I don't want you involved," he mutters, returning to his own seat.

"You mean with your new gangster friends?" I turn away, looking out of the window. It's so bright, I have to squint. Sunshine.

"You don't get to pull the protection card now," I say as the jet comes to a standstill. "I've told you, don't treat me like I'm glass."

"The protection card has been in play since we met, Beau," he replies, standing and taking my hand. I look up at him. "And you *are* glass. Always will be to me." His eyes drop to my stomach. To my wound. To my *womb*. Fragile. And, of course, I can't argue with him.

I let him unclip my seatbelt and carefully pull me to my feet. "I'll walk," I say before he has a chance to scoop me up. "My muscles are dead." I start a very slow wander toward the flight attendant up front, who is freshly painted to see us off Danny Black's private jet. I smile my thanks as I pass her and break out into the sunshine.

"Sunshine on your face," James whispers, resting his chin on my shoulder.

I inhale the salty sea air and let it stream out slowly. "What are we going to do with all our time now you have no one in the vicinity to kill?"

"Have a holiday."

"A vacation."

"Yes, that." He ushers me down the steps, and a driver meets us. He nods and passes us, collecting our bags. "Dinner," James says. "Relaxing, reading, recharging." He opens the car door and looks back. Danny Black emerges from the plane, looking cool and casual in a cream linen suit.

"Strategizing," I add, my face straight when James turns tired eyes onto me. "Am I wrong?"

"You're talking too much about the wrong things."

"I want to know every move you make," I inform him. "*Before* you make it." A wave of something washes over his features, and I tilt me head in question. "Have you got something to tell me?"

"Not a thing." He gently pushes me into the seat as Black approaches, slipping on his shades.

"The driver will take you to the beach hut," Danny says, nodding to the guy who's loading the trunk with our cases. "When you're settled in, we'll have dinner. The four of us."

"Us three and who?" I ask, curious. Don't tell me the Angel-faced Assassin has a girlfriend. I pause for thought, looking at James. The Enigma. How the fuck did I go from being a cop to a gangster's moll?

"My wife." Something shines in his eyes, softening them. "Rose. Something tells me you two will get along great."

"Why?"

Danny looks at James, serious. "Difficult. Was that the word?"

My eyes swing from Danny to James. He's smiling too. "Difficult? Me?" The nerve. "Forgive me for needing to know the finer details of my boyfriend's planned killing spree."

"Thanks, mate," James says, and Danny Black smiles. There's definitely something different about him here. Something lighter. His wife? "Wish me luck," he says. "And if you don't hear from me by morning, you'd better come check I'm alive."

"You're scared of a woman?"

"Terrified. And she's not just *any* woman." He appears to shudder for effect. "She's my wife." He starts backing away, eyes on James, a certain amount of communication happening with that single look.

James nods, understanding, and turns his attention onto me. "Ready?" He shuts the door, rounding the back and sliding in next to me. My cell starts ringing, and I dig it out of my purse. "Oh . . ." I breathe.

"Who?"

"My father." I flash the screen at James. "I've got to take it." It was a cop-out leaving a message with his secretary but explaining why I'm leaving the country seemed like a mammoth task.

"You can't tell him where we are, Beau."

"I know," I say on a sigh. "Dad."

"Beau, what's going on? I've had a message that you've gone on vacation."

"A small break," I say as the driver pulls away. "I'll be back in a week or so."

"Where are you? You should have said, I would have chartered a flight for you."

I smile, looking out of the window at the shiny private jet we just disembarked. "It's fine." James upgraded us. *Into mafia territory.* And yet, undeniably, I feel safe. Did at Casa Black, and now here in St. Lucia.

"So where are you?"

"Somewhere quiet."

"With him, obviously," he says, and I look at James. What happened when I was out cold for a week? Something tells me my father and boyfriend didn't bond.

"With James, yes."

"I see." He coughs. "Well, enjoy. Call me when you're home. We still need to do that lunch. Just the two of us." He hangs up, and I shake my head.

"I'm fine, thanks for asking."

James reaches over and takes my hand. "Still got daddy issues?" he asks, and I laugh under my breath. "I don't want to be an issue for my kids."

I swing my eyes his way. *Where did that come from?*

"My father was a drug tycoon, yours is a conceited wanker. Do you think we'll be shit parents?"

My mouth falls open to speak, but I can't find the right words. Something tells me he's thought about this a lot. I, however, have pushed our loss into a safe box in my brain, never to be opened. It's self-preservation. It's all I can do because the alternative would be bloodshed, and one murderer in this relationship is enough.

What the fuck am I thinking?

I force a smile and look away. "Can we go swimming in the

sea?" I ask.

He doesn't answer the question that was plucked from thin air in an attempt to change the subject. He's still thinking. I'm not sure I like James on vacation.

The beach hut. Biggest understatement of the century. The only thing that makes this four-bed, three-bathroom abode a *hut* is the pure-white wooden-slatted exterior. There's a veranda, an outside kitchen, a dunking pool, and a private path to the beach. But however large and luxurious, it has nothing on the monster villa at least half a mile up the beach. It has to be Danny Black's. Secluded. Private.

Alive.

I drop my glasses back to my nose and rest back on my elbow. James is in the water again. For hours now, he's swam, following the line of the coast as far as he can, back and forth. The water is glistening, the earlier storm passed, but the scent of rain still hangs thick in the air. The sun is warm on my skin. The sand soft under my back. I cast my eyes down my bathing suit. Not a bikini. I can't see myself wearing one of those ever again. It's just another scar to cover. But the mental scars? Will they ever be gone?

And will this nightmare ever end?

I breathe in the sea air and cast my eyes across the horizon. There's nothing for as far as the eye can see. I can hear no traffic, no people, just the lapping of small waves onto the shore and the light whistle of the breeze. We could stay here. Maintain this peace, this nothingness. Just be.

I sigh, content, and search for James again. He's no longer swimming. Now, he's wading out of the sea. I sit up a little, resting back on my hand, and admire the sight. His tight swim shorts. His epic chest. His rough face. I've never seen him look so rested. So light.

When he reaches the shore, he uses his foot to pat around on the sand, and I frown, wondering what he's doing. He drops to his knees, lays his forearms on the sand, and I watch as every muscle in him tenses as he slowly straightens his body until he's vertical. Still. Steady.

Stability.

Focus.

I smile and get to my feet, cursing under my breath at the pull in my tummy and the ache in my arm, and pad through the sand to him, approaching quietly. I circle his upside-down form, taking in every breathtaking inch of him. His back the most. The damage he sustained trying to save my mom's life. Saving *me*.

He's still saving me.

There's always been a connection between us. Something insane and unfathomable, but this scar and how he come to have it propels our connection into another realm. *Unbreakable*.

It's a beautiful notion.

I reach his front and lower to my stomach, resting down gently, propping my chin on my palm, studying his serene face, my cast placed awkwardly to the side. His lashes flicker a fraction, his lips not smiling but not straight either. Even upside down, he's wildly beautiful. Then his lips quirk and mine follow. One eye opens. And with precision and little effort, his straight, lean body, starts to lower over me until his front comes to settle on my back. He buries his face in my neck and inhales, and I rest my cheek on the warm sand.

"Hi," he whispers, and I smile. "It's me."

"Hi, me."

"How's the sunshine?"

"Warm on my back." I lift my butt up into his groin with too much effort, and he groans into my neck.

"I'm your sunshine?"

Warm. Bright. "You're my sunshine," I confirm, wriggling as

best I can without spiking too much pain. But it seems every move hurts. He raises onto his toes and fists, and I turn over, trying to hide the discomfort on my face. He remains suspended above me.

"We're still not done," he says quietly, lowering and kissing my lips gently before rising again.

My sunshine. Warmth where there's cold. Light where there's dark. Happiness where there's misery. "Then ask me again," I say, reaching for the center of his chest and drawing a straight, light line down the middle to his bellybutton. I flick my eyes up to his, relishing his smile.

"If I asked you to marry me," he whispers, "would you say yes?"

"Yes," I reply, and he lowers again, placing another kiss on my mouth, this time remaining lowered. No weight on me, his strong arms and straight legs keeping him hovering above my body. For the first time in what feels like an eternity, he advances our kiss, releasing his tongue and finding mine. Swirling slowly. Lapping softly.

Glass.

I take all he is offering, indulging, feeling.

Loving.

"I have a condition," I murmur around our lips, and he hums, lost. "You don't kill Dexter." As expected, he pulls away, and I smile, almost in apology. "I don't think I could live with myself. I don't think I could look Lawrence in the eye."

His Adam's apple rolls from his swallow, his eyes searching mine. "What are you saying?"

"I'm saying I can live with honest justice where he's concerned." The kind of justice Mom believed in, and which I did too, before I lost her. "I need to know why he did it. How he got in so far up to his neck that he saw *that* as his only out. I need that, James."

His nostrils flare. He doesn't like it, but surely he must understand. "He killed our baby, Beau." He swallows and lowers again, burying his face in my neck, keeping my front free from his weight

"And he'll pay," I say, taking my arm around his back and stroking across his uneven skin. "Okay?"

"Okay," he breathes, but it's reluctant. "Anything else?"

"Yes. Once you've found The Bear, we leave Miami for good." I can't deny him that one kill. I won't truly ever have James until he's exorcized that demon. I know that. And, really, I need it too. It's the missing piece of our puzzle. The path to our eternal peace. Dexter played a part, but he didn't order the kill.

"Where do you want to go?" He lifts and looks down at me. I can already see his eyes darkening. Vengeance brewing.

"I like it here."

"Then I'll buy it." A kiss.

"And what will you do with all of your time?" I ask.

"I'm going to be your constant sunshine, baby." His tongue circles mine slowly, his kiss deep and long, before he starts pecking his way down my neck to my chest.

I sigh and drop my head to the side, looking out at the sea.

And in the distance, vivid and stretching across the horizon...

A rainbow.

ABOUT JODI ELLEN MALPAS

Jodi Ellen Malpas was born and raised in England, where she lives with her husband, boys and Theo the Doberman. She is a self-professed daydreamer, and has a terrible weak spot for alpha males. Writing powerful love stories with addictive characters has become her passion—a passion she now shares with her devoted readers. She's a proud #1 *New York Times* Bestselling Author, a *Sunday Times* Bestseller, and her work is published in over twenty-five languages across the world. You can learn more about Jodi & her words at www.jodiellenmalpas.co.uk

Love Candles? Check out The JEM Candle Library on Instagram. Handmade candles inspired by the characters and words of Jodi Ellen Malpas.

ALSO BY JODI ELLEN MALPAS

The This Man Series

This Man

Beneath This Man

This Man Confessed

All I Am – Drew's Story (A This Man Novella)

With This Man

The One Night Series

One Night - Promised

One Night - Denied

One Night - Unveiled

Standalone Novels

The Protector

The Forbidden

Gentleman Sinner

Perfect Chaos

Leave Me Breathless

The Smoke & Mirrors Duology

The Controversial Princess

His True Queen

The Hunt Legacy Duology

Artful Lies

Wicked Truths

The Unlawful Men Series

The Brit

The Enigma

The Resurrection

Check out Jodi's brand new Regency Romance Series, coming in 2022

Lightning Source UK Ltd.
Milton Keynes UK
UKHW012150210322
400413UK00002B/143

9 781736 057254